W9-BXO-842

Praise for *The Curse of Misty Wayfair*

"Wright creates an inspirational mystery with thrilling finesse, blending chilling supernatural elements with the raw interiority of mental illness, and taking readers on Heidi's haunting search for identity, which is sure to keep them up at night."

—*Booklist*

"The past and present collide in this time-slip suspense, weaving the lives of two women together in a high-intensity thriller. . . . Prepare for a mystery transpiring through time that will stimulate the senses."

—*Hope by the Book*

"With a masterful dual narrative, subtle romance and spine-tingling suspense, Jaime Jo Wright navigates the lives of two young women seeking a sense of identity."

—*BookPage*

"In this thought-proving novel, the contemporary story and the 1910 threads intertwine to explore the consequences of past sins and the way light can break through the dark. . . . With depth and intelligence, Wright explores the role of faith in life."

—*Christian Retailing*

"A pitch-perfect gothic that highlights the extraordinary talent of Jaime Jo Wright. I stayed up past midnight gobbling up this mesmerizing tale and was sorry to see it end."

—Colleen Coble, author of the ROCK HARBOR series

"Stellar writing combined with stellar storytelling are rare. Wright brings both in abundance to *The Curse of Misty Wayfair*. The intrigue starts immediately and doesn't let up until the final pages."

—James L. Rubart, author of *The Man He Never Was*

"Two tales twist together into a story that draws the reader in and won't let go. *The Curse of Misty Wayfair* is deliciously thrilling, with a resolution steeped in light and hope."

—Jocelyn Green, author of *Between Two Shores*

The Reckoning at Gossamer Pond

"The movements between time periods are perfectly done to heighten the intrigue of each unraveling mystery. . . . A complex story with sympathetic characters and many surprises."

—*Historical Novels Review*

"Brilliantly atmospheric and underscored by a harrowing romance, *The Reckoning at Gossamer Pond* pairs danger with redemption and features not only two heroines of great agency but one of the most compelling, unlikely, and memorable heroes I have met in an age."

—Rachel McMillan, author of *Murder at the Flamingo*

"Intoxicating and wonderfully authentic . . . delightfully shadowed with mystery that will keep readers poring over the story, but what makes it memorable is the powerful light that burst through every darkened corner in this novel—*hope*."

—Joanna Davidson Politano, author of *Lady Jane Disappears*

"*The Reckoning at Gossamer Pond* is true to Wright's unique style and voice. Multilayered characters who intrigue the reader and a story the threads of which are unpredictable and well woven together make this a must-read for anyone who enjoys suspense."

—Sarah Varland, author of *Mountain Refuge*

The House on Foster Hill

"Jaime Jo Wright's *The House on Foster Hill* blends the past and present in a gripping mystery that explores faith and the sins of ancestors."

—*Foreword Reviews*

"Headed by two strong female protagonists, Wright's debut is a lushly detailed time-slip novel that transitions seamlessly between past and present. . . . Readers who enjoy Colleen Coble and Dani Pettrey will be intrigued by this suspenseful mystery."

—*Library Journal*

"With one mystery encased in another and a century between the two, Wright has written a spellbinding novel."

—*Christian Market*

"Jaime Jo Wright is an amazing storyteller who had me on the edge of my seat. . . . *The House on Foster Hill* is a masterfully told story with layers and layers of mystery and intrigue, with a little romance thrown in for good measure."

—Tracie Peterson, author of the GOLDEN GATE SECRETS series

ECHOES
AMONG

the
STONES

ECHOES AMONG *the* STONES

JAIME JO WRIGHT

BETHANYHOUSE
a division of Baker Publishing Group
Minneapolis, Minnesota

© 2019 by Jaime Sundsmo

Published by Bethany House Publishers
11400 Hampshire Avenue South
Bloomington, Minnesota 55438
www.bethanyhouse.com

Bethany House Publishers is a division of
Baker Publishing Group, Grand Rapids, Michigan

Printed in the United States of America

Library of Congress Cataloging-in-Publication Data
Names: Wright, Jaime Jo, author.
Title: Echoes among the stones / Jaime Jo Wright.
Description: Minneapolis, Minnesota : Bethany House, a division of Baker
    Publishing Group, [2019]
Identifiers: LCCN 2019024905 | ISBN 9780764233883 (trade paperback) | ISBN
    9780764234798 (cloth) | ISBN 9781493421664 (ebook)
Subjects: LCSH: Murder—Investigation—Fiction. | GSAFD: Mystery fiction. |
    Suspense fiction.
Classification: LCC PS3623.R5388 E24 2019 | DDC 813/.6—dc23
LC record available at https://lccn.loc.gov/2019024905

Scripture quotations are from the King James Version of the Bible.

Cover design by Jennifer Parker
Cover photography by Roy Bishop/Arcangel

Author is represented by Books & Such Literary Agency.

19 20 21 22 23 24 25   7 6 5 4 3 2 1

To Gramma Lola . . .

*You taught me to be strong,
to embrace grief,
and to remember the ones we love
with our eyes lifted toward Hope.*

I will always hear your voice.

It echoes in my heart every day.

CHAPTER I

Imogene Grayson

MILL CREEK, WISCONSIN
JULY 1946

She should have paid more attention to her longtime neighbor, Oliver Schneider, when she passed him on the road at dawn. Her, hiking at an energetic, running-late march, and him strolling the lane, hands in his pockets, and overall straps over thin but strong shoulders. After all, they'd grown up together—albeit more acquaintances than friends—and Oliver rarely said anything that wasn't worth listening to. But, while Imogene had paused for a polite morning greeting, she hadn't taken his words and let them sink into her soul as perhaps they should have.

Oliver gave her his resigned smile—the smile the community of Mill Creek had grown used to since his return from overseas. A sad one, with ghosts in his eyes.

"Red in the mornin'," he quoted, "sailors take warnin'. Red at night, sailors' delight."

Oliver pressed his lips together and raised his brows as if to add a silent apology for the brewing storm. He was an Army

9

boy, but he'd crossed the ocean of the Pacific. He'd experienced war. He knew if the adage was true or not.

Imogene should have listened. Instead, she tossed him a saucy smile, tilting her full lips. "Aw, Ollie. You know nothing is as red as my lips—cherry-apple with a kiss, if you want one. And no one ever sent a warning out ahead of my arrival!"

She glanced at the sky. The morning rays of deep reds and oranges. A thin line of clouds glowing pink and sparkling. The Schneiders' red barn rising above acres of knee-high corn like a marvelous crimson farm mascot.

Red was a color of beauty. Of joy. Of anticipation and excitement of home.

She should have listened to Oliver Schneider that morning on her way to work. But she didn't. The day passed uneventful. She returned home for dinner, for that perfect still evening on the front porch with a paperback as cows mooed and a cat scampered across the drive.

Instead, her day was ending with the beginning of a new war. A more personal one. This time it chose to visit her home. A place that should be secure, should be sacred, should be *safe*.

People hustled around her. Blurs and forms as Imogene stumbled past them. Her breaths were shallow, but they resonated in her ears like hollow echoes, drowning out the commanding voices. She pushed her way through the front door of her home and onto the front porch. An iron shoe scraper by the mat caught her eye. Shaped like a cricket. Bristles dirty with earth. Hazel loved that cricket. She said it was *"unseen but served a purpose."*

Imogene tripped down the porch steps. She planted her feet in the yard, her dress hanging to her calves with its flirty bow tied at the waist. She lowered her head, staring down at her hands. They were turned palms up toward the sky, fingers curled as if cupping the air.

"Red in the mornin' . . ."

Imogene fixated on her hands.

"Sailors take warnin' . . ."

A storm was coming. A storm *had* come. The scarlet stained Imogene's skin, forever redefining the color red.

It was Hazel's blood.

Her sister's blood.

Yes. Yes, she should have listened to the war-weary GI that morning. He knew what red signified. Now Imogene understood it too.

It was the color of death.

CHAPTER 2

Aggie Dunkirk

MILL CREEK, WISCONSIN
PRESENT DAY

It was irony at its best that she stood over an open grave again, two years to the day that her mother's grave had beckoned Aggie to join her. The chasm in the ground that swallowed the last physical remnants of the woman who had raised Aggie Dunkirk to be bold, to be courageous—to stare challenge in the eye and breathe a prayer for strength. None of that had helped the day her mother was buried.

Even rain had a double-edged blade. It could be comforting and cozy on a crisp autumn day like today, or it could be the omen of all things destructive. A thunderstorm. A hurricane. Or, as in this cemetery, a flood.

"This is what I call Fifteen Puzzle Row." Mr. Richardson's stooped shoulders, covered in a wool sweater, hitched up just a bit as he caught Aggie's attempt to conceal a sniff of confused laughter at the nickname. He waved his hand over the expanse of land. "Well? Look at it? Back in the day, when these folks

12

were breathin', anythin' that was confusin' was a fifteen puzzle. And I'd say we're not far from that now."

No. No, they weren't. Aggie adjusted her footing in the soggy grass, not for the last time, cursing the fact she wore red heels that sank into the sod like a knife through butter.

"Any-whose-a-whats-un." Mr. Richardson's brown loafer landed just shy of an overturned headstone that lay half buried in mud. He toed it with the tip of his shoe. Respectful. Gentle. But with an element of resignation. "We were tryin' to map out the plots in this section before the rain came. What with the floodin' two weeks ago, most of this was underwater. Who knew it was a floodplain? But then all them houses that had water in their basements? No flood insurance either. They're callin' it the hundred-year flood for these here parts."

Aggie pulled her heel from the grass and tried to reposition herself. Her pencil skirt was keeping her legs limited as to their movement. Her tailored red jacket was perhaps the only bright spot in the Victorian section of the Mill Creek Cemetery. She stifled a sigh. She hated cemeteries. Hated death. Hated the gloom and the pallor that always settled in places like this. Yet here she was.

Washed up—no pun intended—in her own career, with circumstances thrusting her back into the one community she'd avoided. Her grandmother's hometown. Mumsie with her silly little Midwestern quirks, her persnickety tongue, and her eccentric ideas.

"So, ya up for it?" Mr. Richardson turned, the ground beneath him saturated with moisture, squishing brown bubbles around his heels.

Aggie tried not to grimace, tried not to give the appearance of being too good for Mill Creek Cemetery. Oh, but she was. She really, *really* was!

"I always appreciate a challenge." Aggie gave a quick nod and pushed her long, blunt-cut black hair over her shoulder. Yes. A challenge. Like selling an upscale home in Chicago's Lincoln Park community. Oddly, Lincoln Park had its origins as a cemetery for smallpox and cholera patients who'd succumbed to the tentacles of death. It'd claimed the death of her real estate career too, when she'd failed to make sure the agents under her kept their licenses up to date. Being terminated for something *she* did was one thing, but being given the ax for something those underneath her *hadn't* done . . . well, it was the pitfall of being in leadership. Ultimately it was her fault.

"Good." Mr. Richardson's nod and gravelly voice yanked Aggie from her thoughts. He waved his arm over the muddy earth, the upended gravestones, the plots where the earth had washed away, revealing old wooden encasements and the edges of coffins that held the remains of people who'd passed away before the century had turned 1900, let alone 2000.

"And what is my official job description then?" Aggie ventured.

She'd come here before visiting Mumsie. Before facing the ninety-two-year-old tigress in her dusty, antiquated house. Secure employment. Finances. It was her priority. But Mill Creek's employment opportunities were like looking for groceries in a dumpster. It was this or waitressing.

"Cemetery Secretary," Mr. Richardson barked out. His jowly cheeks tipped in a slight smile, and there was a knowing look in his eye when he said it. "We're not worried about all those highfalutin titles here. You're a secretary. We got a small office in the west corner of the cemetery where you can work. We just got Wi-Fi put in."

Aggie managed a smile.

Mr. Richardson motioned to the asphalt drive that paved its way through the cemetery. "Let's head back. No need to hang around Fifteen Puzzle Row. They're not goin' anywhere, for now anyway. And land's sake, it'll be a trick to figure out who's who and what's what. We're gonna hafta get you to pull records and

14

the old maps. I'll have you work with the archaeologist. He can help figure it all out."

"Archaeologist?"

If they were going to literally exhume the coffins and use paintbrushes to figure out the plots' occupants, Aggie would have to rethink that waitressing job.

"Yep. One of the cemetery board members had some golly-waggled idea that we needed an archaeologist to bring their *expertise*." The way he said the word made Mr. Richardson sound as though he thought archaeologists knew less than he did about dead people.

"I see." Aggie's response was minimal. Best to keep it so. Her heels met with the paved ground, and she glanced down at them. Mud up to the hilt. Aggie squeezed her eyes shut for a moment, collecting herself.

She'd fallen from a lucrative career to this—identifying and plotting out graves in a cemetery. Oddly, one could even argue she wasn't qualified for it, if they cared to. But wasn't that just indicative of her own life?

No one alive really cared.

Aggie was used to that.

Now that her mother was dead.

It took all her courage and then some to knock on the door of her grandmother's house. It'd been eight years. Eight. The last time she'd seen Mumsie, Aggie was a delightfully innocent twenty-four years old. Two years out of business school, already firmly planted with a reputable realty company and ready to conquer the world of residential and maybe, eventually, commercial sales. The world seemed so within her grasp then. Until Mumsie critiqued her dreams to the point of making Aggie question herself. Distance had been her escape, which had turned into a permanent separation.

She could see a person's argument for divorce. Removing negative voices from one's life. Granted, a grandmother was different from a marriage partner, but c'mon. For the sake of the argument, Aggie was going with it. Coming back was like returning to those old, nasty influences that only made her feel small. Insignificant. No. Stupid. Less than. Returning to Mumsie was like returning to an old ex, because you were still tied to them somehow. It was uncomfortable, undesired but circumstantially obligatory.

Aggie held out her hand, poised to knock on the green front door. She glanced up at the roof of the portico. It was triangular, a small shelter, miniaturized by the two-story rise of the old Victorian house with its gables and many crooks.

She was headed for a future of grave plotting and grandmother babysitting. She'd give anything—*anything*—to talk to Mom one more time.

Mumsie sent a letter, Mom. Said she broke her hip and needs assistance. I don't want to go. I tried calling Dad, but he's off in Germany with brunette-headed wife number four. I know what he'd say anyway. Mumsie isn't his mother.

Aggie could imagine her mother's response. Gentle. Calm. Stable.

She doesn't bite, Aggie. She just snaps. Love her. I always did.

And Mom had. She had loved Mumsie with every ounce of her being. Aggie might have separated herself from Mumsie eight calendars ago, but Mom hadn't. Not until she was diagnosed with breast cancer. Not until she had been through so much radiation and chemotherapy, seeing Mumsie would have been a miracle, let alone living another month. And she hadn't lived. She had died, leaving Aggie alone to pick up the pieces of her heart and pack them away someplace where she could piece them together later.

An absentee father. A dead mother. A crotchety grandmother.

Her family tree was enough to make anyone cry—only Aggie hadn't. Not a tear. Not once.

Aggie brought her knuckles down on the door with a firm rap.

"There's a doorbell, you know."

The voice behind Aggie wobbled with age, and Aggie spun on her muddy heels. Mumsie's petite, bent frame came around the corner of the old house. Her walker had tennis balls attached to its back legs, so Mumsie lifted it a bit to maneuver through the grass. Her elastic-waisted pants were navy with pleats down the front, and her flowered blouse brought out the lively green of her eyes.

"I didn't see it," Aggie answered lamely. What a way to say hello to someone's own grandmother after eight years! Yet she couldn't help the tang of bitter she tasted as she noticed the obvious fact that Mumsie's hip wasn't broken. The obligation to come to Mumsie's aid was apparently, as Mumsie herself would have put it, a "falsehood."

Mumsie's face was powder soft, wrinkles lining blushed cheeks, and cheekbones that hinted of faraway beauty. Her gray curls sat on her forehead, permed and poised. She was ninety-two years of perfection, and Mumsie knew it.

The old woman tapped the glasses that hung around her neck on a gold chain. "I've found eyewear to be quite useful for seeing things like doorbells," she quipped, waving her finger at the bell Aggie hadn't seen. "Never mind. It's about time you're here. Come inside."

Mumsie shuffled past Aggie, who sidestepped out of the way of the walker-hoisting artifact that was Mumsie. She watched with a bewildered fascination as Mumsie reached out and opened her front door, then shot Aggie a look over her shoulder as she moved inside.

"You've let yourself go, Agnes. We must fix that."

Welcome home, Aggie sighed inwardly. But it was then she heard her mother's voice deep in her soul.

It is home, *Aggie love. She's all you have left.*

Those weren't the words Aggie ever wanted to hear, let

alone acknowledge. That it was just her and Mumsie left to function through life together. They had nothing in common. Nothing. Except for a family deceased, a runaway father and son-in-law, and a way of eyeing each other with censure that affirmed the other had reached a conclusion and they'd been found wanting.

Aggie pulled the door shut behind her and followed her grandmother through a dimly lit hall into a front room that housed a recliner, a television, and an end table. The table was cluttered with a tissue box, a pair of cuticle trimmers, a bottle of wine-colored nail polish, and a TV remote.

She sniffed. The place smelled musty. The antique architecture was lost to the modernized elements of Mumsie's makeshift living space. Wood paneling wainscot dressed up the walls of the room, the trim an ornate walnut. Aggie reached out and touched the fine wood, recalling how beautiful she'd always thought this old home to be. Dusty and unkempt, with some TLC this place could be transformed into a charming bed-and-breakfast or sold to homeowners who understood classic beauty.

Now? Aggie brought her attention back to Mumsie, who was easing herself into her recliner. Now the house was simply an extension of an old woman waiting for the clock to cease ticking. For time to stand still. Until then, Mumsie would make sure both the house and Aggie had her indifference.

"I was weeding the flower bed in the backyard." Mumsie adjusted herself in the chair, reaching for a tissue to wipe her nose. She did so, then stuffed it in the cuff of her sleeve. She gave Aggie a curious look. "Well? Are you going to just stand there?"

Aggie bit back a sigh. She tugged the hem of her red jacket for something to do rather than to straighten it. Moving to the side, she slid an antique wing-back chair with a worn green velvet seat near Mumsie and sat down. Crossing her legs at the ankles the way Mumsie had taught her to so many years ago. It was what ladies did. No knee-crossing or bouncing a foot like a nonchalant hussy. Crossed ankles, skirt tucked tight against one's legs, and hands folded in one's lap.

She hated to admit it, but the posture had served Aggie well. In sales. Until she'd lost her license, that is. And her career.

Dang. It always came back to remind her with the vicious taunt of failure.

"You don't have a job, then?" Mumsie's hands were folded in her own lap as she gave Aggie a sharp look.

"You don't have a broken hip?" Aggie shot back, then bit her tongue.

"Oh, that." Mumsie waved her hand. "What's an old woman to do to get any help? Stretch the truth a bit, I suppose. I did pull something, I believe, a few weeks ago going up the stairs."

Mumsie gave Aggie such a pathetic look, Aggie couldn't help her instinctual grimace of empathy. Then she straightened her features. No. No! Mumsie had lied. Aggie had been duped into coming, into planning to care for a bedridden, hip-broken grandmother.

Aggie shifted in her seat and uncrossed her ankles.

Mumsie's gaze flitted across them.

Yes. Yes, I did just flip my leg over my knee. Aggie bounced it for good measure too.

They sized each other up.

Green eyes of age.

Brown eyes of a father who'd left when Aggie was eight. Stubborn. Willful. Strong.

"You didn't come after your mother died." Mumsie went straight for the jugular.

"No." There was no use denying the obvious, but Aggie didn't offer any justification for her actions either. There wasn't any justification anyway, outside of the fact she simply did not want to come.

Mumsie noticed. Her eyes narrowed. "And yet you came to care for me now?"

"You said you broke your hip."

Mumsie waved her hand nonchalantly. "Well, you're here now."

"For now." Aggie gave a curt nod, strands of straight black hair falling over her shoulder.

Mumsie offered a small smile that transformed her from being censorious to downright adorable. And she knew it too. Aggie could tell.

"We've much to catch up on." Mumsie reached for the nail polish on the table next to her. "But I'll need your assistance when I'm finished with my nails."

"My assistance?" Aggie was having difficulty following her grandmother's cavalier attitude.

Mumsie looked up. Their eyes met. This time, Aggie saw something flicker in her grandmother's before it hurried away into the shadows of her irises.

"Yes. There's a body in the backyard. We need to bury it or something—before I'm accused of murder and incarcerated for a hundred years to life."

CHAPTER 3

"You *will* let me see my sister!" Imogene shrugged off the grip of a policeman and shoved her way into the front office of the station. The heels of her brown pumps echoed on the wood floor. A burly officer pushed himself away from his desk and stood as she stalked over to it, aware that the eyes of several policemen were watching her.

A war poster still hung on the wall, its edges a bit ragged. For a moment, she almost insisted they rip it off the wall. But that was another battle for a war already over. She was immersed in her own now.

"Now, Miss Grayson . . ." the burly officer started.

"Don't 'Miss Grayson' me, Chet." Imogene sat on the desktop and hiked her knee over her leg, planting her left hand on the green desk blotter in the center of the massive piece of furniture. She eyed her older brother with vehemence. "I want to see Hazel."

Chet snapped his fingers at the policeman behind her. His eyes sparked with a green fire that probably matched her own. "I told you to keep her outta here."

Imogene shot a glance at the officer. Poor Harold Pittman. How he'd become an officer of the law was beyond her. How he'd survived the war was a miracle. The man had all the tenacity of a beaten puppy.

"I couldn't manhandle her!" Officer Pittman defended himself with a whine.

Imogene would have smirked if she wasn't already frantic over seeing Hazel. She gave a saucy tilt to her chin at Pittman and then leveled her glare at Chet.

"Where is she?" Curse her watery voice. The quiver always gave her away. Imogene swallowed back tears. Blinked back the vision she'd seen just that morning. A vision she knew would never, *ever* go away.

Chet waved Pittman off, and the other officers in the room made a respectful pretense of returning to their work. Her brother rounded his desk. He was older than Imogene by a full five years. Made a deputy already and was good at his job. Until today. Today he stood in her way. No one stood in Imogene's way, least of all where Hazel was concerned.

"Chet?"

His hand wrapped gently around Imogene's arm, and he tugged her toward him, urging her off of his desk. Her dress fell around her calves in a sweep of red floral.

"Genie, come with me."

Satisfied she was getting what she wanted, Imogene followed her brother down a short hall and waited as he opened the door. With a quick motion, he pushed her inside and then closed the door firmly behind them.

"Chet!" Imogene set her teeth together in a stubborn gesture.

"No." Chet neared her and put his hands on her shoulders. "You can't see Hazel."

Imogene twisted away from her brother's grasp. "I will. I must! You can't keep me away from her!"

Chet's eyes filled with tears. His voice cracked. "Genie, she's gone. She's at the coroner's. There's nothing we can do. Nothing *you* can do."

"No." Imogene shook her head, the choked argument wrenching from her throat.

"Hazel is gone."

"No!" Imogene's vehemence didn't match the buckling of her knees. She plopped onto a chair that was pulled out from a wooden table. "No, she isn't."

But she was. She *was*! Imogene had seen her—*found* her—lying on the floor of her attic bedroom. A crumpled heap in a dress spattered with red. The floor, a puddle beneath her, and—

"I need to see Hazel!" Imogene's insistence came out in a long moan, and her arms came up to wrap around herself. She cast a desperate gaze on her brother. "Chet, she's not dead. She's not. It was someone else. It wasn't her. All that blood—I can't—"

Chet squatted in front of her, his blue uniform usually so smart, so handsome, now rumpled from his own foray into the pit of grief and family horror.

"Listen, I promise you, once I find who did this to Hazel, I'm gonna let him have it. But until then . . ." Chet cleared his throat when his voice caught.

Imogene locked eyes with her brother. In them she saw the same gut-wrenching grief that was threatening to steal her breath. The same sickening knowledge that Hazel had not died peacefully—had not taken her last breath with any sort of comfort. Only fear. Only terror.

She had to know.

"Did she suffer?"

The silence that followed was the only answer Imogene needed.

—⟋⟍—

She wasn't allowed to return home, Chet said, but Imogene ignored him. The farmhouse, a mile outside of Mill Creek, nestled in the rolling hills and between acres of cornfields, was to be left alone for now. Cordoned off like a museum of sorts. But Imogene never listened anyway. It was why she was here, in the dark, in the shadows of Hazel's death.

Their parents had taken refuge at their neighboring aunt's home, taking with them the memories of their youngest child, nineteen-year-old Hazel. They'd begged Imogene to come, to be with them. But she couldn't look at her heartbroken mother or sit beneath the haunted stare of her father. Not for a moment. It just solidified that Hazel was dead. Reminded her that she was now their only daughter. It was the grief they'd hoped to escape during the war—the grief they *had* escaped—but now? Hazel stained by her own blood was enough of a vision to reconcile for the day. Imogene couldn't wrestle with her parents' grief as she tried to temper her own.

But, strangely, while she wished to avoid her parents, she still wanted to go home. It was empty now. Starkly so. As it had been hours ago when Imogene had returned home from the beauty salon for dinner and her evening porch laze. Hours since she'd given a permanent wave to one of the church deacon's wives. The chemicals from the processing still clung to her white dress that was in her valise to be taken home and washed. She couldn't forget the silence in the old farmhouse as she'd entered their home. The creaking of the screen door as she opened it, laughing at the dog who darted out from the front sitting room and into the outdoors.

Imogene's first hint that something was amiss was that no dinner smells hung in the air. Not a liver loaf or even the pungent smell of cauliflower to go as a side to a roasted chicken. The perks of farm life, they'd not lacked for meat the last few years. Although she could go for a cup of coffee in the evening and a fresh one too—not having to re-brew with yesterday's grounds.

The shadows of rationing still on her mind, Imogene had called for her mother.

Oh yes. She'd taken the car and gone to her cousin's one county over. Imogene had remembered that, and then she'd remembered the fact that Hazel had promised to be home from her work at the powder plant in time to get dinner on the table. Imogene's curiosity took her into the dining room. An empty table. The kitchen. A cold stove. She wasn't sure when the pit began to form in her stomach. If it was when her feet landed on the second floor, peeking into the bedrooms and seeing no one, or when she opened the door to the stairs leading into the attic and Hazel's quaint and secluded bedroom. Her "place of respite," she'd called it. Wonderful for a romantic girl who dreamed of soldiers far away and gave them sweet smiles when they passed by, blushing a bright pink and looking at her feet.

"Hazel?" Imogene had called.

The echo of her footsteps going up the attic stairs still rang in her ears hours later. There had been a strange scent, one she couldn't place. And then it was as if time slowed to a crawl. Imogene's eyes had scanned the attic room. The white iron bed frame. The bedspread neat and tidy across the bed. What looked to be red-spattered paint on the delicate rose wallpaper. Hazel's hope chest at the end of the bed, pushed askew from its normal geometrically aligned position. And then her foot, still with its stocking on, the seam as straight up the back of her leg as when she'd pulled it on that morning. Hazel's crumpled form, lying on her side . . .

Imogene blinked rapidly, attempting to clear the vision from her mind as she stood on the porch of the farmhouse. It was now the dark of night. Chet had no idea she'd left the station and immediately started to hike home. He probably should have guessed, though. Imogene never listened, never obeyed anyone before, so why start now? And something tugged her back here to this dreadful place that had once been a haven of security, filled with childhood memories of growing up moderately poor on a farm during the tight years. Of blowing kisses just five years before to Chet and her other brother, Ivan, as they went off to war. And they had returned home! The rejoicing, it was all a distant dream now. Foggy and muted by the pall of death. Hazel's death.

Imogene reached for the screen door, which opened at her touch. The hinges squeaked their familiar protest, and the chipped white-painted frame was cool beneath Imogene's fingers. Entering the house was like repeating her steps from hours before. She turned on the electric lights, but it didn't seem to clear the darkness. Nausea filling her, Imogene leaned against the wall that hugged the stairs leading to the second floor. Instinct made her squeeze her eyes shut against the memories, only it prompted the vision of Hazel lying in blood, the injury to the back of her head, the way the walls ran red with—

Imogene gagged. Her hand clamped over her mouth as she sagged onto a stair. Her skin was clammy, and though she'd not eaten since lunchtime, it all threatened to come up.

"No," Imogene whispered against her palm, against the sickness. "Hike up your skirts, honey." Her verbal coaching allowed herself the gumption to draw in deep breaths. Her sickness assuaged, she pressed against the wall with her hand and stood.

While staring up the staircase in the direction of Hazel's room, a whiff of roses filtered through the air, alerting her.

"Hazel?" Imogene's voice tremored into the darkness above. The place where Hazel should have been. The place that still held her scent. Only Hazel was no longer here. Just the shell of the room where she'd once been safe. The place she'd curled up and read book after book, dreaming of becoming a librarian someday and putting away her bandanna and coveralls for the factory.

Imogene ignored the nostalgic smells of home and of Hazel. She moved up the stairs, beyond her own bedroom and to the attic stairs. She hesitated. Looking up at the darkened room beyond. The place where someone had invaded and taken Hazel's life. Terrorized her sister and permanently ruined this family farm and its memories forever. Murdered—

"Imogene?"

She yelped, spinning on the bottom stair. Her heart pounded like a locomotive, and she was sure the Glenn Miller band had nothing on her rhythmic pulse of fear. Clutching at her necklace of fake pearls, she met the troubled gaze of Oliver Schneider. Concern was etched in the corners of his eyes, and for a moment she wondered if her neighbor had a glimmer of sorrow in them.

"You frightened me, Ollie," Imogene breathed, rolling a pearl between her forefinger and thumb. Trying to exude an air of casual collection rather than the panicked visage of a young woman standing on a precipice of calm and about ready to careen into hysterics.

Ollie gave her his familiar crooked grin. The one all the Schneider boys were known for. All nine of them. Ollie being the—the what?—the sixth? She didn't know. She didn't care.

"You should go home," he ventured. His voice was gruff, edged with something she couldn't place. It was as though he knew. Knew what she'd seen that morning. Knew how it had seared into her soul like the branding iron on a cow's hide.

"I *am* home." Imogene tried to soften the snap to her voice, but it was too late.

Ollie studied her for a long second. His blue eyes were iridescent. Clear. Knowing. "You don't need to revisit it, Imogene."

"Whatever are you talking about?" She tried to act ignorant— flippant even. What right did Ollie Schneider have to tell her to do anything? None at all. He was a floundering war hero that the world didn't know what to do with anymore.

"Do what you want." He shrugged, his hands sliding into the pockets of his overalls. "If you want to take another gander, have at it."

Imogene pressed her lips together in an impertinent *I won* smile, then turned back to the attic stairs. One. Two. Three.

There were no footsteps behind her.

She turned again.

Ollie stood at the bottom of the attic stairs, looking up at her.

"You're not coming?" Hang! She didn't want to do this alone now that he was here. His presence brought reality crashing into her dreamlike trance.

Hazel wouldn't be alive in the attic.

She wouldn't be there at all.

Just a sordid, vile scene that Imogene had already witnessed. Already had the scream ripped from her throat at the sight.

Imogene couldn't help the desperation that must have fluttered across her face, because she heard it in her voice. "Please don't make me do this alone."

Maybe it was her unguarded moment of vulnerability.

Maybe it was duty.

Imogene didn't know the reason why. All she knew was the fleeting comfort of Oliver Schneider's farm boots echoing on the wooden steps as he climbed the stairs to walk with her.

CHAPTER 4

Aggie

She thought—she'd *assumed*—that Mumsie was exaggerating again. But no. There in the middle of the backyard lay the body, its skeletal remains soiled from earth, as though it had just been exhumed and hauled to her grandmother's yard for reburial. Sans coffin. Or mourners. Or any legal paper work.

"What the—! Mumsie!" Aggie reached for her purse in a frantic gesture but ended up slapping her hip with a purposeless *whack*, recalling in an instant that she'd left her purse inside. She needed her phone. 911. Authorities.

Mumsie perched in the doorway of her kitchen that overlooked the backyard, her wrinkled hand gripping the doorframe with enough pressure to keep her nearly century-old frame standing upright.

Aggie shot the elderly woman another freaked look, but Mumsie appeared quite calm.

"Where did that—? It's a decomposed—it's a *skeleton!*" Aggie's exclamation released in a shocked hiss.

Mumsie nodded, and a curl bobbed over her white eyebrow.

29

"Yes, I quite agree. Female by the looks of her pelvis. Wider hips, you know? For birthing and—"

"Where did it come from?" Aggie all but shouted, trying to keep herself from shoving Mumsie out of the doorway so she could retrieve her phone.

Mumsie's emerald eyes snapped. "How am I to know? I came to the backyard to weed my flower beds, not play archaeologist. Yet there she is, splayed in all her glorious wonder. Although I do believe her bones are lacking calcium at this point. Did you notice the right tibia is—"

Aggie didn't notice. She didn't know one bone from another, let alone a wayward skeleton tossed into the yard like an outlandish horror movie.

"We need to call 911. Why didn't you call the police?" Aggie moved to brush past Mumsie.

"Call the police? And tell them what? Elijah's in my backyard piecing together dry bones?" The dry wit her grandmother possessed was ill-timed as usual. "As a matter of fact, Elijah left that doing to the good Lord, so I figured I'd do the same. And what do you know?" She smiled with a blushed-cheek contentment. "My granddaughter showed up."

Aggie shot Mumsie a look over her shoulder. "This isn't the time for Old Testament references, Mumsie."

"Well, that's obvious." Mumsie turned in the doorway, her legs shaky. "As I don't see the bones regaining any life at the moment."

"I'm calling the cops." Aggie's lip thinned at her grandmother's sass.

"Why?" Mumsie pressed.

"To tell them there's a body in your yard! Perhaps we start with that."

Mumsie clicked her tongue and followed Aggie through the kitchen. Her shoes shuffled on the floor, and she reached for her walker that she'd planted by the sink. "I've no explanation for why it's there. That's what they'll want to know, the police with their incessant and pointless questioning, before they whisk the body to some cold mortuary and rebury it as a *Jane Doe*, along with any evidence, in a Bankers Box marked COLD CASE."

"You watch too much TV," Aggie muttered. She reached for the phone mounted on the wall. A mustard-yellow phone with a rotary dial. "Please tell me this thing works."

"Of course it does. Better than all the newfangled ones you all have nowadays. I've had that phone for thirty-five years."

Of course she had. Mumsie saved everything.

—⁓—

Mumsie had followed her to the front door, eyed her as she rolled her suitcase up the sidewalk from her car, bags slung over her shoulders, and inspected Aggie's stilettos still stained with mud from the cemetery.

"Pumps are more sensible," was all she said.

Aggie silently agreed but had no intention of giving her grandmother that satisfaction. By the time the police arrived, Aggie had kicked off her stilettos and exchanged them for a pair of canvas slip-ons she'd tugged from her shoe bag.

Within moments of their arrival, Aggie led the police to the backyard, and she couldn't help but keep a side-eye on Mumsie, who had grown quiet. Her retorts and quips silenced under the intimidation of men in law uniforms, perhaps? Or maybe something else. Aggie didn't know, yet she couldn't ignore the pang of concern as she watched the blush slowly seep from Mumsie's powdery-soft cheeks to a paler version that reinforced to Aggie how aged her grandmother truly was. Fragile. Life was casting a faux vibrance over the woman so that when one looked closer, they saw that life had instead brought the inevitable weariness a person faced when preparing to bid this world farewell.

One of the cops who'd introduced himself as Officer Benton squatted next to the bones. He shot a look at his partner. "Not exactly in one piece," he observed.

Aggie came up behind them, crossing her arms over her chest, but catching Mumsie's slow lowering of her body onto an iron porch chair from the corner of her eye. She returned her attention to the task at hand.

"I noticed it's in disarray," she nodded. The upper half of the skeleton was intact, while the lower half wasn't, the pieces seeming to have been deliberately laid out in as correct a formation as possible.

Officer Benton stood. His partner snapped some photographs of the scene. Turning to Aggie, Officer Benton frowned, his peppery-gray eyebrows pulling together. "When did you say you found this here?"

Helpless, Aggie turned to Mumsie a few yards away. The old woman's fingertips covered her lips, and she stared past them, her expression lost. Aggie turned back to the officer.

"Mumsie mentioned she found it this morning."

"It's PVC." The male voice invaded Aggie's concentration. She jerked her head toward the sound, as did the policeman who stood in front of her.

"Say what?" Officer Benton turned as a tall man of average build approached them, meandering through the back gate and casting a casual glance Mumsie's way.

His hands were in the pockets of loose trousers, cuffed at his ankles like some English lord from the thirties. His white button-up shirt was tucked in, and suspenders stretched over his shoulders. Ginger hair, thick and wavy, caught her attention. Round, gold wire-framed glasses set on a face that was scholarly but handsome.

Chiseled. That was the word that came to mind. A well-carved face with narrowed blue eyes that hinted they knew more than everyone else did, they were okay with that, and they thought it a bit funny.

Aggie wasn't laughing.

"PVC. Not of very good quality, clearly," he repeated, a hint of a British accent tinging his words. "The skeleton—it isn't real."

Officer Benton turned a questioning glance back down to what appeared to be a worn, decayed, and muddied corpse.

"Collin O'Shaughnessy." The interloper moved toward the detective with a hand of greeting outstretched. They shook over the remains, and Collin nodded at the skeleton. "I'm sorry, chaps, but it's probably from a medical facility or something. A prank maybe?"

Aggie looked between Collin and the police. "A prank? In my grandmother's backyard? What kind of sick joke—?" She extended her hand to the skeleton.

"A prank, Agnes. That's what I've been trying to tell you. Your urgency is very overwhelming." Mumsie's voice wobbled from behind them as she perched on her iron garden bench. She patted the curls at the side of her head. Aggie noticed some coloring returning to the old woman's face.

"Collin O'Shaughnessy, ma'am." The unexplained trespasser reintroduced himself by extending his hand to Mumsie, who took it with a gracious smile and a brief twinkle in her eye. Apparently, even a ninety-two-year-old woman could tell a handsome man when she saw one. Aggie squeezed her eyes shut, willing her emotions not to surge with the impulsive force of her Scottish-English father. The one legacy he'd left to her. No thanks needed there.

Aggie opened her eyes to find Officer Benton, his partner, and Mr. Collin O'Shaughnessy all staring at her while Mumsie picked at a loose thread on her sweater sleeve.

"And no one has gone missing?" Aggie blinked as her gaze collided with Collin's. It was a silly question, really. If someone had, the odds their skeleton would drop from the sky into Mumsie's backyard was about as realistic as expecting Elvis to stride through the yard gate.

"Well, to be sure, if this were the deceased corpse of a missing person," Collin broke into Aggie's thoughts, "there likely would be more decomposition. But if you look closely, you'll see bits of attachments at the bones. See there? The drilled holes? At one point, this entire fake soul was held together by wire of some sort. Note the torso. The silver wiring holding the arm to the socket?"

There was a twinkle in his eyes behind his glasses as he met Aggie's incredulous look.

Officer Benton squatted again and then gave a short laugh. "Well, I'll be. I must be half blind." He shot O'Shaughnessy an appreciative glance over his shoulder. "You're right! Don't get much for dead bodies around Mill Creek. Even had me goin' for a bit!"

Aggie whirled back to Collin, who leaned over the skeleton and peered down into its cavernous, fake eye sockets.

"Well, she's been through a bit, I'd say." Collin chuckled and toed the ground with a polished brown loafer. "Poor model. Must have been discarded from a medical facility."

"In my grandmother's backyard?" It seemed to Aggie that it was all she could ask. Repeatedly, until she sounded like a dim-witted female stereotype.

Office Benton stood. His knees cracked. He shrugged. "Well, we'll take some photos for evidence. Look into a few things. But seeing as it isn't really a—*body*—I'd wager some neighborhood kids were having a bit of fun. Pre-Halloween and all."

"It's the middle of September!" Aggie blinked in bewilderment. Truly? Now children were responsible?

"A swell prank," Mumsie inserted, having conquered the loose thread and readjusted her sweater. She rested her hands on her knees, her pants a bit short and riding above delicate ankles and feet placed neatly in a pair of two-inch, thickly heeled shoes.

"That it is!" Collin snapped his finger and thumb, pointing at Mumsie, who gifted him with a brilliant smile, deepening the wrinkles in her cheeks.

Aggie squelched a gag. She wasn't prone to being overly squeamish, but having only minutes before thought she'd come upon a pile of old bones, she also wasn't in a playful mood. She gave her fingers an agitated rake through her straight hair, allowing the long black strands to fall over her shoulders.

"It's all well and good you all seem to be so comfortable writing this off as . . . PVC. I, however, do not find the humor in it. I expect a thorough and written complaint to be taken down, an investigation made to find out why it was left in this backyard, and—"

"Oh, let's put the kibosh on the whole thing." Mumsie struggled to her feet, and Collin O'Shaughnessy and his yet-unexplained presence or purpose jumped forward to give her his hand. She took it, standing, and shot Aggie that familiar emerald stare, indicating she was finished with the conversation. "Now that we know it's nothing, there's no reason to gaggle around my backyard and play crime-scene investigation. Off with all of you now and leave an old woman in peace."

Mumsie spun—as much as a ninety-two-year-old woman could spin—on her heel and teetered to the back door. Officer Benton gave his partner a quick nod, and the man hurried to take Mumsie's arm and lead her into the house.

"Really, miss, I don't believe you have too much to be concerned about here." Officer Benton lowered his voice, but there was confidence in it.

Aggie searched his face. He would follow the procedures, gather the information, she could tell, but it didn't appear he had any qualms taking the word of the man standing next to her.

"But who is he?" Aggie was anxious to put credibility to the entire situation. She didn't mean his name either. That was clear. As was the fact he was a mishmash of British, American, Canadian, or something. His slang wasn't even consistent with one locale and most definitely not Midwestern United States.

"The archaeologist," Collin O'Shaughnessy answered with a smile. If it was meant to be charming, it was. If it was intended to disarm her, it didn't. "I was doing a ride-along with the officer's partner here. Research and the like. My apologies if I inserted myself where I don't belong. It's just, with my knowledge, I felt a tad responsible to clear the air of suspicion before everyone made it into a beastly afternoon when it needn't be."

Now he sounded decidedly British. Aggie held up her hands. She wasn't a fan of dragging information out of people. In fact, being in real estate sales, she was quite adept at placing a few good open-ended questions and having her clients pouring forth information. But either the circumstances or Collin's ridiculously sapphire-blue eyes had her all turned around.

"Look," she began, shifting her focus between the two men. The more than capable police officer and the, the—"An archaeologist?" Aggie couldn't help how her voice rose into a squeak at the end of her question. She vaguely remembered Mr. Richardson's words at the cemetery. That she'd be working with an archaeologist.

"Yes, as a matter of fact." Collin's right cheek dimpled as his left eyebrow rose above the wire frame of his glasses. "And a writer. I'm also a connoisseur of entomology."

"Bugs?" Aggie's rhetorical question was mumbled in disbelief.

"Insects, actually. Well, not all insects, I suppose. More specifically, the kinds of creatures that waste away the remains of the deceased. It lends itself to quite a—"

Aggie interrupted him by turned abruptly to Officer Benton. "So, there is nothing more here that you need me for?"

Officer Benton cleared his throat and shot Collin an uncomfortable glance. "Uh—no. No, we'll be wrapping up here in just a few minutes."

"And what do I do with—with that?" Aggie looked to the ground where the skeleton's frame mocked her.

Officer Benton gave a short nod. "No worries, miss. We'll take care of it for you."

"Good." Aggie didn't mean to sound rude. She was actually a very nice person, she reminded herself, but today had tested the last of her patience. Finding that a flooded-out cemetery was the fate of her career aspirations and that Mumsie's hip wasn't broken? It wasn't that Aggie wished it *was* broken, but for Pete's sake, today was spinning violently out of control.

"Thank you." Aggie gave the officer a lame nod. She tried to attach a smile but could tell it came out thin. Fake. Confused.

She gave Collin O'Shaughnessy a sideways glance as she turned to walk back to the house. His expression had lost its humor, and instead he seemed to study her, his eyes squinting behind his glasses.

"What?" Aggie half whispered, a bit defensively.

"Nothing," he responded, yet he tilted his head left as if still trying to read something in her face. "Do have a good evening, Miss Dunkirk."

"I will." She swallowed. "Thank you." A polite nod and Aggie hurried toward the old Victorian house with its musty interior that smelled of baby powder and mothballs.

It wasn't until she got inside that she realized she'd never introduced herself to Collin O'Shaughnessy and yet he knew her last name. There was no reason why that should bother her so, but it did all the same. She pushed back a kitchen curtain to peek out the window into the yard. Officer Benton was jotting something down in his notepad, but Collin was staring right at her. He hadn't moved.

Aggie let the curtain fall back into place.

She'd no desire to mingle with a scholarly Oxford-ish type who played around with bugs that ate away dead flesh. And yet it seemed to be her immediate fate. She gave the old kitchen a cursory once-over with her eyes. As did living here with Mumsie. A woman whose tongue could cut sharp grooves into Aggie's confidence and whose eccentricities had a way of always—*always*—chasing people away.

Aggie had never intended to come back here.

This had never been her home.

CHAPTER 5

Imogene

It was a cavern of hollow memories that ricocheted off dark walls, repeating themselves over and over and over until Imogene wished to clap her hands over her ears and scream the remembrances into silence. She sensed Oliver beside her, but he said nothing. What was there to say, after all, with the vision before them, splayed out in all its murderous glory? The aftermath of Hazel's death, staining the rug by her bed. The droplets of blood marring the wallpaper, making a mockery of the beauty of the pink roses and green vines that wrapped themselves delicately across a pale pink background. Hazel had picked out the wallpaper after their parents gave her permission to make the attic into a bedroom. Her "oasis," Hazel said. Her "haven." Now her tomb.

Imogene covered her mouth with her hand, blinking furiously against the hot moisture welling in her eyes. She wanted to erase the mental picture of her beloved nineteen-year-old sister sprawled on the rug. To eliminate the vision of violence and the blatant reality that Hazel was never going to grace the attic bedroom with her smile ever again.

"Close your eyes. Sometimes it's too much to take in." Oliver's soft words were rife with understanding.

Imogene cast him a look and stiffened her shoulders. It wasn't his sister whose blood he'd stepped in, or whose chest he'd spread his hands across, or his screams that echoed in his ears. No. It was hers. Hers. Her Hazel.

And she would make sure she remembered everything. Every detail. Every drop of blood, every out-of-place item, every molecule of dust disturbed. She would remember for Hazel.

Her eyes surveyed the room. Where moments before she'd wished not to look, now she ached to memorize every detail. The box radio, its curved wooden corners and scrolled golden knob. It had a droplet of blood spatter on the number 12 at its dial. It sat on the table next to Hazel's bed. The small piece of bedroom furniture was also marred with dark, burnished splotches. From the corner of her eye, she noticed Oliver's hand rise, as if he were going to rest it in a comforting gesture on her forearm. She took a step forward and away from him, letting her vision drift to the bed.

Hazel's tufted white bedspread over crisp, floral sheets. It was mussed, as if Hazel had sat on it and perhaps even rolled onto her back and stared up at the ceiling as she was wont to do. Daydreaming. Imagining herself a heroine off in a bookish land. Imogene's gaze cast upward as if following the image of Hazel and her vacant stare at the ceiling. The beams of the roof spanned it to the peak. A spider web hung there, neglected and old, long abandoned by the creature that might have borne witness to Hazel's murder—had it not already died long before. There was no blood on the ceiling. There was a nail protruding from one beam, a tiny wisp of webbing hanging from it like a cotton bead.

Imogene's focus returned to the bed. The portion of coverlet that hung over the side to the floor had a bloodstain on it. Dots and splotches. Most of the evidence of violence seemed to be cast away from the bed and against the wall, the table, partially onto the radio, then on the rug. Imogene dared not pause to conceptualize the grief that danced in the shadows of a heart she was purposefully turning cold and distant. Walking forward, she bent and picked up a book that lay on the rug next to where Hazel had fallen. Beneath it, the rug was clean, void of the disturbing evidence. The book itself was clean on its front but had a few spatters of deep burgundy marks on its spine. A Grace Livingston Hill romance. The dust jacket a picture of tranquility, of a rosebud-cheeked young woman with waved hair pulled into a roll on one side, with curls on the other. She looked a lot like Hazel, when Hazel didn't have her hair pulled into a snood, its netting protecting from tangling at the plant where Hazel worked.

Setting the book on the bed, Imogene stepped over a smeared footprint. Perhaps from one of the detectives who'd first investigated the scene with camera in hand? She knew they'd moved Hazel a few times to look for evidence. Fingerprints had been taken off the doorknob and other areas, but so often, Chet had warned them, they weren't matched to anyone in the index-card file.

Disturbed by the motionless chaos of the scene, Imogene brushed past a silent Ollie and moved to the window overlooking the farmyard. She could see the barn, Mother's garden with its tomato plants crawling up cages, a mixture of red fruit and yellow blossoms promising more. Cows dotted the pasture beyond, the black-and-white Holsteins the heartbeat of the farm.

A sob caught in Imogene's throat.

"Genie?"

Oliver's voice tore her from her mental photographing.

She turned and met his deep blue eyes. They reflected some emotion, but she couldn't tell what. Empathy? Pity? Shared sorrow?

"How?" she whispered, fingertips pressed to her bottom lip. "How does God allow something this—this heinous?"

Ollie dipped his head and toed a warped floorboard for a second before raising his eyes again. "I ask myself that every day."

His admission was a stark reminder that he'd seen his own share of inexplicable horrors. The damage mankind could cast on others. The empty lack of soul as one killer drained it from another.

"We should go." Imogene had nothing to add. One couldn't answer for the intentions or oversights of God, and He rarely offered explanations. The clichéd comfort offered at death was a stark underscore to the concept that it could have all been stopped before it ever happened. Had God been watching . . . caring.

Imogene took another lingering study of the room. Hazel's gold locket was draped on the top of her bureau next to a framed photograph of all the Grayson siblings. Before Ivan and Chet went to war. Before the war changed everything. When they lived in a blessed cocoon of contentment, even as others dragged themselves from the pits of poverty caused by the weak economy. Farmers were necessary. Their livelihood shaky but secure long term. The Grayson farm was safe, all was well and—

"It wasn't supposed to end like this." The words escaped Imogene's mouth before she could halt them.

Oliver stood, hands deep in his overall pockets. A strand of dark blond hair draped over his forehead, but otherwise he looked almost spit-shined for church. His shirt was clean, not wrinkled from working at his father's farm. It was almost as if he'd spent the entire day wandering aimlessly and doing nothing, ever since muttering his ominous warning that morning.

"Did you know?" Imogene took a step forward.

Oliver frowned. "Know what?"

"This morning." She blinked, catching the shadow of her black lashes coated in Vaseline to emphasize their thickness.

"When you told me to take warning. Did you know this was going to happen?"

Oliver seemed taken aback by her question. He shuffled his feet and shook his head, meeting her eyes. "No. Of course not. I just . . . it's a sayin'. That's all."

"A saying." Imogene swallowed. Nodded. Trying to accept. Trying to comprehend. "Well, you were right. If I'd only been here, if I'd only told Mrs. Nelson I didn't have time for that permanent. She could have done pin curls, stretched it out longer, and I could've curled her hair tomorrow. Then I would've been home. I would've been here—"

She crossed her arms over her chest, her body beginning to quiver in a tremor she hadn't expected.

Oliver took a step forward in concern.

Imogene stared at the bloodstains on the rug. "Hazel was by herself. She suffered here—I should've been here."

"You couldn't have known." Oliver's sense of reason, of logic, only irritated Imogene. She didn't need to be placated. To be made to feel better. To be let off the hook of blame.

"No. I should have! Besides, it was always left to Hazel. Me at the beauty parlor? Mother off doing her charity work or canning at our aunt's house? Daddy off in the fields with Ivan? For gosh sakes, Ollie! Poor Hazel made dinner for us all after working all day at the plant. You'd think they'd shut it down now that the war's over! What do they need more ammunition for anyway? She works so hard, and I knew she'd be coming home to make supper for us. I should've told Mrs. Nelson her hair doesn't hold a permanent wave, so why bother? She spends so much money trying to look like Hedy Lamarr, but she's over fifty years old and as vain as they come! She'll never look like an actress no matter how hard she tries! She has wrinkles and is downright bat ugly!"

Imogene's words ended in a squelched wail. She clapped her hand over her mouth, red lipstick smearing on her skin.

Her eyes widened and locked with Oliver's. His shoes echoed on the wood floor as he crossed to stand in front of Imogene. His work-worn fingers wrapped around her upper arms, and something in his voice made her keep her eyes on his.

"You couldn't have saved her. We don't know what—*who* killed her. Coulda been you too, layin' there tonight if you'da been here. Mrs. Nelson's hair may not be worth a plugged nickel, but that don't change that you bein' here wouldn't have saved Hazel."

"You don't know that," Imogene whispered.

A shadow crossed his face. He ducked his head, then lifted his eyes. "I don't know a lot of things. But knowin' don't always make it better neither. It don't change what happened. Never can. Never will."

There was something in his voice that told Imogene he'd figured that out firsthand. That there were things he'd like to have changed but couldn't. For a moment, she hung there, suspended in the understanding of his eyes. Then she blinked, and all she could see was beyond Oliver Schneider to the bloodstains of her sister.

Her jaw tightened as she bit down against her grief, against her pain. She sucked in a shuddering breath. "I'll make them pay."

"Genie—" Oliver started.

"If it takes me forever, I will make them fess up for this and then they'll pay for it. She is my sister." Imogene brushed past Ollie, striding toward the stairs. "It's what sisters do. We protect each other. In life and in death."

CHAPTER 6

Aggie

Mumsie had already made coffee. It was the inexpensive grocery-store kind. The kind that left a burnt scent in the air. Aggie shuffled into the kitchen of the old house, her gaze skimming the yellow cupboards with the rounded corner doors, and she sniffed appreciatively anyway. Coffee was coffee, after all, and desperate times required desperate measures. Besides, the kitchen was quaint and vintage, so in a way, high-end gourmet grounds wouldn't have fit. It made sense the coffee came from a can.

Aggie eyed the room with expertise. If she were to sell this place, she could sell it on charm alone, never mind the fact it desperately needed updated appliances. The yellow could be repainted to a weathered teal. The wood floors with their scuffs could be polished. Or leave the scuffs. Maybe it was more charming that it looked worn.

Aggie shrugged off her thoughts. It didn't matter. She was now a *cemetery secretary* and no longer a flourishing real estate agent who sold houses with the ease of someone who also knew how to convince even the worst do-it-yourselfer that they could indeed do it.

Mumsie leaned on her walker that was braced against the counter and poured coffee from the pot into a green thermos.

"Can I have a cup first?" Aggie snatched a mug from the kitchen sink drying rack, barely noticing the orange-painted mushrooms on the ceramic.

Mumsie was still in her pajamas. Cute cotton ones, capris style with purple roses on them. Her baggy sweater hung past her hips, a fluffy cream color, and her hair had a cowlick in the back where the gray-permed curls split where her head must have rested on the pillow for most of the night. She gave Aggie a raised brow. "Do you need creamer?" Mumsie poured some of the black pitch into Aggie's offered mug.

"No. Black is good."

Mumsie gave a wan smile. "Well, at least that's one thing we have in common."

One thing. Yes. Aggie had a sneaking and almost foreboding suspicion they were more similar than either of them realized.

She sank onto a metal kitchen chair, the kind with the vinyl padded seat and the silver studs that bolted the back to the chair with a small swatch of the same green padding. The table was also quaint. Its edges a worn silver, its top an old Formica white mottled with cream flecks and yellowed with age.

Mumsie sat opposite Aggie and took a sip of her coffee, looking out the four-paned window that inaudibly announced cheerily that it was morning and that the filmy curtains in front of it couldn't bar out the sunshine if they tried.

"Happy mornings shouldn't be squandered," Mumsie said with a bit of censure. She set her mug down with a solid *clunk* on the table.

Aggie drew back, cupping her mug with the tenacity of a drowning victim clinging to a life preserver.

"Excuse me?" She couldn't help the squeak of surprise in her voice.

Mumsie tipped her head and raised her brows as if the answer were obvious and she was surprised Aggie wasn't already following her line of reasoning.

"Happy mornings are a rarity, and when they come, one should revel in the delight of them. Regardless of the circumstances. Happiness is fleeting, after all, and you look as though you swallowed a sour apple—or have a doozy of a hangover. I've not decided which."

Aggie's latest sip of coffee went down in a scalding gulp.

"It's not a hangover." Aggie hadn't even had a glass of wine in . . . well, in over a month. It was the first non-necessity to go after she'd been fired from her position. No more one-hundred-and-fifty-dollar bottles of Cabernet, and it wasn't as if she'd ever gotten wasted on wine anyway.

Aggie gave her grandmother a look of consternation. "Who do you think I am?"

Mumsie pursed her lips with an impish smile. "How should I know? You haven't visited in eight years. For all I know, I should be planning an intervention and calling a rehabilitation center to reserve you a spot."

"Good grief, Mumsie!" Aggie glowered, but she didn't miss the twinkle in Mumsie's eyes. She was goading Aggie—and having quite a bit of fun with it too.

"My first stint at rehab didn't go so well." Aggie decided to return the favor.

Mumsie's eyes widened, then narrowed. She tipped her chin up and looked down her nose. "You shouldn't joke about those things. For some, they are very real and very sensitive circumstances."

"Yes, ma'am," Aggie muttered, then wondered how Mumsie was so adept at spinning the fault off herself and on to others.

Shaking past the interlude, Aggie tapped the side of her coffee cup.

A bird twittered outside the window.

A drip fell from the faucet into the kitchen sink.

Mumsie's breath was soft.

Aggie felt as though a bulldozer was shoving its way through her emotions and shattering every piece of stillness she had left inside of her.

"Why didn't you come to Mom's funeral?" The question blurted out with sincerity, though the timing was awful. Aggie immediately regretted the question that had scarred its forever-spot on her mind since the day she'd buried her mother. Alone.

Mumsie blinked, but she didn't respond with impulse. Instead, she looked out the window at the sparrow that hopped across the grassy lawn and over an orange leaf that had floated down from the nearby maple. "Farewells are difficult for me."

"But lying about broken hips isn't?" Aggie shot back, again wishing she had the fortitude to simply bite her tongue.

Mumsie's glance was savvy. "You wouldn't have come any other way."

"I didn't feign a broken hip to get you to come to Mom's funeral," Aggie countered.

"I wouldn't have come regardless." Tears welled in Mumsie's green eyes. She reached up with an arthritic-bent finger and swiped away the offense. "I don't handle funerals well." Her admission was vulnerable but unsatisfactory.

"And if I needed you?" Aggie ventured, softening her voice, a pang of guilt for accusing Mumsie.

Mumsie sniffed. "Well then," she said, and raised her gaze to lock with Aggie's. "I've needed you too, and it seems only now we've come together. So, bygones be bygones. Shall we move forward?"

Yes.

Move forward.

It was what Aggie had been trying to do since the day of the funeral.

And it wasn't working. Not at all.

—⁂—

The Mill Creek Cemetery sloped up a hill and over the ridge, lines of different-sized stones marking row upon row of graves. Aggie pulled her car onto a small gravel patch just to the side of the cemetery office that would be lucky if it boasted more than five hundred square feet. Its boxlike form was sided in white, the paint worn and peeling. But there was an urn stuffed with silk daisies and carnations at the door.

Aggie grimaced. She eased from the car, feeling insecure in just jeans, blouse, and cardigan . . . and flats. Gone were her powerhouse days. Confident and sure of herself in suit and stilettos. Aggie perched her hands at her waist, flipping her black braid over her shoulder. Here were the days of service. Serving . . . dead people.

She blinked and shook her head. Self-pity was going to get her nowhere, and with Mumsie safely ensconced in her recliner with TV remote in hand, it was time to get to work. Whether Aggie liked it or not.

The ground was still soggy beneath her shoes. It squished like stepping on a sponge, and the colorful leaves blanketing the green grass were heavy with moisture and glistening from rain and the onset of mold. Aggie had done a quick browse online the previous night and learned more of the disaster she'd inadvertently been hired to fix. Days of heavy rains just two weeks ago had flooded the lower areas of Mill Creek, making the creek itself crest and overflow its banks. The river to the east of town overtook roads and made traveling on those highways near to impossible. Sandbags had saved some of the homes along the river, but no one could plan for the fact the earth could absorb only so much water before it affected basements, wells, foundations, and even the cemetery.

With the newer section of plots on the acreage in the higher planes, Aggie was left hopping over a rather wide puddle to hike to the iron fence that was open for visitors. In her bewildered state yesterday, she hadn't really taken the time to study the mess. Mr. Richardson, the head of the cemetery board, had prattled on and on about Fifteen Puzzle Row, but now that Aggie was alone, she could do what she did best. Take in the entire vision of the project, much like she'd survey a house she was to sell. See what needed repairing, refinishing, or replacing, and then prepare the perfect pitch to sell it. Of course, she wasn't going to sell plots—not yet. Not until the water surrounding Fifteen Puzzle Row receded completely, the graves were repaired, and—

Aggie halted on the narrow asphalt path.

The ground had eroded, evidently during the heavy rains. In this particular row, Aggie could see the tops of encasements that had once been underground closeting the deceased's casket in a protective vault. Or maybe it was a coffin? One of the tombstones was knocked over and lying in the muck.

"Back in the day, they used to bury a person facing the rising sun."

She wasn't surprised to hear Collin O'Shaughnessy's voice nearing her as he strolled up the path. Mr. Richardson had indicated yesterday that Collin would be meeting her here today. She still wasn't sure she liked the idea or even understood what he was doing here.

"Is that a—?"

"A casket?" Collin followed Aggie's stare at the wooden box corner that peeked up from beneath a pool of water and sodden earth. "More than likely." He nodded. "And you need me, because if you notice, there's no stone to mark that plot."

Aggie frowned. She shifted to look at Collin, who stood beside her with the casual air of someone who was used to daily interactions with the dead.

"I don't understand your point," Aggie admitted.

Collin gave her a sideways smile, the crease in his cheek deepening. "It means there are other graves here that aren't on record. So the plots we *do* know are marked by the tombstone or what we have on record. That one—there's no marker, so we hope we can find a record. If not, then I'll put more of my expertise to work."

"But if you're here to find the record, then what am I to do?" Aggie pulled her cardigan closer around herself as a breeze kicked up, and with it the rustling of dying leaves in the autumn-colored trees.

Collin shook his head. "Oh no, *I'm* here to help determine if there are more unknown graves and also the age of them, et cetera. *You're* here to dig up any records—forgive the pun." His eyes twinkled behind his glasses. "And then draw a new map of the yard. Don't be overwhelmed. I'll assist with that."

Aggie pinched the bridge of her nose, a sudden headache coming on. She drew in a deep breath, but the smell of the cemetery wasn't the crisp, refreshing fall smell she preferred. Instead, it smelled dank, moldy, and wet.

"I don't know why I'm here," she muttered. For a moment, she was captivated by a lost feeling. That deep, disturbing hollowness that captures a spirit and begins to pull it into the pit. Images of her mother's graveside service filtered through her mind. The abandonment loss from her father's absence. The cold reality that Mumsie was probably too old to travel, but not too old to call and express her shared grief.

The emptiness caused her to spin away from Collin and hike up the path. The gentle slope upward meant the water grew less puddled. The grass had troughs cut through the side where the rains had created their own paths, slicing past stones, upending some and unearthing other elements.

She paused, her eyes narrowing. A stone several yards away was tilting precariously to the right, the ground around it having been on the edge of one of the water's miniature ravines. Curious, Aggie tilted her head and frowned.

"What is it?" Collin had followed her.

Aggie pointed. "Are there flowers on that stone?"

Collin's hands were in his trousers, but he gave a nod, a ginger strand falling over his forehead. "It appears to be. Perhaps a rose?"

Aggie eyed the mud and slop, then her ballet flats. Oh well. She stepped onto the grass and felt the squish of the ground beneath her foot. The mud seeped around the sole of her shoe. She could feel water on her foot. Investing in a pair of rain boots was going to be a must.

"Going exploring?" Collin quipped from his dry perch on the cemetery asphalt path.

"*Au contraire,*" Aggie shot back. Her shoe made a suction sound as she took another step forward through the flooded row. She glanced at the stone ahead with the flower at its base. She could make out some of the etching on its front. "I thought this was the old section of the cemetery? Fifteen Puzzle Row?" Aggie tossed the observation over her shoulder, making her way to the next marker.

"It is. From what I've been told," Collin affirmed.

Aggie pointed as though he were beside her. "Then how come that stone is from 1946?"

"I haven't a clue." Collin seemed to debate whether he'd join her in the muck. Apparently, he cherished his leather loafers more than she did her own shoes.

Aggie hopped over a puddle, which sent only a spray of mud onto her jeans as her right foot landed on the sodden earth. She peered over the back of a gravestone to the right of her.

"See? That row looks to be people having died around the turn of the century . . . 1907, 1893." Aggie took a few more tentative steps to survey another marker. "1901?" She looked back at Collin as if he would supply some explanation.

His eyebrows rose over the gold rim of his wire glasses, and he shrugged.

Aggie rested her hands on her narrow hips. She blew out a puff of air to push a strand of hair from her cheek. Yes. All the stones in this row on her left were definitively from the late nineteenth century to early twentieth century.

Aggie skipped over an exposed area of a grave, unwilling to look down into the divot to see if she saw anything other than just washed-away earth.

"Something seems . . . well, dodgy," Collin called to her.

"Dodgy." Aggie muttered the non-American slang expression to herself. Dodgy was right. It was as if someone had slipped a grave into Fifteen Puzzle Row because they'd run out of room. Or something.

She paused in front of the tilting tombstone. It wasn't tall. It was just an average marker of worn gray granite. Nothing fancy. But there was most assuredly a rose at its base. A small pink rose, like a bud that was picked before it could bloom. Picked too early.

Her eyes skimmed the name on the stone.

Hazel Elizabeth Grayson
b. January 19th, 1927 – d. July 18th, 1946

Grayson. The name sounded vaguely familiar, but then it wasn't an uncommon surname either. She bent and lifted the rose, even though she felt as if she shouldn't. As if she was disturbing something sacred.

Who would have sloshed through this muck to put a rose on a grave of someone who had died over seventy years ago?

Aggie moved to put the rose back in its original position when she caught sight of something on one of the outside petals. It was black, inky, with the pigments bleeding into the veins of the flower petal. She frowned, pulling it closer so she could try to interpret it.

It was writing. Writing on a flower petal with what she assumed was a permanent fine-tip marker.

Her breaths came shorter now. She'd stumbled onto someone's homemade epitaph for a long-dead Hazel Grayson.

Not over.

Not over? Aggie drew back. "What's not over?" she mumbled. She turned the rose in her hand, but only the one petal was marred with ink.

"Pardon?" Collin asked from yards away.

Aggie cast him a disturbed look. His smile faded as he caught the angst that crossed her face, probably stretching from her brown eyes to the light spattering of freckles to the corners of her lips.

"Is something the matter?" Concern edged his voice, enhancing his accent.

Aggie frowned, shaking her head. She looked back at the rose, at the petal that slipped loose from its stem and floated toward the ground. It drifted softly until its pink softness rested on the mud at the base of the gravestone.

Not over.

Aggie had no desire to be in the middle of an untold story. A story someone had penned remembrance of onto a rose petal.

She dropped the rose, ignoring the way her shoe crushed it into the messy ground.

"Everything's fine," she called back to Collin.

Lies.

But sometimes lies were far better than the truth. Sometimes, at least, a lie didn't hurt as much.

CHAPTER 7

Imogene

The rain was fitting. Umbrellas created a black canopy over the mourners that gathered beside Hazel's grave. It was open, like a muddy chasm ready to swallow the coffin whole. And it would. Not long after the graveside service, they would return to their vehicles, and the gravediggers would lower Hazel into the ground and shovel the suffocating muck onto her.

The muffled sounds of her mother's sobs wafted through the air and met Imogene's ears. She felt her brother Chet's presence next to her, his uniform of dark blue so authoritative. But he had not used that authority. Four days since Hazel's murder and there was nothing—*nothing*—but the empty echoes of their old farmhouse. The pungent smell of bleach and ammonia drifting through the registers after cleaners had tried to right the evidence of wrong that had been left behind. Staining the moment Hazel drew her last gasping breath.

Imogene wanted to weep, but she couldn't. She wanted to believe the empty platitudes people spoke to her. The funeral clichés. She even wanted to believe people were sorry—and they were—and yet it didn't mean anything. It didn't take away the gut-wrenching agony of loss. Grief was a pond of quicksand,

54

and escaping it was a mythical hope that left Imogene more bereft than when she simply allowed the sorrow to consume her. It was a slow suffocation, but what did it matter? She was practically dead anyway. Without Hazel, without her beloved younger sister, she was . . . lifeless.

The reverend finished his eulogy. Rain puddled at their feet. Imogene looked beyond Hazel's coffin to the gravestones that lined a row—1901, 1919 . . . and now here Hazel was. Some thirty years after, the ground being opened again. Yet there was no family to surround her. Only strangers. Old, dead strangers who wouldn't greet her body with any familiarity at all.

There was no comfort in that.

Imogene watched blankly as her mother placed a rose on Hazel's coffin, her gloved hand sweeping across the wood until it reached the edge. Her fingers curled, and her hand shook. A deep guttural wail, and Imogene's father put his hands on either side of the woman who grieved her youngest child, leading her away.

Her brother Ivan and his wife. They paused, and Ivan laid another rose on Hazel's casket. Imogene heard him sniff. Saw her sister-in-law loop a comforting hand through Ivan's elbow.

Good. Imogene swallowed a massive lump in her throat. Ivan didn't deserve to survive four years of the war, separated from his wife, fighting in the Pacific against God knew what horrors, only to return home to more of the same. To his sister's murder. Ivan had already been withdrawn, prone to long bouts of sullenness. Imogene had heard him in the barn, taking out his pent-up wrath on the cows. Shouting expletives as if one more would be the final bandage over a wound within him that refused to heal. Imogene never judged her brother. She just stayed out of his way.

Now she eyed him, hating herself for the fleeting, rebellious thought that winged through her mind. Ivan. Anger. She recalled the time he'd kicked the barn cat across the aisle and into the wall. Imogene had been furious with him but had waited to run to the cat's aid until after Ivan had left. He hadn't killed the poor thing, but it was stunned, and for sure must've been pained because the tabby had curled up on the front porch in the corner and not moved for at least a week.

Ivan caught Imogene's study as he passed, his faithful wife, her hand, gloved in black, still hooked in his arm.

"Genie—" he choked. Paused. Reached out a hand toward her, then stilled.

Imogene wanted to throw herself into her older brother's arms. As she had as a child. But so much had changed. So much was different now. There were ghosts in his eyes that she didn't understand.

Lifting her hand, Imogene took her brother's, feeling the warmth of his skin through the lace of her glove.

"I'm swell," she whispered the empty encouragement to him. *Don't worry about me.* She was stronger than Mother was. Mother would need Ivan.

"I'll be at the farm later—help with chores an' all." Ivan's comment was unnecessary. He was always at the farm, always helping Daddy. But grasping for words on a day like today meant avoiding the agony of saying goodbye. Simple, straightforward, everyday conversation was about all Ivan would be good for.

"See you later," Genie acknowledged. She met her sister-in-law's sad eyes as they passed. She didn't know her well. Ivan wasn't the social one of the family, and when he left the farm after a long day, he ostracized himself at home with his wife.

Chet moved beside Imogene. He was a bachelor and alone, so he took her arm and led her to Hazel's casket. The other mourners were dissipating into the rain. The motors of several of the cars started up. The rumble of a truck clattered. Voices were low and muttered, reverent and respectful.

Imogene stood next to Chet, clutching her black handbag. She'd worn a black wool suit. One she'd made a few years before when Mother had chided her for being frivolous when the war efforts were on. Spending money on a black frock was ridiculous. But Imogene had to. She had to show her respects to the boys who came home in boxes. Mother couldn't understand it. Said the dresses they had were good enough and folks would understand. But, for Imogene, they weren't. They only showed the boys that what they'd died fighting for was coming true. America was slowly losing, the economy still poor, and the people were emptying of hope. Imogene was proud. Proud of her friends who were never supposed to have died so young.

Now she was proud of Hazel—but it was almost impossible to reconcile her death. There was nothing heroic in it. Just murdering thievery.

"You haven't arrested anyone." Imogene spoke the words less like an accusation and more as an observation. She didn't miss Chet's heavy sigh.

He stared down at the roses on Hazel's coffin. "No. We've few clues."

"There has to be something." Imogene bit her tongue.

"It's not that easy, Genie." Chet's voice was choked.

Imogene glanced up at him. His jaw worked back and forth, holding back grief for his little sister. "Gosh, Chet." She wrapped her arm around his. "I don't blame you. Really. I just don't want him to get away with this. I want you to stick it to him and make him pay."

Whoever this "him" was.

Chet looked down at her. "We're investigating it. Every angle. Trying to figure out who—" This time his words cut off with emotion. He blinked fast and shook his head. With his free hand, Chet reached up and patted Imogene's hand, then pulled away. "I—I—need . . ." He waved toward the police car that sat yards away in line to leave the cemetery.

Imogene saw Chet's escape for what it was. "That's fine. I'm riding with Lola." She referenced her friend, who waited by another car, driven by her husband.

Chet nodded and walked away, leaving Imogene alone with Hazel.

She reached out and laid her hand on the coffin. Oh, the feel of it was cold through her glove. It didn't matter how pretty, how polished, or how detailed the casket was. It was still a box that would eventually decay. It would expose Hazel to the earth, her body becoming the dust from whence man had first originated.

Images scrolled through Imogene's mind like those in a moving picture at the theater. Only Fred Astaire wasn't dancing his way in a lively tap through her memories. It was Hazel. The moments she would throw her head back in laughter, her eyes lighting up the world around her. Those moments when Imogene would catch sight of Hazel, curled up in the hay in the barn loft, accompanied by at least two or three of the many farm cats that roamed the place, with a book in her hand. Usually a Grace Livingston Hill romance novel she'd picked up at the local store. She recalled the quiet humming—always humming—of some song Hazel had heard on the radio. She'd hum while she cooked dinner, hummed while she curled her hair, hummed while Imogene painted Hazel's chipped nails from working at the plant, and hummed as her feet took her into the attic to bed at night.

All music had stopped. It ceased the moment the last breath expelled through Hazel's parted lips, leaving her eyes open, staring up at Imogene as if to beg for help. To beg for life. To beg that everything be put right again.

A tear trailed down Imogene's cheek. She swiped it away, refusing to lift her hand from the casket.

"Miss Grayson?"

The reverend's voice was low. She lifted her head, looking through the wisp of black netting that draped off her hat.

"I'm not leaving her." Imogene knew the reverend was there to urge her to finish her goodbyes. The gravediggers stood off to the left of them at a discreet distance. But it was obvious they were impatient, weary of standing in the drizzle, their overalls dampening with every drop.

"Miss Grayson, I—"

"Leave me." Imogene's direct interruption made the man of the cloth step back. She knew her green eyes snapped when provoked, and she knew she had an edge to her personality that wasn't warm like Hazel's. But for now, she was okay to let that show. There was no hurry, really. It was five hours yet until dark. She could stand here for at least four more of them, and it would be the epitome of rudeness for anyone to escort her away against her will.

The reverend cleared his throat, but when she paid him no further attention, Imogene heard his footsteps squash against the damp grass as he retreated.

She was left alone with Hazel again. Their last moments together. Imogene touched her fingertips to her lips, then pressed them on the coffin.

"My sweet sister," she whispered. "It's not right. Not right what they did to you." Her words choked her breath, and Imogene paused to swallow the emotion. "But I'll . . . I'll make sure it's made right. I promise you, sweetheart. I'll make sure Chet finds who did this to you, and I'll make sure they see justice."

Imogene let her fingers drag from the top of the casket until her hand dropped to her side.

"I'll forget nothing, Hazel, *nothing*. I promise."

It was a promise Imogene fully intended to keep. Even if it took a lifetime.

—⟋⟍⟍⟋—

"And they've found nothing?" Lola, Imogene's best friend, and newly married to her war hero, Ben, poured tea into a cup and set it before Imogene.

Imogene shook her head, running her finger with its bright red nail around the rim of the cup. "Chet told me this morning that since the funeral, they've interviewed a few people who last saw Hazel. From the ammunition plant. She worked a full day, Lola, a *full day* and there wasn't one person who saw anything suspicious!"

"Well," Lola said as she eased onto her chair, her dark curls pinned back from the sides of her face, her longer nose and strong features signs she had definitive German roots. "Hazel had nothing to hide, Genie, we know that."

"Do we?" Imogene retorted.

Lola's brown eyes raised to meet Imogene's in surprise. "You're saying Hazel was secretive?"

"No!" Imogene shook her head, a sigh expelling from her lips. "No, I'm saying maybe there *was* something else. Maybe Hazel was afraid of someone, or—or maybe someone was bothering her and she just didn't tell anyone. Didn't tell me."

"You would have known if Hazel was afraid." Lola took a sip of her coffee, her rose-pink lipstick staining the rim. "You and Hazel shared everything. You'd have been the first to know."

Imogene stared into the corner of Lola's little kitchenette. A small room just off the main living space she shared in her apartment with Ben. The yellow walls were cheery, and it was decorated simply, the colorful porcelain cookie jar in the shape of a pig the most compelling object demanding the eye's attention. It had on blue-painted overalls, and its snout was big. One only had to lift the pig's head to retrieve the temptation inside. And Lola's cookies were a temptation . . . normally.

Not today. Imogene wasn't hungry. She wasn't sure she'd ever be able to eat again without feeling that pit in her stomach clenching with grief.

"Chet said they pulled some fingerprints," Imogene continued, assuming Lola wanted the details, however gruesome they might be. "Nothing came back. They didn't match any of the cards on file. They haven't even found the murder weapon."

Lola paled, but to her credit she didn't react. "I never did hear of—well, of how she died."

Imogene lifted the teacup and took a long drink. It was lukewarm already, its chamomile intending to calm instead coating Imogene's throat and lodging at the lump of emotion that had stilled there. Her breath shuddered as she drew it in, then released it.

"She was—hit. On the back of the head."

"Lan' sakes," Lola whispered in shock, shaking her head.

"More than once," Imogene added. She squeezed her eyes shut. She could see every detail. Every detail that she had promised Hazel she would remember.

"Chet'll find him." Lola reached across the kitchen table and grasped Imogene's hand, squeezing. "He will. Give him time. Someone out there knows something."

"But it's already been a week." Imogene had never been patient. "I swear, Ivan isn't any more patient than me. Chet won't say much. Mother and Daddy may have moved back into the house, but it's silent as a tomb. Daddy gets up first thing and heads out to the cows to do the milkin'. He stays out all day." She paused. The recent events harboring deep inside threatening to bubble up and out. When Imogene met Lola's dark eyes, she could hold it no longer.

"Folks came in and cleaned it up." She remembered the blood. The stained floor. The spattered bedspread. But cleaning hadn't erased the last remnants of Hazel. She and her mother still had to go through Hazel's things, pack or give them away, and shut up the attic bedroom for good.

"Shhh . . ." Lola hadn't released Imogene's hand yet. "Don't bother yourself with it. Things will set themselves right."

Set themselves right.

Could anything ever be right again? Imogene let Lola's soothing murmur seep into her soul, but along with the nurturing reassurances came a darkness that Imogene couldn't ignore. It slithered inside of her, taunting her, telling her that someone had literally gotten away with murder.

Yes. Yes, someone *would* set things right.

Imogene would.

CHAPTER 8

Aggie

She couldn't sleep. Melatonin hadn't helped, and Aggie was about ready to get up and chug a bottle of nighttime cough syrup. Tossing to her right side, she stared through the filmy lace curtain that hung over the four-paned window. Her bedroom in the house Mumsie had moved into when Aggie was a toddler was on the second floor. Its whitewashed wood floors creaked with every step, and she still remembered which parts of the floor were the worst and how to step over the especially loud squeaks. The ceiling slanted downward from the peak of the roof, creating an adorable window-seat area that was piled with old throw pillows. Everything in this house screamed old-fashioned, as though Mumsie had decorated it to match what her home might have been like in her early days. Mom had told Aggie that Mumsie grew up on a farm outside of Mill Creek in what was now a subdivision. Much of the furniture in this house, Mom had told her, once belonged to Mumsie's mother.

Her nighttime perusal of the architecture and décor of her bedroom had Aggie missing how not long ago she'd spent her days identifying selling points in a home, coordinating her pitch to her client, and plain old letting herself reimagine properties.

Man. She'd really messed up her career. People management wasn't her forte. Having a few junior realtors beneath her had been more of a pain than anything of promise. Now here she was eyeing her grandmother's house as though it were listed in a For Sale brochure.

Aggie rolled back toward the opposite wall. The red light on the clock told her it was two in the morning. She was going to be exhausted tomorrow when she had to endure another awkward breakfast with Mumsie, then try to put the files in the cemetery office into some sort of order, so that she and Collin could start working on the new graveyard map.

Aggie growled and sat up, flipping her legs over the side of the bed. Warm milk. Maybe that would do the trick. She couldn't exactly medicate at two a.m. or she'd not wake up until noon.

The doorknob wobbled in its housing, the crystal knob uneven beneath Aggie's hand. She tugged at the door, wincing at the fact that humidity in the house made it stick. The last thing she wished to do was wake up Mumsie, who'd been oddly reserved and lacking opinion at dinner. Mumsie's room was just across the hall. Aggie paused and looked at the closed door, a pang nudging her heart. All these years, Mumsie had lived in this place alone. She was nearing a century old. What if she fell? Why hadn't she moved to a room downstairs where it was safer? Mom would have checked in on Mumsie these last couple of years, but with her gone . . .

Aggie blinked away the emotion. No. Tonight was not the night to consider Mom and her passing. She tiptoed down the hall, the wood floors cold against her toes. Her oxford-style nightshirt hung to just above her knees, the buttons matching the red satin material. Aggie hesitated at the top stair. To the right was Mumsie's study. At least that was what Mom had always called it. When she was little, Aggie had titled it The Room with the Closed Door, because she liked to be super original with titles. She'd caught glimpses inside the room when she'd met Mumsie in the hallway as she came out. Nothing unusual. Nothing mysterious to draw Aggie's curiosity.

But now, for some reason, the moonlight shafting down the hall from the window behind Aggie illuminated the door as if it were asking to be opened. As she complied, the silence was more powerful to Aggie than had the hinges moaned their argument against the intrusion. A waft of musty air met her nose. The kind that hinted of days captured in a treasure box of memories and if she stepped over the threshold, somehow, she would be stepping back into time.

The room held an eerie glow, bluish-yellow moonlight stretching across the wood floor. A large oval rag rug adorned the middle of the room, its hues of reds and pinks and yellows all muted in the nighttime light. Aggie caught sight of an old floor console radio, reminiscent of the thirties. The prewar era when the world was broiling, ready to shatter the lingering darkness of the Great Depression and catapult them into the over-glorified horrors of war that would not leave anyone untouched.

Aggie's fingers clung to the doorjamb. For some reason, she was holding her breath and wondered if in the morning she would still firmly insist she heard the jazzy strains of Billie Holiday rising from the radio. Her gaze skimmed the rest of the room.

A desk with an old yellow vinyl-covered chair, much like one might have seen in a kitchen during the same era. On its top, a porcelain figurine with a pink-hued hooped dress, her dark hair coiffed into a Civil War–era style. It looked as though one might lift the girl by her glass shoulders and she would split from her skirt into a small jewelry box.

Something drew Aggie into the room, into its capture. Mumsie's home was dated in all its rooms, but it had no sentimental ties. Nothing nostalgic. It wasn't an old family home, but rather a house Mumsie bought when she was in her retirement years. But this room . . . something was different. A part of Aggie instantly felt as though she *should* feel drawn to it. As though it housed memories that told stories of family history—even though that couldn't possibly be the case.

Or could it?

Aggie's experienced eye took in the white iron bed with its chipped paint and bedspread of white, with a floral sheet folded in a tight crease over the top. A picture frame, positioned on the bedside table, was strangely empty. The cardboard backing peered through the glass, and the metal frame with its tiny embellishments was tarnished from age. An empty frame. Just the sight of it was sad. Lonesome. Aggie wondered why Mumsie had it there, positioned as if it were waiting for happiness to find it and insert itself behind the glass. Faces with smiles, pleasant memories, or the warmth of a loved one's profile. But it was empty. Ugly and forlorn.

Aggie released a pent-up breath. She'd been holding it, drawn into the emptiness that strangely echoed her own heart. Grief was a lonely occupation, made worse with time's ticking cadence. It passed by each moment as though standing outside looking in at a world that should have stopped moving with death but instead kept striding forward. Oblivious to the pain that screamed just outside its chamber.

The floor creaked, breaking her concentration. Aggie glanced up and her eyes connected with the four-paned window. Outside, the world was dark, modern, and an airplane's red light blinked high in the sky. She pulled her attention back to the room. Against the wall, closest to the bedroom door, was a rather large dollhouse stationed on a straight-legged wooden card table. She hardly registered the coolness of the flooring and the way each floorboard's crease met the bottoms of her bare feet as she approached it.

Aggie narrowed her eyes, reaching up to tuck straight strands of her dark hair behind her ear, tilting her head to note all the tiny features. The front of the dollhouse was open, as if someone had cut a farmhouse—with an architectural style reminiscent of the turn of the century—in half. Aggie couldn't resist the small smile that played at her lips. She lifted her fingertips hesitantly, wanting to touch the delicate rooms, the shingling on the roof, the addition that stretched off the left side of the house.

It was ridiculously detailed. Aggie let her mind embrace the old music that played in her head, the strains of the trumpet, the gravelly voice of Louis Armstrong. Oh, for the time when life slowed to that lazy pace of postwar farm life.

Her finger touched the peak of the dollhouse. It was a vernacular farmhouse. Obviously not designed by an architect so much as pieced together by the hands of someone who used whatever materials and design skills they had on hand. Probably an original house built in the eighteen hundreds, then added on to and eventually becoming the creative version that sat before her, though now in imitation dollhouse form.

Aggie was stunned by the detailing. The shingling was pieced onto the roof with the precision of a roofer. The rooms inside were wallpapered or painted, and the flooring was intricate, down to the detailing of the linoleum kitchen floor and its olive-green squares.

She ran her hand down the center board that divided the house into rooms. Front parlor, living quarters, the kitchen, a small bathroom with pink fixtures, all on the first floor. The second, boasting two bedrooms, a study, and a nursery. Her gaze drifted to the gabled attic. It spanned the entire length of the dollhouse, its walls covered in a delicate paper with tiny roses.

Aggie frowned. Goodness, if the bed didn't look just like . . . She tilted her head and squinted, then shot a quick look over her shoulder at the bed in the room. It was. It was exactly the same. The spread, the sheets, the iron frame.

The moments that had been thick with wistfulness were now replaced by something different that crept in like an uninvited intruder. Aggie couldn't place it. A feeling that something was very wrong in this quaint house replicating days gone by. She bent to peer into the attic room. It was difficult to see without turning on the bedroom light, but she'd no desire to awaken Mumsie and be confronted with the guilt of snooping.

There was something on the wallpaper by the bed. Aggie put her face right up to the open room, straining to see. Her vision traveled down the wall to the floor. The sight snatched her breath from her, and Aggie took an abrupt step backward. She shouldn't be shocked to see a doll in a dollhouse, but this was . . . this was . . . this was no ordinary doll.

The miniature lay facedown on the floor. Red paint was pooled beneath her head and meticulously spotted along the side of the white bedspread. There was red on the doll's fingertips, as if she'd dipped her own hand into the imitation blood. A book lay discarded on the rug beside the bloody doll.

Aggie stumbled back until her hip hit the iron frame of the bed. She whirled and stared with horror at the floor as though the woman's body had appeared there and was lying in her pooled gore.

But the floor was bare.

The rag rug was clean.

The bedspread that touched the floor where it hung over the side was . . . Aggie covered her mouth with her hand, wishing her imagination was simply being overactive in the midnight trance of no sleep. But it wasn't. Stains dotted the white spread. She could see them even in the moonlight. Aggie assessed a few of them. Three on the bottom. Three out of many, but those three were . . .

She hurried back to the dollhouse and stared in. Yes. Yes! The same three stains were brilliant red in the dollhouse and mere pinpricks in comparison to the real blotches that had stained the spread from long ago.

The figurine replica! On the desk!

Aggie's eyes widened, and she spun to assess the figurine on the desk in the room where she stood.

It was the same. Of course it was!

The dollhouse was a morbid crime-scene reenactment, and this room—this room was a modified version!

The room was suffocating now. A cool draft fluttered across Aggie's bare legs, like the breath of a murdered ghost, softly affirming to Aggie they were there. Still there and haunting the room with more than their memories, but also the details of their death.

Aggie shivered.

There were voices here. Old voices hissing to be heard, trapped in the vault of time. *Mumsie's* vault.

She'd had enough.

Aggie hurried to the bedroom door and then skidded to a stop on the floor. The door was closed. She was certain—*certain*—she'd left it open on entry. Grasping the doorknob, the door opened without resistance, and Aggie catapulted into the hallway, dragging the door shut behind her. It closed with a firm latch, locking the phantoms inside. The ones who wanted to come out, to fly away, and to revive the horrific memories that came hand in hand with the Grim Reaper. Grief. Sorrow. That feeling that something precious had been stolen and would never be returned. Ever.

CHAPTER 9

She'd thought they would have dissipated. The ghosts. But they hadn't. Instead, they'd clawed their way into her soul and created a permanent residence there. Even over breakfast, it had taken all of Aggie's reserve not to interrogate Mumsie, seek out answers, and shoo this horrible sensation away. Mumsie had eyed her sullenly. She knew—or it *felt* like she knew—that Aggie had crossed the threshold into the room at the end of the hall. That she had snooped into a reimagined past that was meant to stay shuttered. That she now had questions parading through her mind to an anthem that would not be silenced. But really there was no way Mumsie could have known, not unless she'd seen Aggie. Unless she'd been the one to shut Aggie in the bedroom last night, closing her in with the spirits of the past.

"Are you going inside or are we going to make a practice of opening doors via mind control?"

Collin's lilting sarcasm snapped Aggie out of her vacant stare at the cemetery office's door. The little one-room building wasn't inspiring peace this morning, and she'd been caught clutching the leather strap to her bag that hung over her shoulder and staring at the paint-chipped door.

"I'm just pausing for fresh air." Aggie wished she was witty and capable of responding with quips. But in reality she was practical, and her creativity was reserved for architectural prowess alone.

Collin winked. He was *such* a ginger. More so in the morning light than she'd noticed in the past. Even the light stubble on his cheeks and chin reflected copper, and his wavy hair responded to the sun with a vibrance that made Aggie blink. He was a complete visual of his personality. Cheery. Sunny. Charming.

She, on the other hand? Aggie glanced down at her leather flats, her skinny blue jeans, and the white, tailored oxford shirt that was unbuttoned into a feminine V at the collar. Her hair couldn't be described any less interestingly than jet-black, and yet she knew the freckles that dotted her nose betrayed her otherwise ivory-skinned complexion. Still, she was uptight, dark, boring, and . . . emotionally fried. She was like a burnt marshmallow that once had been sweet but had come too close to the fire and was left crispy and unwanted.

"Do you like s'mores?" Aggie tossed the question out before thinking it through.

Collin pursed his lips, his wire-framed glasses perched with a quirky bent on his nose. "I can't say as they're my preferred. An excellent *flan* on the other hand . . ." He kissed his fingertips and spread them wide. "*Delicioso!*"

Now he was speaking Italian. The man was either a well-traveled conundrum or liked to play up his foreign persona with extra dramatic flair.

"Sure." Aggie shrugged off his happiness. For a fleeting moment, she recalled a time when she'd made s'mores with her mother and had burned a marshmallow and Mom threw it away. Funny how such memories sometimes paralleled life far too closely.

"I'm going in," Aggie said brusquely, as if she'd been waiting for Collin the entire time. She fumbled with the key on her key ring. Mr. Richardson had given her a spare the first day she'd met him here. The first time she'd seen Fifteen Puzzle Row and before she'd begun the slow but steady spiral down into some sort of darkness that lingered over this place.

She moved to put the key in the doorknob, then drew back. The door was already open a crack. Just a hair really, but still, it was unlocked, and all it needed was a nudge of her toe and it would open.

"Weird," she muttered.

"Is it open already?" Collin asked over her shoulder.

Aggie ignored him and pushed the door with her hand. It swung open, silent and slow. Like a small melodrama playing out before her eyes. She stared as daylight stretched into the boxlike office. Her eyes captured the vision that lay before her. She stared for so long that Collin edged by her and poked his head into the office.

"Crikey!" he said.

Aggie lifted an eyebrow. Okay, now he was overplaying the vernacular expressions just a tad too much. British, Australian, or whatever it was he claimed to be, the man was a melting pot of terminology.

Collin gave Aggie a quick glance over his shoulder, obviously missing her look of censure. "Well now, I didn't expect this!"

Okay. British there. It tinged his words with a delightful hint of Mr. Darcy mashed with Doctor Who.

Aggie shook off her question of who Collin O'Shaughnessy really was and followed his gaze. The office had been ransacked. Papers strewn across the desk and the floor. Index cards lay everywhere, from a shelf on the wall to the far corners as if they'd exploded from a confetti machine. The desk chair was tipped over, revealing the metal feet on the bottoms of its wooden legs. And the computer monitor's cords hung unattached, the CPU missing, and with it the contents of the cemetery's digitized records.

"Please tell me they back things up on the Cloud." Aggie couldn't help the desperate whine that escaped her.

"Blast if I know." Even the twinkle had faded from Collin's eyes. He was already reaching for his phone—an old flip phone with a dent in its top.

"Who are you calling?" It was a silly question. Aggie already knew the answer.

Collin replied anyway, no criticism in his tone. "The police, of course."

Aggie moved past Collin into the room, intending to look closer. The warmth of his fingers wrapped around her wrist, pulling her back. Aggie stumbled into him, her shoulder colliding with his.

"Stay with me, Love. They won't want you traipsing over the evidence."

Evidence.

A crime had been committed.

Aggie swallowed back the sudden onslaught of tears. Not the frightened sort and not the terrified sort, but the kind that was married to barely concealed frustration. How had she come so far into the depths of a place she never wanted to visit again? All in the course of a few days? Between skeleton models seemingly falling from the sky to dollhouse murder scenes to roses with cryptic ink messages, and now violated office spaces. Aggie wanted nothing more than to climb into her car and whisk herself back to Chicago.

But she couldn't go back. There was nothing to go back to. No job, no future, and worst of all, no mother. Maybe that was it. This dull nausea in the pit of her stomach. Maybe that was why Aggie wanted nothing more than to flee the cemetery and escape from Mumsie's house and her influence. Every piece of it demanded that Aggie remember Mom. Remember those last days. Remember the days in between the good and the bad. Remember her smile, her scent, her voice . . .

Death wasn't a promoter of healing. It was destructive and wicked, and now Aggie felt as though she were in its employ. It was not a career choice she had ever wanted to make, yet death held too much influence to say no.

———〰———

"You're shaking."

His observation was astute. Aggie looked down at her arms. She'd wrapped them around herself, clutching her elbows until her knuckles matched the white of her shirt.

Collin's hand was warm as he unlatched her fingers from her left arm and wrapped his around her freed hand. He drew her over to his car—a little rusty thing that must run on diesel fuel because she could smell tiny bits of it wafting in the air.

"Sit." He waved at the hood of the car, and Aggie planted her backside on the green paint with the obedience of a child who didn't know what to do.

Shut down. This was what she did in moments of crisis. Well, it wasn't exactly a crisis so much as—Aggie squeezed her eyes shut. It didn't matter. She tried to convince herself she was strong and independent, but really she just wanted security. She had for years. It just wasn't kind enough to offer itself to her. She didn't have words or thoughts or even emotions. She just became a blank on which the moment could write whatever it wanted, and tomorrow she'd awaken and refuse to ever think of it again.

"I'm fine," Aggie insisted, even as Collin pulled an unopened bottle of water from his car and held it out to her. She waved it away.

"Sure you are." He didn't believe her.

She would stay composed. Not fly off the handle, as Mumsie would call it. But everything in her body wanted to launch into a version of her father's raving, arm-waving explosion of emotion. Aggie took deep breaths and regulated her reaction.

"Mr. Richardson is on his way." Collin hoisted himself onto the hood of his jalopy, and the car groaned in protest against their combined weight. "Officer Benton there said it sounds like teenage vandalism. They hauled off with the computer for a lark."

"Curious." Aggie couldn't hide the derision in her tone. "The same way they dropped a skeleton in my grandmother's backyard? I'm suddenly being harassed by the disturbed youth of America."

Collin chuckled. "I believe they always blame kids when there's no other obvious explanation for something."

"Don't they have a surveillance camera?" Aggie inquired.

"Here?" Collin's gaze swept over the flooded expanse of the cemetery. "What for? To catch a ghost?"

"Well, obviously there was something of interest in the office. Something they wanted that computer for."

"Sure," Collin nodded. "To play video games on. Or maybe shoot pellet guns at for target practice."

"Pellet guns?" Aggie raised a dark, well-sculpted eyebrow. One she'd spent time on that morning and now wondered why it'd been so important to look her best for acres of dead people.

Collin twisted off the cap and handed the water bottle to Aggie. "Drink up. My mother says staying hydrated is the best medicine for mental health."

Aggie glared at the bottle, then at Collin. "What are you implying?"

"Nothing. Just that you need water."

"There's enough water around here as it is," Aggie groused, but then she took the water bottle and held it.

"Drink up, Love." Collin directed.

"I'm not your 'Love,'" Aggie muttered as her lips met the rim of the water bottle.

"It's just a nickname. If you keep glaring at me with those pretty eyes, you'll gut me. So take pity on a bloke, all right?"

"Gut you?" Aggie curled her lip and gave him a stern eye. "Really? Pull some more cliché overseas phrases from your back pocket, why don't you?"

"Never mind." Collin slipped off the hood of the car and ran his fingers through his sunshine hair. "This is why I play with insects. They make a lot more sense than a female."

Aggie tipped her head, irritation swelling in her. "A female? Really? You're going all Neanderthal on me?"

Collin's mouth thinned as he surveyed her from top of head to tip of toe. His cheek dimples deepened, and Aggie felt herself flush.

"A man has a right to be a Neanderthal now and then, Love. Same as a woman has a right to be a—well, never you mind."

"Very funny." And it was. That was the part that made her fight the tiny smile that played at her lips. Collin wasn't afraid to speak his mind, even if he encased it with colloquialisms and a dapper smile.

Moments later, Mr. Richardson arrived in his wool sweater and loafers, with stooped shoulders and a bit of a wild-eyed look about him that communicated he was as bewildered as she was at the break-in. It wasn't even typical cemetery vandalism. Damage to gravestones, or flowers and flags ripped from their memorials. This was more direct, and regardless of what platitudes the cops might offer in suggesting it was a wayward teenager, it also felt more deliberate.

Only Aggie couldn't explain why.

—⟋⟍—

Clean it up.

Now that the cops had left, pictures taken, statements made, it was all there, still as messy as ever, and apparently, Aggie had now been tasked with righting the ransacked office before getting back to the job she was hired to do. Connecting the dots from grave to grave, matching them with records, exhuming the history from unmarked graves. All of it was for naught considering the two-thousand-plus index cards scattered about the room, not to mention the random folders of papers and even some old photographs.

"Them cards there. Those are all records of plots." Mr. Richardson gave his arm a broad sweep. "They used to at least be in order."

"We'll set it to rights," Collin assured the elderly man, who raised an eyebrow at him.

"*She'll* set it to rights," Mr. Richardson corrected. "We didn't bring you here to sort through paper work."

"Of course not—" Collin began to affirm when the man broke into his sentence.

"Got thousands of graves in this cemetery—two thousand, I believe—and they all need accounted for. Or found, to be specific."

The graveyard was indeed large, boasting many graves, but Aggie could hardly fathom there being two thousand graves on the acreage. Still, the index cards weren't lying. She picked up one of the cards.

Plot 162
Purchased by: Parkson, Edward
Purchase year: 1964
Deceased: Parkson, Elsie

All the information was there, along with . . . she eyed another card . . . along with all the information that *wasn't* there. The card she skimmed was lacking a purchase year and also the name of the deceased. It was also typed in 1952 for someone who'd purchased a plot in 1929. Apparently, they'd been playing records catch-up for quite some time.

"Yes, well, I'll set right to work on that," Collin was saying when Aggie pulled her attention back to the two men beside her.

"Darn tootin' you will." Mr. Richardson lifted a bushy eyebrow. "You have all that fancy machinery and gadgets. Leastways we'll know there's a body there before we sell what we think is an empty plot and wind up digging old bones up to the surface. And there isn't a one of those plots already flooded that's gonna return their contents to their original glory. So, let's be sure those bodies are marked and stay underground."

Aggie cleared her throat, and both men turned to her. "How do we mark the graves once Collin identifies them? What if we can't find their gravestones?"

"Gravestones?" Mr. Richardson barked. "Heavens, woman, are you thinkin' Mr. O'Shaughnessy is goin' to uncover the plots and find some fancy nametag in the dirt to tell us who's been buried there?"

Aggie opened her mouth to respond, then snapped it shut. Really, that was a good question. "Well, how *do* you figure out who was buried there?"

Mr. Richardson gave her an offhanded wave of arthritic fingers. "Well then. There're the records that were on the computer, but we can't cross-check those anymore. Then there's alllllllllllll this." He dragged out the word as if he were talking to a juvenile. "Paper, m'dear. Paper. It's why it's gotta get sorted and logged. Then you chat with people who might know somethin', if you can't find a lead from the records. Pretty much everyone in town is connected somehow. Heck, my seventh cousin pastors the Lutheran church and we don't even share the same last name, but we know we're cousins. People around here know the local history."

Seventh cousin? Aggie grimaced. Either Mr. Richardson and his townsfolk were all historians and ancestral geniuses, or she needed to rethink her own view of family history. She could maybe identify a second cousin—under duress.

Collin and Aggie exchanged glances over the mess. "So," Collin started, "you're suggesting that if the records don't match an unmarked grave, we simply interview residents of Mill Creek at random in hopes we stumble upon someone who happens to recall the death of a distant relative who was buried without a headstone in plot number eight-two?"

Aggie bit her bottom lip at the cynical wit emanating from Collin's eyes.

Mr. Richardson shook his head. "Naw. Ain't no one goin' to know what you're talkin' about if you talk in plot numbers. Plots, man, plots! Families! If there's an unmarked grave near a mass of other graves, stands to reason they're probably related and in the family section of the graveyard." The old man tugged on his sweater, muttering to himself, "Young folks these days don't use their heads. They have *search engines* to do their thinkin' for them."

Aggie was feeling the weight of the monumental task before her and Collin, and honestly, more on her simply because Collin at least had equipment and expertise to put to use.

"And you, missy!" Mr. Richardson gave her a curious look. "I don't know what young man is in your back pocket, but we'll expect you to keep your love life off work hours."

Aggie choked, cleared her throat, and blinked. "Excuse me?"

Mr. Richardson wasn't paying her much attention. Instead, he was once again mumbling under his breath as he stepped over a manila folder on the floor. "Sendin' flowers on work time."

She followed his reach as Mr. Richardson lifted a pink rose off the desk. Its petals appeared manhandled and smashed, nowhere near its original glory. He handed the rose to her, a glimmer of sternness in his eyes. "A rose is right nice and all, but it's not the place here."

Not the place here. Aggie nodded with a blank expression, reaching for the long-stemmed rose, a frown firmly etched between her brows. "But this isn't—"

"No excuses now," Mr. Richardson said as he neared the door. "Let's just get to work and get goin' on this before the cemetery board is down on my head and makes me have a stroke." He stepped into the daylight and gave a haphazard flop of his arm. "I ain't even bought myself a plot yet!"

Then he was gone.

Aggie and Collin stood in silence in the middle of the trashed office, the wilting rose bending in her hand.

Finally Collin spoke. "I take it you know nothing about the rose?"

Aggie shook her head, giving him an incredulous look. "Nothing. I know . . ." Her eyes drifted across the petals, and she noted darkness staining one of them. Lifting it closer, she fingered the petal, pulling it gently off its stem.

Not over.

The ink bled into the veins of the petal, making the words difficult to read but still obvious in their penmanship.

"What's this about?" Collin's breath tickled her neck as he looked over her shoulder.

Aggie sensed that coldness returning. The same draft that had brushed by her legs in Mumsie's room last night. The same sensation that visited her in the wee hours of the morning when all she could think of was her mother and the look on her face after she had passed away. The frozen, empty expression that firmly planted an exclamation point at the end of her life. It was over. It was very much over!

She turned to give Collin a confused shake of her head. "I don't know. Death puts a finality to everyone's story, doesn't it?"

"In my experience." Collin gave her a nod, his brow furrowed as though trying to follow her train of thought.

Aggie lifted the petal for Collin to see. "Then who believes it's 'not over'? Who sees something here as still very much alive?"

Collin didn't answer for a moment, but a breath released through his nose in a studious sigh. "Or," he ventured, "who wants to be certain someone isn't forgotten?"

Someone.

Aggie's head snapped up. She met Collin's inquiring eyes. "Hazel. Hazel Grayson."

"Who?"

"The other day. In the flooded graves. There was a pink rose with the words *not over* written on a petal by the overturned stone of a Hazel Grayson."

"Who, might I ask, is Hazel Grayson?" Collin's eyebrow rose in a sharp angle over his left eye.

Aggie rubbed her thumb against the petal, her other hand still gripping the thornless stem of the rose. "I don't know." She swept her gaze over the tossed office. "But I suppose her story is in here. Somewhere."

"Or . . ." Collin's voice had dropped to a lower tone, void of any humor. Aggie sensed her concern rise as he continued. "Or it's her story that we won't find. That they didn't want us to find. That they made virtually impossible to find."

"A needle in a haystack." Aggie nodded, toeing a pile of index cards on the floor.

"That it is," Collin agreed.

But it wasn't. It couldn't be. For the two penned words on the rose petal had accomplished exactly what its author must have intended. It wasn't over. Hazel Grayson, whoever she was—or her memory—was being kept very much alive.

CHAPTER 10

Imogene

The powder plant stretched across thousands of acres of farmland. It had been erected quickly as the war progressed and the need for ammunitions became a demand. Now the demand was significantly decreasing, and chatter already had rumors flying that the on-site housing would close, and jobs would significantly decline. But for now, Imogene sat on the bus transporting workers from town to the plant grounds, her trousers loose around her legs and cuffed just above her leather loafers.

Just like *Hazel's* loafers. And just like Hazel's trousers with the wide legs and belted waist. And . . . Imogene took a subtle but deep breath, breathing in the scent of Hazel's fading perfume. She had rummaged through her sister's closet and now wore Hazel's red-and-white-checkered blouse with the feminine tucks at the shoulders creating tiny puffs. It made her feel closer to Hazel somehow.

Imogene had spent the morning teasing her black locks into two victory rolls that framed her oval forehead and then finished the look off with a floral scarf that looped from the base of her

81

neck and tied off at her crown. It was difficult not to primp further. She was never meant for factory work, war or no war. Imogene was schooled in fashion—pinup-girl fashion—to her parents' dismay.

She stared out the window as the bus clattered down the road. Trees rose on either side while it curved and wound through the hillside. Imogene would never be a pinup girl now. Not a model or an actress. Even her work at the beauty salon was thwarted in the wake of Hazel's murder. She ran her damp palms down the navy trousers. She was Hazel now. Or at least she would walk in Hazel's footsteps. Someone knew why Hazel died. It hadn't been random—that much Chet had leaked to the family. There was no prying open of locked doors, no evidence of intrusion other than the struggle in Hazel's room. A boot print had been discovered in the hallway, left on the carpet runner. The dirt had been examined and labeled as your typical earthen substance, mixed with small samples of manure and gravel. Nothing out of the ordinary for anyone in the Mill Creek area to have on the bottom of their shoes. The boot print was only a partial print, of normal size, not at all indicative of its owner. In fact, Chet said, it could even be their own father's.

The case was growing cold fast and it'd only been two weeks since Hazel's passing. Chet had warned Imogene to stay out of it. Not to pry or try to play detective. He tried to convince her that he was working on it—wouldn't stop working on it—but she found it hard to fathom that Chet would pursue the case with ongoing passion. He might be Hazel's brother, but he was also a law officer in Mill Creek with many distractions. His intentions would be sincere, but his time limited.

Imogene wasted no time obtaining work at the plant. The cafeteria needed help, and if she wasn't working with the powder itself, being near those who did would give her access to the people Hazel had brushed shoulders with daily. She'd been in laundry. Washing the coveralls of the men who stripped out of them after each shift, the residue and chemicals needing to be carefully cleaned from the fabric. Imogene had hoped Hazel's position in the laundry would be open, but it'd already been filled, leaving only the cafeteria as an option. The Mill Creek Ordnance Works wasn't hiring. If anything, they were letting people go.

"The war is over, after all."

The lilting voice broke into Imogene's thoughts—words that fit perfectly with what she'd been musing about. She turned from the scenery out the bus window and looked across the aisle. A woman, not much younger than Imogene, smiled at her with a gentle ease. For a brief flicker, Imogene was jealous of the peaceful sparkle in the girl's blue eyes and the frizz around her shoulder-length curls, indicative of a natural wave rather than a permanent.

"I'm sorry." The young woman folded and unfolded her fingers as though she were shy and for some reason intimidated by Imogene. "I didn't mean to bother you. I was just thinking about how bright the sun is. But it makes sense, you know? With the war finally being over now?"

"Of course." Imogene offered a smile, but doubted the sun cared whether the world was at war or at peace. She gave the young woman a quick once-over, knowing instinctively and not at all pridefully that she was far prettier than the girl across the aisle. Maybe that was why she was timid.

"I'm Ida. Ida Pickett." The girl lifted her hand in a small wave. She waited, and Imogene mustered another smile.

The bus drove over a pothole in the road, and they lurched in their seats.

"Imogene Grayson." Imogene offered her name and was surprised when the stranger's eyes instantly dimmed.

"Ohhhh." Ida put her fingers to her lips, which had no color on them to begin with. "Are you related to Hazel?"

The piercing agony of reality was never going to diminish at the mention of her sister's name, Imogene was sure of it. "She was my sister, yes."

"I'm so sorry." Ida reached for her handbag and pulled a handkerchief from it. She dabbed the corners of her eyes. "I'm sorry," she repeated. "I don't mean to make such a scene when it's *your* sister who's been lost. But I used to ride with Hazel. Every day to the plant, we'd sit right here." Ida glanced at the empty seat beside her, then fell silent.

Imogene hesitated only a moment before clutching her purse and rising from her crouched position, ducking to keep her head from hitting the roof of the bus. Struggling to keep her balance, she waddled across the aisle and plopped down onto the empty seat—Hazel's empty seat—and resolutely tilted her chin up. She tried to muster a brave and confident smile as she looked down her pert nose at Ida. "I'll fill her seat," Imogene announced, swallowing back her grief.

Ida offered a tiny smile in return. "That's awfully sweet of you." Imogene had no intention of letting this opportunity go to waste, yet she knew with someone as reserved as Ida Pickett seemed to be, that she'd need to temper her personality or she'd frighten the heebie-jeebies out of her.

"Did you—were you close to Hazel?" Doubtful, Imogene had already determined, but it was a polite way to inquire as to the terms of Ida's friendship with Imogene's sister. Hazel had never mentioned an Ida Pickett before. But then, Imogene admitted to herself, Hazel hadn't mentioned anyone from the plant.

Imogene tucked the realization away in the back of her mind as Ida tucked a curl behind her ear. "Oh, we were close enough, I suppose. Considering we shared the bus together most every day." Ida gave a small laugh. "I work in the cafeteria, and Hazel is in—*was* in—the laundry . . ." Ida's sentence dwindled.

Imogene snatched the opportunity. "I'm going to be working in the cafeteria."

"You are?" Ida's head snapped up, and she met Imogene's eyes. The friendly twinkle was back. "How lovely!"

"I hope I do well." Although Imogene was confident that making sandwiches and serving the workers wasn't going to be any more difficult than wrapping old Mrs. Puttaker's hair.

"You'll do just fine, I'm sure." Ida patted the back of Imogene's hand, and for a moment it stunned her. It was as though Hazel had somehow reached out of the grave to touch her. To be a part of reassuring Imogene that she was on the right trail. And to thank her for it.

Then Ida's hand lifted, and the moment was gone. Imogene studied Ida's profile as the young woman stared ahead, the bus turning into the entrance of the massive plant. Her cheeks were rounded and blushed. She was plain, sensible, everything that Hazel hadn't been. She'd been a dreamer—a responsible dreamer—trapped doing laundry at the plant instead of marrying some GI back from the front. Always dreaming, that was Hazel. Dreams that had ended in a nightmare.

—⟋⟍⟍⟍⟋—

"Didn't expect to see you here." Oliver Schneider's voice brought Imogene's head up with a snap. She met his solemn eyes and had a moment of brief appreciation for his handsome smile. While it was reserved, there was warmth in it. The kind that seemed to imply had he a different past, his future would have been brighter. As it was, it seemed quite a few of the men Imogene had already served lunch to shared that *look*. The look that implied they'd seen things another human being should never see, and that they had stories they would never repeat, never shape into words and retell.

"Well, Ollie Schneider." Imogene didn't even have to force the flirtatious tone into her voice. Good or bad, it came naturally, even if her insides were raw with grief. "I thought your daddy would have you working the fields, not brewing up potions at the powder plant."

The smile teased the corner of his mouth again, and he bobbed his head. "Seems he got used to havin' me gone."

Oh. Imogene swallowed hard. There was no good response to that. Everyone knew that the Schneiders had lost two of their nine boys to the war. Ollie's homecoming was tainted with sorrow of a different kind than Imogene's, but sorrow nonetheless. Sometimes that sort of hardship made the good things go unnoticed. Grief cast shadows over places of happiness and left them in permanent darkness.

"Are you—farin' all right?" Oliver's question was delivered with a kindness that almost made tears spring to Imogene's eyes. She hadn't forgotten the way he'd traveled up the attic stairs with her to view the scene where she'd first found Hazel. Hadn't forgotten that he'd helped her down the stairs after she'd memorized every piece of that room and then tried to descend from it with legs that had turned weak. His arm had been strong. Thin but strong.

"Swell," she lied.

He knew it. Oliver's eyes darkened, and he gave her an understanding nod as she handed him a sandwich on a plate. Turkey. No mustard. Just a decent slice of cheddar cheese between two slices of white bread.

"Well," he said, shuffling his feet awkwardly, "you have a good day now." His expression told her he recognized his lame attempt at etiquette. They'd stood together over the drying pool of Hazel's blood. A "good day" was far, far from Imogene's future—if ever.

She spun around, thankful Oliver was the last worker through the line. The next hour was spent cleaning the kitchen. She skirted Ida several times as they wove in and out between two other women doing dishes in the massive sinks. At this rate, Imogene was hard-pressed to see how she'd ever get to know anyone, let alone find any clue, any *anything* about why Hazel had been killed. Let alone who had done it.

As Imogene wiped down the counter with a wet rag, she second-guessed her decision to take a job at the plant. The day had been long. The conversation limited. A sick feeling formed in the pit of her stomach that she was on a wild goose chase. Not to mention, Chet was going to have her head on a platter once he found out what she was up to.

She tossed the rag into a pail of dishwater.

"Life doesn't move along fast enough sometimes."

Well, for Pete's sake! If Ida Pickett didn't have a way of breaking into Imogene's thoughts with just the right phrase to make Imogene wonder for a moment if Ida was somehow in her head.

"No, it doesn't," Imogene responded.

Ida smiled as she untied the apron from around her waist. "Days here get so long, I sometimes feel as if I'm trapped in an unending cycle."

Imogene drew a deep breath.

"Walk to the bus with me?" she offered to Ida.

Ida gave a quick shake of her head. "I'd love to, but I need to go to the administrative offices. My brother works on one of the lines, and he asked me to pick up his paycheck."

"Can't miss that, then," Imogene acknowledged, squelching another wave of defeat. She wouldn't even be able to nudge through Ida's memories of Hazel.

Ida gave Imogene a wave, and the plain girl walked away, her simple dress floating around her legs like a curtain of brown.

Imogene stood in the now-empty kitchen. Even Oliver had disappeared from the cafeteria, along with the last shift of workers for the day. The dishes were all washed. Her sigh echoed in the kitchen.

"Miss Grayson?"

The strident voice startled Imogene. She spun on her heel and met the sharp gaze of the cafeteria manager, Marjorie

Harris. Mrs. Harris's hawkish nose and beady eyes reminded Imogene of a vulture.

"Best leave now. The last bus heads into town at 5:35. You miss that, you'll be here all night."

"Thank you." Imogene tipped her head and furrowed her brow as she brushed past the older woman. She sensed Mrs. Harris's eyes burrowing into her back long after she exited the building.

Shrew. Imogene hiked down the walk. The grounds of the Ordnance Works were akin to a small town. In the distance, she noted the administration building Ida had referred to. To her left were the Clock Alleys, where the workers punched timecards upon arrival and departure. Beyond them, the Change Houses, where they stripped out of their work clothes and returned to wearing street clothes.

Even now, a large group of men and women seemed to be drifting her way. The last of the shift for the day. Some split off toward the barracks, originally intended for Army housing during the war, but now simply housed permanent staff and their families. Others neared Imogene until she was surrounded by a cluster of folks waiting for the string of buses to take them back to Mill Creek. It registered in Imogene's mind that Hazel had done this every day and every evening. Waited here for the bus that would drop her at the stop, and then she'd walk the last two miles to the farm. The only difference was that Hazel's shift ended at 3:30.

Imogene scanned the people around her. All were unfamiliar faces. Except for one. Oliver stood several yards away, oblivious to the fact she watched him. He seemed lost in his own thoughts. A shoulder banged into Imogene. She stumbled, hitting a woman to her left.

"I'm so sorry!" She reached for the woman, who tripped forward, even as she tried to catch sight of whoever had slammed into her. There were too many people to identify and no one brave enough to come forward with an apology.

Regardless, Imogene made right with the woman, who assured her she was fine. She gripped her purse tighter to her side and then realized it'd come unclasped. Looking down, Imogene moved to clip the latch of her clutch together, then paused. An envelope stuck up from the innards. White, with no stamp, no penmanship on the outside, and yet sealed.

Frowning, Imogene slipped the envelope from her purse and ripped open its end. A thin sheet of blue paper pulled out at Imogene's tug, folded in half, with typewriting on the inside. She unfolded it, her fingers rubbing the indentations from the typewriter keys on the back of the page.

It's over.

The message made absolutely no sense. Imogene glanced around her as the mass of workers readying to get on the buses and return home grew thicker. Even Oliver had disappeared, and for a brief moment, Imogene felt a pang of fear stabbing through her. She rotated on the platform. There were a few men behind her, chatting amiably. The woman she'd knocked into had stepped forward a few paces and was laughing with another lady, who was so rotund she took up the spaces of three women. But they were happy.

Everyone was happy.

The war was over.

The powder being crafted here at the plant would now go to fueling rockets instead of smokeless grenades made to blow off the arms and legs of enemies overseas.

Yet . . .

Imogene's attention shifted back to the two words on the typewritten page.

It's over.

Whoever had slipped it into her reticule as they'd, more likely than not, purposefully bumped into her was delivering a very pointed message.

Little bumps rose on Imogene's arms. She made quick work

of refolding the paper and slipping it back in its envelope, ignoring the way her heartbeat increased.

It was obvious the war was over, and the powder plant was a new setting for Imogene—starkly different from the beauty salon. Yet someone had already noticed her. Recognized her? Made plans to leave her a cryptic note that, if it didn't imply the war, could only have one other association with Imogene's newly acquired position in the cafeteria.

Hazel.

As the buses rolled to a stop and the throng pressed forward to gain their seats, Imogene crammed the envelope into her purse. One could make the argument that Hazel was, indeed, over. She was dead. In which case what point did it serve to remind Imogene of that? Unless someone wanted to make certain that Hazel stayed dead. In everyone's minds. And that the case around her murder became colder than the icehouse in the back of the Grayson family farm.

CHAPTER 11

Imogene was resistant to admit it even to herself, but by the time she'd gotten off the bus and started the two-mile walk home to the farmhouse she was loath to return to, she was thoroughly shaken. What had at first seemed to be a simple stumble now grew in its ominous undertones.

It's over.

They might as well have typed the words *Stay the heck away.* Stop nosing in what was nobody else's business. Let go of Hazel and leave it to the police. Or maybe . . . Imogene halted on the side of the road, gravel crunching under her feet. Maybe this didn't have anything to do with a threat to stay silent. Maybe it was a consolation. A short, stilted recognition that Hazel was gone, that Imogene needed to move on, that . . .

Footsteps behind her made Imogene spin on her heel. Oliver strolled toward her, his hands in his overall pockets, the calm look on his face set as though not much could dislodge it. It wasn't much unlike his expression the morning of Hazel's murder.

"Going my way?" Imogene opted for a half smile and a lilt to her voice. Anything to ward off the concern that flickered in Oliver's blue eyes and then disappeared.

"Yep." His one-word answer relieved her. Anyone else would

have probably asked a dozen or more questions as to how she was holding up. Or "Has Chet made any breaks in the case?" Or "How's your mama faring?" Or since this was Oliver, he could straight-out ask her how she was managing after seeing all that gore. The kind of horror no human eyes should ever behold. But he didn't. Instead, he moved beside her and matched her steps.

One, two, three, four . . . Imogene found herself counting them. Distraction. Anything. She was light-headed, dizzy even, as a wave of exhaustion and emotion raced unexpectedly through her. To cover it up, she looped her arm through Oliver's and hugged it. He tripped against her and cast her a bewildered look. She was quick to cover it up with another red-lipped smile.

There. More distraction. His eyes dropped to her mouth, then quickly back up to her eyes.

"Thank you, Oliver Schneider." She sincerely meant it, even if she did sound a bit flirtatious.

"For . . . ?"

They continued to walk, and she continued to cling to his arm as though she had a mad crush on the boy and was quite khaki wacky. In reality, the world ahead was swimming in a blur.

"For not badgering me with incessant questions and not expecting me to be sobbing like a weeping mess in the corner."

Oliver gave a sniff and then chuckled. "Imogene Grayson isn't known for being a mess."

"No." She gave a definitive nod, blinking fast to clear her gaze. "That's not to say"—gracious, she realized how callous and bitter she sounded—"I don't have emotions."

Oliver paused on the road and tipped his head. A strand of dark blond hair fell over his forehead, and his brows drew together. "No one ever said you didn't."

Imogene hadn't released his arm. She noticed the firm tone of it, in spite of his rather lanky appearance. She didn't want to let go, and the unwarranted feeling that surged through her surprised her. He was safe. Oliver—*Ollie*—was safe and non-threatening and . . .

"Thank you for understanding me," Imogene murmured with sincerity. For he did. She could tell. He saw through her flirtatious façade to the wounded, broken heart beneath that she refused to let show. She'd let him into it the night she'd climbed the stairs to Hazel's room.

Ollie twisted toward her, dislodging her arm from his. A red-winged blackbird swooped over their heads, chirping its warning call. It must have a nest somewhere nearby. Imogene's attention was snagged by the bird as it landed in the tall grasses bordering the road, the green rows of corn just beyond that, with the glimpse of the Schneider barn in the distance.

"Genie . . ." His voice tugged her attention back, and Imogene met his eyes. "Why did you take a job at the plant?"

She didn't want to tell him. He'd try to talk her out of it and for no good reason other than it was police business. Let Chet handle it. Hazel's murder wasn't hers to unravel, to resolve with any sort of justice.

It's over.

The words were burned into her mind, right next to the image of Hazel's bloodied body that had lain like a rag doll on the floor.

"No, it's not," Imogene protested aloud, shaking her head.

"What's not?" Ollie tilted his head. She could tell he was trying to get a read on what she meant. That her face was more likely than not emblazoned with consternation and fury didn't help.

"It's not over, Ollie. Hazel died for a reason, you know? I can't believe it was random. There had to be a cause. And—and no one can tell me it's over and done with. No one!"

Ollie rolled his mouth together and drew a deep breath as though carefully weighing his words. "People dyin', no, you're right. It's never over."

"I can't just let it be, Ollie." Imogene heard her voice tremble.

93

Hang it all! She turned into an emotional puddle whenever she was around Oliver Schneider and she didn't know why. She'd known him all her life as that "Ollie boy" down the road, as her parents called him. Though he was only one year her senior, they'd never played together much. He was a boy, rough and tumble, throwing around a baseball and pretending to be Babe Ruth. But now? Now there was something deep and hidden behind those sky-blue eyes of his. Something that hinted he had his own secrets of horrors he'd seen. That maybe, out of everyone in Mill Creek, Ollie understood the terror she experienced when she closed her eyes. He understood that one couldn't just close the book on the sight of someone's lifeblood draining from their body.

"Was it awful?" she whispered.

There, on the side of the country road, Ollie lifted his fingertips and grazed Imogene's cheek with a gentleness that took her by surprise.

"Awful can't begin to describe it."

Imogene blinked back a sudden burning of tears. She knew they balanced on her dark Vaselined eyelashes, probably making her green eyes shimmer emerald, like Daddy always said they did when she cried. Which wasn't often.

"Then you know why I'm saying it isn't over?"

Ollie's jaw muscle jumped as he seemed to bite down against his own conflicted feelings. He peered beyond her, over her shoulder at the cornfield on the other side of the road. "It'll never be over."

His words drilled a hole in Imogene's heart, and with them followed the haunting reality that death branded its mark into a person's soul, and time healed no pain. It never would.

—⟶⟵—

Imogene had nothing to go on but a typewritten note, the memories of Hazel's room the day she discovered her, and a new job at the powder plant doing the type of service work she'd swore she would never do. Imogene sat cross-legged in the middle of her bed. She'd stripped out of her hosiery and the dress she'd worn for supper and had slipped into pajamas. She busied herself setting her hair in pin curls for the night as the jazzy strains of the music from her radio filled the void of silence in the room. And now she sat on her bed, staring across the room at the window.

Closing her eyes, she let herself float back on the memories to the night she'd climbed the attic stairs with Ollie. Every creak of the steps, every pounding heartbeat . . . she could recall it all in vivid detail. For now. She could even smell the faintest hint of Hazel's perfume. A sweet scent tipped with rose. Hazel used to spray it on liberally after coming home, to get the smell of the powder plant out of her nose, she'd always said.

Another strong whiff made Imogene's eyes snap open, and she fixated on the window opposite her, the dark night sky drenching the familiar in blackness. Right above her room— *right above her!*—was Hazel's attic bedroom. There was nothing worse, nothing more awful than reliving every moment of the discovery of Hazel's battered body while in the same house. Sleep was not going to be her partner tonight.

She blinked, clearing her burning eyes from their unblinking stare at the night sky. Taking a deep breath, Imogene imagined Hazel still alive. She would have perched herself beside Imogene on the bed, probably wearing those silly yellow pajamas her sister had gotten for Christmas when she was thirteen. They were a bit snug now, but Hazel loved them. They'd—

"They served me well during the war, why not still?"

Imogene smiled back at her imaginary Hazel. She reached out, her hand swiping the air where the vision of Hazel sat.

"Because they're silly and threadbare." Imogene's voice echoed in the empty room.

Hazel's form cocked her head to the right, and she gave

Imogene the sweet smile she always did when she wanted to insinuate that although Imogene was her senior by four years, Hazel's maturity far exceeded hers.

"There are a lot of people still in need. The war has left us all in a fit, Genie. Why should I spend money on nice pajamas?"

Why indeed? It wasn't as if Hazel didn't plop every coin she earned into Daddy's hand to help keep the farm afloat. She deserved new pajamas.

Imogene's throat tightened with emotion. The kind that warred between an imagined moment and reality.

"Hazel, you need to come home." Her whisper floated like a feather across the room.

Hazel's face wavered for a moment and then became clearer. Her smile was sad. *"You know I can't."*

"I know." Imogene picked at a loose thread on her spread. "Chet said they took all sorts of photographs of your room. I don't know why he won't let me see them."

Hazel's response resonated in Imogene's mind. *"Because you don't need to keep seeing me. Not like that."*

"I need to help find out who killed you." Imogene drew in a thick, shuddering breath. Why did the police take photographs? What did they hope to learn from them? She recalled Chet saying the police would look at several factors. Fingerprints, for one, but since they matched none on record at the station, it'd be tough to figure out who might own any strange sets they might have lifted from the scene. Dust displacement. Whatever that meant. Maybe if something had been moved in the room, or a foreign substance was left behind, like—like red clay traces when the soil at the farm and surrounding area was mostly sand? Perhaps. But Chet hadn't let on that there was any dust displacement outside of the footprint that had proven to be a dead end.

"Who killed you?" Imogene repeated, this time as a question. The image of Hazel flickered before her eyes. Hazel wasn't looking at her now. She was staring out the window as if she would float away into the night sky. As if she *could* float away. *"I can't tell you that."* Hazel's words carved their way through Imogene's mind. No. Of course she couldn't. She wasn't really there. She was a conjured fragment of Imogene's broken heart.

"Then what can I do?" Imogene uncurled her legs and pushed off the bed, padding across the floor on her bare feet to the window. She glanced to her side. In another life, with a different direction, Hazel would be studying her closely from the bed. Imogene could almost sense her there, and the pain that riffled through her soul was poignant. If she could just turn— just close her eyes and spin around and open them—and Hazel were really sitting there. On the bed. In those silly pajamas.

"You can remember me. Every part of me. Every moment. Every item. Every stain. Every footstep. Every smell. Everything."

Imogene did spin then. Right as the saxophone belted out a lilting tune through the radio's speaker. Just as the moon passed behind the clouds. Just when she heard the creak of the mattress bedspring. Her gaze raked the bed, the floor, the dresser beyond, and she saw her own reflection in the mirror. The bed was empty, and even the mirror boasted one face only. Hers. Black hair in silly pins, green eyes wide with both hope and horror, her hand clutching the V of her pajama top where the button met the first hole.

Remember. Yes. Photographs. Yes. Chet wouldn't let her see them, but she didn't need to. She already had memorized everything, and in doing so she would uncover something. Something Chet had missed, something the police had overlooked. If she could walk in Hazel's footsteps during the day, then she could theorize in Hazel's room at night. Every single memory poured into one room. One house. The Grayson farmhouse.

The shrill high pitch of the saxophone followed Imogene as she bolted from her bedroom, her purpose fully intact.

CHAPTER 12

Aggie

She'd never been fond of the saxophone, or any brass instrument, but the peals filled the house as Aggie opened the door, Collin behind her. What inspired her to invite him for dinner still left her questioning herself. But he was there, behind her, and in front of her was the overwhelming flamboyancy of true music of the forties. Clarinet, trumpets, a chorus of them, with a peppy tune that made Aggie feel as though she were stepping into a time machine. Even the kitchen into which they stepped heralded that feeling. So did the hallway with the coat tree and the wool coat hanging from a peg, its collar fringed in mink. Maybe real, maybe faux, but mink nonetheless and very much not current-day winter coat style.

"It's real," Collin muttered as they passed it, his hand brushing the fur.

Of course it was. Mumsie wouldn't concern herself with animal welfare. She was of the era of the Depression and entered adulthood when blackouts were practiced, even throughout the rural countryside, in case Japan or Germany decided that Wisconsin was high on their target list. Concerning oneself with whether an animal had the right to live or trim a coat with its fur was a shallow, purposeless question, considering human plight and the last grasps of holding on to the golden-age vanity of the twenties.

"Mumsie?" Aggie called with a brief glance over her shoulder at Collin, who was eyeing the musty old architecture. She waved at him to follow her. "Mumsie, where are—?"

"Well, for pity's sake, child, are you trying to raise the dead?" Mumsie's wobbly but vibrant voice caused Aggie to jump back into Collin as the old woman appeared in front of her, having stepped out from a hall closet Aggie hadn't noticed before. It was small and under the stairs, but one could go in by ducking, and Mumsie apparently had. Her large silver flashlight in her hand, she pulled shut the closet door behind her and reached for her walker.

Adorable was too cutesy of a word for Mumsie, and yet she was. Her curls were perfect around her angelic face. She looked past Aggie at Collin, who had steadied Aggie by gripping her elbow.

Mumsie's green eyes sparkled. "There's the looker from the other day!"

"Mumsie!" Aggie widened her eyes in embarrassment.

"What?" Mumsie gave her a quizzical look. "He is. That hair—all that ginger—and yet he's manly." She sidestepped Aggie and lifted up her chin, studying Collin. A tiny smile tilted her mouth, the wrinkles that feathered off her lips deepening. "I say, do you have a girl?"

"Mumsie!" Aggie hissed through clenched teeth.

Collin dipped his head congenially. "I daresay no."

Mumsie clicked her tongue. "It's amazing that a boy like you hasn't been snatched up by the first dame who'd have you!"

"They've tried." Collin winked, adding a playful tone to his words that made Aggie raise an eyebrow at him. "But I'm hard to catch." He dipped his head conspiratorially. "And equally as hard to hang on to."

Mumsie's laughter filtered through the hallway. "Oh, I'm so glad you brought your young man home for dinner." She patted

Aggie's arm as she sidled past, her slippered feet shuffling on the wood floor, and her polyester button-up blouse of vivid purple leaving behind a whiff of baby powder and perfume.

"He's not my young man!" Aggie protested without thought, chasing after Mumsie. She shot Collin a desperate look. He shrugged. Aggie rolled her eyes. *Oh, Mumsie, Mumsie, Mumsie!*

Mumsie deposited the flashlight on the kitchen table and moved to the kitchen sink and the hand-washed dishes in the dish rack. Actually, they were plastic sandwich bags. Mumsie reached for one and lifted it, eyeing its clear insides and the few drops of water that remained.

"Oh, these take forever to air-dry." She reached for a dish towel of yellowed white linen with embroidery on it and lacy tatting on the edges.

"What—why are you washing baggies?" Aggie couldn't stop her bewildered question.

Mumsie's look was innocent in return. "Why wouldn't I? They're perfectly good and reusable. Now, I've not prepared a decent meal for dinner. But I do have some canned green beans and mushroom soup. That would make a perfect side dish to the leftover roast beef from Sunday."

"Brilliant!" Collin chimed.

Aggie spent the next few minutes hand-cranking the can opener to open the cans, not particularly looking forward to the combination of their innards. Collin rifled in the pantry, and he called out, "By any chance would you have some French-fried onions?"

"Bottom shelf. To the left," Mumsie responded with the sharp memory of one well practiced in not forgetting, even if one hundred years was staring her in the face.

Aggie sank onto a kitchen table chair and watched in puzzled silence as Collin and Mumsie worked side by side. Collin mixed the beans and soup in a pan on the stovetop, his round glasses sliding down his nose, but his square jaw making up for any boyishness that might have been tempted to shine through. Mumsie cocked the glass lid sideways on her glassware container and popped the roast into the microwave. She punched a button, hesitated, Collin reached over and hit another, and with a playful smile, Mumsie punched the start button with her crooked finger.

"Now . . ." She made her way to the table and pulled out a chair, slowly easing her old bones onto it. "You're here to pry, I can see it all over your face. If you played poker, Agnes, you'd be out on the first hand."

"I'm not here to pry!" Aggie defended herself. Collin's smile appeared again, but he remained focused on the pan and mixing the green beans so they didn't scorch.

Mumsie drummed her fingers on the tabletop. "Mmmm-hmm. I'm quite sure you've been adept at pulling the wool over many of your house-buying clients, but you cannot weave it over mine."

There was a deep, pointed gleam in Mumsie's eyes. One that made Aggie squirm and shoot another despairing look at the oblivious Collin. Mumsie knew about her midnight jaunt into Mumsie's room, didn't she? That Aggie had seen the horrid dollhouse with its crime scene in miniature. Or did she? And what if she did know? It couldn't matter. Fine. She really wanted to interrogate her grandmother about the disturbing scene, her room that sported a bloodstained spread, and the nagging sense that there was something hiding behind Mumsie's eccentricity that made Aggie more than a little bit concerned.

But she would start simple.

"The cemetery office was broken into this morning. The entire room was trashed." It wasn't a question or a prying into anything. She was merely interested to see if it sparked anything on Mumsie's face. Not that it should. But something nagged at Aggie.

Mumsie's small laugh surprised Aggie. She exchanged looks with Collin, who was dumping the green-bean soup mixture into a bowl.

"What were they after? Old bones? Buried treasure?" A swift intake of melodramatic breath, and her eyes widened.

"Neither." Collin popped open the microwave and poked at the leftover roast with a fork. He'd apparently taken over the cooking. "Although, I daresay, that would cause quite the kerfuffle if it'd been dug-up graves."

Aggie frowned. "You know, that is odd. A skeleton—no matter that it was fake—in Mumsie's backyard. The cemetery office ransacked. It's sort of as if a grave had been, you know, messed with."

Collin shrugged and sprinkled fried onions over the green-bean casserole that apparently was going to be served straight from the stovetop and never see the inside of an oven.

Mumsie didn't say anything, yet Aggie could feel the old woman's eyes on her. Aggie met her grandmother's stare. Frank. Open. Wary. They were both equally cautious of each other, it seemed. It was difficult to trust.

Collin continued. "I don't believe a grave could be any more *messed with*, as you say, than the flooding. We're going to need the office space tidied straightaway so we can get to work putting it all to rights. Some of the graves can be instantly tied to their markers. It's obvious. But some of the graves that have no marker, no place in the cemetery records? I find that curious."

Aggie nodded, sniffing the air. Maybe that casserole wouldn't be so awful. "And also why you have a section like Fifteen Puzzle Row and stone after stone of markers from the late eighteen hundreds and turn of the century, and then smack in the middle is a grave from the forties."

Mumsie didn't have much of a reaction to that. Aggie had been watching her closely. Mumsie was for certain alive and living in Mill Creek during the war, that much Aggie knew. So, she'd been hoping Mumsie might spark at the small implication. Maybe even know right away whom Aggie was speaking of. Mr. Richardson had, after all, implied the "old-timers" of the community knew all sorts of things about those buried in the cemetery.

It was unfortunate that Aggie had never made a point to listen to old stories of family history and experiences. But then she couldn't remember Mumsie ever saying much of anything about her years before Aggie's mother had been born. Frankly, she rarely even mentioned Aggie's grandfather. Ancestry had never been Aggie's interest, not even slightly. Now she wished perhaps she'd been a bit more savvy and asked questions of Mom, instead of having to wheedle information from the tight-lipped Mumsie.

The memory of the rose petals with inked words hadn't drifted far from Aggie's thoughts, and the more she dwelled on them, the more curious she became. Curious and unnerved now that she'd made the conscious tie between the fake skeleton in Mumsie's backyard and the break-in at the cemetery. Maybe it was farfetched to draw a line between them, but there was the fact that *she* was a common denominator between the two incidents. Agnes Imogene Dunkirk. And now the words *It's not over* felt a bit ominous. Like a storm cloud that was drifting over the horizon. Not remarkably threatening, but looming all the same and moving closer, leaving questions as to its predictability, severity, and intention.

"Mumsie," Aggie said, deciding to jump in with both feet, "did you know a Hazel Grayson?"

"No." Her response was quick. Clipped.

Aggie waited a moment, then asked, "Do you know anyone who might know her?"

"Why?" Mumsie skewered her with a frank look. "What's important about her?"

"Well—" Aggie began.

The third chair being pulled out from the table scraped its interruption against the floor. Collin straddled it and crossed his arms over the chair's back. His strawberry-blond eyebrows were raised, and the laugh lines at his eyes deepened, though not with humor. Instead, his eyes seemed to hold a warning for Aggie.

She furrowed her brow at him.

Collin reached out and patted Mumsie's hand as if she were

a child to be placated. "Never mind, sweet lady. Your grand-daughter is just beginning to explore the cemetery records, and sometimes a name just has a beautiful ring to it."

Mumsie's face softened, and she smiled at Collin. "I see." She unfolded and refolded a cloth napkin in front of her. "Is the roast ready?"

"Dinner will be served forthwith." Collin stood with a flourish, and Aggie noted his accent became more pronounced. He was so genuine—most of the time—and yet so . . . not fake? What was it? So surface. He was all surface. Aggie knew not one thing about the man who could charm his way into a dinner invite.

She caught his eyes and the small shake of his head. His look of caution made Aggie bite her tongue. For now.

—⟨⟨⟨—

"What was that all about?" Aggie hissed in Collin's direction as they stood side by side at the sink hand-washing the dishes, Mumsie having retired to her recliner and TV in the other room. She took a rinsed plate from his hand and applied her dish towel to it, but her glare pierced him. Supper had been a superficial affair, with Mumsie's charming-but-frank opinions being well-matched against Collin's witty personality and equally talented quick thinking. Aggie had sat in silence, processing Collin's redirection of the conversation and absently trying to draw a conclusion as to whether his accent and random colloquialisms were authentic or manufactured.

"What was what all about?" Collin hedged.

"Cutting me off with Mumsie. About Hazel Grayson." She opted for answers to the more pressing question.

He gave her the side-eye. The kind Aggie recalled her father giving her mother in the days when they had gotten along and would have general conversations about life. It hinted at disinterest, yet disguised the deep attention behind it.

"You didn't notice, did you?" Collin asked.

"Didn't notice what?"

"Your grandmother's hands. They were clenched and white-knuckled the moment you said Hazel Grayson's name."

"Oh." Aggie rested the dry plate on the stack of two clean ones. "But she said she didn't know her."

"I believe I am relatively safe in saying your grandmother was lying to you." Collin waggled his eyebrows with a sympathetic grimace. "You don't truly believe she's being that honest?"

He pulled the plug on the drain as the dirty, soapy water began its slow whirlpool spiral. Collin's shoulder brushed hers as he reached past her. He smiled and gave her a wink, his arm stretched in front of her face. "Pardon me."

Aggie couldn't ignore the scent of spice and citrus. Delightful. She squirmed and backed up a step to avoid the surge of unwelcome attraction.

Collin tugged a recipe book from the shelf above the sink and laid it on the counter in front of Aggie. It was old and worn, the edges bent. He opened it, and his index finger rested below a handwritten signature.

"I noticed this earlier while you and your grandmother were bickering back and forth like two clucking hens."

Aggie sputtered, but her gaze drifted down to read the faded ink.

Hazel Grayson

Her astonished look flew up to meet Collin's self-confident understanding.

"It's—it's Hazel's," Aggie whispered. She shot a quick glance at the doorway that led from the kitchen to the hall where Mumsie had disappeared after dinner.

Collin allowed the book cover to shut on its own. "Apparently, your *Mumsie* knew Hazel Grayson quite well and has no intention or desire to speak of it."

CHAPTER 13

Aggie tugged on her rain boots, anticipating a day of sloshing around the muddy, soggy grounds of the flooded cemetery. Mumsie had fallen asleep early last night, and Collin took his leave not long after Aggie's realization that Mumsie had indeed known Hazel Grayson. But it was the come-to-Jesus moment she'd had with herself that left Aggie feeling melancholic this morning. Clearly, Mumsie was also continuing what seemed to be a lifelong pattern of avoiding the truth. It ate at Aggie's gut as she slipped her arms into a cardigan. She wanted to march into Mumsie's sitting room and demand answers, but she didn't dare. She couldn't. It would be confrontational. Aggie knew that, and since she was being truthful with herself, she wasn't willing to risk the potential rift that might form between them. A rift that would turn the ditch that seemed to keep them at odds into a canyon. It would be irreversible. She was enough like Mumsie to know this.

Maybe Mumsie having Hazel's old cookbook was nothing more than a garage-sale purchase coincidence. Or maybe they were just old friends from long ago and time had erased Hazel's memory from a senile old woman. Or . . . Aggie reached for her car keys. Or maybe there was much more to it.

The upstairs bedroom and Mumsie's dark little world of

a dollhouse-staged murder was an omen that couldn't be ignored. An omen of what, Aggie didn't know. She'd spent half the night snooping around, but there was nothing to inspire a trip into their family history. Leastwise nothing she could find. And racking her brain for anything Mom might have passed on to her about Mumsie's younger years, Aggie had either forgotten or simply hadn't heard anything. Mumsie did know Hazel Grayson somehow, but tying that together was like trying to tie shoelaces without knowing where the tips were.

Aggie slipped out the front door, not disturbing Mumsie with another goodbye. They'd shared coffee that morning and exchanged glances over the rims of their mugs. A few superficial comments, Aggie having an internal debate as to whether to be bluntly honest and just ask outright or to give Mumsie space and gently prod the truth about Hazel Grayson from her. Then it was too late. Mumsie had wandered from the room. Aggie heard her footsteps as she climbed the stairs, step by step. Her walker's feet hitting the stair above while her shoes clomped the stair below. She reached the second-floor landing, and then Aggie heard the soft thud of the bedroom door closing. Mumsie's study. The secret place barred from the rest of the world. Aggie had followed, intending to use a goodbye as an excuse to poke her head in, but then she heard murmuring coming from behind the door. As though Mumsie were having a conversation with someone. Perhaps she had a phone in the room that Aggie hadn't noticed the night of her trespass.

Either way, Aggie chickened out. She'd refer to Google for answers. Later. After work. A search for Hazel Grayson of 1946 had to turn up something.

Now she hurried to her car, tapping the key fob to unlock the doors. She rounded the front bumper just as her phone rang. Digging into her bag, she pulled it out. "Hello?"

"Aggie, I need you." Collin's shaking voice startled her. He wasn't his normal cheery self.

"Are you all right?"

"Just—come. To the office." The call ended abruptly.

Aggie jumped into her car and drove the eight miles to the cemetery. She noted Collin's car parked in front of the office. Some sort of electronic equipment sat on the ground next to it, looking half like a lawnmower and half like a moon rover. Collin's ground radar maybe? He'd mentioned last night it was one of the tools he used to identify where old graves might be if they couldn't be found on a map.

The office door was open halfway.

"Collin?" Aggie called.

She heard a mumble from inside and hurried to the door, pushing it wide with her palm. "What on earth!" Aggie's eyes widened at the sight of Collin. He leaned forward in a chair, elbows on his knees, pressing a wool sweater to his head. A trickle of blood trailed down his face. "I'm calling 911." Aggie lifted her phone.

"No. No, don't," he grunted and raised a hand to stop her.

Aggie stared at him incredulously. "You need medical care!"

"It's not that serious. Just a beastly head wound."

"Looks serious to me!" Aggie knelt in front of him, clutching her phone. She ignored Collin's dismissive snort, then his soft moan. "I'm calling."

"No." His tone was sharper this time, and Aggie leveled a shocked look on him. The man was pale as a ghost, made more so by the golden-red stubble on his cheeks.

"Fine. You're as stubborn as Mumsie," Aggie snapped. "I'll be right back." She rose and hurried to her car, popping the trunk to grab her first-aid kit. Silly man. Her rain boots slopped around her skinny jeans, and when she returned to the office, they squeaked as they connected with the linoleum floor. Kneeling in front of Collin again, she gave him a fast once-over.

"Just a minute," she muttered. Snatching a rubber band from her wrist, she made quick work of tying back her ebony hair into a messy knot. She unzipped the kit and stuffed her hands into a pair of purple latex gloves.

"You're not going to pass out on me, are you?" Aggie asked. It was so dumb she was listening to him and not calling 911. She lifted her head when there was no answer.

Collin was swaying in the chair.

"Hey!" Aggie reached for him as he fell forward into her. Again the smell of his cologne tickled her nose. His forehead leaned on her shoulder, and his wavy hair brushed her lips as she reassured him. "Okay, move forward with me."

He followed her instruction until she had him lying on the beat-up floor. Yanking off her cardigan, she reached for an abandoned cardboard box and rolled the sweater, putting it on top. "Lift your legs." Aggie helped Collin raise his legs so the sweater and box braced him below the knees, elevating his feet above his head.

"I'm fine." He waved her off.

"Yeah. Right." She reached for the sweater he was still clutching to his head and tugged just enough for Collin to drop his hand. Aggie pulled the sweater from the wound. He was right. It appeared relatively surface, but being a head wound it had bled profusely. It seemed to have been stanched by the pressure he'd applied, but . . . well, if she wasn't a bit woozy herself! Fine pickle they'd be in if she passed out.

"There's a reason I didn't go into the medical field," Aggie scolded. His eyes were closed, yet a smile made the creases in his cheeks deepen. She noticed for the first time he wasn't wearing his glasses. Even his eyelashes were a golden red.

Aggie rummaged through the first-aid kit. "I'm going to have to clean off this blood."

"Go ahead," Collin mumbled. His color was returning.

"Hydrogen peroxide. It shouldn't sting," Aggie assured him.

"I called it 'bubbly stuff' when I was a lad." Collin's weak chuckle gave her the confidence she needed. Aggie poured it over some gauze and started dabbing at the wound, cleaning the blood away.

"Better if you just pour it on," Collin said.

"Better if I called 911," Aggie argued.

"Don't." Collin winced as she tipped the bottle of peroxide and watched it darken his hair, made redder by the blood that was matting around the wound.

"Why not?"

"Insurance." He grimaced.

"Please tell me you have health care wherever you're from." Aggie set the peroxide bottle on the floor and snatched up a fresh piece of gauze.

"Brilliantly expensive health care."

"Well then." Aggie worked at wiping away the blood. She was more than aware of how soft his hair was. For some reason, she had always been fascinated by auburn hair, as though the color would rub off like hair chalk. Only it didn't. She resisted the random urge to run her fingers through the thick mass.

"So, what happened, Romeo? Are you a klutz, or did someone lie in wait and whack you over the head?"

"The latter." Collin's eyes opened just as Aggie leaned closer over him to get a better view of the semi-cleaned wound.

Their eyes connected for a moment, and something twisted inside her. His eyes were . . . honest. Regardless of her questions about who he truly was, one couldn't fake blatant honesty, not unless he were a psychopath.

"Wait." She blinked, breaking the connection. "Someone whacked you over the head?"

"Yes. Now, if you please, it's not deep, is it?" Collin pointed to the side of his head.

"Whoa, whoa, back up!" Aggie lost a bit of empathy for his head wound and drew back on her heels, eyeing him. "You were attacked and refused 911 and instead called *me*? What if your attacker is still out there? You're putting me in danger!"

Collin gave her knee a little pat with his palm. "They went for a run right after. I even heard them drive away. There was no danger, only of me bleeding out and of you calling 911 and stiffing me with a massive medical bill."

"You have all the sense of an addlepated muskrat." Aggie heaved a frustrated sigh and leaned in again, ignoring the way she could feel his breath on her neck.

"Muskrats are misunderstood creatures—"

"Shush!" Aggie pushed his hair away from the cut, losing patience with the ridiculous man. "It's not bleeding as bad. It looks surface, but I'm no doctor."

"Splendid!" Collin's grin was followed by a wince. "I'll be fine then."

"Except that someone *hit you on the head!*" Aggie was in no frame of mind to let him—or his attacker—off the hook.

Collin squeezed his eyes shut. "Oh, well. Perhaps I'm not thinking as clearly as I believed. I forgot about that thing."

"That thing?" She followed the direction of his waving fingers. On the floor by the door lay a shovel. She'd not bothered to pay attention to it. "Tell me you weren't hit in the head with a shovel?"

"I know." Collin opened his eyes again. "Archaic, yes? In this day and age, using a shovel as a weapon seems quite dated."

Aggie reached for a wad of gauze and pushed it against Collin's cut, then stretched for a strip of first-aid bandage. "I'm wrapping this on your head and then I'm calling the police."

"Let's not overreact." Collin grimaced as she not-so-gently lifted his head to wrap the bandage around it.

Aggie tossed him an incredulous look. "It's common sense, and I think whoever was lying in wait for you knocked it clear out of your head. Not to mention, there is no way the police can say this was a *teenage prank.*"

"There is truth in that," Collin groaned as he tried to sit up. Even though Aggie protested, he leaned against her. She braced him with her arm as he pulled his legs off the box, her cardigan falling to the floor. She waited a moment longer before dialing 911 with her free hand to summon the police.

"They'll bring an ambulance too," Aggie informed Collin. His eyes shot daggers at her, the first sign of crankiness she'd seen in the man. "Don't look at me like that," she tossed back. "You're on the job. It's workers' comp."

"I'm a consultant." Collin seemed to nestle against her. "But do what you will to me. Send me into bankruptcy from medical debt. I'm at the mercy of a beautiful woman."

Aggie eyed him warily, sure that if he turned his head, his nose would bump into hers. But she couldn't very well release him, charming flirt though he might be. "Be quiet."

He smiled.

She tried not to.

It didn't work.

A siren pierced the air in the distance, and Collin gave his brows a wag. "I do believe they're coming for you."

"Shush," Aggie instructed again. She needed to. There was absolutely no sound reason for enjoying a moment where someone had just accosted her colleague with a shovel. Yet she was. And that was almost as equally disturbing.

—⟨w⟩—

She was shaking now. Full-on tremors. The adrenaline had worn off. Collin's head was properly tended to, and sure enough, he *had* needed a few stitches. Aggie was a bit too satisfied that her instincts had proven to be more than correct. The police had taken Collin's statement regarding the assault and done a thorough investigation of the cemetery office, bagging the shovel and taking it with them as evidence. Aggie was hard-pressed to believe that anyone would be able to pull off incriminating fingerprints. Half of Mill Creek had probably used that shovel at one time or another in the hours of volunteer services apparently poured into the old acreage that hallowed the dead.

Aggie stole a quick look at Collin, who had finally been released from the ER and now sat in the passenger seat of her car. His hair was slicked back where they'd wet it down to administer the stitches, making it appear a deep cinnamon color. Only he smelled like antiseptic and the hospital. Two smells Aggie hated. They always took her back. The beeping of the heart monitor, the endless stream of medical tests and treatments, and in the end, Mom lying in the bed with her own head of hair barely growing back into a pixie. Aggie shook off the memory and its lurid detail she'd vowed to forever lock away and not revisit. There was no need to. Life went on. It *had* to go on.

"Do you want me to drive you—home?" Aggie directed her question to Collin, hesitating over the word as she'd no clue where he resided during his temporary consulting work for the cemetery.

Collin sniffed, wincing. "I've got a blinding headache. But I wanted to show you something I discovered this morning, before you arrived."

Aggie thought it unwise, and she steered her vehicle down the side street lined with orange maple trees in full autumn foliage. "You can tell me, you don't need to show me."

Collin waved her off. "No good to sit and chatter on about it. I'll be fine. It's at the cemetery office, Love."

She refused to answer him or indulge him. "Where do you live? I'll take you home."

"Blast, woman! You're worse than your grandmum for stubborn!"

Aggie's lips thinned, and she shot him a side-eyed glare. "Fine," she gritted out and turned the car in the direction of the cemetery.

Collin stared blankly out the windshield, and for the first time his face became a bland mask void of any expression. Gone was the merry twinkle of his eye, the charming smile tipped with dimples, and the lighthearted look he owned so beautifully as he viewed the world through his glasses.

"Are you all right?" Aggie ventured, turning onto another side street, the cemetery looming closer.

"Most definitely." Collin cast her a quick smile. "I'm simply not a fan of incidents that end in bloodshed. I'll be better after a cup of tea and a nap, I suppose."

"Which you won't get at the cemetery," Aggie shot back, her willful self a bit annoyed at him.

"Ahh, well." He expelled a sigh, his accent tinging his words. "If the dead can't have their tea, then I don't see why I should be so privileged then, eh?"

"Eh," Aggie muttered in response.

"You're a moody one today, Miss Dunkirk. Don't let this get your knickers all in a twist. I'll be fine." The teasing expression was returning. "Although I was never one to put off a pretty woman's tender loving care, to be sure."

"I'll relieve you of it myself then," Aggie countered.

The creases in Collin's cheeks deepened. "That's it. Stand your ground."

Aggie ignored his shallow mockery and turned the steering wheel as her car's tires crunched on the short gravel drive that led to the office. The place was deserted now. Dark inside, the front door shut. She stifled a shudder. Goodness knew she'd little desire to be here in the first place, let alone now.

The sloping yard was still a sodden mess. Nothing had changed in the last day or so, least of which the graves in Fifteen Puzzle Row were still flooded and upturned into a mud heap.

"You didn't find a body, did you?" Aggie had to ask. Blunt was better, and she was being dishonest if she didn't face her darkest fear outright. Who wanted to help re-map cemetery plots when a good portion of their oldest ones were at risk of literally giving up their dead?

"No. No body. The corner of a casket, though. But that just needs some tending to and it'll be back underground in no time."

"A casket? Aren't they put in cement vaults when a body is buried?"

"Today, sure, but back in the day, no. They dug a hole and dropped them in."

Aggie paled. This was getting worse by the minute. She looked at Collin as neither of them had moved from their seats in the car.

"So you're saying, after a hundred or more years, the wood from a casket hasn't rotted through and exposed a corpse?"

"More likely a skeleton. Which is partly why I found it so amusing that a fake one ended up in your Mumsie's backyard. The irony that you'd just been employed by the cemetery was not lost on me."

"Well, I found it morbid, and now increasingly concerning considering someone saw fit to whack you over the head with a shovel this morning."

Collin shrugged. "It wasn't the first time I've taken a beating. Fistfights after a lost game of rugby can turn quite violent, you know?" He reached for the car door. "Now, would you like to see what I found?"

"No," Aggie responded honestly, but disembarked from her car all the same.

CHAPTER 14

Imogene

Her father's barn had often been a place of respite for her when she was little. Usually because kittens scampered about the hay and were the source of hours of entertainment for Imogene. Until they grew and became mousers, some getting stomped on by the cows and sent to their early doom. Not unlike Hazel.

Imogene shuddered as she rolled the barn door to the side on its rollers. The wood creaked and slapped against the frame, the red paint chipping beneath her hands. Daddy's barn was nowhere near as pretty as the Schneiders', who seemed to repaint theirs every five years. The Graysons were good, decent farmers, but making a living had been the primary focus, not creating a vanity of outbuildings. Especially not after Daddy worked so hard to hold on to the farm when things got bad around the time Imogene was born. Money had been tight, work almost impossible to find. They were lucky there was still a demand for dairy, although even that had significantly dropped in value and was still making its comeback. War ravaged more than just people. It could demolish entire economies and strip communities of their futures with just one explosion.

Mother's voice sounded from the front porch, and Imogene looked over her shoulder. Her mother had aged—aged in days, with new streaks of gray in her upswept bun. She gave Imogene a halfhearted wave.

"I'm going to take Daddy's truck into town. I need to stop at the market and drop my shoes off to get resoled."

Imogene nodded. "Bye, Mother." Her acknowledgment went almost unnoticed as Mother hurried down the porch steps, pinning a hat to her hair, her purse slung over her elbow.

Normal. That was what they were all reaching for. A new normal that didn't satisfy any of them.

Imogene blinked, her eyes adjusting to the barn's dim lighting. She watched hay-dust particles dance in a shaft of light that shone through the vents on the portico. The stanchions for milking the cows were in the lower level, while this floor was heaped with mounds of hay as high as the loft rafters. The beams that spanned the vaulted roof had hoists and pulleys attached to them. Ivan's Farmall B, hitched to a trailer, was parked beneath. Along the side wall to her left stood his workbench. Her brother spent hours in here, tinkering with the tractor's motor, jury-rigging tools and such to suit his needs for whatever maintenance project he embarked on.

Imogene wrapped her arms around herself, eyeing Ivan's bench. Tools lay scattered across the top, greasy rags, bolts, and parts of an engine. It didn't help that she also remembered hearing Ivan cursing in here too. The sound of a pipe wrench launching across the barn and hitting the wall. His temper had always been just below the surface, but since the war . . . And he'd never been close to Hazel. He was the eldest, she the youngest. Imogene hated where her thoughts were inadvertently leading her for the second time. No. There was nothing—*nothing*—in her memory that would lead her to believe there was enough animosity between Ivan and Hazel to cause Ivan to strike his own sister.

But the war had changed so many. The Depression prior to the war as well. It was almost as though the entire world had tilted off its axis and there was no one strong enough to right it. Not even God himself.

She reached up and tightened the bandanna she'd rolled and tied around her head. Touching her fingertips to the top button of her dress, Imogene heaved a sigh knowing exactly where she must go next.

"I'm so sorry, Hazel," she whispered.

It's all right. It won't do me no good anymore anyway.

Imogene winced as she heard Hazel's voice in her ears. A quick sweep of the barn told her she was still very much alone. She hurried across the straw-strewn wood floor to a side stall where they would occasionally house a sick or injured animal. It was empty—it had been for some time. Ivan didn't have much patience for animals. That was Daddy's role. Daddy had begun to work with those animals in the lower level. Even he was leaving Ivan alone lately and giving him his distance.

She reached the dark stall, shadowed for lack of lantern light. But Imogene didn't need any. She knew where to go. She knew Ivan wouldn't question her either. He and Hazel might not have been close, but they both found their respite in the barn's upper level.

In the far corner of the stall, a bulky object was covered under canvas. Imogene approached it, giving her eyes time to adjust to the darkness. Without much hesitation, she swallowed any angst and set her jaw with determination, reaching out and dragging the canvas to the floor.

There it stood. In all its beauty and glory. Hazel's masterpiece.

"Oh, Hazel," Imogene breathed. Her eyes took in what she'd seen before but now seemed to see for the first time. Hazel's artistry. Her to-scale, handmade dollhouse of the Grayson home. It was open, revealing all three floors. The bottom with the kitchen, dining room, living area, pantry, even the small mudroom off the back porch. The second floor with the bedrooms.

"And your room." Imogene caressed the empty attic bedroom. Hazel had gotten so far as to paper it with tiny scraps of the original wallpaper.

Her sister had been an artist. An artist of miniatures. Even the roof had hand-cut shingles, meticulously laid as though a roofer himself had transformed into someone tiny and spent a week nailing them all to the framework.

Where Ivan was talented in machinery and engines, Hazel had found her forte in delicate beauty. Accuracy and eye-pleasing finesse. Now she would never finish it. Never reconstruct the house to the homey glory it had been prior to her death. Before blood had stained the walls and the floor. Before the tenuous thread of peace the Graysons had was broken by the intrusion of someone unknown and evil. Someone whom Hazel had trusted, had allowed into their home and—

Imogene startled, snatching her hand away from the attic replica. No one had said that Hazel knew her attacker. Chet had implied there'd been no forced entry, yet that didn't mean Hazel had *known* her killer personally. So why was she consumed by the sudden feeling that Hazel had willingly walked to the screen door, smiled as she opened it for her killer, the hinges squeaking in hospitality?

"You talked to them, didn't you? Greeted them as you would a friend while you bid them to follow you into the kitchen so you could get supper started?" Imogene positioned her fingers in thought around her lips. "You would never have opened the screen door for a stranger."

Of course, one could argue a screen door was not much of a barrier if someone wanted to enter the house. But what Chet hadn't known was that there *should* have been signs of forced entry, unless Hazel absolutely *knew* her attacker and trusted them.

"You always hooked the lock on the door." Her whisper filtered through the shaded stall and echoed in the empty rooms of Hazel's dollhouse.

Because I was sure if I didn't, some traveling salesman would come and have his way with me.

Hazel would have said it with a laugh. The kind that indicated she understood how farfetched her fears were and how her imagination exaggerated realistic possibilities. Nonetheless, she would have flipped the metal hook into its latch. So, a stranger would have to at least kick in the door—easy, for sure, but leaving obvious damage—or rip the screen and reach through with their hand to flip the hook from its metal ring.

Imogene backed away from the dollhouse.

"You knew them. You *knew* them," she repeated to the darkness. It was something she needed to tell Chet right away. Hazel didn't have many friends. The circle of trust had to be small, which meant the narrowing of suspects.

Imogene surged forward and dragged the canvas back over the dollhouse. She arranged it so the pigeons that sometimes fluttered in and out of the barn couldn't leave their droppings on the piece of artistry. Once convinced it was properly covered, Imogene pressed her fingers to her lips in a kiss, then stretched her hand out to leave the kiss on the covered dollhouse.

"I'll be back." It was a promise. An addendum to the promise she'd already made to Hazel. Her death would not go unsolved, and now her dollhouse would tell its story. A story that screamed unintelligibly from every drop of blood Hazel had left behind.

—⚬⚬—

"Where ya goin'?" The motor on the Ford pickup truck hummed as a distinct scent of gasoline mixed with motor oil wafted to Imogene's nose.

She hiked along the side of the country road toward town, cursing every step in her black pumps and wishing she'd thought to exchange them for more sensible walking shoes before high-tailing it to town to find Chet. A quick call to the police station might have sufficed, but she couldn't rightly discuss Hazel's death on the party line. All the busybodies would be listening in—since they didn't have anything better to do—and with two shakes of a lamb's tail, Imogene's theory that Hazel knew her killer would be front and center in the *Mill Creek Gazette*.

Now she shot a glance at the man who drove the truck, his arm dangling out the open window. A lazy grin tipped his mouth, and green eyes met hers with a similar spark. Interest? Maybe. Flirtation? Definitely. Only she wasn't in the mood, not like she might have been even three weeks ago. A stranger in a truck who seemed vaguely familiar now held only suspicion to her. Yet he was a stranger, so perhaps that meant he was safer than those Imogene knew.

"I asked ya where you were goin'?" There was a chuckle in his voice.

Imogene concentrated on walking a straight line on the shoulder. Her dress swished around her shins, and out of the blue she wondered if her stockings were straight or if in her rummaging through the barn the seams had shifted cockeyed to the back of her legs.

"The road goes in one direction, so if you have half a mind, you'd know I'm heading into town." Imogene allowed her tone to include a snap. The man could interpret it either as flirtation or as being put in his place. Whichever was fine with her, but she wasn't about to be coerced into giving him details.

"Need a lift?" he asked, his voice inviting and not at all sinister.

Imogene halted, immediately wary. Her own theory about Hazel's killer swirling in her head didn't leave her of the mind to befriend strangers. Of course, in Hazel's case, it seemed *friends* might have been more likely the concerning factor.

121

The man braked. His smile stretched wide and reached the crow's feet at the corners of his eyes.

"Jeepers!" Imogene exclaimed, allowing the full force of her sauciness into her voice, offsetting her nervous shudder. "You're rather brave to offer a ride to a girl you've never met before."

The twinkle sparkled in his eye. He reached his hand from the side of the truck door. His left hand, but he extended it anyway.

"Sam. Sam Pickett."

Pickett. She'd heard the name before. Something about the Picketts, years ago, only it wasn't spouted in a pleasant way like respectable families were. Troublemakers. Rum runners. Hidden distilleries. Who knew if the rumors were true? But then war came, the Picketts seemed to have scattered, and now, apparently, only Sam had come home.

"Well, hello, Sam Pickett." Imogene braced her hands on her hips and eyed him.

Sam tossed a glance through the windshield and down the road before looking back at her. "Your pegs are goin' to get tired fast if you insist on hiking all the way to town."

"My *legs* will be fine, and I do it on a regular basis." Imogene began to walk again.

The truck started to roll forward. "I'm just sayin' I'd give you a lift is all."

"Oh really?" She tipped up her chin and kept walking.

"And don't you have a name?" he ventured, allowing the truck to slowly parallel her.

"Of course I do." Imogene bit back a smirk. He'd have to work for it.

"Lemme guess. Betty?"

Imogene kept walking.

"Susan."

It was more of a declaration than a question.

"Frank?"

Imogene spun to face Sam Pickett. "Listen here!" Again her

hands found her hips, and she perched them there while doing her best schoolmarm impression. "I've no intention of accepting a ride with a man I've never met before."

"I promise you I'm a gentleman."

"Says the fox in the henhouse." Imogene matched his smile. He was rather charming, but then charm could be deadly too.

"Let the poor Marine help a gal in need, why dontcha?"

Oh, honestly! He wasn't the first soldier-come-home to use that line, and yet it always smacked her right in the heart. The boys had seen so much, *done* so much for them . . .

Pickett. Ida Pickett.

Imogene startled as she realized she knew another Pickett. The potential connection had never dawned on her. After meeting Ida on the bus to the powder plant, Imogene had all but forgotten her. She stared up at Sam. "Do you have a family?" One more test of his credibility to ease her overly suspicious state of mind.

At first, Sam seemed a bit taken aback. Then he gave a nod and said, "Sure. Got a sister. And a brother too, but he's buried somewhere in France."

"What's your sister's name?" She ignored the twinge of empathy for the loss of his brother.

"Ida, and my brother was Ralph." He rattled them off without hesitation.

"I know Ida."

"You do?" He raised an eyebrow. There was still humor in his eyes.

"I do. Where does Ida work?" This would tell if he was who he said he was.

"The plant, of course, like I do. Like half of Mill Creek does."

With that answer, Imogene stiffened her shoulders and gave him a pert nod. "Very nice to meet you." And she kept walking.

Imogene snuck another look at Sam. The idea of thinking so suspiciously about those she met was foreign to her. She was a small-town girl, and small-town girls were supposed to be able to trust people. Everyone knew everyone for the most part, and if you didn't, only one or two relations separated you from commonality.

"If it helps," Sam offered with a sly wink as the truck rolled beside her at a snail's pace, "I go to the Baptist church every Sunday too."

"Well . . ." Imogene straightened her back and ran her hands down her dress. "There's the problem. I'm a Methodist."

—⁓⁓—

The truck pulled up in front of the station with a rattle and a puff of exhaust. Sam had been the perfect gentleman—so far—and remarkably annoying but funny as he'd rolled alongside her the entire length of the trip to town.

"This was the most ridiculous escort," she muttered under her breath to him and gave him a snippy smile that should have left him cold. Instead, Sam held up a hand, indicating she should wait, and he shoved open his door, hopping down onto the sidewalk next to her.

"Can't have you thinkin' I'm no gentleman, now, can I?" A wink. A flicker in his eyes, and Imogene narrowed hers.

Not able to restrain herself, she leaned forward and tapped the end of his nose with a customary boldness her parents used to lecture her about but Imogene rather enjoyed. She pulled her finger back as Sam cocked his head to the right and smiled, which communicated he was enjoying the exchange. "You may be a hunk of heartbreak, cookie, but I've gotta keep my date."

"With the police?" His broadening grin indicated he found her shallow flirtation intriguing.

"Never say a woman can't be trouble." Imogene tossed him a saucy smile and flounced past.

"I better keep my distance, then." Sam winked as she breezed away, leaving him behind.

Pulling open the station door, Imogene waltzed inside, then leaned against the door as it closed behind her. Her increased heart rate told her all she needed to know about how she felt regarding Ida Pickett's brother. He made her both nervous and warm inside at the same time. His brooding good looks and the way he could dish it back to her . . . well, she'd never met anyone like him.

Imogene finally allowed herself a dreamy smile.

"What're you doin' with Sam Pickett?"

Ollie Schneider's voice came out of nowhere and echoed across the linoleum floor, bouncing off the ceiling. Imogene yelped and clutched her neck.

"Holy Joe, Oliver Schneider, you scared the wits out of me!"

Ollie observed her with his sad eyes. He reminded her a bit of a lost dog. One that had once been a strong, vibrant pup but now was so beat, he might whimper if someone moved at him wrong.

"Sam—um, escorted me to town," Imogene answered belatedly. She adjusted the belt at the waist of her dress and patted her bandanna hair band with an absent gesture.

Ollie shrugged and glanced out the window that skirted the door. "Oh."

"None of your business anyway." Imogene couldn't help being coy as she brushed past her neighbor. It was in her blood and was the perfect deflection for anyone asking her how she really was. What would she say if she had to be honest?

Heartbroken.

Hearing her dead sister's voice in her head.

Having *conversations* with her sister . . .

Spinning, she planted a fingertip on the bib of Ollie's overalls. He looked down at it and then back into her eyes.

Imogene opened her mouth, poised to say something witty, charming, or sassy. Instead, the depth and sadness in Ollie's expression was like a bullet piercing her soul. Somehow he knew—he knew it all. The pain, the horror, the agony, the tears that were filling up a hidden well inside that she could only pray were held back by the wall she was carefully building.

125

CHAPTER 15

S he knew who killed her." Perhaps she should have worked on easing into her theory, but Imogene hadn't the patience and her nerves were a tad raw after meeting Sam Pickett and then running into Ollie. Why he had been at the police station was probably something she'd never know, though it did raise a curious question mark in her mind.

"Genie." Chet's voice held a hint of warning. He extended his arm toward the hall and the room he'd taken her into the first time she'd charged into his station.

One of the officers passed them as they wove through the desks, a low whistle emanating from his lips. Imogene was vaguely affirmed that her appearance hadn't taken too much of a hit on her hike into town.

"Knock it off, Ed." Chet's command made his point. He opened the door to the room, and Imogene slipped past him. She could already feel her confidence waning now that she was here. What seemed so obvious back in the barn at home, standing there in front of Hazel's miniature house, was now . . . well, it would have to stand up not only to the scrutiny of the law but also to that of her brother. Chet was the master at playing the opposing point of view and finding all the angles one might have overlooked. Withstanding his critical assessment was sure to prove difficult.

But when Imogene sat in the straight-backed wooden chair Chet pulled out for her, she met his eyes as he sat down opposite her, the table between them. There was concern there, weariness etched into his face, and a resignation that made her breath hitch for a doubtful moment.

"What is it, Chet?"

He drummed his fingers on the table as if debating whether or not to tell her. "It's bad business all around, Genie. What happened to Hazel is—well, let me hear your thoughts. Now that we're not in the middle of the station."

On another day, in a different topic of conversation, Imogene might have chuckled at her brother's passive admonition. Today, though, she tilted up her chin with what she hoped was a look that expressed certainty and even a bit of defiance. "She *knew* her killer, Chet. She had to have known him."

"Him?" Chet's eyebrows rose.

"Honestly!" Imogene rolled her eyes. "Let me explain without you interrogating me before I get to my point."

He managed a smile. He'd always had infinite patience with her, even though Imogene knew she could come across as headstrong and even spoiled at times. She tempered her expression and allowed her genuine fondness for Chet to come through.

He nodded. "Carry on."

Imogene leaned forward, her elbows on the table. "Hazel always locked the screen door. Always. She wasn't a fan of traveling salesmen and the like, and you remember that time Mother was cooking that awful meat loaf of hers and she turned around and that salesman had just walked right into the kitchen? She hadn't even heard him knock? I doubt he even did."

"And?" Chet pressed for Imogene to gather her thoughts more definitively.

"And, so, Hazel said it was downright creepy, especially with our place being out in the boondocks. So she started locking the screen door just for her own peace of mind when she was home alone. And you know as well as I do that she got home from the plant before Mother and Daddy."

"A screen door doesn't tell us much, Genie." Chet's sigh matched the agitated rake of his fingers through his already-cropped hair. "I don't get why you think she'd know a person based on that."

"Must I spell it out?" Imogene's mouth tilted in a small tease. "Was it kicked in? The screen cut? No. Even you said so. Did anyone bother to look to see how the hook dangled? It was unlatched. *Unlatched.* Hazel must have walked over and greeted the person, smiling, and she probably . . ." Her words faded as the implications of what she was so glibly spouting out chopped off her energy like an ax to a tree branch. "You know what I'm getting at, don't you, Chet?"

Chet nodded, his nostrils flaring a bit as he took another deep breath. Releasing it, he seemed to expel every ounce of oxygen before looking to the ceiling as if beseeching God for help—or wisdom. "I'll go over the photographs again. I'm sure we can attest to your theory being correct—the door was not tampered with. But, Genie, that doesn't mean anything. Hazel may not have locked it. She also may have forgotten to, okay? And even if she had, it's not hard to slip a thin card through the door seam and flip the hook to unlock the screen door. I've done it myself a time or two."

Imogene's hope deflated like a popped balloon.

"Now," Chet continued, "I need you to listen close." His words seemed squeezed, as though he was choking up and trying to hide his emotion. He looked down at the table for a moment, collected himself, then returned his gaze to Imogene. "Our sister was—she was murdered. I need you to let that sink in. I need you to realize that whoever did this, whether they knew her or not, is bad news. Dangerous."

"Of course they are!" Imogene nodded, playing with the necklace around her neck.

"Also, Mother rang me last night. She told me you'd taken a job at the powder plant."

Imogene blinked. "Well, yes. I did."

Chet tilted his head and looked down his nose at her. He had a bit of a superior air to him, probably not unlike the one she often bandied about. "Genie, I can think of only one reason why you'd go and do that."

She stubbornly tapped her finger on Chet's shoulder. "The beauty parlor isn't paying near what I need to make if I ever want to move out and live on my own. Let alone move to Hollywood, where I might make something of myself. Ladies just don't have the money for that sort of thing yet."

Chet thinned his lips. The look he gave her indicated he wasn't falling for her manipulative skirting of the truth. He pushed her hand away. "Workers at the plant are paid less than two years ago when the war was full on. How come you didn't work there then? I hear tell the plant may soon have to lay some of the workers off. I think folks around here are done with war and making ammunition, at least for a while."

"Maybe." Imogene shrugged. "But truly, Chet, the extra money will do me good. And you know how Hazel helped Mother and Daddy with her wages? She's not—well, that won't happen anymore and—"

"Genie, some people may fall for your attempt at benevolence, and while I love ya and think your intentions are good and you're a true pistol of a woman, your snooping around trying to figure out what happened to Hazel is only gonna put yourself at risk of the same thing."

Imogene studied her brother, her eyes narrowing. He was one of the few people who saw through her façade and could read her intense loyalty and her always-analyzing brain. She leaned back in her chair and crossed her arms, acquiescing to the fact that nothing but scrupulousness would work with her brother.

"Honestly, Chet, you'd think I was a criminal."

"Hardly." His smile was sad but still good to see. "You're just willy-nilly with your emotions, and while I know you're trying to piece it all together, just like I am, you can't charge headlong into battle like a soldier with no rifle."

"So you *do* think it was someone Hazel worked with?" Imogene raised an eyebrow, ignoring her brother's warning.

"Imogene." He dragged out her name, lowering his voice in a scolding manner.

"Well? You're not telling us anything, Chet. What am I supposed to think? Far as I'm concerned, it's as though Hazel's case is already cold and your investigation got buried alongside of her!" Imogene knew her eyes shone with tears, and she successfully blinked them away. "Hazel never talked of anyone at the powder plant. Not one soul. Why was that? But she had friends. Ida Pickett for one, who I met just yesterday. Did you know that? Have you talked to Ida? Or her brother, Sam, who also works at the plant?"

Chet's jaw set as Imogene exploded the full of her pent-up angst on him. She couldn't stop now, though something inside of her said it was better if she did.

"Hazel never, *never* forgot to lock the screen door. And she couldn't have been home for long either, because she hadn't even started making dinner, which would've been her first priority. Did you realize that? Did that even catch your attention? And these photographs your men took of the scene—of *our house*—where are they? Why haven't I seen them?"

"Genie!" Chet broke into her rant that had fast grown watery as tears welled in her eyes again, this time spilling over. "I can't let you see them."

"Why?" The severe wobble in Imogene's voice annoyed her—betrayed her. "I already *saw* her, Chet. I stepped in her blood, and I screamed her name. There isn't anything a picture is going to show me that I haven't already seen—except maybe important details missed."

"Like the screen door," Chet finished lamely.

"Yes." Imogene swiped the tears from her cheek with the back of her hand and rolled her lips together to even out her lipstick.

Chet looked away from her, toward the wall, staring at the gray paint with an empty expression. When he turned back to her, his eyes were resigned. They told her that her brother would tell her nothing. Nothing noteworthy, and certainly nothing that would jeopardize the confidentiality of his position.

All she could envision was the musty, straw-scented stall and Hazel's unfinished dollhouse. The details. The details would have to come from Imogene's memory if Chet wouldn't let her see the pictures.

Imogene might be accused of many things, such as being too bold and brassy, with an edge of stubborn beauty that was enough to catch her a man. Yet no one had ever noticed that she saw things too, like Hazel did. The tiniest things that others missed, stepped over, walked by, and disregarded. She might not build dollhouses for a hobby, but she was good at the beauty parlor because she was an artist.

The horrible idea that her sister's murder would now become the focal point of Imogene's artistic concentration both unsettled and motivated her. She would draw her own blood if necessary to re-create that dreadful day.

Sunlight blinded Imogene the instant the police station door opened and she stepped out onto the sidewalk. It was the last thing she remembered clearly before an explosion jolted her, tossing her back into the building as if she were a bale of hay being tossed onto the hay wagon. She recalled a fierce cloud of dust and debris from just across the street, all of it catapulting toward her. Maybe it was a brick, or a fragment of a brick, perhaps wood, but it slammed into her head just above where her bandanna tie skirted her hair.

Genie, wake up.

Hazel bent over her, eyes filled with concern.

Genie, you must pull it together now. Honestly, you walk into trouble worse than I did!

Hazel's face went out of focus. Imogene blinked several times as her sister's silhouette shifted from her wispy frame to that of a man's solid one. Then she was back again, and Imogene tried not to blink for fear Hazel would disappear.

Genie, now stop this nonsense. The post office just got blown helter-skelter, and you lying here isn't going to help anyone. Least of all Chet.

Hazel patted Imogene's cheek. Her hand was rough, callused, large. Her figure distorted as Imogene blinked again, and this time a different face came into view.

". . . Chet." The male voice was finishing a sentence.

Chet returned, his words carrying an urgent tone. "But my sister!"

"I got her. Now go and figure out what in tarnation happened!" The man was talking fiercer than Imogene ever remembered hearing him. She recognized his voice but not the commanding nature of it. It didn't suit him. Not the shy soldier who jumped when a car backfired or a cow mooed.

"Thanks, Ollie." Chet's hand folded around Ollie's narrow shoulder, and then Imogene saw her brother charge into the fray. The chaos was becoming clearer.

A baby crying, and a young child.

A mother was consoling them, but the wail in her own voice betrayed her fear.

Men were shouting.

In the distance, the scream of the fire truck from the firehouse.

A few policemen were waving, directing folks about.

There was a car with its wide hubs perched halfway onto the sidewalk, its windshield cracked like a spider web.

Ollie's hand patted Imogene's cheek again. He came into focus now. Light blue eyes narrowed not in concern but in concentration as he studied her. His finger lowered and gently lifted her eyelid. Imogene whimpered and tried to pull away.

"Shhh." Ollie did the same to her other eyelid. He clicked his tongue and gave his head a quick shake. "All bets you've smashed your head in good enough to make you a bit loony."

She had no idea what he was talking about.

Imogene struggled against his hand that now pressed some cloth to her head. She tried to sit up. The world spun, making her stomach nauseated.

"Don't try an' move yet," Ollie instructed, but Imogene gave him a feisty smirk. She wasn't dead, and she wasn't some blown-up GI in a foxhole.

"I need to get back to Hazel."

"See now, you ain't makin' a lick of sense." Ollie gripped her chin as he stared into her eyes.

Imogene frowned. Who had gone and made her world explode and turned Oliver Schneider from a timid farm boy into a sergeant?

"Hazel . . ." She pushed against the sidewalk, vaguely realizing there were crumbles of clay and debris beneath her palms. She stumbled to her feet, falling into the crouching Ollie and bracing herself with her hand pressing down on his shoulder in a way that kept him from standing.

Her stomach roiled, then calmed, then—

"Holy Joe" were her last muttered words before she released the contents of her stomach. It splattered on the walk, but mostly on Ollie's back.

"Oh!" Imogene clamped a hand over her mouth as Ollie's hands wrapped around her arms and he stood. She swayed, blinking her eyes furiously, fighting the black curtains someone was pulling over her eyes. Ollie let her fall into him even as she focused on the man just beyond Ollie's left shoulder.

"Sam Pickett," she breathed. Then her eyes went dark, and all she could feel was Ollie's shoulder and chest as her body relinquished to his care.

CHAPTER 16

Aggie

The shovel that had threatened to collapse Collin O'Shaugnessy's skull had revealed over fifteen sets of different fingerprints, and every one of them was accounted for with a reliable alibi or they were unidentifiable because they were partials rather than registered in the system.

"Well, that doesn't surprise me," Mumsie mumbled with her rose-stained lips against her teacup just before taking a sip. The smell of lemon and mint drifted into Aggie's senses. "Every citizen of Mill Creek has touched that shovel since the day Floyd Barber bought it for the cemetery and practically screwed a brass dedication plate into its handle."

She lowered her cup, and her green eyes twinkled. A sassy twinkle with a hint of a smile that was far too knowing. "Honestly, you'd think he could do better for his dead wife than dedicate a gravedigger's shovel to the place he buried her."

Aggie choked on her tea—not sure whether it was the pharmaceutical flavoring of it or her grandmother's comment.

It'd been a monotonous several days since Collin had been assaulted. Nothing—absolutely nothing—had happened. Aggie didn't know if she should feel resentful for the beginning touches of small-town boredom starting to affect her attitude, or grateful she had the opportunity to toy with boredom in the first place. She'd searched Google for Mill Creek history and Hazel Grayson's name. So far, no luck. It seemed Mill Creek was as much off the internet map as it was off the national map. Small town, little interest, and no one seemed to care enough to give Mill Creek more of a web presence than a landing page with links to a few of the businesses in town.

"I'm less worried about the shovel and its fingerprints and more concerned about what Collin found at the cemetery," Aggie muttered, unsure as to why she was taking Mumsie into her confidence tonight.

Mumsie clicked her tongue with an impish scowl that perched on her face below her permed curls that still had strands of black woven through the otherwise steel gray. "He's an archaeologist, Agnes, so *of course* he's going to find a grave."

Mumsie's reference to Collin's revelation of finding new graves brought back the same creepy sentiment that had invaded Aggie the first time Collin had showed them to her. Right after getting stitched up from his head wound.

"But *two* unmarked graves in Fifteen Puzzle Row?" Aggie mused. She still couldn't figure out how people could bury anyone and not mark it on something. Collin was wading through the politics and ethics of analyzing the graves for age. No one seemed too excited to find out *who* was buried there, or when or why, so much as to make sure they were put on the map. Mr. Richardson had paid her a visit the day following the discovery and insisted Aggie catalog them "asap." Apparently, the cemetery board had hired Collin with less of an intent on uncovering historical details than identifying potential issues for future sales of plots.

"But—they were *unmarked* graves." Aggie frowned, staring blankly at the television opposite Mumsie's recliner that had a game show flipping letters and taunting them with word riddles.

"Not everyone had the funds to buy a marker by which to flaunt their dead relatives." Mumsie sipped her tea again, then smiled. "Dancing in the Dark!" she announced to the television.

"No." Aggie shook her head. "It's Dancing in the Deep."

"It can't be," Mumsie argued with a tilt of her head. A curl bobbed. "The *a*'s have already been turned. There's an *a* in the last word."

Fine. Let Mumsie win the game show. Aggie continued as though they hadn't interrupted their prior vein of conversation. "Most people at least put out a simple marker."

"Not always." Mumsie pursed her lips and tore her attention away from the puzzle that had proven to make her even more right than she'd been just a minute before. "Some people are as poor as a hobo hopping trains during the Depression. The last thing they were going to do is pay someone to practice art on marble."

"But it's Fifteen Puzzle Row," Aggie protested. "The graves are all from the late nineteenth and early twentieth centuries. Before the Depression."

Mumsie feigned a surprised look. "So, there were no poor people before the stock market crashed? Well, I'll be!"

"You know what I mean, Mumsie."

Mumsie's eyes narrowed. "Of course I do. All I'm saying is I understand why they won't let your young man dig around and upset those old corpses. For pity's sake, let the dead rest in peace."

"I don't think he'd have to do a full exhumation." Aggie pulled her feet up to rest on the seat of the cushiony chair on which she sat beside Mumsie. "Collin mentioned samples."

Mumsie's face contorted. "Cutting off the flesh?"

"No!" Aggie tried to temper the roll of her eyes. "If they're that old, there wouldn't *be* flesh. It'd just be bone. Decomposition would have completely run its course by now."

"Not completely," Mumsie countered with another wave of her wrinkled hand. "If there are skeletal remains to be found, then decomposition is most certainly still in play."

Aggie bit back a sigh.

"And for that matter," Mumsie added and gave her a side-eyed look of censure, "you deliver quite the evening morbidity for conversation."

Aggie didn't know whether she wanted to hug Mumsie around that adorable old neck of hers or strangle her—rhetorically speaking, of course. She chose neither.

"Well, it's all strange to me. I've been looking at the cemetery plotting map, and it's a mess. Not to mention, there's a grave smack-dab in the middle of it all from 1946." Aggie squelched the small niggling of guilt as she took the cowardly way out and subtly baited her grandmother.

"That Hazel Grayson again? You don't let sleeping dogs lie, do you?" Mumsie set her teacup on the narrow side table between them.

"Well, it's odd." So was everything else about Mill Creek since her arrival here. Aggie had been keeping a mental inventory, and it was one weird event after another. Mumsie's continued skirting of Hazel Grayson when Hazel's cookbook sat front and center in the kitchen was just another strange loophole in a mystery Aggie wasn't even sure was a mystery. Then there was the dollhouse, the bedroom upstairs—okay, now that created a real shiver.

Aggie hadn't revisited it since that night over a week ago. Something about it felt . . . *sacred*, or maybe that wasn't the right word. Not sacred. Perhaps raw? She felt as though, if she were to pry into it even a little bit, it wouldn't be that unlike someone pouring straight-up whiskey over a gaping wound. No one wanted to be the victim in that scenario, but then no one wanted to wield the whiskey either. So, Aggie kept quiet.

She continued to study Mumsie, who hadn't responded now

and whose eyes were so trained on the game-show host, one might tease her she was afraid he would disappear. Aggie didn't have the heart to taunt her grandmother, even though she knew Mumsie certainly would have were the tables turned.

"Who was Hazel Grayson?" Aggie didn't bother to mince her words.

Mumsie's cheek twitched, its pastel pink circle where she'd applied a powder blush that morning the only color in the old woman's face.

"Mumsie? You *did* know her. I found her cookbook in your kitchen."

Mumsie turned her head, the twinkle and sass gone from her eyes. "Oh, that thing. I bought that years ago at a church rummage sale. Don't make a story where there's none to be had."

"But you knew her?" Aggie pressed. She could see Mumsie teetering on the edge. The woman's mouth opened as if she were going to speak, and then it snapped shut.

Mumsie's eyelids closed, perhaps to collect herself or her thoughts. Aggie watched her profile, the high cheekbones, the fine curve of her brows, the delicate lashes and wrinkles that, if turned back in time, would have been on the verge of Elizabeth Taylor beauty sans the violet eyes.

"Yes." Mumsie's admission was quiet. Low. As though someone had dragged it from her and she was resigned to having to speak the truth.

A thrill of confirmation shot through Aggie. She dropped her feet to the floor and twisted in her chair. "How? Were you friends? Acquaintances? I'm just so curious as to why she's buried in the middle of Fifteen Puzzle Row when all the other graves from the forties tend to be up the hill in another section of the cemetery. And—" Aggie hesitated—"why would someone put a rose on her grave?"

"A what?" Mumsie's head snapped around to level Aggie with an intense emerald stare.

Aggie sensed the first pang of regret. "A r-rose?" The word rolled off her tongue with a question mark at the end. The hesitant kind that accompanied Aggie's wince.

Mumsie's mouth tightened into a fine line. Her lipstick staining some of the minuscule wrinkles at the edges of her lips. "No one knows Hazel Grayson anymore." Her whispered words were edged in stunned surprise.

Aggie reached across the side table and laid her hand on Mumsie's sweater-covered arm. "Mumsie?" She was worried now. She shouldn't have pressed. The woman was staring down her own imminent death, considering how old she was. The last thing Aggie wanted on her conscience was inducing her grandmother into a stroke.

"I'm fine, Agnes." Mumsie gave Aggie's hand an absent pat. She sniffed delicately. "I just—they say the war ruined lives . . ." She met Aggie's eyes, and a haunting sadness lingered in hers. "But no one tells, no one accounts for the aftereffects. How it altered everything. No one was the same again. Ever."

Aggie didn't respond. She allowed the clapping of the game-show audience to fill the room. The *ding* of the monetary reward being selected. The contestant yelling out a letter.

"Well, isn't that funny?" Mumsie was watching. An ironic smile touched her lips now. "The puzzle. It's an event. The Battle of Normandy." She sniffed. "Horrible as that was, no one remembers the smaller battles. The ones we fought for years, long after the bombs stopped falling."

Aggie waited, but Mumsie had nothing more to say.

—————

It was predawn, the sky still dark outside her bedroom window, the stars still twinkling. Aggie rustled through her suitcase, yet unpacked, for a sweater. Shoving her sleeves into its knitted coziness, she wrapped it around her torso and eyed the planner she'd tossed on top of the antique dresser. She didn't need it anymore. Well, she never really had, not since she used an app to keep track of her schedule. Even so, it was nice to have something tangible, something she could still mark with a pen and pretend her life was organized when really it wasn't. Aggie thumbed through the pages before closing it and dropping the planner into the wastebasket, which teetered at the sudden weight but didn't topple.

Goodbye, old life. Goodbye, dreams and aspirations.

Aggie grabbed her phone and couldn't help but swipe it on to access her photo gallery. Her mother's smile filled the screen. The sparkling green eyes, the healthy blush to her face, the age lines around her eyes, and the gray streaked through her dark hair.

"I miss you," Aggie breathed into the empty bedroom. She looked around. There was no one to hear her speaking to the dead. To her mother, who'd stopped fighting when Aggie finally gave her permission. The moment was etched in her memory more clearly and poignantly than the worn stones at the cemetery.

"It's okay, Momma. I'll be fine. You go now and rest, all right?"

She could still almost feel the warmth of her mother's pale hand beneath hers. Momma's eyelids fluttering as though she heard, her eyes sunk into her face, her frame a skeletal version of happier days. Pre-chemo days.

Before that, Aggie had been Momma's cheerleader. Phrases like "You've got this" and "Kick cancer's butt" weren't uncommon. But that night? That night Aggie heard the labored breathing, smelled the inevitable tinge of loss in the air, and witnessed her mother's strain to keep fighting carved into every shadow and crevice and bruise on her face.

Aggie had bent over Momma at that point, releasing her hand and embracing the shell of her body, laying her head on her mother's shoulder. Her face pressed against her mother's neck, she kissed the skin there and stroked her mother's soft cheek with her left hand. Tears burned as the knowing—the *knowing*—became all too real for Aggie. There was no more fighting. There was no more to be done but to breathe that last deep breath of life, release it, and with that breath release one's spirit.

Fly, Momma. Fly.

And she had.

Now Aggie sensed her legs give out beneath the weight of a memory she'd long suppressed. The stress of the last week was catching her off guard, lowering her defenses with exhaustion so that now she was remembering with clarity.

"Oh, Momma . . ." A tear trailed down her face as Aggie sank onto her bed. She swiped at it, running her thumb over her mother's face as she smiled back at Aggie from the phone's screen. It was after Momma had passed away that Aggie lost motivation for her career, began to let things slide, and even cut ties with her father, who, for all sakes and purposes, had left them over a decade before.

"I don't want to admit it," Aggie whispered to her mother, "but I think that's why I came here. I knew Mumsie was fibbing. She always fibs to get her way . . ." A chuckle mixed with a sob escaped Aggie's throat. "But she's—a part of you." Two more tears, both parallel to each other on Aggie's face, ran their course and trailed down her cheeks and chin, landing on the screen. Her raven-black hair fell in thick, straight strands over her sweater, and Aggie swept it back over her shoulder.

"Mumsie is a part of you, and I need you, Momma. I need you."

She sucked in a sob, opening her mouth to say more but halting suddenly as she heard a voice. A chill ran through her. "Momma?"

Startled, Aggie lifted her head. But Momma wasn't there. There was no ghost, no spirit visiting from heaven, just an empty room. Aggie frowned, straining to listen.

Sure enough. She heard a voice.

Standing, she tossed her phone on the bed and crossed the room to her door. Gripping the knob, Aggie turned it, opening the solid wood door a few inches.

The hallway was dim, except for dawn beginning to awaken out the window at the end of it. The wood floors were uneven and dark, the walls covered with a printed calico wallpaper, void of any pictures.

Mumsie's door stood open. Aggie tiptoed across the hallway and peeked in through the six-inch gap. The four-post bed lay empty, its quilt and sheet tossed aside.

"Mumsie?" she murmured softly, pushing the door wide. The distinct scents of rose water and baby powder met her senses. Aggie gave the room a quick sweep of her eyes and noticed Mumsie's walker was missing too.

She turned her back to the room and peered down the hallway. Mumsie's study.

Aggie's heart pounded a bit harder, the momentary wallowing in her own bitter grief fast fading in the curiosity and concern of the present.

A voice came from the room. Faint. Watery. Unrecognizable.

Aggie hurried to the door, which was closed tight. The only sign someone might be inside was the soft glow that escaped from the crack between the bottom of the door and the floor.

She gave a light rap on the door. "Mumsie?"

Silence.

Aggie's hand fell to the knob, but as her fingers met its coldness, she paused, unsure if she should twist it or not. It had to be Mumsie in there, but her reception would more than likely not be welcoming to Aggie.

Another murmur, followed by a strangled cry, and Aggie twisted the doorknob without further thought. "Mumsie!" She surged into the room, her bare feet sticking to the hardwood floor as she stumbled to a halt. "Mumsie?" Aggie held her hand to her throat and steadied her breathing. "Mumsie, what's . . . ?" Her words trailed as Aggie took in the sight before her.

Mumsie sat curled in the middle of the floor. Beside her was her walker, its metal frame waiting for when she chose to stand. The bed with the stained spread was behind her, a backdrop of something frightening, something dark that enhanced the shadows on Mumsie's face.

The elderly woman held a framed picture in her hand. She ran her fingers over the face in the photograph, not unlike Aggie had with her phone only minutes before.

Mumsie lifted a shaking hand and wiped tears from her cheek, still somehow unaware of Aggie's presence. She focused on the photograph, and a watery smile tipped her lips. "It's never over," she murmured. "Never over."

Not over. The words from the rose left on Hazel Grayson's gravestone and in the cemetery office were like a cold slap to Aggie's face.

Mumsie lifted her eyes but looked past Aggie, and her face was awash with a bright smile, one that made her ninety-two years fade away and leave behind someone much younger, more youthful, one who still had hopes that were bound to come true.

"Honestly, you've taken long enough to show me." Mumsie's voice had a chiding, almost teasing tone.

Aggie looked beside and behind her grandmother. No one was there.

Mumsie's eyes were gentle and warm, and she released a small sigh. "You always were the dreamer."

"Mumsie?" Aggie regretted calling to her the instant she uttered her name.

A shutter fell over Mumsie's eyes. She blinked and focused on Aggie instead of whoever it was she'd been seeing or talking to. Now their eyes met in a mutual pain, raw and guarded.

Aggie ignored the hesitation inside that made her want to pull back, retreat, and distance herself with the bitter edges of independent strength. Instead, she padded across the floor and knelt beside Mumsie, reaching out to her grandmother and placing her hand over Mumsie's. She moved Mumsie's fingers aside gently, revealing the face of the person in the photograph.

A young woman, no more than twenty, in black-and-white. A vibrant smile, and eyes that seemed to dance, with a crown of black hair set in pretty rolls.

"You?" Aggie ventured with a soft whisper.

Mumsie shook her head. Her index finger traced the woman's jawline, and she dropped her gaze to watch its path across the photograph. "No. Not me."

A tear dripped from Mumsie's face. Aggie caught it in her hand. She closed her fingers around it, knowing. "Hazel?"

Mumsie swallowed and gave a short nod. Her fingers splayed across the glass, and she refused to look up. Her head shook, but it was the shiver of age and nerves that kept Mumsie in movement.

"Who was Hazel Grayson?" Aggie lifted her hand that had caught Mumsie's tear and rested it on Mumsie's nightgown-clad shoulder.

They both stared down at the photograph as Mumsie moved her hand away.

"She is my sister," Mumsie murmured.

"*Is?*" Aggie found the present tense to be a bit disturbing.

Mumsie's eyes were confused as she lifted them to look squarely at Aggie. "No. She was. She was my sister."

A sob caught in Mumsie's throat. The desperation that filled her face tore into Aggie with the revelation that Mumsie's agony was not unmatched to her own. Instead of plying Mumsie to answer all the questions swirling in Aggie's mind, she scooted closer to her grandmother. Reaching around the aged, fragile shoulders, Aggie pulled her near and rested her cheek against Mumsie's hair.

"This is why I came," she whispered.

Mumsie sniffed. "Nonsense." But the quiver in her voice belied her stubbornness.

"It is," Aggie insisted. She didn't know of Hazel—Mumsie's dead sister—she'd never heard of her before. The surname of Grayson? Not even a hint of it. But the pain that laced Mumsie's voice, the raw grief reflected in her eyes? Yes. Aggie knew that. She understood that.

Grief made its own indelible mark on a person's soul, and only those who toiled through its muck could understand the exhaustion that came with it. Of the final never seeming final. Of the proverbial strain of one's hand as they reached into the darkness to somehow touch for just one last time, the person who had left before anyone was ready to say farewell.

There was never a good time for Death to visit.

There was never a time that Grief would leave.

CHAPTER 17

Neither of them said much. Aggie made the coffee while Mumsie shuffled to the front door and retrieved her morning paper. Aggie preferred to read it online or just skim the national headlines, but Mumsie might be one of the few remaining people on earth who still snapped open the black-and-white newsprint every morning over breakfast.

"Do you want cream in your coffee?" Aggie heard Mumsie shuffle back into the room and asked without looking up. When there was no answer, she lifted her head to glance over her shoulder.

Mumsie stood by the table, the newspaper discarded, and a padded envelope in her hand. "This was on the porch for you."

Aggie put the coffeepot back on its warmer and frowned. "For me?" She wiped her hands on a towel, damp from the steam that had drifted from the pot. Reaching out, she wasn't quite sure what to make of Mumsie's drawn brows. Of course, the morning hadn't been conducive to rest and relaxation, so it was no wonder that stress showed on Mumsie's face. She must know that Aggie had a litany of questions just waiting to cascade out.

Hazel Grayson—the roses saying "not over"—why?

And being buried in Fifteen Puzzle Row?

Aggie stuffed the questions to the back of her mind for the

moment and took the brown envelope from Mumsie's hand. It wasn't large, but she felt the bubble padding between her fingers as she ripped the top off. She reached inside, fumbling for paper or whatever object made the envelope puff out. Her fingers came out empty.

She pursed her lips and caught Mumsie's curious look. "Must be small." Crossing the kitchen, she held the opened envelope over the table and tipped it upside down.

"Holy Joe!" Mumsie's exclamation filled the room, her hand clamped over her mouth.

Aggie dropped the envelope as if it were laced with poison. "What is that?" She eyed the pile of debris that littered the tabletop. It appeared to be a cream ceramic substance turned brown with time. But the variance of color in its minuscule edges made Aggie curl her lip in horrified worry.

"It's bone," Mumsie stated matter-of-factly, but the shake of her hand as she reached for the edge of the table reminded Aggie to care for her grandmother first. She made fast work of pulling out a chair for the elderly woman.

"Sit, Mumsie."

"Of course I'll sit. You sit. Let's all just sit." It was nervous chatter coming from her now. She tapped the Formica table with her index finger just shy of the supposed bone fragments. "I am not amused by this."

"If that's what it is," Aggie inserted quickly. Heck, the first day she'd arrived here, there'd been a fake skeleton tossed into the backyard. Who was to say this wasn't fake also? She voiced her suspicions.

Mumsie's lips thinned as she considered it. "Who is it?" There was a tinge of fascination in Mumsie's voice that surprised Aggie and made her shoot a quick look of shock in her grandmother's direction.

"Don't touch it!" Aggie half shouted as Mumsie reached for a piece.

"Why not?" Mumsie lifted it.

Aggie snatched it from Mumsie's hand and dropped it back on its small pile of bony friends. "Because it could be evidence!"

"Evidence of what?" Mumsie's expression was innocent enough, yet the sharpness in her eyes made Aggie narrow her own as she realized Mumsie seemed less flustered by this than she did.

"I-I don't know."

"Call your young man," Mumsie said.

"He's not my young man," Aggie muttered as she fumbled in the pocket of her flannel pajama pants for her phone. "And I'm calling the police is what I'm doing."

Mumsie tossed her hand in a flimsy wave. "Oh yes. Because we must file this as another prank."

Aggie tended to agree, but she wasn't about to exclude the cops from this any more than she was intending to exclude the bone master himself. It shouldn't have surprised her then when Collin answered the phone. She'd intended to call the police first and had misdialed by subconscious instinct.

"I need you," she rasped, staring at the bones.

"Ahhh, turnabout's fair play, I'd say." Collin's teasing lilt brought little comfort to Aggie's jagged nerves. "I do pray no one has taken a shovel to you."

"Worse!" Aggie hissed.

"Worse?" Collin's teasing drained from his voice.

"Someone sent me bones!" Aggie stared at the pile as if they might come alive.

"Bones." It was more a statement of disbelief.

"Yes." Aggie gripped her phone tighter while eyeing Mumsie, who had once again lifted a fragment and was holding it up to the window as though lifting a diamond to judge its clarity.

"Well, isn't that a fine kettle?"

"Get over here now." Aggie wasn't one to mince words. She caught Mumsie's wobbly smirk. The old woman was reviving from the morning's emotion and regaining her spit and vinegar. Well, Aggie certainly wasn't! "I need you, Collin, please."

She wasn't clear why she all but whimpered and completely shamed herself and those of her sex by begging Collin to race to her rescue. But she had no desire to figure this out on her own. Not with a picture of Mumsie's dead sister still lying on the floor upstairs, and the words *Not over* replaying in her mind like a broken record.

"On my way, Love."

She didn't even bother to tell him not to call her that. Now wasn't the time, and for some reason it made her feel a little better.

—⁓⁓—

It was definitely bone, Collin confirmed. The police had scooped all the evidence off the table in CSI style while Aggie bristled in the corner of the kitchen, cupping her mug of coffee like a lifeline.

"We won't know if it's human," Collin whispered in her ear, "until a lab looks at it."

Aggie glowered at him. "Is that supposed to comfort me?"

Collin raised ginger brows. "I suppose it might, especially if it turns out to be pig bone."

Aggie grimaced. "Something still had to die."

"Ahhh," Collin nodded. "Isn't that the way of things, eh?"

"Aren't you supposed to know what kind of bone it is? You're an archaeologist, for pity's sake." Aggie heard the annoyance in her voice, though it didn't seem to bother Collin one bit. He had to understand it was her nerves. And nerves made her brittle, sometimes snappy.

"Well"—his breath at her ear moved a few strands of her black hair and tickled her neck—"you haven't exactly provided me with a full skeleton like before. Fragments are hard to identify. And I'm an archaeologist, not a forensic anthropologist."

"What's the difference?" Aggie didn't really care, but her nerves were making her chatty.

"Archaeology is a part of anthropology, but I'm afraid I make more of a study of the people, the culture, and the time periods than I do the scientific analysis of the bone itself."

"Then why did you want samples from the two unknown graves at the cemetery?"

Collin grimaced as though he knew he wasn't explaining it in a way she could comprehend. Especially considering that the detective was dropping the padded envelope in which the bone fragments had been delivered into a plastic evidence bag and had pretty much snagged her full focus.

"It's my business to discover the graves, their origin, the people, the story per se. And it's a forensic anthropologist's business to identify, classify, and often date the remains. While I have some experience in it, I would need to collect the samples and send them to a laboratory to be analyzed. I can made educated guesses, but without a macroscopic analysis, perhaps a CT analysis—"

"Fine. Fine." Aggie waved off the impending science behind the explanation. "So you're Indiana Jones, not a lab tech. Got it."

"Hardly a fair comparison and on multiple levels." Collin's glib response was lost on Aggie as her eyes connected with a slip of paper under the table. Maybe a receipt. Aggie moved toward it mindlessly. Something to do. Pick up the clutter. She wove between the police, ignoring Collin, who was calling her name. Bending, she reached under the table and pulled the paper out, glancing down at it.

It was not a receipt.

She didn't deserve death. He didn't deserve life.

"What is this?" Aggie's hand shook as she lifted the paper toward an officer.

The detective reached for it, his hand encased in a glove. He gave Aggie a discriminating look. "You shouldn't be handling things, ma'am."

"I-I saw it under the table."

"Was this in the package?" he asked.

Aggie shrugged. She really had no clue. She hadn't seen a note—unless Mumsie had—and her grandmother had taken to her recliner and the morning news in order to avoid the chaos. "I don't know. It must have been," she finally answered.

"Any idea what it means?" the detective inquired.

"None. Nor do I have any concept as to why someone would send me bones." Irritation crowded Aggie's throat. "Heck, it wasn't even mailed. It was set on my grandmother's front porch with her newspaper! How hard can this be to figure out? It is *not* a teenage prank." Her last comment was delivered with a scowl.

Collin's breath was in her ear. "Shhh, Love, you're going to need the law on your side."

Aggie gave him a withering glare, but the look Collin returned was innocently blank of emotion.

The detective offered an empathetic smile. "I understand this is all a bit weird." He shot a glance at Collin's stitched head. "And that."

"And the break-in at the cemetery, and the skeleton dummy in my grandmother's backyard . . ." Aggie chugged her coffee now.

"Ma'am—"

"Miss," Aggie corrected.

The detective stifled a sigh, and she could see him run his tongue along the inside of his cheek as if to squelch his impatience with her. She needed to temper her emotions—or rather temper her temper.

"*Miss*," the detective tried again, "we are taking all of it seriously. A thorough investigation will be made."

"And you'll be as slow about it as molasses on a cold winter's day." Mumsie's aged voice filled the room. She tapped her walker forward as she moved into her kitchen. "Just like always."

"Excuse me?" The detective didn't appear amused to be sandwiched between the older smarty-pants version of Aggie.

Collin, however, appeared to see the humor. The dimple in his cheek deepened.

Aggie opened her mouth to speak. She really needed to smooth the situation over. Collin was right. No need to sour the police against them.

But Mumsie was ahead of Aggie and wasn't shy about it either. Having walked up to the detective, Mumsie tilted her head to the side as if assessing him. Her cap of gray curls made her green eyes sharper, but her wrinkles softened them—a curiously cute and stubborn contrast at the same time.

"Mill Creek doesn't have a grand record of solving crimes." Mumsie tapped the detective's chest, her finger bouncing off the button on his uniform.

Aggie bit the inside of her cheek.

"But you do your darndest, Detective. And I'll do mine."

Apparently, Mumsie was going to pull her own Miss Marple on the police force of Mill Creek.

CHAPTER 18

Imogene

There were good outcomes and bad ones when frightening circumstances struck. Imogene was trying desperately to focus on the good—one being positioned against Ollie on her right while jostling against Sam Pickett on her left as he transported her home in his truck. But the bad was so difficult to ignore as they passed another car with a concerned driver apparent behind the wheel.

"How many were hurt?" She couldn't ask how many were killed. The idea of the post office exploding into smithereens was awful, but made horrifying when considering potential loss of life.

Sam shot her a glance. She noticed his knuckles whitening on the steering wheel as he gripped it tighter. "I'm not sure. Hopefully no one."

Ollie shifted, and it caused Imogene to lean further into him. He'd removed his soiled shirt at some point, and now his overalls were rolled down to his waist, and his white T-shirt was all that was between Imogene and his skin. While her head was pounding, she wasn't going to show squeamishness even if she was aching to crawl into bed and sleep off the headache.

"Reminds me of . . ." Sam's mouth tightened, and he didn't finish his sentence.

Silence filled the truck's cab as cornfields whisked by on either side. The window was down on Sam's side, and Imogene drew in a deep breath of warm country air, touched with hints of manure and cornstalks.

"The war?" Imogene finished for Sam.

His fingers adjusted on the steering wheel. She sensed Ollie stiffen.

"Aw, shucks," she mumbled. "I'm sorry." Imogene knew Ollie never spoke of his experiences overseas. Having just met Sam, she couldn't decipher whether he was one who would revel in the retelling of stories or turn into himself. But today it'd be poor taste to find any glory in war. Not when the explosion of the post office was a grim reminder of what the boys had faced every day for years.

"Who would do such a thing?" Sam craned his neck to see the road and steer around a pothole.

"Blow up the post office?" Imogene inserted.

Sam nodded.

Ollie braced his elbow on the open window and rubbed his nose as he looked at the passing fields. But Imogene also noted with vague and painful curiosity that his left arm had wrapped around her body, holding her more firmly. It felt better. Her head hurt so badly, and the stabilization made a difference. She ignored propriety or appearances and allowed herself to rest her head against his shoulder. Though Ollie didn't acknowledge her, she noticed Sam's sideways glance.

"Some meatball, I'm sure," Sam offered. It was his explanation as to who the culprit might be.

"Sure, but *why*?" Imogene was always asking why lately. Disorder had followed the boys home from the war. Whoever thought they could all move on with their lives needed to take a trip to the loony bin.

"Your brother will figure it out." Ollie's voice silenced Sam's. Imogene felt the bony thinness of Ollie's shoulder. He'd lost a lot of weight overseas.

"Chet?" Imogene mumbled against Ollie's shirt. A light-headed feeling washed over her, and she closed her eyes. "Chet's got other things to do."

"He's gonna be busy now, though." Ollie's observation knifed into Imogene. She tried to lift her woozy head and glare daggers at Ollie, but it didn't work.

"Nothing's more important than Hazel." Her words were muffled by Ollie's shirt.

"You're right," Sam reassured her. His statement held an indefinable edge to it, and if her eyes weren't closed, Imogene wondered if Sam was shooting Ollie warning glances to *shut it*.

"We don't always get justice for the ones we lose." Ollie's observation was so quiet, it was almost swallowed by the truck's noisy muffler and the breeze whipping through the open windows.

This time, Imogene did muster the energy to lift her head and open her eyes. She narrowed them at Ollie, irritated by his lack of sensitivity. "You wouldn't know what it's like to have someone you love murdered. That kind of talk is ignorant."

Ollie turned his head from the view out the window, and the blue of his eyes pierced Imogene's soul. There was such sadness in them, such beaten-down determination, that Imogene wanted to apologize for snapping at him—even if she was right in what she'd said.

"I know what it's like." He didn't blink, and there was such honesty in his expression, Imogene felt more pain, this time in her very soul. "I had buddies blown to bits, and what justice did they get? War isn't fair, Genie." Ollie turned back to the window, but she caught his words just before she drifted off into oblivion. "It isn't fair abroad or at home."

—⁓—

"Thank the Lord, you're awake." Lola's worried voice filled Imogene's senses. She opened her eyes against the light shining through her bedroom window. "Your mama's downstairs making cookies. She's just about mad with worry."

Of course she was. She'd already lost one daughter, and now her other was blown into the side of the police station in an explosion. Imogene grimaced as she moved to sit up against the pillows.

"Ollie and Sam Pickett brought you home. Chet called ahead and let your mama know and then he called me. Of course, I already knew because Mrs. Nelson had heard on the party line, and she didn't waste time rushing next door to tell me the news." Lola helped adjust the pillows, then held a hand to Imogene's forehead as if she were feverish. "What is this world coming to? Honestly, Genie, the blast put three people in the hospital. You're the lucky one! Just lightly concussed, no doubt."

"Was anyone killed?" Somehow, Imogene was able to push out the words.

"No. Not killed. Thank the Lord."

Yes. The Lord. Imogene winced inwardly. Oh, for the old-time religion to be as sweet as it had seemed when she was a child. The church with its white clapboards and Sunday-happy bell ringing. A little bit of Jesus and Sunday afternoon potlucks were the memories she'd expected to carry her through her entire life.

Not anymore.

The church had become tarnished by war vigils, where the women had knitted socks for soldiers. It was the catchall for the donation of food to help those who didn't have as much and were running out of rations. It was the doorway through which Imogene had ushered Hazel into her eternal rest, singing hymns over her casket as though somehow that "hope of Jesus" would shine down from heaven and relieve their weary souls.

It hadn't.

He was silent.

156

"Why were you at the station anyway, Genie?" Lola's question was soft but insinuating.

Aside from her pounding headache, the last thing Imogene was in the mood for was justifying her reasons for holding Chet accountable to solve their sister's murder. Or the fact she was trying to do it for him.

"It doesn't matter." Imogene picked at a piece of lint stuck to the cotton sheet that covered her.

"Well"—Lola allowed Imogene her reasons—"they said they saw someone running away from the post office just after the blast."

That snagged Imogene's attention. Her eyes snapped up to meet Lola's. "And?"

Lola shrugged. "No one could recognize him. And a few others said everyone was running away from the post office, so just 'cause some saw a man running doesn't necessarily mean anything." Lola crossed her legs at the ankles and tucked them behind the foot of the chair on which she sat. Her large brown eyes were inquisitive. "Rumors are already flying around that someone made a homemade bomb. They probably stole the powder for it from the plant."

Imogene hadn't expected that, and she knew surprise must have registered on her face. "How could anyone—?" She left her question hanging. Nothing made sense anymore. Peaceful Mill Creek had borne the shock of a murder and now the post office's destruction.

"You'd best be cautious, Genie." Lola's eyes darkened with concern. "It's not hard to figure out why you stopped working at the beauty salon and took a job at the plant. Now with this? Makes me wonder . . ."

"Wonder what?" Imogene leaned forward, reading her friend's face in hopes someone else would justify her own thoughts and suspicions.

Lola crossed her arms over her chest and pursed her lips,

raising an eyebrow and staring down her strong German-ancestral nose. "What did Hazel get mixed up in, Genie?"

The question hung between them like an omen—a bad one. Imogene locked eyes with her longtime friend. She couldn't answer for the pounding in her head and her throat, which seemed clogged with tears of relief that she wasn't the only one to harbor such questions.

"I don't know," Imogene finally admitted, "but I aim to find out."

Lola shook her head and stood, her cotton dress falling around her shins. She crossed the room to look out Imogene's bedroom window, keeping her arms wrapped around herself. She was a pretty silhouette, the white filmy curtains pushed back, the flowery print on her dress, her bobby socks at her ankles, and her sensible oxfords on her feet. Lola's dark hair was permed and pinned on the sides, just like Imogene had taught her.

Lola sniffed and shook her head again, speaking over her shoulder. "I know Chet isn't a numskull. He'll figure this out without you putting yourself in harm's way."

Imogene bit her lip. She only ever truly second-guessed herself when it was Lola criticizing her. She respected her friend, wanted her approval, and more she saw Lola's intuition for what it was—wisdom. But that didn't mean Imogene always listened.

"It's been almost a month, Lola." Imogene shifted in the bed, pulling her knees up and dragging the blanket over them. "The longer it goes since the day I found Hazel, the more I believe every clue Chet won't share with me is just getting colder. Pretty soon—" her voice hitched—"pretty soon they're gonna box up all of Hazel's files and put them away in a closet somewhere. That can't happen. You know it isn't right. No one would just—*kill* Hazel. It was someone she knew."

Lola turned, a question on her face. "How do you know that?"

Imogene didn't dispel her own theories with Chet's arguments of earlier. She believed her theories. She had to or no one else would. "Because the screen door was unlocked. Because Hazel didn't fight. She didn't fight until she was in the attic."

Lola blanched at the idea.

Imogene continued, bouncing her reasoning off her friend. "She wasn't injured either. There wasn't any blood downstairs. No smearing of it on the walls like she was fighting anyone off or . . . or that they dragged her upstairs. She just walked them up the stairs to her room. Hazel knew her killer, Lola. She *trusted* him."

Lola walked back to her chair by Imogene's bed and sat down, leaning forward and reaching for her friend's hand. Her gaze was sincere and searching. "Or someone could have just come into the house. A stranger. A vagabond. They could have found her up in the attic and, well, you know . . ."

"No." Imogene shook her head. "Nothing happened to Hazel outside of being bludgeoned to death."

"Genie!" Lola flopped back in her chair and covered her mouth with her hand.

"Well?" Imogene snapped. "If no one is willing to say it aloud, then I shall! There was blood on the *wall*, Lola. The wall! They didn't just hit her by accident and cause her death. They didn't come with lust in their eyes. They intended to do away with her for a very specific reason. And they made their point over and over and over again until Hazel was good and dead."

Lola's throat bobbed as she swallowed hard. Her eyes were watery. But Lola was tough too, and the breath she drew in, while it shuddered, also bolstered her. "And you don't think Chet sees the same story?"

"I don't know if he does or not." Imogene waved her hand dismissively. "He won't tell me anything. And who did Hazel know enough to trust to take them to the attic? Family, most likely. That's all she had was family. She didn't have *friends*. At least not that she spoke of."

"Which," Lola mused, "I always thought a tad odd, didn't you?"

Imogene frowned.

Lola held up her hand as if to beg for Imogene's patience. "Hazel wasn't shy, Genie. 'Course, she wasn't outright flamboyant and a flirt like you—"

"Hey!"

Lola dipped her chin and looked down her nose at Imogene. "You know as well as I do that if you had three men hanging on your arms at the dance joint downtown, you'd be happier if there was a fourth to balance it out. But Hazel was . . ."

"Friendly." Imogene nodded. She had to agree, for it was the truth.

"And doesn't that inspire *friendship*? So why didn't she have any close ones?" Lola asked.

Imogene drew in a contemplative breath. "Which is why I took a job at the plant. Hazel had acquaintances at church and in town. Of course, you were her friend, but what reason could you possibly have to kill Hazel?"

"Thank you," Lola mumbled.

Imogene kept musing aloud. "So then, if everyone loved Hazel, but no one *knew* my sister, who did *she* know well enough to invite into her private room?"

Lola smiled a sad little smile. "What if Hazel's death and the post office explosion are somehow related?"

Imogene frowned. She could see where Lola's reasoning was taking them, although it didn't make clear sense. "Powder."

Lola nodded.

Imogene wrestled with the idea, because it was the only common factor between Hazel and today's explosion. Yet Imogene was certain Hazel hadn't been smuggling materials out of the plant in order to blow up the town of Mill Creek and then later murdered for it.

Well, almost certain.

CHAPTER 19

Imogene pressed the back of her hand to her brow and let her eyes rove over the tables in the powder plant's canteen. She'd made enough sandwiches to last her a lifetime in the last week since she'd returned to work after her mild concussion. If she never saw another marriage of two slices of bread with condiments and meat in the middle, she'd be happy. Truth be told, she missed the pungent smell of the perming chemicals and the sweet scents of the shampoos.

Men rammed food into their mouths during their short lunch break. The fact the room was filled with men might have once been the only bright spot in a dirty, glamourless place such as this, but it now brought little interest to Imogene. She caught threads of conversation, and it squelched any healing that could have possibly come to her soul since Hazel's death.

"Fact is," she'd heard one man say yesterday as he stood in line for his lunch, "they can't figure out whodda been dumb enough to blow up the post office, let alone the why of it."

"Maybe one of them Comm-you-nists?"

That was the newest thing since the Nazis had been bested and the Japanese regime pushed back after the war. Communism. Imogene wasn't even sure she knew what it was—what *Communists* were—and she wasn't sure she cared.

"Nah. Why blow up the U.S. Mail?"

Why indeed? That was the question on everyone's minds. What was worse, it was also the foremost question on Chet's mind. Which meant the foretelling of Hazel's death becoming less of an urgency was coming true.

"Genie?" The voice nudged her from her mental puzzle solving.

"Oh! Ollie." She worked a warm but fake smile to her face. He was so . . . unsettling. Even now his eyes drove into her, but somehow the blue of them still reminded her of a gentle summer sky and not the sharp point of an icicle. It was a stark contrast—the meekness of the man and the decisive command of Ollie the day of the explosion.

"I was thinkin' maybe I could stroll by later tonight and we could take a walk?"

Imogene stilled and drew back. She blinked a few times, completely taken aback that he was asking her to walk with him. As a date? Or for other reasons? To assess her well-being?

"Well, Oliver Schneider, you do beat all!" She mustered her best flirty smile that covered the unease settling in her stomach. Unease or anticipation or maybe a bit of both.

"It's just a walk." His bland response made Imogene's smile droop.

"Never 'just a walk' when it's a pretty gal next to a man." The voice that interrupted them was one Imogene had heard in her mind several times. Sam Pickett's voice. Somehow these two men seemed to show up near each other, and the pattern made her raise her eyebrow. Knowing full well the effect of her winged, upward swoop of one black brow matched to the geometry of her high cheekbones and red lips, Imogene cocked a hand on her hip and looked between the men.

"Now, now. One of you asked, and the other interrupted. So, are we planning another war, only this time it's over me?"

It was tactless. That much was apparent by the way Ollie's

gaze dropped to the floor. He wasn't embarrassed or disappointed in her toying with the two men. He was disappointed *in her.*

But Sam laughed. His smile took over his entire face. A mix of Cary Grant's Hollywood brooding charm and just the good ol' hometown wit of a local boy. A local boy with a family name that meant trouble. Reckless trouble. Somehow the temptation of throwing caution to the wind was juxtaposed with the caution in her heart since Hazel's death. Imogene hadn't one story to pin Sam to anyway. It wasn't as though he had a rap sheet to match John Dillinger's, who, rumor had it, had been spotted not far from Mill Creek ten or so years ago. Sam Pickett was—well, he was a stranger to her, a distraction, with the exclamation point of danger that might have intrigued her before Hazel's death, but now . . . well, she had to admit, she was still intrigued.

"Ida!" Sam spotted his sister across the room and waved her over. A timid smile stretched across her simple face, which had hints of Sam matching in the shape of her eyes and mouth. "Get on over here!"

His joviality did something to Imogene's insides. It took everything dark and made it light—if even for just a moment. She caught Ollie's careful study of her. She chose to ignore it.

"Who would you choose?" Sam gestured between himself and Ollie as he addressed his sister.

"Choose for what?" Ida's response was almost mousy in comparison to her brother's friendliness. But the kindness in her eyes when they met Imogene's once again warmed Imogene. Hazel had found a friend in Ida. A friend . . .

Imogene's conversation with Lola had never been far from her mind. Ida was a friend. But no. That was ridiculous. She was a petite little thing and had the gumption of a church mouse.

"To take a stroll down Lovers' Lane, arm in arm and all that." Sam's voice interrupted Imogene's sudden suspicion. She swung her attention to Sam. Had Hazel been friends with Sam?

"Lovers' Lane?" Ida's smile quirked up on the side as she began to catch on to the drift of the conversation. She crossed her arms over her uniformed chest, the cotton coveralls not doing much to enhance her appearance. "We don't have a Lovers' Lane in Mill Creek, do we?"

"So literal." Sam biffed the curl on the side of her head, and Ida ducked, giving a little laugh. Her face had brightened under her brother's attention.

"Well . . ." Ida looked between him and Ollie, whose only expression now seemed to suggest he was looking for a way to excuse himself from the awkwardness of the conversation. "I'd not trust you alone with a girl, Samuel." Ida's laugh was quiet but teasing. "So I'd have to pick Ollie."

Ollie glanced at her. Disinterested in all of them, Imogene could tell. Something inside her compelled her to make it up to Ollie. Her insensitive comment about another war . . . no one wanted to think about war for at least a hundred years.

"Yes, Oliver Schneider. I'd be happy to take a walk with you."

He lifted those sky-blue eyes, yet there was no hope or joy or even excitement in them. They were dull and resigned. Still, he gave her a nod. "I'll see ya around eight." And then he moved on, as if content that he could do so now without appearing rude.

Imogene watched him walk away. His tall, thin frame so familiar. They'd known the Schneiders their entire lives. Ollie was their friend. Hazel's friend . . .

Holy Joe! Imogene blinked several times to clear her thoughts. Any more of this and she'd have accused all of Mill Creek for murdering Hazel. She needed to narrow it down—find more clues and signs that she could piece together. Just casting suspicion on everyone who'd crossed paths with Hazel was unfair.

Sam shot Imogene a wink. "He ain't no Casanova."

"He's my friend," she retorted, still not sure why she felt the need to defend Ollie to Sam.

"Sam, are you riding the bus tonight?" Ida's simple question slipped into the banter with a naïve inquiry. "I think Glen would love it if we could pick him up from Auntie's early."

Sam's smile waned as fast as it had brightened his face. "Glen can wait," he muttered. Then he gave a fast nod to Imogene before moving away almost as fast as Ollie had.

There was an awkward pause as both women watched Sam crisscross the canteen and head for the door. The shift whistle blew, and everyone stood in a mass flurry to return to their positions on the lines. Ida cast Imogene an apologetic smile that touched her brown eyes with sincerity.

"I'm sorry."

"No need to apologize." Imogene waved it off, although every ounce of her wanted to know who Glen was.

Ida was quick to supply an answer to the question that must have reflected in Imogene's eyes. "Glen is my nephew. Sam lost Bonnie—his wife—a few years ago. They married, quick-like, before he shipped out. You know . . ."

Yes. Imogene nodded. It hadn't been uncommon. Quick marriages threatened by war, death, a future that might never be. Many had found their way down the aisles at young ages to spit in the face of a dark future and believe for a moment that dreams could come true.

"Bonnie, she . . . well, she had Glen right after. Poor little guy, never knew his mama."

"She passed away?" Imogene held her breath.

Ida nodded. "The birth—it wasn't easy. The doctors knocked her out so they could take the baby without painin' her, but then Bonnie never woke up. Our aunt has helped raise Glen, especially since Sam was over in the Philippines. Now . . ." Ida glanced over her shoulder, where Sam had disappeared with the throng of workers. "Well, it was hard to come home to a dead wife he'd barely had time to love and a boy he didn't know."

Imogene nodded, even as a small piece of her shattered on

behalf of Sam. On behalf of his wife, Bonnie, and their little boy, Glen.

"I swear, Ida," Imogene heard herself say, the words almost bitter as they passed through her lips, "I wish we could erase the last six years and start over."

Ida's eyes were teary, and she nodded, even as one slipped out and ran down her cheek. "I'd like that. To start over with all the ones we loved before."

Imogene bit her bottom lip so she didn't follow Ida's watery example. "With all the ones we loved before . . ." she repeated softly.

The lantern lit the stall with its warm glow. Imogene stood over her table of supplies. Paintbrushes. Paints. Glue. An assortment of necessities she'd collected from Hazel's supply of miniature-making crafts. Her insides curdled as she turned her attention to the dollhouse itself. She was certain this wasn't what Hazel had imagined when she'd set out to re-create the family farmhouse. So much of her work was already finished. Loving details, down to a tiny replica of the mantel clock that Momma said had sailed over from Germany with her grandmother.

Imogene ran her finger over the tiny piece of wood. Hazel must have stood in front of the real clock for long moments, studying every detail so she could remember it later. Like a camera, only in her mind. Imogene and Hazel used to play games remembering details until finally one of them tripped up with a lapse of recollection. They could go for hours. Hazel usually won, but Imogene had never been far behind.

Now she shifted her focus to the attic bedroom and the tiny furniture Hazel had so delicately crafted to match her own precious space of respite, which had careened into an event that would collect her very blood instead.

Imogene shivered at the thought. She picked up a tiny paintbrush. Her breaths came in short, quick successions as she lofted the bristles over the small jar of red paint. That she had to paint her own sister's demise on the walls of the precious and beloved dollhouse Hazel had constructed! Its ominous undertones of realism twisted Imogene's insides, and she felt her nostrils flare as she sucked in a breath and held it for five long seconds. Releasing it, she dipped the brush into the paint.

Remember, there was a spatter of polka dots on the wall just a few feet above my head.

Imogene squeezed her eyes shut, picturing, remembering the horrible details as Hazel's voice recited them in her mind.

As if someone lifted something from the blow to the back of my head in an arc over their shoulder.

"Only to repeat it again and again." Imogene dotted a pinprick point of red paint where she recalled the first part of the spatter. The meticulous detail was so tiny, yet it glared at Imogene with the vigorous assault of the actual attack.

How many times did they strike me?

"I don't know." Imogene applied another tiny dot.

I wonder if you could tell how many times if you could pattern the blood on the wall precisely the way it looked when you found me?

"My memory isn't that remarkable." Imogene smirked as though Hazel was really standing there to be the recipient of the dry sarcasm. "And why . . . ?" Her words waned as she frowned. There was a picture on the bedside stand. It was turned up and facing her with the sketch of a black-and-white landscape. Too tiny to be exact replicas of the real picture and too tiny to be identifiable.

"This wasn't there." Imogene held her paintbrush in the air, staring down at the minuscule picture replica while retracing the details of the room as she recalled it. "There wasn't a picture by your bed the night I went back to see."

Are you sure? There's one here in my dollhouse.

Hazel's question nagged at Imogene.

"I-I don't . . ." Remember? She had to remember. She remembered details far more obtuse and difficult than a sketch of some landscape! But perhaps the picture or painting was so mundane, so a part of life that she'd grown so used to it that . . . "Hazel, I don't remember!"

Imogene's gasp was followed by a deep voice from the doorway of the stall.

"Who are you talking to?"

Imogene spun around, paintbrush lofted like a weapon. Her preoccupied vision collided with the reality of Ollie's very real form and confused gaze. His eyes scanned the barn stall, squinting to see into the shadows where the lantern light didn't cast its blaring focus.

"Are you all right?" He stepped into the stall.

Oh. The walk. The "stroll down Lovers' Lane," as Sam had so casually teased earlier in the day. Imogene had completely forgotten.

"Is it eight o'clock?" She dropped the paintbrush onto the table, clattering it against a jar of brushes and sending a metal paint lid bouncing along the surface. Imogene slapped her hand on top of it to keep it from careening over the side into the straw on the floor. Flustered, she lifted it, her hand shaking.

You can't remember?

She was still hearing Hazel's voice.

"No!" Imogene mumbled, still trying to pull herself from her jaunt deep into her memory.

"Genie?" Ollie took another step toward her, his brow furrowed. The shadows only emphasized the crags and crevices on his face. Ones that hadn't been there four years ago when he'd left for the war as a young man and returned home an old, dying soul.

"I don't remember," she whispered. Agony welled up within her. The kind that mingled with panic and shock. When one's habitual tendencies failed at just the pivotal moment you relied on them the most.

"Remember what?" Ollie captured her gaze with his own, and he neared her but didn't reach out to touch her. He tilted his head to his right as if by doing so he could somehow burrow deep into her vision and see what Imogene was seeing.

Nothing. She was seeing nothing. She wasn't hearing anything either.

Hazel's voice had gone deathly quiet.

CHAPTER 20

Aggie

Mumsie had fallen asleep in her chair. The morning—and probably their predawn meet-up in Mumsie's dollhouse room—had worn the poor woman out. The police left, and now Aggie leaned against the front door, letting the latch click into place. She paused for a moment, collecting her nerves, and then swung about, coming nose to nose with Collin O'Shaughnessy and his cheeky smirk.

This time she didn't let it bother her—neither the annoyance nor the butterflies in her stomach. She grabbed Collin's hand and started for the stairs.

"That's a bit bold, don't you think, after just rifling through someone's bones?" Collin's teasing lilt followed her as she tugged on his extended arm and started up the stairs. He continued his friendly mockery. "I don't think we know each other well enough to be heading upstairs to your room, Love."

"Shut it, Romeo." Aggie dropped his hand as they reached the top of the stairs. She wagged her finger. "Come. I need to show you something."

It was a violation of Mumsie's privacy. But who else did she have to share it with? After Mumsie's not-so-subtle challenge to the detective, things were starting to fall into place.

Hazel, Mumsie's never-spoken-of sister.

A dollhouse that was a literal crime-scene reenactment.

The stained bedspread . . . Aggie stumbled to a halt outside the room.

Collin's spicy cologne filled her senses with a calming effect. "What are we doing?" His whisper lifted some of the hairs by her ear. Aggie patted them down and stepped away from Collin. She swung open the door, stretching her hand out in an arc as if to announce a big reveal.

"My grandmother's room." Her statement meant little to Collin. He peered in with a vaguely curious gaze, then shifted his attention back to her through the lenses of his round glasses. Heaven help her—his dimples were still visible even when he didn't smile!

He appeared genuinely perplexed. "Forgive me, but . . . why are we in your grandmother's room?" Collin's voice rose a bit in question.

Aggie stepped into the room, an eerie sensation raising the hairs on her arms. The pieces beginning to make only a smidgeon of sense, but enough to know this room was the coffin that held Mumsie's broken heart.

"Welcome to Mumsie's past." She gave her arm a broad sweep that ended with the flicking of the light switch. The lamp on the bedside stand shed its warm, muted tones across the room.

The wood floor creaked beneath Collin's step. He rolled his lips together in confused contemplation and raised his eyebrows—a ruddy shade darker than his hair—over the rim of his glasses.

"Aggie, what are we looking at? Why did you bring me here?"

Aggie led him to the dollhouse, to the disturbing scene splayed out in its attic bedroom. "This. And Hazel Grayson. And . . . the messages on the rose petals."

Collin shoved his hands in his trouser pockets. Darn it if the man wasn't wearing suspenders like some English professor, looking as though he could stroll the quaint streets with the calm air of a man on an adventure.

"Hazel Grayson," he murmured with a nod.

Aggie reached out with her index finger and glided it slowly across the unmarred portion of the miniature attic room. She eyed Collin's reaction with a sideways study. His gaze followed the trail her finger left until the tip of her manicured nail touched the imitation pool of blood that had drained from the head of the woman whose body sprawled facedown on the floor.

"Dreadful." Collin's expression held a strong hint of curiosity. He bent forward, craning his neck to examine the interior of the dollhouse. "But this miniature shows remarkable workmanship. I mean, it's *splendid*! The detail is stunning!"

Aggie didn't wait for Collin to piece anything together. He had no reason to outside of the vague clues she'd dropped. "Hazel Grayson was Mumsie's sister."

Collin shot her a quick look, and then he returned his attention back to eyeing the blood spatter on the tiny wall.

"I believe—I *think* this is how Hazel died." Once the words had left Aggie's internal musing, the harshness of her statement stilled her tongue. It was a conclusion she'd been so sure of in her head, but now that she'd spoken it out loud, she wasn't certain it would all fit together.

Collin must have thought the same. Aggie realized he had stilled and turned his head, even though he was still bent over the dollhouse. His cinnamon eyes roved her face. "You're serious?"

Aggie gave a short nod. A strand of hair fell from behind her ear, and she pushed it back before giving a dismissive wave of her hand. "I know it's crazy, but I . . . what else could this be?" She gestured toward the minuscule crime scene. "And did you notice?" Grabbing hold of his arm, Aggie pulled Collin away from the dollhouse to the room behind them. "Look. The bed.

172

It's the real-life version of the tiny one in the dollhouse. That entire side of the room is the *actual* furniture."

"So it is." Collin was grave now. He strode across the room, eyeing the wallpaper. "But the wallpaper is a different pattern."

"Do you suppose the murder happened—" Aggie swallowed hard—"happened here?"

Collin shook his head, scrunching his lips in thought. "Doubtful. The floorboards run in the opposite direction as the ones in the dollhouse. I would wager it's a different house altogether."

"What if you're wrong?"

"No." Collin's reply was confident. He turned back to the dollhouse. "The attention to detail is too particular for the artist to have made a very general mistake such as directionally juxtaposed flooring."

"Of course," Aggie nodded. Bewildered. "I-I wouldn't have noticed that."

"Why do you believe this is Hazel?" Collin touched the model person that served as the murder victim. The dress she was clothed in was real cotton, woven green with tiny navy-blue polka dots.

"Because . . ." Why indeed? Mumsie had only admitted to being Hazel's sister. She'd given no further detail that her sister had been violently murdered or that this was a reenactment of the crime scene.

Collin didn't wait for Aggie's response. "This is really quite genius. Have you ever heard of the Nutshell Studies?"

"No." Aggie drew her brows together.

Collin straightened from his perusal of the murder victim. He gave Aggie a slight smile. "Francis Glessner Lee. She was the godmother of forensic science." He pointed at the dollhouse. "She created crime scenes in dioramic form. Students who wished to learn the investigative techniques of forensics would attempt to solve the murders by examining the clues she planted in the scene."

Aggie's attention was drawn back to Mumsie's dollhouse with magnetic force. Collin continued to explain. "It was in the 1940s that Francis Glessner Lee began making the dioramas. I'm quite intrigued your grandmother did the same. I highly doubt she would have known of Lee."

Aggie nodded. She had to agree. If recollection served her well, Mumsie had been a beautician, not a forensic scientist. Not in the slightest.

"How many of the students solved Lee's crime scenes?" Aggie tried to wrap her mind around what they were looking at.

Collin shook his head. "Frankly, no one knows. Lee never actually gave them the truth of the crime or the killer—although I have to imagine she had one in her story. The miniature scenes were merely to be used as tools of observation. Piecing together clues into a puzzle. As with any crime, the evidence must be used to draw a conclusion, but it's not as if the dead rises to confirm one's theory. This is why the science must support it. In many ways, it's archaeology only moments after a person's death rather than dusting aged bones."

Bones. Aggie twisted to give Collin her full attention. "Do you suppose . . . ?"

He cocked an eyebrow. "Suppose what?"

Aggie tried to tamp down the nagging suspicion. "The bone fragments just sent to Mumsie. The fake skeleton in the back-yard. The break-in at the office. And your assault . . ."

"Are you imagining they're somehow tied together?" Collin's eyes never left hers.

Aggie shrugged, the red wool of her cardigan-covered shoulder brushing her hair against her ears. "Nothing is *tied* together, obviously, or there'd be a distinct connection the police would be making by now." She cast him a look of exasperation. "But I also don't believe in coincidence. There have been too many oddities since I arrived in Mill Creek to turn a blind eye to or make justification for. Even if I ignored the dummy skeleton in the backyard as a mid-September Halloween prank—which still seems ridiculous—everything else is too coincidental. And I can't disregard it or look at them as anything but a conglomeration of random evidence that needs piecing together."

Collin must have spotted something on her sweater. He reached out and plucked at it, his fingers brushing away a piece of lint. Aggie blinked. A bit surprised that his platonic and absent-minded gesture would make her catch her breath.

"I'm the last person you'd ever need to convince that pieces of a puzzle create a larger picture." His words soothed Aggie's frayed nerves. It justified her direction of thought and validated that she wasn't turning into a bitter-edged woman like Mumsie with eccentric ideas and off-the-wall theories.

She blinked, breaking eye contact with Collin, who for some unknown and most likely meaningless reason had yet to do so himself. Aggie cleared her throat. "All right then. The common denominators seem to be Hazel Grayson, the cemetery, your attack, and bones."

"That's an awful lot of denominators." Collin's mouth quirked in a half smile.

"Well, what do you suggest? I was never good at mathematical equations." Aggie rolled her eyes.

Collin's smile broadened. "Perhaps we should learn the culture and history of the time, so we understand the subject better?"

"Spoken like an archaeologist," Aggie grumbled.

"Spoken out of sheer logic," Collin corrected. "Because truly, who was Hazel Grayson—aside from your grandmother's sister—and why, after all these years, have you never known she existed?"

———⁂———

Aggie wrapped her arms around her chest as she stood in the doorway of Mumsie's house. The afternoon sun was brilliant as it illuminated the trees along the street, whose leaves were beginning to show definitive tinges of autumn reds, yellows, and oranges.

Collin's question about the existence of Hazel Grayson bugged her. She waved goodbye as he pulled away from the drive. She'd told him she would meet him at the cemetery in an hour. The flooded graves would not wait for bone fragments to be identified and Aggie's family history to be fully revealed. She still had a job to do, although the thought of continuing the arduous task of entering each gravesite's index card information into a spreadsheet on the new computer was not at all as intriguing to her as helping Collin search for more—if there were any—unmarked graves.

Two was probably enough. But those buried in them, especially seeing as they were in Fifteen Puzzle Row, made Aggie question their stories too.

"One story at a time," she muttered to herself as she stepped into the house and closed the door behind her. She went to the doorway of Mumsie's sitting room and peeked in. The old woman appeared so delicate in her sleep. The stubborn lift of her shoulder having relaxed into the thin, fragile body. Her impish look was replaced with the sweetness of slumber. Her wrinkled face telling the depths of the story she'd lived for almost a century, a life filled with untold tales.

Aggie scanned the room. For the first time, she noted there were no family pictures on any of the ledges, shelves, or tables. An oil painting of five kittens playing in an old Victorian-style trunk hung on one wall. A pair of glossy ceramic lovebirds perched next to a few Zane Grey novels. A strange read that Aggie credited to someone Mumsie must have once known, for the large-print romances piled on the floor next to her recliner was evidence that Mumsie wasn't an Old West type of reader. Maybe they'd belonged to her grandfather. Another shadowy figure from her ancestral tree whose name was just a name and whom no one seemed to have any memory of. Aggie's mom had grown up fatherless. His legacy left behind—a couple of Western-genre novels? Maybe.

She crossed the hall and peered into the all-too-familiar kitchen. A quick glance at the table and Aggie squelched a shudder. The envelope with the bone fragments and cryptic message had been confiscated by the detective. The kitchen looked bland. Outside of the vintage linen towels hanging on the oven door and the shelf of old cookbooks, there wasn't much else to bring homey touches to the room.

Frowning, Aggie drew back into the entryway and glanced at the walls. Another painting of a Wisconsin farm. She ignored the bathroom, assuming no one would bother to put family photos in there, and hurried back upstairs. Avoiding Mumsie's study, Aggie moved to Mumsie's bedroom. It was cozy but nondescript. If she were to sell this place, Aggie would have advised that the rooms be given some serious staging. Go vintage, and go vintage *all the way*. Mumsie's room was a hodgepodge of an ivory-colored wooden bed frame with a shelf acting as the headboard. Mumsie had a box of tissues perched on the shelf, another romance novel, a flashlight, and a small Asian-styled jewelry box.

No photographs.

Aggie tiptoed to the bureau as if it were the middle of the night and she was afraid of awakening Mumsie. A narrow, embroidered dresser scarf spanned the length of the bureau. A few strands of faux pearls lay on top. A comb. A box of matches next to a used-up candle. There was a pile of letters, and Aggie made quick work of thumbing through them. Mostly advertisements for credit-card approvals, a letter from Aggie—she realized sheepishly it was her last letter to Mumsie, which she'd sent over a year ago—and a *We Miss You* card from a local church.

Church?

Aggie tried to recall whether Mumsie had ever mentioned a

church she attended often enough to have them miss her. Was this another side to Mumsie that Aggie had somehow missed?

A sense of guilt filled her and curled her nerves. How much was there to Mumsie? To her past? How much had her own mother known? Aggie wondered if it was those untold stories that maybe her mother might have been aware of. Perhaps this helped to spawn more empathy from Mom, more understanding. A side of Mumsie that the rest of the now-almost-extinct family line never really knew.

Aggie moved to the bookshelf. It was piled with everything from classics to well-worn paperback romances. Grace Livingston Hill. She'd heard of her. Aggie pulled one out and thumbed through its yellowed pages. The woman on the cover was dressed very much in the garb of someone who'd existed in the thirties or forties. She flipped to the inside first page.

Hazel Grayson

The name was written in a thin, loopy cursive. So, Hazel had been a romance reader also? A dreamer perhaps.

Aggie slipped the book back into its place.

A small picture frame sat on one of the shelves. A picture of Mom. Aggie ran her finger over her mother's face. Mom was young in the photo, perhaps in her late teens or early twenties. Beautiful, like Mumsie had been. Aggie knew she took after both of them, and though her ego was modest, it felt natural to recognize the dark beauty of the family and appreciate it for what it was.

It was the only photograph in the bedroom. Aggie stepped back and sank onto Mumsie's bed. The room with the most artifacts of Mumsie's life was the room with the god-awful dollhouse and stained bedspread. It was almost as if Mumsie had created a time capsule and returned there frequently. As if life for Mumsie had somehow stopped in 1946 when Hazel had died, and though she'd continued to build an existence, Mumsie had never really continued to live.

CHAPTER 21

"H eard tell they were pig bone." Mr. Richardson's sudden declaration behind Aggie caused her to jump in her chair and choke on a scream. It was unnerving working in a cemetery to begin with, let alone in the cramped little office where someone had not so long ago taken a shovel to Collin's head.

"Excuse me?" Aggie couldn't hide her annoyance at being surprised.

The older man peered at her through his thick plastic lenses. He tugged on his sweater, the hem of it frayed and a string of wool dangling against his navy-blue trousers. "Them bones someone sent to your grandmother."

Aggie drew back in shock. It'd been several days. Several days with very little answers. Mumsie had been remarkably quiet, napping a lot lately. Before leaving for work, Aggie would call and ask a local volunteer from the Center for the Community on Aging to come sit with Mumsie and make sure she didn't— God forbid—pass away alone in her sleep. Aggie wasn't certain Mumsie was ailing so much as the undetermined letter and bones had made her turn inward.

"I'm sorry . . ." Aggie shook her head and eyed Mr. Richardson. "Pig bone, you say?"

179

"Yep. I saw Harold Pittman downtown, and he said that his wife heard that them bones were pig. Not human."

Lovely. The entire town was playing a verbal game of telephone surrounding the facts of Mumsie's sordid and freakish events.

"Mr. Richardson," Aggie began, "the police haven't even confirmed that with us."

"Oh, they will. Eventually." Mr. Richardson shuffled to the desk where Aggie sat and scooped up a pile of index cards—some of them typewritten, some written in faded handwriting. "Police here in Mill Creek have always been slow as molasses."

"So I've heard." Aggie grimaced. She paused, then proceeded as an idea struck her. "Mr. Richardson, what do you know of Hazel Grayson's gravesite?"

His head popped up from his perusal of the cards. "What don't I know? I know everything about this here cemetery."

Not really. Aggie wanted to point out the two unmarked graves Collin had discovered. He was still waiting on the legalities involved before he could exhume the graves and have samples sent to a lab to determine exact ages, dates, and logistics of the remains. Until he received the go-ahead, the bodies would stay where they were, encased in the earth.

"Then enlighten me." Aggie prodded the older man's ego. He grinned, revealing crooked front teeth, stained from coffee and maybe tobacco use years before.

Mr. Richardson scratched his chin. "Well now, I was a lad when it happened, so I don't recall all the details, mind you."

"How old were you?" An age would help Aggie to know how firmly she'd choose to believe the cemetery curator's story.

"Five? Yes, ma'am. Five years old." Mr. Richardson smiled again, this time with pride. His eyes were alert, his expression rife with eagerness to tell the tale of Hazel Grayson. "She was murdered, Hazel was." His voice dropped an octave, as though bringing Aggie into some circle of need-to-know information.

Aggie tried to ignore the pang of regret that snagged her when Mr. Richardson confirmed her suspicions. She managed her facial reaction so as not to show the man how much his blunt acknowledgment had affected her. "Oh?"

"Yes, ma'am!" He shifted his feet and reached for a metal folding chair. Plopping onto it, he slapped his knees with his hands. "My daddy told me that Hazel was found in her attic bedroom. Facedown. Blood everywhere. Like someone had taken a hatchet to her."

Aggie leaned back against the desk, gripping the edge of it. "That's, um, interesting." And morbid. And tragic. Her chest constricted with the sensation of empathy filling her. The kind that predicted tears would soon follow. She took a deep breath to quell the instinctive response.

Mr. Richardson nodded. "For sure it was. Wall was covered in blood and—"

"Okay." Aggie waved him along.

Mr. Richardson halted and assessed her briefly. "Anyways, my daddy told me it was your grandmother that found her. Came home and went lookin' for her sister, and there she was. Dead as a doornail and still a bit warm."

Aggie blanched. "And then what? Who killed Hazel?"

Mr. Richardson shrugged his sweater-clad shoulders. "There's the mystery of it!"

"No one was ever convicted?" Aggie stiffened, frowning.

"Nope."

"What about DNA?" Aggie asked before thinking it through.

"DNA?" Mr. Richardson's laugh sounded congested. He coughed and cleared his throat. "Ain't no one know nothin' about DNA. Fact is, what you young'uns are so used to seein' on all those crime shows on TV? We didn't have much of that back then. Photographs. Fingerprints. Common sense. That was what they used to solve crimes."

Aggie's arms suddenly had goose bumps on them. The very

idea of a young Mumsie calling for her sister, walking up the stairs, opening that attic bedroom door . . .

She blinked. "So the police found nothing? No one?"

Mr. Richardson shrugged again. "All I know is, they buried Hazel Grayson in Fifteen Puzzle Row, right between two graves from 1901 and 1889. There she is, all these years later, a dead woman from 1946 smack-dab between a three-year-old and an old lady. Know why she's buried there?"

Aggie leaned forward, her breath catching in anticipatory eagerness for *something* to be answered. "No. Why?"

Mr. Richardson drew back, tucking his chin in and creating an extra roll of flesh around his neck. "Well, I don't know why! I was asking you!"

Aggie bristled. "How would I know?"

He gestured to the desk and the computer. "That's what you were hired for! Put the records together. Make sense of it all. Build up a well-plotted map of this place so we can answer those questions. Who wants to buy a plot of dirt to lie in someday if the only empty ones are in old sections of the graveyard, or in the brand-new sections where the trees have hardly grown taller than a few yards?"

"I've no idea what you're talking about." Aggie tempered her voice so she didn't allow her irritation to show. She'd learned this skill after years of selling real estate. Picky, presumptuous buyers, entitled spouses, and the like.

"People like to have *trees* over them when they're dead! No one likes those baby ones the cemetery board had us plant two years ago. Buyin' those four acres was stupid is as stupid does. Especially when we got open plots here already. Sell what we got, I voted for, and fill 'er up first. Then spend money on more land."

If Mr. Richardson didn't stop spinning circles around her, she was afraid she was going to reach out and slap the old man silly. Aggie folded her hands in front of her to avoid any such extreme and overdramatic reactions. "But you just said that no one would want to be buried in an old section of the cemetery."

"Sure! Of course I did!" He gave her a wide-eyed nod as if she should understand.

Aggie didn't. Not in the slightest. She mustered a smile, laced with a simpering sarcasm she was all too familiar with. Summoning Mumsie's spit and vinegar, Aggie patted the old man's hand. "No one likes to fill up a graveyard like one would fill up their gas tank."

Mr. Richardson narrowed his eyes as if trying to follow her. Ha! Now he knew what it felt like! Riddles and circles and spinning woven tales with no endings.

"But, Miss Dunkirk," Mr. Richardson said, seeming to want the last word on the subject, "graveyards *do* fill up. Point is, people want to be buried in a pretty place. No one wants to be laid to rest in a hole in the bright sunlight with no big trees around and no real landscapin'. And no one wants to be dropped into a hole in the middle of a bunch of old graves. People'll forget to look for ya if you're stuck in some old section. But I say a grave's a grave. You get what you can pay for, and the fact is we sell those cheaper."

A thought struck Aggie, and she pushed herself off the desk. "You say the graves are cheaper in the old section?"

"Sure. Who can say why some plots never sold and others did. Although now we got random one-offs stuck there among established dead families. People want their kin together. They're not gonna be having no party where they're laying, but I suppose the idea of being dead next to relatives is comforting, I mean if you're still alive to think about it."

Aggie nodded. "So, it's difficult to sell gravesites that allow no space for family to be buried nearby."

Mr. Richardson nodded. "That's a fact, ma'am."

Aggie bit her bottom lip and pondered for a moment, squinting as she tried to picture the gravestone of Hazel Grayson.

"If Hazel's family couldn't afford a nice plot in their family's section, then they would have perhaps just bought one that was available, right?"

"Sure seems like that's what happened." Mr. Richardson nodded as though their entire conversation had been heading in that direction to begin with.

Aggie frowned. "And where is the Grayson family section?"

Mr. Richardson snorted, shaking his head as though Aggie's question was the most ridiculous thing he'd heard all day. "Ain't no Grayson family section. Never was. Prob'ly never will be."

"Where's my grandfather buried then?" Granted, Mumsie's husband obviously hadn't been a Grayson, seeing as that must have been Mumsie's maiden name, but for certain family burials had to be *somewhere* in the Mill Creek Cemetery.

Mr. Richardson appeared confused. He pursed his lips and gave his head a little shake. "Your grandfather isn't buried here."

"Then—where is he buried?"

"Don't know. Never even heard much about him."

"John. John Hayward," Aggie supplied. His name was the *only* thing she knew for sure about him.

Mr. Richardson gave her a blank stare, wagging his head back and forth. "Nope. Sorry. Never heard of him."

Aggie thumbed a stack of index cards. Cards that would never lead her to any more family graves. Mumsie's family was missing, and not even their graves existed by which to name them.

—⁂—

"I'm not even sure where to begin." Her admission pained her as Aggie spoke it aloud. She ran her finger around the rim of her coffee mug and lifted her eyes to meet Collin's.

He off-loaded a duffel bag of equipment onto the floor of the office. His normally combed hair flopped onto his forehead in a damp mop of copper waves. The autumn weather was gifting them with mist and a cloudy, dismal day. Moisture glistened on Collin's shoulders, clad in a brown fisherman's sweater that hung to his waist over a pair of olive-green pants, which had a pressed seam down the front of each leg.

Classy, even when playing with dead people in the mud.

"Begin what, Love?" His back was to her as he hoisted the duffel onto a table.

"Figuring out what happened to Hazel Grayson and why Mumsie has a crime scene reconstruction in a dollhouse. And that stained bedspread? I'd place bets that it's the actual spread from Hazel's attic room where they found her murdered, and that creeps me out."

"And how do you come about that?" Collin jotted down some notes in a small notebook. His glasses had slid down his nose.

Aggie was distracted for a moment, then shook her head to clear her mind from vacant admiration of the man who had somehow won her trust and without telling her anything personal about himself.

"Mr. Richardson was here earlier today. I asked him what he knew. It's all hearsay, of course, but it sounds like Mumsie's sister was murdered in 1946 and no one knows for sure who did it. He thinks it's likely the Graysons buried Hazel in the most affordable plot available at the time. In Fifteen Puzzle Row. Can you imagine? Not being buried next to family?"

"I can't fathom it." Collin's response was vague as his face scrunched in concentration. His pencil squiggled more in the notebook.

"So where's my family buried then, if not here in a family section of the cemetery?"

"Somewhere else, obviously," Collin said. His reply was hardly helpful.

"Yes, but where? And why not here? I mean, where exactly is my grandfather buried? Why would someone kill Mumsie's sister? Was there a supposed motive? Was she assaulted first—

like a random attack on a female? I can't imagine that was all that prevalent in 1946."

"What wasn't prevalent?" Collin looked up from his note-taking.

Aggie set her coffee mug on her desk with a *clunk*. She widened her eyes, hoping the green of them would shoot daggers of *no-duh* into his senses. "Abuse against women."

"I'm sure it *was* prevalent," Collin muttered.

"Abuse, yes, but I meant . . . rape." Her voice waned. Saying the word was so—*violent*. She prayed that wasn't Hazel's story.

Collin shut his notebook and stuck the pencil behind his ear. He contemplated her for a moment, rolling his lips in thought, which caused his dimples to deepen. "Seems to me whoever killed Hazel Grayson pulled a blinder."

"A what?" Aggie drew back.

Collin blinked as if confused, then realization entered his eyes. "Oh, uh, 'pulled a fast one,' you might say."

Aggie nodded. "No doubt. If what Mr. Richardson said is true. Still, I can't imagine Mumsie living with her sister's un-solved murder for over seventy years."

"What are you going to do about it?" Collin cocked an eye-brow and pushed his glasses back up the bridge of his nose.

"And we circle back." Aggie rolled her eyes. Not so much at Collin, but at the situation. "I don't know where to begin." The nagging questions were only growing stronger, and it was becoming more unsettling as she pondered the fact that there were no family pictures in Mumsie's home. Not even the eighth-grade picture Aggie specifically recalled sending Mumsie of herself, so excited she was that her freckles had faded, and her bobbed black hair made her cheekbones stand out much like Mumsie's. She was an eighth-grader proud of looking like her grandmother's younger version. Apparently it hadn't moved Mumsie enough to keep the picture on display.

"Ah, well, that's a pity."

"Is everything okay?" Aggie frowned. She could tell Collin was trying to be invested in their conversation, yet he kept glancing at the notebook he'd set on top of his duffel bag.

"Mmm?" His brows raised in question, as if she'd startled him. He gave his head a quick shake. "Oh. Yes. Quite well, thank you."

Aggie tilted her head. "I don't believe you." And he should at least share something with her since she'd word-vomited her entire considerations regarding Mumsie and Hazel.

"It's just, I thought this job was going to be especially simple. What with the flooding, the graves mark themselves, or so it would seem. Outlined by sinking and that. It should be as easy as mixing milk in my tea. But I'm a bit gobsmacked now."

"By what?" Aggie watched the confusion furrow his brow again, and when he met her eyes, there was concern in his that had completely erased the typical twinkle that resided there. "What is it?" She leaned forward.

Collin raked his hand through his hair and shrugged his shoulders. "I found another grave. Another unmarked grave. That makes three now."

"You're in Fifteen Puzzle Row. It stands to reason some old, ancient graves might have lost their markings, doesn't it? That was the whole reason the cemetery hired you." Aggie reached for her coffee mug, more out of something to do with her hands than the need for a warm drink.

Collin nodded. "One would think. But this one . . . it's not where I'd expect one on the grid survey. The other two graves I found, I was able to calculate depth and position of the grave based off the imagery on my GPR. This grave is not only *horizontal* to the other two graves, it's also not the average depth. Quite close to the surface actually."

"You mean your radar? That thing I can't make sense of with all the ripples and lines and shadows on the screen?"

"Yes."

"So, this supposed grave didn't wash away in the flood?" Aggie took a sip of coffee.

Collin shook his head. "From what I can tell, there's nothing for the earth to sink around or wash away from."

"I don't understand."

Collin gave a long sigh, his frown deepening. "Meaning, there is no grave. More specifically, no cement vault, no casket or coffin. At least from what I'm able to detect with the equipment I have at my disposal."

"But you said it's a grave."

"Yes. Yes, I did. There's something inside of it, but the measurements don't fit a coffin. They're not typical. It's more compact. As if . . ."

"As if what?" Aggie was going to throttle the man if he didn't just spit it out.

"As if a body was buried there. Just a body. Nothing else."

Aggie winced. "So, not only did people buy grave plots cheap because they were in random spaces, but they skipped buying coffins too?"

"And were buried sideways," Collin concluded.

"That sounds . . . unbelievable." Aggie shook her head.

"Unbelievable? No." Collin met her gaze. "Atypical, most definitely. It raises many questions. Many, many questions."

"Such as?" Aggie led.

"Well, pardon my bluntness, but it begs the question as to whether Hazel Grayson was the only murder victim laid to rest in Fifteen Puzzle Row."

CHAPTER 22

Imogene

She was in no mood for a moonlit stroll. Hang it all if Hazel's murder wasn't seeping the last ounce of fun from her life! Imogene dared a sideways glance at Ollie, who took lazy strides beside her, hands in his overall pockets. Dusk was settling fast, and the tips of the cornstalks in the fields appeared dark against the sunset that blended into the dark violet of the night sky. Tiny pinpricks of stars were beginning to pop up across the sky. A cool breeze lifted strands of Imogene's black hair. Wisps of carefully preened hair curled into their rolls and pulled up on each side with a comb.

And being in no mood to toy with a teasing dance around the truth of it, Imogene chose to simply ask. She tempered her tone so her voice didn't sound sharp or annoyed. "Why did you want to take a walk with me?"

Ollie didn't bother to look at her. Instead, he surveyed the gravel road they walked on. The toe of his boot sent a stone skipping ahead of them.

Imogene heard a whippoorwill lilting its nighttime lullaby.

"Well?" she pressed. Truth be told, she was embarrassed

about her reaction back in the barn. Ashamed that Ollie saw her close to being driven bonkers by it all. Everything. Hazel. The dollhouse. Her own raging mind filled with details and nuances and riddles.

"Figured you needed to get out for a bit," Ollie finally offered.

"Out?" Imogene couldn't help the slight raise to her voice. She stopped and turned to face Ollie, her shoes crunching on the loose gravel. "Out? Do you think now is the time I want a boy to come calling? In the wake of Hazel being *murdered*?"

She put her hands to her hips, wishing not for the first time that she'd thought to grab a sweater. Her bare arms were chilled with goose bumps rising on her forearms. From what Imogene could make out in the waning light, Ollie's facial expression shifted slightly, and he looked at her through sad eyes. "I wasn't callin' on you."

Oh. "Oh."

"I thought you might need to get *outside*. Take a breather. Too much comin' at a person and they're like to lose their mind."

Imogene bit her bottom lip and shifted her arms so they crossed over her chest. She looked away and mumbled, "Well, my mind is quite intact, thank you very much, Oliver Schneider."

"Can't be too intact if you're lookin' to hook up with Sam Pickett." Ollie's under-the-breath chastisement brought Imogene's head back around in a swift motion.

"Now, what is that supposed to mean?" She'd no intention of *hooking up*—not with anybody—she convinced herself.

"Supposed to mean what it sounds like." Ollie shrugged. He still hadn't taken his hands from his pockets. The bib of his overalls dipped in the front, revealing more of his blue, plaid cotton farm shirt that buttoned up the front. "Sam Pickett is bad news."

"I don't know about that." Imogene gave her crossed arms a stubborn jolt over her chest as if tamping down a fit. She lifted her chin, aware of the fact that her emerald eyes would reflect enough of the remaining light to show him how temperamental she was becoming. "I think Sam's swell. So is Ida."

"Ida's all right." Ollie nodded. "Sam just—he ain't all he's chalked up to be."

"I've heard the rumors about boys with the Pickett name," Imogene admitted, but she could hear the defensive edge to her voice. She had little right or reason to defend Sam. She'd known him all of two shakes, and even with that, she didn't know much about him other than his charming personality belied a deep grief and a son he could hardly face. That alone was sad. That alone grabbed every loose thread of her empathy. "But I never met Sam until recently, and he doesn't seem so bad. What'd he do to make him bad news?"

Ollie shrugged. "Ain't much of a father to his boy, you know? Goes out drinkin' on Friday nights."

Imogene rolled her eyes. "So does just about every man in town. Gosh, Ollie, I never knew you to be so petty."

"I never knew you to be so naïve," he retorted.

They glared at each other as the darkness embraced them, wrapping moonlit arms around them as if the dying light were trying to soothe them.

Ollie kicked at the dirt.

Imogene sniffed.

Ollie seemed intent on keeping to a stony silence.

Imogene broke it. "Fine then. I don't know if I can trust him any more than I can trust half of Mill Creek right now! Someone murdered Hazel, Ollie, but heck, what am I supposed to do? You think he's dangerous?"

"I just said he's bad news. Don't know if he's dangerous or not." Ollie's admission made Imogene's frustration dampen into a lost feeling. The kind a person had when wandering in the darkness and wanting to just accept it as safe, but still worried about what lurked in the shadows.

But everyone had shadows. She was suspicious of everyone.

Sam. Her own brother, Ivan. Yet she couldn't ignore the empathetic side of her—the side that wanted to believe it all away. Believe that the black evil that had visited her home and stolen Hazel's life had somehow left in its wake some small smidgeon of hope. Of friendship. Of camaraderie. Didn't the boys say they made buddies of men in the foxholes they'd have never been friends with outside of the war?

"Ida told me that Sam's had it rough, you know?" Imogene stated blandly, without emotion, even though she ached for Sam, for his son, for anyone who'd experienced loss. She knew what it was like now. "He lost his wife."

"I know." Ollie nodded and stepped closer as the darkness became stronger than the light. Peering down into her face, Imogene could catch the slight narrowing of his eyes. "We all lost a lot."

Yes. Ollie had. The Schneider family would never be complete again—not after the war.

"Then you know how Sam feels," Imogene concluded, not sure whether she was defending Sam or defending her right to try to find goodness in the wake of dreadful grief.

"I do," Ollie nodded again, but something in his expression showed worry—concern—for *her.*

"Oh." Once again it was all she could think to say. Then she found her words again. "So you're, what, all high-and-mighty good, while Sam's just the town-rumored bad news a girl's gotta steer clear of? That's not very Christian of you."

"Christian," Ollie laughed, though it lacked humor. He appeared to stifle a sigh. Of exasperation? With her? Imogene wasn't sure. "Genie, bein' Christian ain't got nothin' to do with having a good head on your shoulders and bein' able to see what's in front of your own nose."

"What are you saying it is, then?" she challenged.

Ollie regained the step he'd lost a moment before. "I don't rightly know, I guess. But makin' good choices is one of them.

I may not have much more than an eighth-grade education, what with havin' to help my daddy with the farm, but I know God created us with the smarts we need. I know bein' Christian means showin' love to others, but also knowin' when to keep your distance with certain ones before they hurt you."

"Hurt me?" Imogene gave a saucy laugh. The audacity of Ollie Schneider lecturing *her* about befriending Sam Pickett! "I daresay you're just jealous, Oliver Schneider. What do you think he's going to do? Get drunk and make me cry? I don't need Sam Pickett to make me cry. I have enough reason as it is. Maybe I should toss a few back too, huh? I heard tell it helps a person not feel so sad all the time. I can't say as though I blame Sam—if drinking is all that you can find wrong with him."

She glared at him, daring Ollie to contradict her. Why she was growing so angry and defensive, she wasn't completely sure. Sam Pickett meant nothing to her. But Ollie did. Ollie was her neighbor, her friend, so for him to lecture her . . .

Ollie didn't say anything but took another step closer.

For the first time, Imogene wanted to draw back but couldn't.

Something in the shadows on his face made her freeze where she stood. Her breath caught as she drew in a whiff of the farm, manure and . . . cinnamon? The pungent, sweet scent of a farmer. Of a man.

"I just want you to be careful, Genie." Ollie's voice dropped almost to a whisper. She could feel his breath on her nose as he leaned even closer. It seemed he was trying to see her face in the darkness, but his nearness just about sent her into a tizzy of unexpected and inexplicable emotion.

"Are you threatening me?" Her tease came out in a breathless laugh meant to tamp down her frustration, and now her racing heart.

He moved closer still. This time, Imogene felt his overalls against the thin cotton of her dress. His work-worn hands folded around her forearms, his flesh warming her chilled skin. Ollie drew his mouth close to her ear, his cheek grazing hers.

"I'd never threaten you, Genie. But there's no tellin' what I'd do if anyone messed with you."

More than his breath against her ear warmed her then. His words were delivered with undertones of loyalty, of protectiveness—and something else she couldn't quite put her finger on. As though Ollie had deep, hidden feelings and he was allowing her just a tiny glimpse of a broiling inside his quiet soul, passionate and fierce.

"No one's gonna mess with me, Ollie." Darned if her words didn't come out breathless.

"No. They won't." His words, however, were decisive.

She had a soldier. Whether she wanted one or not.

—ɯɯ—

Imogene was exhausted. The kind of exhaustion that made a person ache clear down to the soles of her feet. She leaned back against the bus seat, not bothering to look out the window at the powder plant she was leaving behind for the day. She should quit. Return to the beauty salon and do what she was born to do, instead of thinking she was going to stumble across a connection to Hazel. Across an explanation that her sister's premature death came by the hand of a vile human being who slipped in and out among the throngs of workers Imogene served every day. She'd had no more cryptic notes or bodily collisions with anyone. No more clues. No more . . . anything.

"Have you seen the post office? All that destruction. It's so awful." Ida shifted in her seat next to Imogene.

Imogene nodded. "Yes. My brother won't say a thing about it. I keep asking him if he's got any suspects to take the blame for the explosion, but he keeps telling me to stop meddling."

Ida gave a gentle chuckle. "He's protective of you."

Imogene rolled her eyes. "No. He's preoccupied and distracted from my sister's murder, that's what." Her bitterness was growing. Slowly but surely, Imogene could feel it seeping into her bones. The police, Chet, even her parents were moving on. Moving on? Hazel was barely buried in the earth—in that pathetic cheap little plot sandwiched between two graves of people they didn't even know.

"Have you—have you been to see her?" Ida's question was hesitant, but Imogene offered her an expression of gratitude for asking straight out and not pretending that Hazel wasn't dead.

"I have." Imogene nodded. She didn't expound on the fact that while her *seeing* Hazel had to do with visiting her grave, she also *heard* Hazel. In her head. During the quiet times when she could interact, and they could work toward justice together.

"I have too."

Imogene started at Ida's confession. She smiled sadly. "You have?"

Ida played with the straps of her purse. "I know Hazel and I weren't very close, but she was always kind to me. It took me a bit to find her grave, though." A question lingered in Ida's voice, but Imogene knew Ida was far too polite to ask it.

"We needed something affordable," Imogene offered, though it wasn't any of Ida's business, and Momma would probably have her hide for admitting it out loud.

"Don't you have a family section?" Ida inquired. Then her gloved hand rose and touched her lips. "I'm sorry. I didn't mean to intrude."

Imogene didn't care really. It was nice to have an honest conversation with someone other than Lola. Ollie's intentions were—well, who knew what they were outside of butting into her private affairs. Her stomach curdled at the thought, and she fought back the sensation. Chet had refused to have a conversation with her about Hazel's case. He said he didn't want her snooping around and asking questions of others either, that it wasn't safe. Meanwhile, her brother Ivan remained his sullen, loner self, becoming more so as time went on. Just the other day, Imogene saw him lift a cat by its belly with the toe of his boot and fling it across the cow yard. Even though she'd scolded him for it, she knew Ivan wouldn't change. *Couldn't* change probably. The war had injured him in a way none of them could understand.

"Imogene?" Ida broke into Imogene's thoughts.

"Oh. No, no intrusion at all," she reassured Ida, whose worried expression melted. "We don't . . ." She hesitated. Ida was right. Truthfully, it was none of her business. "We don't have a family plot at the cemetery," she finished.

Ida gave her a tiny nod. She didn't ask any more questions. The bus rolled along, jolting and rocking as it hit potholes that hadn't been repaired since before the war broke out.

"How's Sam?" Imogene asked politely.

"Fine," Ida replied. "He's fine. He has a late shift today."

Imogene nodded. That explained why Sam wasn't on the bus. She looked out the window, watching the scenery go by. She needed to get back to the barn tonight. To work more on Hazel's dollhouse. What other details would she notice were amiss as she crafted the attic room? She still couldn't recall what the picture on Hazel's stand had been of. It was recently put there. That was all Imogene could theorize.

"You're good for him, you know?" Ida's quiet voice bounced off the bus window.

Imogene turned. "For who?"

"Sam." Ida ducked in a shy gesture. As if she shouldn't have said anything but did anyway. "He seems—well, he seems more like Sam when he's around you. You bring out a bit of his playful side again."

It was a compliment she was willing to take. Imogene gave Ida her full attention. "How so?"

Ida sighed softly. "Sam's always been lively, but since Bonnie died and he came back from overseas . . ." Her voice waned, and then she swallowed and lifted her eyes to Imogene's. "Well, he's fun again, when you're around. He teases—he doesn't even tease his boy. I can see a little bit of the old Sam, you know? When you're around."

When you're around. It sounded like a song title to Imogene, or something maybe Bing Crosby would croon. Her cheeks warmed.

"I think all the boys came home different," Ida observed.

"Yes. Yes, they did." Imogene paused for a moment as a thought struck her. "Ida?"

"Hmm?"

"Did Hazel have—?" Imogene stopped and cleared her throat. "Speaking of boys coming home, was there anyone you knew of at the plant who Hazel was interested in?"

Ida's look of surprise was genuine. She lifted her shoulders and grimaced. "I don't know. She never really said anything to me. But like I said, we weren't very close."

"Mmm." Imogene nodded, accepting Ida's answer. Just another dead end. Maybe she *was* being too harsh on Chet. Maybe there really *wasn't* much to go on, no matter how hard one looked.

"Although . . ." Ida's hesitation snagged Imogene's attention again.

"Yes?"

"Well, I did see Hazel talking to a young man several times. It was usually before the bus would pull out after the shift's end. They'd be off to the side in conversation. I just assumed they were acquaintances, but maybe—maybe not?"

"Do you know his name?" Imogene tried not to appear too eager and scare off Ida.

Ida offered a tenuous smile. "I think—I think he was a Schneider boy. Not Oliver, but one of the younger ones who never got shipped out during the war."

"Harry?"

"Maybe," Ida responded. "I don't know them all that well.

197

I mean, Mill Creek is a small town and all, but since the powder plant was built . . ." Her words hung in the air between them.

"I know," Imogene affirmed. "So many new people. So much housing went up around the plant, and the poor farmers who had to sell their land, I didn't know most of them. But I heard they all relocated." She didn't expound on her thoughts—on the way it had affected her own family. Their loss had been small in comparison to the farmers' livelihoods. Still, it was a loss.

Ida exchanged sad smiles with Imogene. "Sam said the farmers weren't offered near the proper amount for their land, and yet they had no choice but to sell."

Imogene shrugged. "Well, at least they can take comfort in the fact it was for a good cause. The boys needed ammunition, or we'd have lost the war."

"Yes," Ida acknowledged.

"So, Hazel and Harry would frequently chat while waiting for the bus?" Imogene mused, not wanting to be sidetracked by the plight of the relocated farmers.

Ida furrowed her brow. "Like I said, I don't know for sure who it was."

Imogene gave her a reassuring smile. But she knew who she would ask to verify it. Demanding an answer if necessary. It could be nothing—or it could be everything.

CHAPTER 23

Her eyes flew open and were met with the thick blackness of her room. Even the window, its filmy curtains waving in the midsummer breeze, refused to cast much light. The moon appeared to be asleep, along with the rest of the world.

Something had startled her awake. Imogene could sense it, the little hairs on her arms standing straight up. She rose, grabbing her wrapper from the end of the bed and slipping her arms into it as she stood poised in the middle of her bedroom. Listening. Her ears strained for something—anything—that might give definition as to why she'd awakened.

Crossing the room, she looked out the window, peering across the yard and down the drive toward the barn. Its windows were black, gaping holes that stared back at her. Its doors pulled shut as if it were forever holding silence regarding what it witnessed at night, in the shadows, while everyone was asleep. Had the barn watched Hazel's killer step onto the porch and walk through the unlatched front door? Perhaps the barn still registered Hazel's screams deep in its wood-slatted sides. Its red sides, glowing in the aftermath of violence that had forever marred the Grayson farm.

Imogene shivered. There was nothing amiss. Nothing that

should have awakened her. Shivering, she tugged her wrap tighter, tying the satin ribbon around her waist. "Ohhh, Hazel," she breathed, then blinked multiple times. Imogene resisted the tears that threatened to spill out. Resisted the grief.

Don't forget me, Genie.

Imogene could see Hazel's smile. It reached her eyes and drove into Imogene's soul. Her sister. Their spirits. Always meshed. So different, yet so much alike.

Don't forget me, Genie.

Every laugh they'd shared. Every whispered dream. Every tightened hand hold as they huddled under blankets to hide the light of the radio during a mandatory blackout. Only a few years ago, their father had walked the streets of Mill Creek, keeping vigil, as if the Germans or Japanese would even think to somehow invade the small town. No lights on. Nothing. Nights like tonight, when not even the moon was strong enough to smile. When Hazel's white-knuckled grip on Imogene's hand was the only grip on anything familiar, anything real, anything—

A floorboard creaked.

Imogene yanked her head up and stared at her bedroom door. Even her breathing was too loud. She held it.

Nothing.

She dared to swallow. Then took a step toward her door, hesitating as she neared it, her hand resting on the knob, the metal cool beneath her touch. Imogene glanced at the light switch and longed to push the button and flood her room with the security of chasing shadows into hiding. But she couldn't. It would also chase away whatever had awakened her, and she wanted to face it. To confront the injustice of all that had befallen the Grayson home.

Turning the knob, Imogene tugged on her door. Its wood had swelled with the summer humidity and it stuck. During the day, she would have just yanked it open without thinking and without much effort. Tonight, she restrained such force and tried her best to pull it open without scraping or squeaking. Successful, Imogene held the open door stable, leaning her forehead against its coolness and peering into the dark hallway.

"Mother?" Her whisper was too loud. But if it had been her mother, awake and visiting the bathroom, then perhaps she'd creaked the floorboard and this was all Imogene's foggy imagination of being caught in sleep. "Daddy?" He had a habit of visiting the bathroom at night as well.

But the hallway was empty. Imogene stepped out, her bare feet cold against the wood floor. It was an uneven floor but familiar. She skipped over the squeaky floorboard and tiptoed to her parents' bedroom. Their door was ajar a few inches. Imogene peeked in. Her father's snore grazed her ears. Her mother's form was curled next to him, a handkerchief clenched in her hand. Had Momma cried herself to sleep?

Pain squeezed Imogene's heart. Poor Mother. She existed with shoulders square and her head held high. She'd returned to life without Hazel, pretending, like they all did, that the violation of Hazel's death hadn't forever altered their home.

The slam of the porch screen door downstairs startled Imogene and she jumped, hitting her cheek against the doorjamb of her parents' room.

"Daddy!" she hissed, too terrified to do anything but summon help. "Daddy!"

His snore choked, and he coughed, then sat up. "What—? Genie, what is it?"

Mother whimpered and rolled over, still asleep.

"The porch door, it just slammed shut," Genie whispered, her tone urgent.

Her father threw back the covers and eased out of bed. He reached for his shotgun that lay beneath the bed. "Probably just the wind."

His explanation made sense, only Imogene was sure she'd

hooked the lock before bed. Like Hazel had always said to do. A lot of good that had done her.

Imogene's father moved past her, releasing the hinge of his break-open shotgun and shoving two shells into the breech. He latched the gun closed and pulled back the hammer. "Stay behind me," he directed Imogene. "Better yet, stay here."

Of course, she wasn't going to listen to him. Instead, she followed her father down the stairs, the tip of the shotgun's barrel preceding them both.

The porch door banged again, and Imogene leapt back, pressing herself into the wall the stairs hugged. Her father raised the shotgun to his shoulder and took the remaining three steps with steady feet. He swung in front of the door. The shotgun's blast resonated through the house with the violent impact it served up with the exploded shell. The shell casing flew back and hit the floor, rolling until it bumped into the edge of the carpet runner.

Imogene sank to the stair, her knees giving out. Every part of her quivered. She held her hands over her mouth to stifle her scream.

"It's all right," her father said over his shoulder. "It was just a coon."

A raccoon? A little masked bandit? Imogene saw spots as her breath released in a whoosh. She willed herself to take deep breaths, releasing them as her fear eased.

"Roy?" Mother called from the upstairs hall, concern in her voice.

"It's okay, Mother," Imogene called back. "It was only a silly raccoon."

"Did your father get it?" There was a quiver in Mother's voice too. Imogene could relate. So much tension. So much unspoken but underlying terror.

"Yep!" Daddy shouted. "He's dead." Daddy turned to Imogene and leaned the shotgun against the wall. "I'm gonna go drag the carcass off so it's not in front of the stairs when your mama comes down in the morning."

Imogene's hand moved to her throat, and she gave a weak nod. Of course. Hide it. Blood. Corpse. It was difficult to stand, but Imogene did, reaching for the wall to steady herself. She needed something to drink. Something to steady her nerves. Finishing the last few steps, Imogene walked through the doorway, away from the open porch door and into the kitchen.

She halted, a frown crossing her face as her gaze swept over the empty room. Something wasn't right. Something was out of place. She glanced out the window to her right and saw her father striding across the yard, a big raccoon hanging from his grip.

A raccoon. But she'd latched the porch door before bed. There was no way a raccoon would have the wits to slip anything through the crack between the door and its frame and unhook the lock, like Chet had tried to convince her was so possible.

The porch door had slammed. Twice. It was windy enough for that to be the explanation. Still, if the door was latched as she remembered . . .

Imogene grabbed for the back of a chair at the table by the window. She reached for the light, pushing the switch. A yellow glow flooded the kitchen. Familiar. Welcoming. Secure.

Or it would have felt secure if the light hadn't revealed what sat on the kitchen table. Hazel's teacup. The one she always had tea in when she couldn't sleep sat there on the table. Steam rose from the tea that filled it. And beside the cup and saucer was the tea bag. Lemon and mint. Hazel's favorite.

She had been here tonight. More than a voice. More than an imaginary vision. Hazel had been here. Or at least her ghost had. *Someone* had.

Imogene opened her mouth to scream, but this time her voice

was strangled. Much like Hazel's must have been the day she died.

Chet stood over the cup of tea, like Mother and Daddy had that morning before Daddy took to the field and Mother headed to town for groceries. Imogene was thankful it was a Saturday. She was still shaking—though she'd never let anyone see it—and part of her wanted to whip the teacup out into the corn and have it disappear. Have it *all* disappear. The memories, the images in her mind, and the fact that Hazel was dead.

"I would give anything for Hazel to walk through the front door," Imogene mumbled. Would it be horrible if she admitted to Chet that she wondered if Hazel *had* walked through the door? There was no way she could voice that suspicion out loud.

Chet nodded, but his eyes weren't on the cup. They were surveying his sister's face. The dark blue of his uniform made his green eyes fleck with tiny spots of blue as Imogene met them with her own frank stare in return.

"Hazel wasn't here, Genie." He said it like he was worried she didn't believe it. Imogene hated that he so easily read her thoughts.

"Have you talked to Harry Schneider?" she asked, hoping Chet was following her train of thought.

He frowned. "What's Harry got to do with anything?"

Imogene eyed the teacup again. "Ida Pickett said she saw Hazel chatting it up with Harry at the bus stop after their shift ended. Several times."

Chet drew in a deep breath, but he didn't let it out. It seemed he was tempering his reaction, and when he spoke, it was with care. "You told me Ida wasn't sure it was Harry. 'Sides, Hazel talked to many people. That doesn't make them suspects."

Did her brother never see possible ties and theories? "Chet!

What if Hazel and Harry were interested in each other? What if Hazel didn't accept his advances and he got mad?"

"Mad enough to kill her?" Chet's voice rose. "Have you lost your ever-lovin' mind? Next thing I know, you're gonna accuse *me* of Hazel's death!"

Imogene crossed her arms and tightened her lips, turning to look out the window at the barn, the corn, the cows, anything other than Chet. Now was certainly not the time to admit she'd pondered their brother Ivan's temper for committing the deed.

"And this Ida?" Chet tipped his head, trying to get her to look at him. "She's Sam Pickett's sister, right?"

"So?" Imogene glared at her brother.

"Sam's been arrested a few times, you know. Disturbing the peace."

"What peace?" Imogene muttered.

"Listen to reason, sis. He may be nice, but he hides a whole lot of baggage."

"So do you!" Imogene shot back, her gaze colliding with Chet's. "Besides, I'm not courting Sam, and I'm hardly friends with his sister. So stop your worrying about me and do your job!"

He paled and stepped back. She could tell he chewed the inside of his lip as he ran his finger around his collar as if it were too tight. "I'm just sayin'—"

"You were asking about Ida," Imogene interrupted. "I never said a thing about Sam." And she certainly wouldn't now.

"I'm only looking out for you."

Imogene skewered him with a look. "And I have need to be concerned about *Ida*?"

"Aw, heck, Genie!" Chet slapped the table. The teacup rattled on its saucer, cold tea sloshing over the side. "You're on a wild goose chase that isn't yours to chase. You're gonna get yourself into trouble."

"So what if I do?" Imogene half shouted back. It almost

felt good to yell at Chet. To release the pent-up anger that had been building since the day they'd laid Hazel to rest in a cheap grave. "What are *you* doing about Hazel's murder? I don't see anyone behind bars. You're too busy trying to figure out who blew up the post office!"

"It endangered the entire town!" Chet was shouting now, his arm swinging out in the direction of town. "People could've been *killed*! It could happen again! I have to focus on that investigation as my top priority."

"So, Hazel's murder doesn't matter?" Imogene was so furious, her chin quivered and her voice wobbled, losing its sharp edge.

"I never said that," Chet said, more quietly now.

"Then do something, Chet. Find the one who killed our sister. I can't stand this much longer. The not knowing. There must be clues you're not seeing. Things you're overlooking."

Chet grabbed Hazel's teacup and in a swift motion launched it against the wall. Cold tea splattered on the kitchen wallpaper, not unlike the blood of their sister in the attic. The cup shattered, falling to the floor in shards and slivers of glass.

"Why did you do that?" Imogene flew toward the mess, bending to try to pick up the larger pieces. She shook one at Chet. "This was Hazel's favorite cup! You broke it!"

"I'm sorry, all right? I'm sorry!" Chet dragged his hands over his head. "I'm doing what I can."

"It's not enough," Imogene countered. She tried to ignore the hurt that flashed over her brother's face. She tried to avoid the anguish and helplessness in his eyes. Instead, she repeated herself, as though by saying it somehow it would awaken them all to the truth of what had happened so they could lay Hazel to rest. "It's not enough."

CHAPTER 24

Aggie

The coroner has to sign off for a body to be exhumed." Collin set the pen down, having completed filling out the disinterment form. "He's going to think I've lost my blooming mind. This is the third one I've filled out."

Aggie set a plate of cookies in front of him. Chocolate chip ones. Out of a package. Because, well, baking wasn't exactly her forte. She pulled out the chair from the kitchen table at Mumsie's and plopped onto it, snatching a cookie for herself. Stress eating wasn't a good habit, and she didn't do it normally. But today it felt like a necessity.

"He has to understand your role at the cemetery."

Collin ran his hand over his hair, the golden-red strands on fire in the early autumn sunlight streaming through the nearby window. "One would think. Although, I must admit, I have my doubts as to whether the cemetery board intended on my doing anything more than simply locating unmarked graves. Opening a grave is a sensitive matter. Coroners—or medical examiners—I've found are often reluctant to disturb the dead without a darn good reason."

Aggie chewed and spoke around the cookie, not waiting for manners to take precedence for her to swallow. "But if they've been dead for a hundred years, does anyone really care?"

A sharp glance from Collin told her she'd unwittingly communicated her insensitivity.

"One should always care, Love." His voice softened, along with his eyes. "There's a sacredness in death. Your grandmother, for instance. Can you imagine the emotional toll if we petitioned to exhume her sister?"

Aggie winced. He had a point. Yet the odds of the unmarked graves having any family still alive who might claim them was slim.

She reached for another cookie. "Why do you think this most recent grave is potentially . . . well, a crime scene?"

"Not the scene. The dumping ground."

"Okay, the dumping ground." Aggie thought that sounded harsher than her earlier comment about exhumation. "Why would anyone commit murder and then bury the victim in the cemetery of all places?"

Collin shrugged. "Who would look for a murder victim in a cemetery? Call it a hunch. The grave matches none of the average specifications when I help remap cemeteries. Certainly, graves will vary in sizes, depths, and so on, but they all take the same general shape. They all tend to follow the same direction. What's more concerning is the absence of encasement. It's either a body sans coffin or something entirely different."

"It's probably a dead deer carcass," Mumsie's wobbly voice announced from the kitchen doorway. She pushed her walker with its tennis ball feet onto the linoleum. Her green eyes were vibrant. Behind her, a young aide from the senior center hovered as though Mumsie would collapse at any moment.

"A deer carcass?" Collin's mouth twitched. He did seem to find Mumsie amusing, whereas Aggie struggled to accept the sharp edges to her grandmother's sweeping declarations.

"Of course." Mumsie shuffled across the room toward the

lidless kitchen garbage. She'd spotted something, it seemed, and was on a mission. "Hunters will often dump the remains of their hunt after disembowelment."

Aggie grimaced. "I highly doubt it's a deer carcass, Mumsie."

Collin seemed to agree. "At the risk of offending you, sweetheart, I would have to argue a hunter would dispose of animal remains where he cleans the carcass. Typically, in the field or woods where the animal is harvested."

"This is all a bit violent, don't you think?"

Mumsie waved off Aggie's aversion. She reached into the garbage, lifting a plastic zip-seal baggie from its innards. "I became immune to violence years ago."

An instant quiet fell over the room. Collin exchanged a raised-eyebrow look with Aggie. Aggie glanced at the aide, whose blue eyes were wide with innocence and not a small bit of shock.

"This one here," Mumsie said and waved her hand in the aide's direction with a cheeky grin, "she's unsure of me. I don't blame you." Mumsie directed the tail end of her sentence to the aide. "Poor Rebecca, you do try and all, but when you reach my age"—she shook the plastic bag in Aggie's face—"you realize there's no point in changing."

Aggie snatched the delinquent, crumb-filled bag from Mumsie's hand, but Mumsie speared her with a stern eye.

"We wash the baggies. We do not throw them away."

Aggie crumpled it in her hand. "Mumsie, they're less than a few cents a bag."

Mumsie shook her head and shot poor Rebecca the aide an exasperated look that must have been intended to gain Rebecca's mutual agreement. The smart girl remained expressionless.

Mumsie pursed her lips—newly rouged in red lipstick, it appeared—and returned to lecturing Aggie. "A few cents go a long way. Didn't your mother ever teach you that?"

Again, silence. Even Mumsie seemed tripped up at her own words.

Aggie's rush of unexpected emotion and hurt sent a flush into her cheeks, and she squeezed her eyes closed to compose herself.

Collin cleared his throat.

Rebecca shifted her feet, her tennis shoe squeaking on the linoleum.

Mumsie's hand reached out and cupped Aggie's, her skin cool and the baggie crumpling even more between Aggie's fingers.

"I'm sure your mother did." Mumsie's response was belated. But there was also a tremble in her voice that made Aggie look up and into the old woman's eyes. Hurt reflected there, like a mirror, mimicking the image seen in Aggie's eyes. That deep, dark kind of hurt that held on to the tail end of any potential happiness a person could find and dragged downward until succumbing to the weight of it was the only option—and to survive it, one must build up a good defense.

Aggie had no desire to try to make amends. Mumsie might be ninety-two and almost adorable to the naked eye, but she had sharp edges that sliced so fast and quick, one bled before they even had time to feel the pain of the wound.

"Excuse me." Aggie pushed back in her chair, made a point of dropping the baggie back into the garbage, and hurried out the back door.

She heard Mumsie's choked "Agnes!" Whether from tears, worry, concern, anger, or annoyance, Aggie had no intention of trying to decipher it.

Her feet planted her in the middle of the fenced-in backyard. This time, it was void of a fake skeleton—much to her vague relief—and her flats sank into the cushiony green grass and crunched a few early fall leaves that had floated to the earth.

Mill Creek was worse than Chicago for getting away from people! At least there you could go for a walk and get lost in the throngs of passersby you'd never see again—never care about. But here, the backyard was adjacent to a young family whose mother now played in their own yard with her toddler,

210

lifting her hand in a wave that demanded a polite wave back. One could find aloneness in a crowd, but in Mill Creek? A small town? The place suffocated Aggie.

"She didn't mean to drive you away, Love." Collin's lilting voice brushed her ear. Aggie crossed her arms over her chest, avoiding looking at him, and lifted her eyes to the tops of the maple trees in the neighbor's backyard. She could see her thick eyelashes as she blinked. She could also feel their wetness on her cheeks.

Aggie swiped her eyes, recrossing her arms. "She never *means* to. She just—does," Aggie acknowledged.

Collin seemed to be examining the very same treetops. He didn't demand her attention, yet Aggie could sense him weighing his words carefully.

"You've both experienced losses."

Well, that was an inane observation! Aggie glanced at him, ready to say so, but then realized she'd sound as snippy as Mumsie. Blunt, tactless . . . Maybe they were one and the same after all.

"It's beyond time you ask your grandmother directly what happened to Hazel. It's more than apparent that Hazel's death somehow shaped your grandmother's entire life. Dancing about and hoping she drops a hint or two is a pathetic way of getting to the bottom of it all, don't you think?"

Direct. Apparently, Collin could dish it out too.

Aggie bit her bottom lip, then retorted, "I don't know that I want to get to the bottom of it all."

Collin nodded. "So I thought. You're far too assertive otherwise."

Aggie rolled her eyes at the trees. Assertive. It'd served her well in her last job. But now? It did her no good. It was misdirected into a long-standing family dysfunction and a more-than-confusing exploration of the local cemetery. Neither of which had ever been on her bucket list of things to be assertive about. Which was why she was holding herself back.

"Let yourself do what you're good at." Collin's words rifled through her frayed nerves.

Aggie turned to look at him. "And what is that?"

He shrugged. "I don't know you that well, Love, but I do know you're the image of your grandmum. Both outside and in. I don't believe your *Mumsie* really wants you to cower around her. She needs you to push her. Let's be frank, she's not long for this world, and I'm sure she'd like to know what happened to Hazel too. That rose you found was right about one thing— it's not over. For either of you. Your grandmum can't teach you how to grieve and heal, not until she's found out how herself. Until then, you're both just treading water and you're bound to get tired."

Aggie stared at him, surprised by his astute read of the situation, and confused as to where he found his wisdom.

"And you?" she pressed gently. "What are you good at?" Besides suspiciously contrived accents and slang, keeping his private life like one kept secrets of the Vatican, and turning her defenses into mush with one red-lashed wink of his eye.

Collin reached out and lifted strands of her dark hair, rubbing their fineness between his index finger and thumb as he contemplated. "Ahh, well." A strange shadow flickered across his face. He frowned, the furrows between his brows deepening almost into a bothersome scowl. Then they faded as his features relaxed. He'd come to terms with something in his own mind, she could tell.

Collin met her eyes. "I'm a genius at finding a hidden grave."

But the humor was gone from his voice, the wit vanished from his eyes.

Aggie didn't know why she was compelled to, but she moved closer, studying his face. All his insight was directed into her or to Mumsie or others around him, of which he was especially observant and even spot-on with his assessments. But the door to who Collin O'Shaughnessy was remained firmly latched.

"Who are you, Collin?" she whispered.

His eyes dipped to her mouth, then lifted and collided with her gaze. There it was. The same hidden hurt. The same darkness lurking behind his irises. Yet there was something different in them too. A tiny flicker of health, of hope, as though he were mending, and she and Mumsie were left behind in an emotional ICU.

"I'm just an archaeologist, Love." He released her hair and trailed his finger down her cheek. "I help uncover dead things and bring their stories back to life."

CHAPTER 25

Dinner was eaten in silence. Collin had departed for a meeting with Mr. Richardson, the cemetery board, and hopefully the county coroner, who was the one who needed to sign off on the disinterment paper work. Apparently, they could all only manage to gather at suppertime. Aggie had a missed call on her cell from Mr. Richardson, but she listened to the voicemail requesting she attend the meeting and take notes. Too late. They'd have to figure out how to do that without her. Aggie knew her devotion to her work was sorely lacking.

Not to mention, Aggie couldn't shake the interlude between them in the backyard that afternoon. Couldn't avoid the way his whispered words pierced her, wondering if he knew more of her pain than she realized. Comprehending that his story—who Collin O'Shaughnessy was—surely surpassed her initial assessment of him. Archaeologist nerd who studied insects on the side and dressed like an English lord in casual wear from the twenties.

"If you're not going to go after that nice boy with the glasses, perhaps you should consider finding a man." Mumsie forked the chicken that balanced on her TV tray as the game show played on the TV in front of them.

Aggie glanced sharply at her, her own fork stopping midway to her mouth. That wasn't the silence breaker she'd expected as they ate together in Mumsie's sitting room, Mumsie in her recliner and Aggie on the stiff chair that begged to be tossed on a bonfire.

"You're making an assumption I want a man." Aggie ignored the flash of Collin's image in her mind.

"Now you sound like one of those females who believe men are the spawn of the devil," Mumsie snapped.

"Not at all," Aggie responded quickly. "I believe men are a creation of God. I'm just not racing into the trenches to find one." Although some days, if she were honest, her independence fell just shy of enough and she desired companionship. A partner. Now more than ever, if truth be told. Loneliness was that strange partner to grief. Somehow grief ostracized a person from intimacy of any kind.

"Men are necessary for procreation."

That wasn't the sort of intimacy Aggie had been thinking about. Still, she blushed as though Mumsie had somehow read and misinterpreted her thoughts. "I've no desire to procreate."

"How would you know? You haven't a child to gauge that by." Mumsie stared at the TV and the word puzzle with the intensity of an actual game-show contestant.

"One doesn't *rent* a child to measure one's disposition to be a parent." Aggie fumbled with her fork and jammed it into her mouth so she had something to chew before she said anything more snippy to her grandmother.

"And why not? It makes far more sense than bringing an unwanted little thing into the world to fend for themselves."

"Mumsie!"

"Well?" It was time for the infamous Mumsie stare of condescension. "If you're not going to find a man—like that Collin fellow—then go help a child in need, for pity's sake, and stop this infernal loafing about in my business."

"I'm not—"

"Of course you are." Mumsie waved Aggie away. "I've seen

you in my room upstairs when I'm not in it. You didn't even get the hint when I closed the door on you the first time."

"That *was* you!" Aggie glowered.

Mumsie smirked a little. "Well, you're nosy. I thought perhaps if you thought a ghost was afoot, you'd take your leave."

"I don't believe in ghosts," Aggie retorted.

"So I've discovered. However, I know allllllllllll about the fact you interrogated Mr. Richardson about my sister. You've probably even looked up town records and know more than you should. There're other things to do with your life than nose into mine. Find a hobby. Go dancing. Knit a scarf, for heaven's sake. You need to make something of yourself. It's pitiful, really, you don't even go to church."

"I don't like churches." Aggie had stopped chewing and stared incredulously at her grandmother, who had yet to take her eyes off the TV. "I don't know if I even believe in God."

"Fancy that." Mumsie lifted her dinner roll. "Your mother certainly didn't teach you that."

The offhanded comment was launched without any attempt at apology or retribution this time. Aggie caught Mumsie's quick glance from the corner of her aged green eyes. She knew what she was saying, and she intended it to have its impact.

"No." Aggie remembered the worn Bible by Mom's bedside. Remembered the years growing up when she took Aggie to Vacation Bible School, enrolled her in church camp one year, and when her father wasn't around to care—which was often—took her to church on Sundays. Truth be told, while it was nice and all, Aggie hadn't really needed faith, church, or God. She'd been successful on her own. Until Mom died. Then she for sure didn't need faith, church, or God.

"God has never pulled through for me." Aggie heard the words, perhaps the excuse, and at the same time was never more certain she believed it.

Mumsie glanced at her, then pointed her fork in Aggie's

216

direction. "And that, right there, is the problem with today's *Christianity*. Such entitlement. I never."

"Entitlement?" Aggie drew back. "Is it too much to ask an all-powerful God to save my mother from cancer?"

Her question reverberated in the room. The game-show host announced something. The audience clapped. Mumsie studied Aggie's face, and they had a showdown between their locked eyes.

Mumsie cleared her throat. "There are some things we cannot explain, Agnes. One being the greater mind of God."

"There's a comfort," Aggie quipped, more to herself than anything.

"No." Mumsie stabbed her fork into a piece of chicken. "There is truth. It's why we must have faith and believe in His goodness."

"What a dreadful way to live. What if His goodness fails us?" Aggie dared Mumsie to retort with wisdom that would trump her own cynical faith.

Mumsie gave her a small smile. "I've no Scripture to blubber your way, and I refuse to offer you a biblical cliché, Agnes."

Aggie stared at her grandmother, who chewed her chicken and then swallowed it. "Needless to say," Mumsie continued, "your end result changes naught if you choose not to believe in God's goodness. You'll still have a dead mother, the same as I have a dead sister, and our grief will still cling to us like a spider web we can't untangle from. However, your outcome changes significantly if you *do* believe in God's goodness."

"How so?" Aggie challenged, unsure how to interpret this spiritual side of her grandmother.

Mumsie pursed her lips and nodded. "Hope. You have hope. I don't believe it's blind hope either, or"—she lowered her eyes—"frankly, I wouldn't have survived to be ninety-two with a penchant for smiling in the most inappropriate times. I've been able to muddle through a life with wounds that still bleed profusely. But muddle through I have. By God's good hope."

Aggie stared at Mumsie.

Mumsie eyed her back.

"I'm not getting a man," Aggie insisted belatedly, avoiding the poignancy of Mumsie's observation with a weakened tone of voice.

Mumsie tapped the TV tray. "Of course you're not. You're too much like me, and someday you'll die, alone for the most part. Old and persnickety, but precocious enough for people to still care enough to love you a little . . ."

Their eyes met.

Aggie hated it when Mumsie was right. She felt the weight on her chest and heard Collin's prompting in her mind.

Be assertive. Just ask.

Mumsie had all but told Aggie to butt out, but when did Mumsie ever listen to her own advice?

Aggie opened her mouth to ask, *What happened to Hazel?*, when the phone rang, startling them both. Mumsie's fork slipped out of her hand and clanked on her plate. Aggie jumped, staring at the telephone that balanced on the table beside Mumsie's chair, as if the corded, fossil-like form of ancient communication between humans had come alive.

"Doesn't anyone text in this town?" Aggie muttered, peeved at being interrupted, unnerved by the unexpected spiritual turn in the conversation that left her more bewildered by Mumsie's very non-evangelical style of faith in comparison to Aggie's almost complete lack thereof.

She moved the TV tray to the side so she could rise and get the phone for Mumsie. Mumsie stopped her with a look. "I can answer my own telephone." Her hand reached out gracefully, lifting the receiver from its base. The keypad lit up with the backlight of a 1980s handset. There wasn't even a digital face for caller ID. Mumsie was going in blind.

"Hello?" Mumsie's voice was clear. She tapped her finger against her plate as she listened.

Aggie watched Mumsie's face, as though by doing so she could surmise who was on the other end of the line and what they were saying. The old woman was impassive. She just listened. No sound. Not even a *mm-hmm*.

Assuming it was a telemarketer, Aggie redirected her attention to her plate of warmed-up chicken and half-eaten, non-gluten-free dinner roll. She had to pull herself together. Find that inner-Aggie who had been a skilled real estate agent instead of a career idiot. Be the courageous, outspoken woman she'd always thought Mumsie must have been, once upon a time. Heck, even seek faith like Mom had so vibrantly committed to and Mumsie seemed to have some remnants of still.

She couldn't shake the memory of Mom passing, the soft smile the last thing to die on her face. A smile of faith, of expectancy, of hope—and this on the face of a woman whose husband had abandoned her and her daughter. Whose father had died when she was a little girl. Whose mother was so eccentric she was hard to love. Who was dying of breast cancer and joining a long list of names and statistics.

"Stop." The tone of Mumsie's voice brought Aggie's attention back to her grandmother. The woman had gone ashen, her eyes widening with some emotion Aggie couldn't tag with an adjective.

"Mumsie?" Aggie pushed her TV tray farther out from in front of her.

"Stop," Mumsie repeated, only this time there was a distinct trembling to her voice. She gripped the handset tightly, her arthritic knuckles turning white.

"Mumsie, give me the phone." Aggie's defenses rose fast at the weakened look of Mumsie's body. The woman's spit and vinegar had been exchanged for the pitiful look of a lost puppy that was desperate to be rescued. "Give me the phone!"

Aggie demanded again, her whisper coming out harsher than she intended.

"You've no right," Mumsie muttered into the phone. She stiffened, her eyes searching desperately until they met Aggie's. She clung to Aggie's gaze. "You've no right at all. It *is* over," she whispered just as the phone fell from her hands and Mumsie slumped forward, crashing into her plate of food, the TV tray, and sliding to the floor.

───ⱳ───

"I want to know who called my grandmother. I want a detailed call list. I want the police here now, and I'm reporting harassment!" Aggie paced the waiting room at the hospital.

"It's eleven o'clock at night, Love." Collin watched her from his chair.

Yes, she'd called him after she'd dialed 911 and an ambulance had been dispatched. No, she didn't know why she kept reaching out to Collin when she needed something. Aggie ran her fingers through her hair, black strands falling like silky ribbons around her shoulders. She couldn't stop her pacing. Couldn't stop second-guessing everything. Couldn't stop overreacting when she knew she needed to calm herself. Hydrate. Breathe. Compose.

"I don't care what time it is. I want the call log." Aggie bent until she was nose to nose with Collin.

He blinked and then pushed his wire-framed glasses up the bridge of his nose. A ginger stubble shadowed his jaw, making him appear far less English debonair and more like a regular guy. A guy who'd been dragged into the night to respond to an emergency, but who still looked remarkably impeccable in his dark, pressed jeans and a striped T-shirt, with a Mr. Roger's–style sweater buttoned over it.

Collin's dimples deepened, and he raised both eyebrows. "Best of luck then," he quipped.

"Gah!" Aggie straightened and stalked across the room, then turned and stalked back. She knew she was being irrational. But they'd taken Mumsie in for emergency scans. A stroke caused by a blood clot. Of all things! And whoever had called her and whatever they'd said had catapulted the clot straight into its damaging action. At least that was how Aggie saw it. Factual or not, someone was to blame for Mumsie's current condition.

"Why doesn't she use a cellphone?" Aggie plopped onto a chair next to Collin.

"Not everyone embraces the rigorous routine of today's technology." Collin gave her knee a patronizing pat. "Why didn't you dial *69 to redial the caller?"

Aggie looked sideways at him. "I'm a Millennial. I have no clue what you are talking about. And please tell me you have a cellphone."

"Of course I do. You've seen it before. What do you think you ring me on all the time?" Collin pulled his phone from his pocket. That's right. An old-style flip phone. One that for certain wasn't equipped to browse the internet.

"Good grief." Aggie sagged back into the waiting room chair and looked to the doors where she silently begged the doctor to walk through. To tell her Mumsie was going to be okay. To release her from the fear of losing the last remaining person in her life who *meant* something to her.

As if her hopes had conjured him, the doctor entered the waiting room, and of course his face was completely unreadable. Aggie squelched a sigh. Even his eyes were emotionless. He was a walking robot, probably trained that way so he didn't sway waiting families toward too much hope or too much despair.

"Dr. Patton?" Aggie urged him to update her.

"We've stabilized Imogene." His monotone use of Mumsie's first name brought Aggie to sharp attention. No one referred to her as that. Come to think of it, everyone she knew called Mumsie, "Mumsie." It was as if she'd graduated into the name

221

eons before Aggie had been born. "Imogene" seemed foreign, as if they were discussing someone else entirely.

". . . but she hasn't regained consciousness yet."

Aggie registered the doctor's statement. She stood. "What's the prognosis?"

Dr. Patton tempered his expression. "It's hard to say. Her age is a factor here. It isn't in her favor. Did you know she has congestive heart failure?"

"What?" Aggie blinked. The words came out of left field and smacked her in the proverbial face. She sensed Collin rise to stand beside her. "What do you mean?"

Dr. Patton allowed himself the liberty of a slight grimace. "Ahh, I see. I'm not Imogene's primary caregiver, but her records state she was diagnosed with the disease over a year ago. While it doesn't appear to be progressing too rapidly, the stroke tonight may speed up the process."

"The process of what?" Aggie didn't care that she sounded snippy—challenging—daring Dr. Patton to say what she knew she abhorred him saying. So she said it for him. "Dying? You're saying Mumsie is dying?"

Dr. Patton shot a glance at Collin. If she wasn't already tipped over the edge of rationality, Aggie would wonder if there'd been some desperation in that glance. A plea for help. It seemed Dr. Patton expected Aggie to know far more about Mumsie than she did.

"Is Mumsie dying?" Aggie repeated. Insisted. No. Demanded.

She felt Collin's fingers take her hand, enveloping her fingers in comforting warmth. Aggie pulled away and crossed her arms in front of her. The touch, the gesture—she didn't know what to make of it.

Dr. Patton sighed and gave a noncommittal tip of his head. "If—when—your grandmother regains consciousness, we'll need to run more tests. You'll need to meet with her primary doctor, and a full prognosis can be drawn up at that point.

However, it was a massive stroke. So, I must warn you, there may be some paralysis as a result. She may have difficulty speaking or moving, and more likely than not, walking. All of this has some of the wait-and-see elements."

"This is assuming she regains consciousness?" Collin interjected with the question Aggie was loath to ask.

Dr. Patton looked between them, then gave a subtle nod. There was honesty in his eyes now. It made him more human. "Sometimes the elderly are just tired. They don't have enough reason to fight to come out of a trauma like this. You should be prepared, in case she slips away."

"Mumsie won't give up." Aggie shook her head, tightening her arms around herself. Neither Dr. Patton nor Collin knew Mumsie—really knew her. Mumsie was too strong-willed, too persistent to just give up and accept that it was her time to go.

But an old, familiar wave of predilection washed over Aggie. She remembered that night in Mom's room as she struggled to breathe, to fight, to live. In the end, her body had given up her spirit anyway, regardless of what she might have wanted.

Death didn't give a person a choice. It just came and stole. Whether you'd finished what you wanted to do with your life or not. Death was a thief, and there was no justice that could imprison it from stealing again. And if God provided hope in the midst of Death's evil . . . Aggie was willing to beg to see it. Just once.

CHAPTER 26

Imogene

Lola took two steps to Imogene's one. Imogene could feel her friend darting nervous, sideways glances at her as they strode down the sidewalk toward the corner drugstore. The drugstore where Harry Schneider worked the soda bar.

He's just a kid.

Imogene could hear Lola's argument in her head.

He couldn't have done anything to hurt Hazel.

The Schneiders were lifelong neighbors and friends to the Graysons. Besides, Harry didn't have a vindictive bone in his body—just like Ollie.

Just like Ollie.

Imogene pursed her red lips tighter as she marched toward the door with the cream-painted words spanning the top of the store's windows that bordered it.

Cigars. Candy. Prescriptions.

And on the other window: *Cosmetics. Films. Aspirin.*

She reached for the long brass door handle. Lola's hand on her bare arm stopped her. Imogene met her friend's concerned eyes.

"Let's think about this first, Genie." Lola's words were almost a whisper.

Imogene shook her head. "There's nothing to think about. Ida saw them together."

"Talking. That's all she said they were doing was talking—*if* it was even Harry! Heck, Genie, I *talked* to Hazel the day before she died! That doesn't mean she said something to make me mad enough to—" Lola cut her sentence off sharply.

Imogene sucked in a breath. All right then. She'd think about it. In an effort to waste time, Imogene glanced at the toothpaste sign in the window, *1 cent*. What a waste. They'd used baking soda for most of the war. There was no reason to waste money on paste.

Was a fifteen-second hesitation long enough?

Imogene swiveled her head back to look at Lola, her hand still clutching the door handle. "Well, I thought about it."

Lola's expression fell into one of exasperation mingled with worry. "Genie" was all she could get out before Imogene tugged the door open.

The bells tinkled their welcome as the ladies stepped into the drugstore. The long soda bar was the first thing to their left. Stools lined the bar, with only two occupants. Children. Their mouths puckered over paper straws sucking in chocolate malts topped with whipped cream and sprinkles.

Harry's back was to them. From behind, he looked almost identical to Ollie. When he turned, the warmth in his eyes startled Imogene. She'd conjured him into a ruthless killer. A jealous, thwarted lover. Gosh. Lola was right. He was just a kid. A nineteen-year-old kid like Hazel.

His eyes dimmed a bit as he recognized her. Sadness reflected in them. Not the lingering, soulful kind like Ollie's, but the kind that hinted he'd lost out on some possibility in his future and had also lost a friend.

"Genie." He motioned to the stools. "Lola. Have a seat."

Gentlemanly. Pretty fine for a farm boy.

Lola slid onto a padded stool, adjusted her dress so it fell modestly around her shins, brushing her stockings. Imogene stood beside her but couldn't sit. If she did, somehow she felt less confident. Less sure of herself. It was already waning fast beneath the questioning look of Harry Schneider.

Cold-blooded murderer?

Imogene exchanged glances with Lola. Okay. Fine. Lola was right. She needed to think first.

"How well did you know my sister?"

Lola's shoulders sagged as Imogene blurted out the question. So much for thinking.

Harry's eyes widened. He glanced around and leaned forward on the counter. "Did you want me to step outside for a second?"

"No. Just answer the question." Imogene rested her hands at her hips and cocked her carefully curled and pinned head of raven-black hair. She summoned her best Hedy Lamarr savvy yet sultry look and softened her demand. "C'mon, Harry, it's just a question."

Harry cleared his throat. "I've known Hazel since we were kids, Genie, you know that."

Imogene couldn't glean any signs that he was nervous, outside of being flustered by her assertive nature.

"Harry, we're just trying to figure out what happened to her," Lola interjected.

Harry glanced at her. "I'm s'posed to know? Don'tcha think I'd say somethin' if I knew?"

Imogene leaned against the bar. "You were seen several times in deep conversation with my sister. At the plant."

"Yeah? So?" Friendliness fled from Harry's eyes, but his answer affirmed Ida's observation that it had been him. "Gosh, Genie, I don't know what you're thinking, but just 'cause I talked to Hazel don't mean I know why she—she was killed!"

The children's heads popped up from their malts, and their

eyes widened. Harry shot them a reassuring grin before returning his attention to Imogene and Lola, lowering his voice now.

"Listen. Hazel was a good girl. You know that. What happened to her—well, she didn't deserve it. But we were just friends, and I was only trying to help her."

Imogene pulled back. "Help her?"

Harry glanced at the children again, then nodded. "Yeah. You know? It's what neighbors do, right?"

Lola reached out and rested her hand over Harry's in an almost sisterly-like reassuring gesture. "It is, Harry."

Imogene bit her tongue. Maybe Lola would draw more bees with honey.

"What did Hazel need help with?" Lola asked the same question Imogene wanted to ask, only her voice was gentle, prodding, and far less forceful.

Harry directed his attention to Lola. "That's just it. I'm not quite sure. She kept talking to me almost in riddles, you know? Kept saying stuff like, 'If I say something, people I care about will be hurt, and if I don't say something, people I don't know will be hurt.'"

"What's that supposed to mean?" Imogene snapped.

Harry shot her a glance. "Heck if I know. I kept trying to get her to tell me what was bothering her so. She said she couldn't, but she kept asking me what I'd do. Like she was in some big moral dilemma, and whatever she did, well, the outcome didn't suit her."

"So why talk to you?" Imogene pressed, not able to ignore the hurt that Hazel hadn't just come to her if she was hiding something, or knew something about someone, or whatever the case might have been.

Harry ran his fingers through his hair. The look on his face was not unlike the resigned expression Ollie seemed to tender often. "Probably 'cause I was familiar. Someone she trusted. She didn't do too much with folks at the plant. She just did her job and went home, you know? I don't even know what she might have stumbled on to put her into such a tizzy."

"She worked in laundry," Imogene mumbled, her mind searching for something—anything—that might help to move her forward.

Harry nodded. "Yeah. The only thing I could gather was that she learned somethin' about someone. And it pained her—a lot."

"But what was it?" The question slipped from Imogene's lips, even though she knew there wasn't going to be a satisfactory response.

Harry shrugged as he grabbed a washrag to wipe off sticky drips of soda syrup from the bar. "I've no idea." He stopped wiping and looked up for a moment, directly into Imogene's eyes. "Funny thing is, she mentioned once she never thought the war would come home after it ended. I mean, I lost family and she knew that too, but that wasn't what she was meaning. It was as though, for Hazel, the war wasn't over yet."

—m—

Imogene bid Lola farewell at the front door of Lola's house in town. It was a subdued farewell. Both had expressed theories, conjecture, and Lola had made sure to bring up again the fact the post office had been blown apart. But outside of Harry's vague account of his conversation with Hazel, there was nothing to take to the police to investigate, outside of what they would already think was a "wild theory." Still, she'd share it with Chet later, when he came for dinner. If nothing else, maybe it would trigger something in Chet. Something he knew that she didn't.

Besides, Imogene argued with Lola, while it seemed plausible to them in theory, it wasn't consistent with Hazel. If she'd known someone was going to plant a homemade bomb at the post office, she surely would have told Chet straightaway. She would have been too concerned for the citizens who so easily could have been seriously wounded or killed.

Such thoughts were swarming in Imogene's mind as she walked along the road toward the family farm. A robin swooped in front of her and pecked at the gravel. It fluttered away as Imogene's toe kicked a pebble in its direction.

"Yes. Fly away." Imogene wished she could too. She needed to work on the dollhouse tonight. But her insides revolted against the idea of once again visiting the scene of Hazel's death in her mind. But with the little bit Harry had told her, maybe she could see things differently if she looked at them again. Perhaps she could remember what had been in the empty picture frame. Or maybe that was of no importance and something else would surface that would trigger a more logical theory.

She walked faster, but her body felt as though someone had hold of the back of her dress and was tugging her away from the dollhouse at the same time.

There's something I didn't tell Harry. Hazel's voice resounded in Imogene's mind. She glanced behind her. No one was there, no one pulling on her. It was a vacant, imagined feeling.

"Then what was it, Hazel?" Imogene asked aloud, her voice startling a few sparrows in the long grasses by the road.

Keep asking. You'll find out.

"I can't right now. I told Mother I'd make dinner tonight." But she didn't want to return to the farmhouse. She didn't want to force herself to work on the dollhouse, to remember sweeping up the shards of Hazel's teacup Chet had launched against the wall. She didn't want to try to stop her mind from spinning, asking why had the teacup been on the table in the first place? Worse, she didn't want to admit that the only person she could think of angry enough to blow up a government building and potentially even take Hazel's life was . . .

Ivan.

Hazel's voice stopped Imogene in her tracks. Her shoes

crunched on the gravel. She covered her mouth with her palm, stifling a gasp. Clear as day. She'd heard Hazel's voice clear as day. She was going crazy. Losing her marbles!

Imogene turned to look behind her again. All she saw was the long stretch of country road, the distant rooftops of town rising in the distance over a wide hill bordered by cornfields and trees. She twisted back and looked ahead of her. She could see the Schneider barn peeking over the knoll ahead. Beyond that would be their farm. But now? The road was empty. It was only her and the voice of her sister accusing their older brother Ivan of horrible, terrible things.

But it made sense.

If what Harry had implied was true, she would hurt someone either way if Hazel had known about the plan to blow up the post office and told or didn't tell. If she didn't tell, civilians could be horribly affected. If she did tell . . . and if it were Ivan . . .

"Why would Ivan build a homemade bomb to destroy the post office? What's in the post office he'd even care about?" Imogene's questions floated away on the wind. She waited, lost in her thoughts, still paused on the side of the road. "Ivan wouldn't do such a thing!"

Family loyalty warred against the nagging sense that Hazel's voice might not be one hundred percent imagined. Maybe she *was* speaking from beyond the grave. Now. Too late to save her or the post office, but maybe now she'd found a way to speak so as to avoid any further trauma. Any more horrid mistakes that Ivan might make.

He'd know how to build a bomb.

Imogene put her hands over her ears, shaking her head back and forth as though Hazel stood next to her. "Stop it. Stop. It wasn't Ivan!"

He's angry. Ever since the war, he's not the same person anymore.

"But he—" Imogene's argument cut off as she heard a car engine behind her. She'd been so wrapped in her own world, she hadn't heard it in the distance. Now it was directly behind her. She spun and screamed as the front bumper of a black pickup grazed her hip. The motion flung her to the ground, mixing her cry with the scraping of gravel against her arms and legs. She rolled a few times, her body tangling with grass and dirt.

The truck stopped. Imogene could hear the door open as she lay facedown, dazed. Blackness warred with her vision as she tried to lift her head. Her hip throbbed, but worse than that was the petrifying sensation of someone watching her. Someone glaring at her from the vehicle. Imogene could feel their eyes boring into her back. Hatred. Anger. She didn't even need to look up to know they had intended to do more than simply catapult her body into the weeds.

They'd intended to kill her.

Imogene's fingers dug into the dirt, desperately trying to shove her body upward. The world was a spinning carousel. Cornstalks just behind the ditch blurred together. She tried to roll over, but the pain in her side caused a moan to escape her lips.

She heard footsteps. The engine of another vehicle coming swift behind them. Shoes crunching on the gravel as the driver sprinted back to the truck.

Then, silence.

A door slammed.

Stones spit from the rear tires as the truck peeled away. Imogene lifted her head, trying to see the truck, its color, make note of the driver. Though her vision was blurry from tears and pain, she saw a hat pulled low over the driver's face and nothing more. The truck was nondescript, not unlike many of the trucks she'd ridden in. Even Daddy owned a black truck like that.

A sob escaped Imogene. She tried to roll over on her other side and this time succeeded, her eyes connecting with the brilliant blue summer sky as she lay on her back. Puffy white clouds like balls of cotton mashed together floated above her.

"Genie?"

The voice came from just above and to the right of her, and the quiet rumble of a vehicle's motor greeted her ears.

"Genie?" The voice again. Male.

She screamed.

A hand touched her shoulder.

Imogene screamed again, clawing at the offender. She'd be darned if she died without a fight. Vivid memories of Hazel's blood spattered across the wallpaper, the bedspread, and pooled on the floor gave Imogene more energy. The pain in her hip became nonexistent as her fingers gripped the cotton of the man's shirt.

"No!" she screamed again, the words ripping from her throat, mingling with sobs of horror and a desperate bid for her life. Her hair flew in front of her face, blinding her as she hit and scratched the man.

Large hands wrapped around her wrists, holding her away from him. His grasp was ironlike and it pinched her skin. "Genie, stop! It's me!" The voice broke through her terror. "It's me! Ollie!"

Imogene's struggle weakened. She flipped her hair from her eyes and blinked several times. Her fingers were still curled into claws, ready to fight, like a cat that had been cornered. Then her eyes connected with Ollie's, the gentle blue in them faded, matching the color of his old pair of overalls.

"What'n heck happened?" Ollie's grip loosened on her wrists as he must have seen recognition flash in her eyes. "I saw a truck pull away, but can't figure who was drivin' it. Looked like your daddy's truck."

"It wasn't Daddy," Imogene mumbled. She knew that much. Daddy would never hurt her. Never. She looked down the road.

There was no truck other than Ollie's, which idled on the shoulder just beyond them.

"Someone tried to—someone hit me. They were going to kill me." Imogene swallowed back a sob, not even attempting to hide the fact she was terrified. Not trying to cover her insecurity and fear with any façade.

Ollie released her. "Okay. Okay. Let's get you to a doctor, and we'll get the police."

"No!" Imogene reared back. "No—I—Chet will be angry with me."

Ollie reached for her, his touch gentle on her arm. "He won't be," Ollie reassured her like one would a child. "Genie, honey, he won't be. Let's get you help."

Imogene felt the hot trails of tears running down her face. Her body began to shake, and she barely registered it in her mind when Ollie wrapped an arm around her shoulders and helped her to stand. All she recognized was his warmth and the security he provided. The way her unassuming neighbor held her against himself. It was necessity, it was need, it was familiarity that made Imogene melt into Oliver Schneider. She needed him to fight this war for her. Just today. Just this moment. For her strength had dissipated and left a chasm of fear behind.

CHAPTER 27

Y ou're lucky you didn't get yourself killed." Chet's stern
look, with his arms crossed over his chest as he stood over
Imogene's hospital bed, affirmed why she'd not wanted
to tell him to begin with.

Imogene glanced at Ollie, who stood off to the side. He
didn't look as though he planned to insert himself into their
sibling dispute.

Pity.

She ran her fingers across her forehead. First a mild concussion in the post office explosion, and now being hit by an
automobile?

Before she could respond to Chet, the door to her room burst
open and Lola hustled in, Imogene's mother and her brother
Ivan close on her heels. Imogene couldn't help but give his face
a quick study.

"Oh, sweetheart!" Mother brushed past Chet, her cool hand
pressing to Imogene's forehead as if she were sick with the flu.

"I'm okay, Momma." She met Ivan's eyes, searching them.
Hazel's whisper echoed in her ears.

Ivan cursed softly. But he was looking at Chet now, his arm
stretched out toward Imogene. "What are you doing about this?"
he demanded.

The similarities between her brothers stopped at their looks. Similar height, build, same green eyes, dark hair, and square jaws. From there, Chet's calculating personality contrasted sharply to Ivan's explosive one.

"If everyone would leave me be with Imogene, I'd get a statement from her," Chet snapped.

"A *statement*," Ivan growled. He flung his hands in the air. Glowering. "That's all you do these days. Collect statements and make notes. You haven't solved a darn thing! You're just a paper-pusher!"

Lola covered her mouth with her hand, a shocked and awkward expression on her face. Imogene's gaze swept to Mother, who straightened and leveled both of her boys with a glare.

"That's enough! Both of you!"

"He's worthless," Ivan spat.

"Shut your mouth," Chet shot back.

"Boys!" Mother snapped.

"Please. Everyone, please stop." Imogene inserted her lame attempt at calming the situation.

"Can't even figure out who blew up the post office and murdered our sister! You're a joke!" Ivan's accusations hit their mark. "Now Genie? If something happens to her, it'd be your fault you know!"

Chet staggered back a step.

Mother's quick inhalation was evidence of how fresh Hazel's death still was.

"Stop." Ollie's deep command ripped through the tension. He didn't shout, but there was authority that resonated through his one word and the stance of his body.

Lola edged closer to Imogene and reached out her hand, resting it on Imogene's shoulder. It was nice to have that comfort. She hadn't regained her composure to add anything to the argument one way or the other.

Ollie took a step forward, joining the small circle that had gathered around Imogene's bed. With him at her left and Lola at her right, Imogene sucked in a deep breath, feeling her confidence beginning to seep back into her.

"This ain't the time to solve your family squabbles." Ollie looked between Imogene's brothers. "Lord knows you all got pains, but throwing punches ain't goin' to help none."

Imogene noticed Ivan unclench his fist. Holy Joe! She'd not observed that he was standing in a position just shy of slugging Chet.

"Now, Mrs. Grayson, Genie's goin' to be fine. The doc was here and they're goin' to release her shortly. If you an' Ivan want to wait downstairs, you can help get her home. She'll need to rest." Ollie commanded the room. "Lola, I think Genie would appreciate you stayin' with her, if that's right fine with you, Chet? You can ask your questions then."

Silence followed.

Chet cleared his throat.

Mother nodded, tears glistening in her eyes. She leaned over Imogene and pressed her lips to her daughter's cheek. "Sweetheart . . ." The endearment was rife with a weepy realization. Imogene could only imagine how shaken her mother was. The threat of losing a second daughter within a two-month span had to be overwhelming.

Mother straightened and rested her hand on Ivan's forearm. "Come, Ivan."

Ivan hadn't released Chet from his furious glare. His jaw clenched. Imogene assessed him. Ivan certainly wasn't the picture of a man who had it in him to kill his own sister. Maybe his brother, but not a sister.

Imogene closed her eyes. Nothing was clear or made sense. All she knew was that someone was very unhappy with her, angry enough to want to do her harm. She'd somehow stumbled into the same web Hazel had, but worse than Hazel, Imogene didn't know what web it was or how to even begin to free herself.

Ivan helped her out of his car. Mother hurried ahead of them into the farmhouse to prepare a place for Imogene to rest. Imogene faltered as she stared up at the house, her eyes drifting to the attic window. To Hazel's room.

Ivan's hand on her arm tightened. "You okay?"

"Huh?" She tore her stare from the window and met her brother's eyes. "Oh. Yeah. Swell. I'm swell."

"Best get you inside before Mother has a fit."

"Seems like you're the one who's been having fits." Imogene spoke before weighing her words more carefully. It wasn't that she was frightened of Ivan, and yet that nagging suspicion played louder in her mind.

"Chet's an idiot," Ivan muttered.

"Well, you didn't have to snap your cap at him," Imogene said.

"No matter. He'll just pass the buck anyway. Sheriff's got him workin' this or that, and he ain't found no evidence one way or the other. He likes to grandstand with that uniform of his and parade around actin' like he's the bee's knees."

"That's unfair." Imogene frowned. She recalculated what Chet had done to solve Hazel's case, and she couldn't think of much. He'd shared next to nothing with them. So maybe the question was more about what Chet *hadn't* done.

"Is it?" Ivan scowled.

"Do you have any theories?" She might as well just ask. It was what she'd do anyway, even if she didn't have that niggling warning in the back of her mind not to press her brother too hard—not to anger him.

"Theories?" Ivan gave her a quick glance. They hadn't moved from their position by his car. "Nah. I got nothin'."

"I need to show you something." She didn't know why she

said it, but she did. Maybe she wanted to see Ivan's reaction to it. Maybe a part of her thought Ivan might take her more seriously than Chet was. Regardless, Imogene motioned to the barn, and Ivan assisted her as she limped toward the open doors.

In a few minutes, they were in the stall. Hazel's paint supplies and miniatures spread across the table she'd erected. The dollhouse stared at them from the back of the stall. What appeared to be a child's plaything carried with its gaping front an ominous air.

"Hazel's dollhouse?" Ivan looked at Imogene, a question in his voice. "I've seen it before. She used to work on it out here all the time."

"I know." Imogene limped toward it, tugging on her brother's sleeve. "But I've added to it."

Ivan frowned, moving forward until they both stopped directly in front of the miniature house. His scowl deepened as he bent over it, taking a long hard look at the changes Imogene had added.

"Are you playin' some kinda sick joke, Genie?" His whisper was hoarse as his eyes skimmed the attic crime scene she'd been re-creating in the evenings when she wasn't at the powder plant.

"We gotta remember, Ivan. There're clues here. There must be! I know the police took photographs, but they won't let me see them."

"But to re-create it in a dollhouse—*Hazel's* dollhouse?" Ivan furrowed his brow. "I don't see what starin' at it in miniature is going to do, except traumatize you."

Imogene heaved a sigh. She didn't know any other way to draw the picture for Ivan. "Don't you remember? Those times during the war? When something awful happened?"

Ivan's expression went blank. He averted his eyes from Imogene and locked them on the attic bedroom scene, scanning the painted-on blood that dotted the wall in tiny pinpricks and stained the edges of the bedspread on the model bed.

"'Course I do," he muttered gruffly.

"I remember what it looked like—when I found—when I found Hazel. I've gotta get it out of me, Ivan. I've gotta put it here so I can study it. Maybe see things that we missed, or that will help us understand what happened. I promised her I'd not rest until we found who did this to her."

"So you don't trust Chet to figure it out either?" Ivan asked.

Imogene was starting to regret how she'd approached this with Ivan. "It's not that I don't trust Chet . . ." Her voice waned. Hazel's death was going to destroy their family if Imogene wasn't careful. She shouldn't plant needless doubts in anyone's mind. Let herself be haunted by rude suspicions and disloyal thoughts. It'd do no good to inspire the same in either Ivan or Chet. "I just can't wait for Chet."

Ivan's jaw worked back and forth. He rammed his hands into his trouser pockets. Finally, he turned to her and said, "Genie, this is dangerous."

"How so?" she challenged.

Ivan's cheek muscle jumped. "Oh, c'mon! Use your noggin! Someone tried to hurt you today. Someone already killed Hazel. I don't think anyone's safe right now, what with the post office explosion and all. Whatever's goin' on, you best not put yourself in the middle of it."

"I'm just trying to find justice for Hazel."

"Justice?" Ivan scoffed, his face darkening. "There ain't no justice. Trust me. Justice is never served up when it should be." There was more to his words. Stories Imogene knew he was never going to share. They were locked in his war vault of memories.

"I promised Hazel." Imogene pointed to the small bedside table. "That frame there. I can't make out what was in it. And the replica is too tiny to be detailed enough."

"So?"

"Do you remember it?" Imogene caught her lower lip between her teeth in hope.

Ivan rolled his eyes and slapped his hand against his leg. "I don't know! I never went in her room, Genie! Now leave it alone!" He spun and stalked toward the door of the stall, bracing his hand against the frame. Ivan spoke over his shoulder, and when he did, his voice adopted a dark tone. Imogene recognized it as barely concealed temper. The kind that often brewed deep like the calm before a storm. "I'm tellin' ya, Genie. Stay outta it."

"I can't." Imogene held on to the table as her hip throbbed. She caught Ivan's stare and refused to look away. She dared him with her eyes to tell her the truth. Tell her everything he knew, suspected, or needed to confess.

Instead, he growled at her. "It's safer that way."

He marched out of the stall. Imogene heard his foot connect with a metal bucket, sending it flying across the barn and slamming into a wall. A cow mooed from below them in the yard. Ivan swore at it, shouting with a curse that stung Imogene's ear. It mooed again as if to taunt her brother. Ivan's intense yell in return chilled Imogene to her core.

"Want me to beat you? Bash your head in with a shovel? Stupid animal!"

Then all was silent, Ivan having stormed from the barn and yard. Imogene sank to the floor, tendering her hip. Every muscle in her body shook. Every part of her ached. Every ounce of her insides wanted to curl into a ball and pretend it all away. But she couldn't.

Imogene reached up to Hazel's table and grasped a small doll. It was wearing a shirtdress not unlike what Hazel had worn the night of her death. It was time to place the body in the crime scene, to remember every part of Hazel. No matter what Chet said. No matter how enraged Ivan became. Imogene had made Hazel a promise, and she loved her sister too much to break it.

Don't do it, Genie. Just let me go. Hazel's voice argued with her as she studied the doll in her hand.

"I can't," Imogene whispered. "I can't ever let you go."

There weren't enough tears in the world to assuage the agony of grief. In that moment, Imogene knew that whether or not she found justice for Hazel, she would always carry the pain of it with her. The murder, the images, the suspicions, but most of all, the sorrow. Grief changed a person. Imogene could already feel it stealing away her reckless, fun-loving nature and replacing it instead with the tiny seeds of cynicism.

No wonder Ivan had become a raging version of his old self.

Violence stole any semblance of peace. One could never get rid of it. Its impression was a tattoo on her soul. On Ivan's soul. Even God couldn't make that right. Not today, not tomorrow. Not ever.

CHAPTER 28

Aggie

S he was surprised when a few ladies from the local church
showed up at the hospital and offered to sit with Mumsie.
Aggie wasn't prepared to leave her grandmother—at least
not emotionally—and now that she was eye to eye with the
possibility, if not probability, of Mumsie's impending passing,
Aggie couldn't squelch the clingy feeling she had. The kind that
made her hold Mumsie's hand while she balanced a plastic mug
of hospital coffee in the other. The kind that had her curling
into the fetal position in a chair with a stiff hospital blanket
over her, trying to catch some sleep.

It'd been two days. Collin had stopped in, as had Rebecca,
Mumsie's caregiver. Rebecca had been a saint and relieved Aggie
so she could go work at the cemetery office. But working all
day digitally logging index cards was draining any extra ounce
of energy from her.

But Aggie was taken aback by the elderly ladies who bustled
in with clicking tongues, shaking heads, and expressions of
utter kindness on their faces. There were three of them. Mrs.
Donahue, Mrs. Prentiss, and Jane. Jane refused to be called

Mrs.-anything, she'd instructed. She might be eighty-one, but it still sounded like her mother to her ears.

"You need to go rest." Mrs. Donahue patted Aggie's hand. Her gray curls were permed tight to her head. Her brown eyes were narrow, hooded but soft.

"She needs more than rest," Jane inserted. She was plump and rosy-cheeked, and all she needed was a red mobcap and she'd look just like Mrs. Santa Claus—but with a first name because, after all, she didn't like the title *Mrs.*

"She needs a glass of wine," Mrs. Prentiss said. She was the tallest of the three, with long legs encased in polyester slacks of forest green, and long peppery hair pulled into a braid.

"Oh, heavens no!" Mrs. Donahue patted Mrs. Prentiss's shoulder. "Spirits aren't the answer to one's problems."

"No. Jesus is." Jane gave a firm nod of her head.

"Yes, yes. That's right," Mrs. Prentiss acknowledged, as if she'd somehow forgotten that Jesus came before wine, even if He had done His first miracle by turning water into wine.

Aggie had conversational whiplash. She could feel her eyes burning not just from exhaustion but from bewilderment. "How do you all know Mumsie?"

"From church!" they cried in unison.

Oh, wonderful. Aggie blinked fast to relieve the dryness in her eyes. First Mumsie starts acting vaguely spiritual, and now she finds out Mumsie had a church *and* friends. It was Sunday. Bets were the ladies heard about Mumsie at church that morning, though how the church had found out, Aggie had no clue.

"I-I didn't realize Mumsie went to church often enough to be missed." Aggie winced at her unfiltered admission.

"Oh, she doesn't," Jane responded bluntly. "She used to. When you get old, church gets overwhelming, poor dear. And she's too old to figure out how to ring an Uber for a ride."

Aggie coughed to cover a chuckle. Apparently, Jane figured she was quite a bit younger than Mumsie.

243

"She's very Baptist," Mrs. Donahue offered with a smile. "Been a member of First Baptist since, ohhhhhh, I think the early seventies?" She cast a questioning glance at Mrs. Prentiss, who nodded in agreement.

"Yes," Mrs. Prentiss confirmed. "Although she was raised Methodist, as she always reminds us. Regardless, Imogene joined the church a year after Mildred Benning ran off with Esther Halloway's husband."

Aggie's eyes rounded.

Jane rolled her eyes. "That Mildred. I didn't like her in grade school, and I still don't like her."

"Now, now." Mrs. Donahue patted Jane's arm. "We must still show love and not judgment. It's not our place."

"One has to have standards!" Jane protested.

"Well, of course. But even then, love wins every time," Mrs. Prentiss corrected gently.

Aggie cleared her throat, both to keep from bursting into tired, hysterical, and emotional laughter and to stop the old ladies' ramblings. Here she'd thought Mumsie was a character. No wonder she'd made friends with these three, albeit her juniors. Aggie smiled at the thought. If a person being in her eighties could be considered "junior."

"Ladies, I appreciate you coming, but I don't intend to leave Mumsie." And she didn't. Yet a part of her was tempted to take the ladies up on their offer if for no other reason than to start some serious digging into who had called Mumsie and what exactly had happened to Hazel. They had to be tied together somehow. Mumsie's last mumbled words "It is over" was so similar and yet so contradictory to the roses Aggie had found. And the cryptic note that was delivered that had yet to be explained.

She didn't deserve death. He didn't deserve life.

Her blasted job toiling over old grave plot records hadn't been conducive to having much free time, and Mr. Richardson had left her a friendly note to "Stay focused, your grandmother will be fine." How lovely was that?

"We know you'd never leave your Mumsie without good reason." Mrs. Prentiss's affirmation was given with an encouraging smile.

"No, of course not," Mrs. Donahue nodded.

"But you should leave her," Jane inserted.

Aggie blinked.

"Yes, you should," Jane repeated. "You need to go. Get some fresh air. Sleep. Your eyeliner is almost gone, and what's left makes you look like an albino raccoon."

Oh. Well, how thoughtful. Aggie bit her lip.

"Is there such a thing as albino raccoons?" Mrs. Prentiss tossed a quizzical glance at her friend.

"You must trust us and go get some rest." Mrs. Donahue ignored her cohorts. "Not to mention we have cellphones!" Mrs. Donahue dug in her purse and pulled forth an old bar phone the size of a block of cheese. Aggie couldn't believe it worked, but Mrs. Donahue showed her the black-and-white digital readout. Yes. There was a signal.

"If that doesn't beat all," Aggie muttered, using one of Mumsie's favorite phrases.

"Yes, and so if something changes with her condition"—Mrs. Prentiss waved at Mrs. Donahue's phone—"then we will call you. You can rush right back."

"But there'll be no reason to rush," Jane added quickly. "I'm sure Imogene will be just fine."

Aggie hesitated. She hated the idea of leaving Mumsie, but the more time that went by, the less likely she'd uncover who the caller had been. The phone company hadn't been helpful at all. Because she wasn't authorized on the account, they wouldn't release any call information. Aggie would have to get a court order for the information to be obtained, that or show proof of power of attorney. The police said no crime had been committed, so they had no reason to investigate. When Aggie had inquired as to the fake skeleton, the assault on Collin, and the strange note, she was given a "We're still looking into it."

So where did that leave her but to try to fit the puzzle pieces together herself? And Aggie hated puzzles. But she also hated loose ends and unresolved issues. Much like Collin was determined to get the graves exhumed, she was committed to once and for all understanding what had happened to Hazel Grayson.

"All right. Let me give you my number." Aggie wrote it down for Mrs. Donahue, who didn't have a clue whether or not she had a contact book in her cellphone. She gathered a few items, her jacket, purse, water bottle, then nodded her thanks to the group of old ladies. "Thank you all. I'll be back as soon as I can."

"You take your time, dear." Mrs. Prentiss patted Aggie's arm.

"No hurry," Mrs. Donahue parroted.

"We need to pray," Jane announced.

"Excuse me?" Aggie blurted.

Jane stared at her. Faded eyes set in a round face. "You pray, don't you?"

Of course she did. Had . . . Aggie swallowed. "It's . . . been a while."

"No time like the present to start!" Jane smiled, her cheeks full. "Now, let's pray."

The three little ladies bent their heads, closed their eyes, and Jane launched into a prayer. Aggie stood there uncomfortable for numerous reasons. One being she didn't know the last time she'd prayed, let alone prayed corporately and out loud. Two, the memory of Mom praying came back in a rush. The déjà vu familiarity of walking into a room and seeing Mom curled in the chair, her head covered in a turban, her body thin and dying, but her lips moving in prayer and a look of sheer hope written on her face.

Aggie scanned the faces of the ladies beside her, hovering around Mumsie's still body. She heard the *beep beep beep* of the heart monitor. The air from the oxygen. The pump on some machine Mumsie was hooked up to. Jane's voice praying in simple conversation.

For a strange, almost surreal moment, Aggie was flooded with warmth. Not a physical warmth, and nothing uber-charismatic or spiritual. She just felt . . . cared for.

". . . In the Lord's precious name we pray, amen," Jane ended.

Three sets of elderly eyes lifted and looked at Aggie.

It was strange. So strange. She'd hardly shed a tear since Mom had passed away. Not at the funeral. Not afterward. But in this moment, her throat was clogged. It took everything in Aggie's power to nod and walk from the room, keeping her burning eyes from spilling over.

Thankfully, the Mill Creek Library was open with shortened Sunday hours, and their newspaper archives had been digitized. Given how tired her eyes were, Aggie wasn't looking forward to scrolling through microfiche. She typed the year 1946 and the key words *Hazel Grayson* into the database and was soon greeted with several links to newspaper articles surrounding Hazel's murder. It was more than she'd found in her Google searches. These document files were unique to the library's database.

Aggie skimmed them, trying to learn the story she'd not asked Mumsie about soon enough. A lot of it matched Mr. Richardson's cursory explanation. Mumsie, or "Imogene Grayson," the older sister of the victim, had found Hazel in the upstairs attic bedroom. There was no sign of forced entry. The investigation was being headed up by . . . Aggie squinted at the names listed, then scrunched her face in surprise. *Chet Grayson.* She alt-tabbed to an online family tree she'd found on an ancestral site. Okay, so Chet was Mumsie's older brother. He'd been dead for twenty years already.

She kept skimming. The articles covered the bulk of the first few days following the murder. No further leads. No suspects had yet to be taken into custody. Aggie clicked the link on the next article. It popped up on the monitor, only the headline had nothing to do with Hazel. In bold letters it announced an explosion at the post office.

"All efforts to investigate Hazel Grayson's brutal murder have been paused as Mill Creek police have launched an investigation into yesterday's explosion at the post office. Four people were hospitalized . . ."

The article went on to name a few people. Two individuals were injured and later released from the hospital, including Hazel Grayson's sister, Imogene, and the young son of Hargrove Thompson and his wife.

Apparently, the paper had seen fit to draw a tie between the investigation of Hazel's murder and the weird explosion of the post office. Blowing up a post office sounded like a modern-day version of terrorism. More than likely, that was why the investigation into Hazel's death appeared to have stalled.

Aggie sagged back in the uncomfortable library chair, stifling a yawn as she clicked another link. This one read, *"Search for Grayson Woman's Killer Gone Cold."* The headline came roughly eight weeks after Hazel's death.

"Gosh, Mumsie," Aggie mumbled to herself, shaking her head. How had she coped, never knowing? The agonizing unresolved death of her sister no doubt had catapulted Mumsie in a whole new direction in life. Emotionally, maybe physically, and for all sakes and purposes probably spiritually. Aggie knew it was bad enough to try to move past her own mother's death. But that had a reason. Cancer was the enemy. Boldly making a claim on its victim. In spite of the disease's relentless brutality, Aggie at least knew what to blame. But Hazel?

Aggie clicked on another link.

"Mill Creek law enforcement has confirmed the use of a homemade explosive device in the destruction of the post of-

fice one week ago. Also confirmed were similarities between the ingredients used and those manufactured at the powder plant. Police are investigating any ties to the plant, but so far no suspects have been named."

Powder plant? Aggie scrolled down. The links trickled out. A few small mentions of Hazel's murder, but no resolution at all. No one convicted. No answers.

Aggie exited out of the database and logged off the computer. Grabbing her notebook, she stuffed it into her leopard-print bag that had been one of her last expensive splurges before she was blindsided by losing her career. She approached the library desk, where a man smiled kindly at her, his balding head crowned with graying brown hair, and a pair of tortoiseshell glasses perched on his nose.

"Can I help you find something?" he asked.

Aggie adjusted the bag's straps on her shoulder. "I was researching an article from the late 1940s and ran across one about an explosion at the Mill Creek Post Office."

"Ah, yes. My dad was actually there that day."

"Really?" Aggie raised her brows, intrigued.

"Mm-hmm." The librarian pointed to his nametag. "I'm Ronald Farber, and my father was a postman back in '46. I wasn't born yet, but my dad told me later that the explosion blew off the side of the post office. Injured a few, I believe." Mr. Farber scrunched his face in thought and raised his eyes to the ceiling, considering. "Mmmm, I don't think anyone was killed."

"No. The article said it was just injuries," Aggie said, confirming Mr. Farber's memory. She reached for her notebook, pulling it from her bag and flipping open to the notes she'd jotted down. "The article mentions that Hazel Grayson's murder case was put on the back burner in light of the explosion? And that they thought some of the bomb might have been resourced from the local powder plant?"

Aggie had a vision of a factory that produced compacts of

face powder like one would find in a store's cosmetics department. She was tired enough to feel like giggling at the idea of blowing up a building using makeup.

Good grief. She needed sleep.

Mr. Farber reached for some books that had slid across the counter as a patron dropped them there and walked off without looking back. He started to restack the books so he could check them back into the system. "I'm not familiar with any murder cases from back then. But I can't imagine that a government building getting attacked right after the war ended didn't take front and center after that. The powder plant? Yep. That was Mill Creek's claim to fame for quite a while. The U.S. government built it in just a little over ten months in 1942 to manufacture ammunition for the war. It stayed in production until well after the Korean War. Not sure, but they might have still been producing ammunition for Vietnam. I don't recall."

Aggie had never heard of a powder plant before, let alone one dropped in the middle of south-central Wisconsin on acres of farmland. She imagined that being something they would have built on the East or West Coasts. Maybe the strategy at the time was that German or Japanese bombers wouldn't be able to fly this far inland to form an attack?

"Is the plant still active?" she asked the librarian.

"Oh, no. The ammunitions plant was put on standby in case of a war, but the government pretty much shut down all ten thousand acres of it. Sort of turned into a ghost town, minus a few offices that were left open. But then, about ten years ago, the property was put up for sale by the government, and they took bids on the land. It's owned by a few different organizations now. Most of them are private, even the company that secured the cemetery."

"Cemetery?" Aggie looked up from the notes she was taking.

Mr. Farber hefted the books he'd stacked and bent down to

set them in a bin behind the counter. His voice ricocheted off the floor as he spoke. "Yep. When the land was purchased during World War II, it had been family farms up until then. A family cemetery was there too. Like an acre maybe? I'm not sure."

"So families just sold their land in support of the war effort?" Aggie was impressed. Back then, having just come out of the Depression, families who owned land, let alone farms, had to be some of the lucky ones.

Mr. Farber straightened and sniffed, rubbing his nose. "I remember my dad mentioning they were offered X-amount for their property from the government. But I didn't get the feeling they had the choice to decline it either."

"They were forced off their farms?" That seemed archaic for the U.S. government. But then maybe not, considering America didn't always have a shining history when it came to honoring people's land rights.

Mr. Farber shrugged. "That's where my know-how ends. I'm not a historian, just a local librarian."

"Do you have a historical museum here I could visit to get more information?" Aggie inquired. Perhaps they'd have more documentation surrounding Hazel's death as well.

"We did, but it shut down two years ago. Ran out of funds. It doesn't seem like a lot of locals care much about our community's history. Those Millennials, you know?"

Aggie bristled at the stereotype that was in error. "Actually . . ." She started to correct the older man and educate him on how community-minded Millennials had proven to be, but then stopped. It'd do no good. "Do you have any suggestions as to where I could find more information about local history in that era?"

Mr. Farber shook his head. "You can keep looking through the archives here. Or you can just take a gander down at the local nursing home. There're a few old-timers there who might remember some of it. Probably not too many from World War II, but I know there's a few Korean War vets there who worked at the plant."

Aggie offered the librarian a smile. "Thank you for your time." She had turned to go when Mr. Farber's voice stopped her. She spun back around and was surprised by the serious expression on his face.

"You know, they've bulldozed most of the ammunition plant. They said it used to be haunted, so now there's really just a few small buildings left over."

"Haunted?" Aggie raised an eyebrow.

Mr. Farber nodded. "Ghosts. From the family cemetery. I guess quite a few people saw them over the years. Causing trouble. Sorta like they were out for revenge."

"Vengeful ghosts?" Aggie blinked.

Mr. Farber chuckled. "Well. Who knows. I heard my dad say once that someone thought maybe they were behind the blowing up of the post office."

"Why would—um, ghosts—blow up a post office?" *Not to mention how,* Aggie finished in her thoughts.

Mr. Farber chuckled again and waved her off. "Aww, it's just my daddy's hearsay, and he liked to tell stories. But he figured if the families who lived there were forced to sell out to the government, the loved ones they left behind in the earth couldn't have been none too happy with the government."

"Soooo they blew up the post office?" Aggie couldn't hide her cynical tone.

Mr. Farber smirked and rolled his eyes. "Well, that was the only other government building in town at the time. Except the town hall."

"And the town hall is still standing," Aggie concluded.

Mr. Farber shook his head. "Oh, the town hall now isn't the one they had back in the forties. No, that one isn't standing anymore."

This was getting weird. Aggie took the bait and allowed Mr.

Farber's unfinished theory to tempt her. "So, what happened to the old town hall?"

Mr. Farber waggled his brows as though he'd always believed his daddy's ghost story. "Town hall burned down. Not long after the post office explosion."

"Burned down?" An eerie sensation knotted Aggie's insides. She envisioned poltergeists swooping through the night air, exacting their revenge for the loss of family land and the desecration of their graves.

"Yep," Mr. Farber said. "Now you see why, if there was a murder around that time, it probably took a backseat to the sabotage on government property."

"I can't believe Mill Creek was accustomed to having someone murdered here, so it's hard to imagine they'd just stop investigating it." Aggie threw out the comment, playing devil's advocate.

Mr. Farber nodded. "One would think that, yes. Mill Creek wasn't known for violent crimes, and isn't today either. But you could head out to the ammunition plant too, if you wanted. They have a small museum there. Not sure what you'd learn, but there you be."

Aggie allowed the silence to stretch between them. When Mr. Farber offered no further explanation, she gave him a polite nod and another "thank you."

Explosions, murder, disappearances, and ghosts.

Mumsie's personality of eccentric self-preservation made more sense now. Mill Creek was a strange little town, with a past of postwar mysteries it seemed no one had ever succeeded at solving. And Hazel Grayson's murder appeared to have been the impetus to it all.

CHAPTER 29

So you just take your time now!" Mrs. Donahue's voice filtered through Aggie's phone and into her ear.

"Thank you." Aggie tossed her phone onto the passenger seat of her car. Mrs. Donahue had been kind enough to call with an update on her grandmother's condition. Aggie wished she hadn't, because the moment her phone rang, she had a surge of panicked adrenaline that left her feeling nauseated. She wanted to tell the elderly woman to call her only if Mumsie had awakened, or worse, had died. Calling to let her know nothing had changed after only two hours was thoughtful but going to put Aggie on an emotional roller coaster.

She turned off the ignition and adjusted the rearview mirror so she could take a quick inventory of her face. The ladies were right. She did have raccoon eyes. Aggie rifled through her bag and pulled out a tissue, wiping the black from beneath her lower lashes.

Great. Now her eyes looked washed out—except for the long eyelashes she'd inherited from Mom, who in turn had inherited them from Mumsie. Her brown eyes were fawn-colored and tired looking, the pupils tiny due to the sunlight. She ran her fingers through the raven hair and pulled it up in a messy bun. A few more swipes of her hands to her face succeeded in brushing away an errant lash and remnants from the sandman in the corners of her eyes, leaving behind the smattering of freckles that matched the color of her eyes. Typically, they were light enough to cover with concealer. Aggie gave up. She didn't know why she was primping anyway. She was at the cemetery of all places, and she highly doubted the dead looked any better than she did.

But Collin looked . . . smashing. Aggie wanted to duck down into the driver's seat as he exited the cemetery office, Mr. Richardson behind him. In her exhaustion, she almost did. She hadn't expected Mr. Richardson, let alone Collin, to be at the office on a Sunday. Her hopes of privately scouring paper work with the sole agenda of finding information about Hazel were thwarted.

"Agnes!" Collin's use of her full name halted her in her position behind the open car door.

She couldn't hide the shocked look that spread across her face, which left her speechless. Only Mumsie called her that—well, and Mom had.

"Ah!" Mr. Richardson edged in front of Collin, waving a document at her with a big grin. "We've had success!"

"Pardon?" Aggie's bewilderment wasn't getting any less.

"Exhumation!" Mr. Richardson all but did a happy dance in his orthopedic shoes and gray slacks. His sweater looked like one from the nineties, with big squares of blue, purple, and green splashed across it.

Even Collin appeared a tad too pleased.

"Have you been drinking?" Aggie scowled.

"Brilliant deduction!" Collin flashed her one of his golden grins that creased his face in all the right places. "But horribly wrong. Although I did have a tonic water a bit ago."

Aggie rolled her eyes and stepped away from the car, shutting the door, trying to collect her thoughts and wits and the twist from her intentions.

Mr. Richardson held the document toward her. Aggie took it but looked at Collin, a question in her eyes. He winked.

"That, Love, is approval to open the mystery grave I discovered."

"What about the other two graves?" She didn't know why it mattered. Apparently, one disinterment was enough morbidity to bring a brilliant twinkle to both Collin's and Mr. Richardson's eyes.

"Not approved!" Mr. Richardson replied. He glanced at Collin as though he might have overstepped the bounds of announcing the bad news. "The coroner saw no reason to exhume the poor souls. There's nothing suspicious about the graves, and based on Collin's calculations and mapping, they appear to fit the time frame of the other graves in Fifteen Puzzle Row."

"Except for Hazel Grayson's grave," Aggie inserted.

"Well, yes." Mr. Richardson waved her off. "But we have good reason to figure why she was buried there."

Of course they did. Aggie bit her tongue and mentally chided herself. She was going to cross the border into serious snippyland if she wasn't careful. For a moment, she had the startling realization that she was becoming more like Mumsie than she realized.

"And the third grave?" she asked.

"We're all quite curious to see what we find." Collin reached for the approval paper work that Aggie had just skimmed. "I'm hoping it's not the remains of a family dog."

Aggie's lip curled. "You think it could be?"

"One never knows for sure until one digs." Collin waggled his ginger brows. Good grief. The man was borderline giddy over the idea of digging up a dead body.

"Well, it'll take you forever with your paintbrushes and picks," Aggie joked, trying to be funny but falling miserably short.

"We called in a backhoe!" Mr. Richardson's volume of excitement made Aggie think in all caps and exclamation points. He was going to give her a headache soon.

"Won't that destroy what's in the grave?" Aggie directed her question to the expert. "You said there's no vault, no coffin."

Collin nodded. "It will enable us to clear away the topsoil. I can map how deep they can go and then I'll proceed from there."

"The coroner wants to be present," Mr. Richardson added, "and the police will have personnel here as well. You know, in case it's more than a dead dog or someone accidentally buried backwards."

"You mean a murder victim?" Aggie recalled Collin's ominous thought the day he'd discovered the grave.

"One never knows," Collin answered, his excitement leveled out a bit.

Mr. Richardson shook his head. "Doubtful. Very doubtful. I'm more convinced it is an old burial ground for Native Americans."

"Good heavens!" Aggie gasped. "You can't exhume that! That's sacred."

Collin cast a slightly irritated glance at the old man, then shook his head at Aggie. "There's nothing to indicate such. No evidence of Native American anything in this area. Reason being, the cemetery would never have been started here if this had been sacred burial grounds."

"Unless no one knew!" Mr. Richardson waved his index finger in the air to make his point.

"What if it is?" Aggie wondered if tribal representation would also attend the exhumation.

"Again, from an archaeological perspective," Collin said and shot a look at Mr. Richardson, who opened his mouth and then snapped it shut, "there is nothing to indicate such. If we were to find anything that did, exhumation would cease immediately. From what I've been able to surmise, the grave is by no means older than a century, which eliminates the possibility altogether."

Mr. Richardson finally had no response.

Aggie looked at the cemetery behind the two men. It was dried up now. The last few weeks had been sunny with autumn winds that helped the earth release moisture. The graves in the lower area were still sunken with tilted stones, but at least the mud had turned into a hardened clay. Tomorrow, she'd walk the upper-east section of the cemetery with the old map to see if the stones there matched up to the document. Any new ones that failed to be added needed to be marked so that a new map could be created.

She didn't at all feel like doing it.

"How is your grandmother?" Collin asked.

Aggie tore her gaze from the expanse of graves and drew in a deep breath, letting it out through her nose and trying to squelch a yawn. "She's still non-responsive."

"Oh. Yes. So sorry to hear about Mrs. Hayward," Mr. Richardson said.

Mrs. Hayward. Imogene Grayson Hayward. All names Aggie never associated with Mumsie. She was just persnickety Mumsie, with faded beauty and a wit as sharp as a blade.

"The cemetery board will understand if you need to take some time away." Mr. Richardson's sympathy seeped through the cracks in Aggie's barely maintained composure. She hadn't expected that it would be the old man who'd make her want to cry again. What was with all the old people in this town anyway? All so curiously stubborn in their ways but with a gold streak of kindness that almost—*almost*—made Aggie wish she'd grown up in Mill Creek.

"Thank you." Aggie nodded. "I-I might do that."

"You need to get some rest, Love." Collin stepped toward her.

Aggie took a step back and reached for her car door. If he touched her, extended a hand toward her, or gave her that warm, caring gaze one more time, she'd become a puddle. That was not acceptable. She reached inside herself for strength and stamina. Not that there was anything wrong with weakness, but she wasn't ready to be weak. She wasn't sure she ever would be.

"I think I'll do that." Aggie opened the door.

"I'll pop in straightaway after I'm finished here," Collin said.

He didn't need to "pop in," and Aggie opened her mouth to say so but stopped. He wasn't family. He was a co-worker. Okay, a friend. But a friend of short acquaintance, and really she didn't want him babysitting her.

"You don't have to," Aggie finally managed to say, giving Collin an offhanded dismissal.

The warmth of his eyes penetrated her. "I know."

———

The afternoon sun was waning. Aggie needed to get back to the hospital to relieve the Three Stooges. Larry, Curly, and Moe. That was the only way she could think of the three ladies she met just hours ago. They'd imprinted themselves on her for more reasons than their entertaining personalities. She couldn't wipe Jane's sincere praying out of her mind. Couldn't seem to tamp down how much it reminded her of Mom. Couldn't explain how the Three Stooges' steady natures made her own world seem like it was completely spinning out of control.

Aggie straddled a straight-backed chair, her arms crossed over its back, the lamps turned on in every corner of Mumsie's study. She stared at the dollhouse. The creepy, awful thing with the imitation murdered body of Hazel sprawled on the floor. She studied the stains on the miniature bed, twisted and analyzed the stains on the real bed behind her. Almost to perfection.

Mumsie's attempt at early forensics was impressive to say the least. Aggie chewed on her cinnamon gum, popped it, and chewed some more. Apparently, after seventy years, the dollhouse had yet to shine light on any clues strong enough to draw a conclusion to the mystery of Hazel's violent death.

Aggie glanced at her open notebook on the floor.

The ammunition plant—once called the powder plant—it really had no connection to Hazel, but somehow it felt as though it did. Of course, if she'd just asked Mumsie sooner, instead of tiptoeing around it, she'd know far more than she did now. If Mumsie never woke . . . well, did it matter if she ever helped Mumsie find closure to Hazel's murder?

But then—Aggie tried to line up all the events in her mind— whoever had called Mumsie and sent her into a panic that caused her stroke, *they* mattered.

"Aarrrrrrgh!" Aggie spit her gum against the wall.

Mumsie would have a fit if she'd seen that.

"I don't think one is supposed to launch chewing gum at the walls."

Collin's voice interrupted the beginning of Aggie's frustrated tantrum. She startled backward, the chair flipping out from beneath her, and landed on the hardwood floor.

"Way to let a person know you're here!" Aggie winced. She'd also fallen on one of her stylish boots she'd taken off when she sat down. The red ones with the three-inch heels.

"Here." Collin extended a hand. "Let me help you up. It's my fault if you injured your bum."

Aggie shoved herself off the floor, ignoring his hand and swatting at her jeans to knock off dust. "I didn't injure my *bum*."

"Splendid." Collin directed his attention to the dollhouse and crossed his arms over his button-down oxford shirt. Aggie shot a glance at his pants. Tiny embroidered trout dotted the pressed khakis. Fish. Of course. The man dressed to the nines all the time. She wondered if he even owned a pair of basketball shorts or flannel pajama pants.

"Do you sleep in dress pants?" It slipped out before she could stop it.

Collin raised a brow. "No. But I do press my pajamas. There's nothing in the world as splendid as wearing pressed cotton."

Aggie had nothing to say to that. It was so . . . un-American to iron pj's.

"Any further clues?" He motioned toward the dollhouse.

Aggie averted her thoughts from Collin in pajamas. "I don't even know why Mumsie keeps that horrible house. She's stared at it for over seventy years, and still no one knows a darn thing about what happened to Hazel."

She hurt for Mumsie. She ached for whatever Hazel had gone through. She wanted closure for them all. Most of all, she longed to bounce all of it off Mom, but two years after her death, Aggie only heard Mom's voice in her head. An imaginary one telling Aggie all things she *thought* Mom might say in a situation, but none of it being from Mom herself.

"Have you checked with the local police department?" Collin inquired. "Perhaps they still have the evidence from the crime scene?"

"Seventy years later?" Aggie couldn't hide the high level of doubt in her tone.

"It's possible." Collin tipped his head in affirmation of his suggestion. "Although, I'd wager not likely."

"Well, I doubt they ever throw out evidence, but whether it's anywhere anyone can find would be the trick." Aggie considered the possibility. She supposed it'd be worth a visit to the precinct. The worst thing they could do was confirm her suspicions that none of it was available.

"So then, we assume this is all we have. The miniature and this very room." Collin turned to the bed, the small table, the empty picture frame.

"Trust me, I've been staring at it all for two hours." Aggie pinched the bridge of her nose.

Collin gave her a sideways glance. "And your grandmother has been staring at it for seventy years."

Aggie tipped her back and released a sigh toward the ceiling. "I don't even know where to look. I don't know why seventy years later anyone other than Mumsie would even care. But the roses, the note . . . and good grief, you had someone hit you on the back of the head! That's probably connected too. Someone isn't happy with Mumsie. They're not happy with us at the cemetery. This whole thing is so blown out of proportion. There's hardly a soul alive in Mill Creek who was an adult during World War II, so why would anyone still care?"

Her rant ended with a watery choke. Aggie held her fist to her lips and bit the skin on her thumb, attempting to compose herself.

"Take a breath, Love."

"I am!" she retorted.

"Agnes," Collin started.

"Don't—call me that," Aggie snapped.

"Fine then. Love."

"Or that," she snapped again.

"Splendid. I will refer to you as 'You.' So, You there, I believe there's a tear in the corner of your eye."

Aggie swiped at it. If she broke down now—well, she wouldn't.

Sometimes, Agnes, you must step outside of your own strength and realize there's a greater Strength waiting to hold you.

Now wasn't the time she wanted to recall that specific admonition of Mom's. Aggie turned away from Collin.

"You." Collin's teasing nickname brushed her ear, his breath against her cheek as he came up from behind to speak into her ear.

"Don't call me that, please." Aggie knew she had breached the epitome of Mumsie's record for being persnickety.

"Then I'm back to 'Love.'" Collin's fingers tucked a stray piece of hair into her messy bun on her behalf. "So, Love, I daresay it's time for you to lie down and sleep. You're trembling. Attempting to solve a seventy-year-old cold case while your grandmother's in a coma and you haven't slept in forty-eight hours is foolhardy."

You're so much like your grandmother. Stubborn. Willful. Not asking for help. Not listening to wisdom.

If Mom were still alive, standing here saying the words out loud, Aggie knew she would have argued back. Instead, she closed her eyes against long-overdue tears.

"I don't want to sleep," she whispered.

Collin's hand on her arm nudged her to turn toward him. "You need to. It will help you heal."

"Heal?" Aggie pulled back and glared at him. "Heal? What on—what gives you the right to—who said I need to heal? I need to solve a murder! I need to give Mumsie this one last thing in her life! Resolution. Vengeance! Whatever it is, it should be hers. *I* don't need anything. I don't need to *heal*. I'm fine. I am one hundred percent fine!"

Collin crossed his arms and met her glare. "Splendid. You had me duped."

"Shut up," Aggie muttered, looking away. "As if you know anything about me." She swept her eyes back to his. "What about you? Mr. I Have No Problems in the World! You just dig up dead things and play with bugs for a living. You're educated and . . . and have a sexy accent that isn't consistent with just England, I'll tell you!" Aggie wagged a finger in his face. "But you haven't spit a word out about who Collin O'Shaughnessy is. So, until you let me into your world, don't try to insert yourself into mine!"

Drat.

A hot tear trailed down her cheek, defiant against her struggles to keep it and others contained. Collin stared at her. His mouth was clamped shut. His eyes stormy but not angry. Bothered but not desperate. Aggie locked eyes with him, her chest heaving from her verbal rampage. Another tear escaped her willpower.

When Collin spoke, his voice was low. Not resigned. Not regretful. Just straightforward and truthful. "I lost my sister when I was twenty-one. We were twins. My father was a government contractor from the U.S., and my mother was from England. I rarely saw my father, so my mum took care of Cadie and me. We lived in England for much of my youth, then moved to Egypt for a year in hopes of reconnecting with my father, who was in the Middle East at the time. From there we hopped to Canada to live with my mother's brother. By the time I was sixteen, we were in America living in New Jersey with my father's mum. Cadie and I enrolled in college there. We went out for our first drinks the day we turned twenty-one. You know, all that youthful thrill about having our first legal drinks."

Aggie didn't say anything. She hadn't expected Collin to open up without being pried open like a vault. Apparently, he hadn't been hiding anything behind what seemed like a contrived accent. He was just a wanderer, at the fault of his parents, and for all sakes and purposes he appeared to be an open book. He was transparent, though sadness laced his voice.

"I wasn't ready to go back to the dorms that night. Cadie was. She took the car, and I said I'd call a cab. She should have called one too. The next morning, we found her car wrapped around a tree. The grace of God kept anyone else from being injured."

The clock ticked.

The bloodstains on the bed, over half a century old, glared at Aggie.

Mom's voice fell silent in Aggie's heart.

The dollhouse stood testament to all their grief.

"I'm sorry," Aggie finally mumbled out. "I didn't know."

Collin laid his palm against Aggie's cheek, his thumb rubbing across her clear skin and touching the freckles she always kept hidden. "Sleep, Love. But don't say you don't need to heal.

You can't compare your grief to another's. Not Mumsie's, not mine. It's yours to hold, and yours to heal from."

"You can't come back from sorrow," Aggie whispered. "It locks you in a prison and leaves you there." Her voice caught as the agonizing pain she'd shoved deep inside made its way into her chest, constricting it with every pent-up sob she hadn't cried.

"I know Someone who holds the prison key."

"If you say God . . ." Aggie let her sentence fall away.

Collin's smile was small but knowing. "Then I won't. I don't appreciate clichés any more than you do. But sometimes clichés become such because they're true."

CHAPTER 30

Imogene

Imogene sat gingerly on the bench outside the cafeteria, her chicken-salad sandwich wrapped in paper and a Coca-Cola balanced beside her on one of the bench slats. She'd been awake for almost forty-eight hours, and nothing good ever came from her lacking in sleep. She either got remarkably sharp-tongued, became overly flirty and fun-loving, or just was an all-around basket case. Today she was on the verge of tears plus giggles. She stuffed the sandwich in her mouth and ignored the plant workers who were on break and passing by. The waft of cigarette smoke from one of them tickled her nose, then grew stronger. She looked up and met the sideways grin of Sam Pickett.

Honestly. The man could make a nun fall for him. It seemed while boys like Ivan and Ollie had brought home morose and serious dispositions, a boy like Sam had learned how to see the world for the best it had to offer. It was refreshing. Or else she was just feeling reckless.

Imogene sent a saucy grin his way and hoped her eye makeup hadn't smeared. "Well, hello, Sam Pickett."

"Same to you, Miss Grayson."

Imogene smiled and took a smaller, more ladylike bite from her sandwich. She waited. Sam picked up her Coca-Cola bottle and sat down beside her, holding it between his hands.

"You're looking mighty fine," he observed.

Imogene raised an eyebrow. "Well, a girl has to try."

"Don't try too hard or Hollywood will come looking for you and make you into something way bigger than a cafeteria girl."

"I'm all right with that." Imogene had a sudden rush of sadness. She missed the beauty salon, the smell of perming chemicals, the fun of helping someone apply lipstick for the first time. Heck, she missed the afternoons of daydreaming that someone would paint her image on the side of a plane. A pinup girl. Mother would have to fan herself from a dead faint if she knew what Imogene's silly dreams had been. Hazel's death saved her from pursuing them. Funny, for she didn't feel saved at all.

"Does it ever weigh on you?" Sam's more serious inquiry startled Imogene from the flirtatious moment.

"Does what weigh on me?"

"Fact your sister used to work here at the plant?" While Sam's question was stabbing, Imogene melted a little inside. She kept forgetting he was a widower. It had to be difficult trying to maneuver through life when memories of your dead wife were everywhere—including in the face of your child.

"Sometimes," Imogene admitted. She wasn't sure how much to say. Transparency with her brothers and Ollie hadn't gone over well. "Hazel didn't work the cafeteria, though. She was in laundry."

"Yeah." Sam nodded.

Imogene eyed him. "You knew Hazel?"

Sam shot her a surprised look. "Well, sure. She was Ida's friend."

Imogene twisted in her seat. Eagerness filled her, mixed with hope. "Tell me, did you ever have conversations with her? I mean, beyond just saying hello?"

Sam turned the Coca-Cola bottle in his hands. "Sure. I mean, I asked her to a dance once."

"You did?" Imogene drew back. In another lifetime she might have been jealous of her younger sister.

Sam offered her a sheepish grin. "She told me no and pretty much gave me the cold shoulder. Not sure why. I always figured she had someone else, but I never saw her with anyone other than Harry Schneider."

"But they weren't together?" Imogene was a bit sorry she baited Sam.

Sam turned the bottle of soda in the opposite direction. "Haven't a clue. To be honest, I was sorta glad she turned me down. I don't think—she was too sweet. Man like me didn't deserve her."

Vulnerability splayed across Sam's face for a moment, then was wiped away as he tossed her a smile.

"I don't think you're all that bad." Imogene offered an encouraging smile in return, Chet's and Ollie's warnings pinging in the back of her mind.

Sam's eyes clouded. He pressed his lips together and shook his head. "Wish the rest of Mill Creek thought that. But nope. I'm a Pickett, and with that comes the reputation."

Imogene shifted, and the paper-wrapped sandwich crunched in her hand. "I never heard the rumors before—well, I suppose I didn't pay attention."

Sam handed her the bottle of Coca-Cola. He met her eyes, and there was a restlessness in his, a turmoil he didn't try to hide. "Mill Creek ain't the friendly town everyone always thinks it is."

Imogene didn't know what to say. She could ask, could pry for an explanation, but something made her bite her tongue.

"But!" Sam's face perked up and he straightened, offering her a grin that rivaled any darkness that had now fled from his eyes. "I'm ready to prove that a Pickett can be a gentleman. Especially to a pretty dame like you."

"Oh!" Imogene felt a warm blush creep up her neck. She elbowed him. "You're trouble in a handbasket."

Sam didn't answer, but reached up to adjust the cigarette that hung lazily from his mouth. He scanned the stretch of buildings and busy streets. He narrowed his eyes, then removed the cigarette and ground it out on the cement at their feet. As he sat up, he glanced at Imogene. "Used to be this was all farmland around here."

Imogene nodded. "I know."

"Yeah?" Sam gave her a funny twist of his face. "Not anymore."

Imogene felt that familiar pang of empathy for the folks who had been forced from their land. It'd touched her family too, but nowhere near as dramatically. At least as far as her daddy was concerned. Mother, on the other hand, she hadn't taken it as well.

"My family owned some of the acres here," Imogene confided in Sam. "Daddy used to farm part of the land." Imogene remembered a few years back when Daddy came home and said the U.S. government wanted to buy them out. He hadn't protested too much. It was difficult to maintain acreage this distance away from their actual farm. He'd only kept it because it'd been part of Mother's family and they had a small family cemetery there. Grandpa and Grandma on Mother's side were buried in the cemetery. And two of Mother's babies who never made it. An uncle. Some cousins. It was where family was. It was where Hazel wasn't. The government said they'd care for the existing graves, but they couldn't add new ones. Imogene could only imagine the heated argument Mother must have had with Daddy behind closed doors, coming to terms with burying Hazel all alone in the old section of the Mill Creek Cemetery.

"We owned land here too." Sam made a clicking noise with his tongue. It drew Imogene's attention to his chiseled lips, his square jaw, and his eyes. They weren't stormy, but they were vacant. Defeated. His jovial flippancy had disappeared again. "Now I play with nitro instead of plowing a field."

"Are you angry?" Imogene ventured.

"Me?" Sam shook his head. "No. I don't know what I'm cut out to be, especially now."

Imogene took a sip of her Cola. She sensed Sam watching her. Watching her mouth, then roving her face with his eyes until she startled as he rested his hand on her knee.

"One of these days I'll ask you to dance."

"Oh!" Imogene squeaked. She eyed his hand. It wasn't overtly improper—she supposed—but it did funny things to her insides. She wasn't sure if she liked the advance or wanted to bat it away.

Sam removed his hand before she could react. He winked. "Just need someone to schedule a dance." He stood and gave her a haphazard salute before walking away.

—⁓—

Sirens were wailing as the bus pulled into town after her shift was over. Imogene scrambled for her purse and exchanged glances with Ida. "What do you suppose happened now?" she whispered.

Ida responded with her customary wide-eyed look of hesitation.

Imogene pushed past her friend and urged the people in front of her to hurry off the bus. "What's going on?" She craned her neck to try to see out the bus window.

"Fire!" someone hollered down the aisle.

Seconds later, Imogene was hit with a blast of fresh air as she stepped off the bus, but it was quickly followed with the distinct tang of smoke. She noticed plumes rising above the roof of the grocery store and the butcher shop.

"Town hall is burnin' down!" a man yelled as he sprinted by.

"Oh no!" Imogene breathed. Hopefully, in the middle of a weekday, it wasn't packed with people.

A hand grabbed her elbow and dragged her away from the throng of people getting off the bus and running toward the fire.

She yelped as she fell against Ollie.

"Honestly, Ollie! I swear you follow me around!" She wasn't sure if she was perturbed or flattered.

Ollie ignored her and half shouted in her ear over the din. "Come with me!"

"Why?" She gave him a curious look.

He tugged her, and she followed, realizing that at this pace, her bruised hip was going to quickly start bothering her.

"Ollie, where're we going?"

"C'mon." His grip slid down her forearm until he grasped her hand. They rounded a corner, and he led her toward the city park. Tall trees stood in full foliage around a small fountain. Of course, it was completely empty now, as everyone had deserted it for the shock and horror of the town hall going up in flames.

"What's going on?" Imogene stumbled to a halt, trying to yank her hand back from Ollie.

He didn't release her, but glanced down at their hands. His overalls were covered with soot, as though he'd gotten too close to the fire. There was ash streaked across his face, and a reddening swell of flesh on his free hand.

"Heck, Ollie!" Imogene cried. "You're hurt!"

He glanced at the burn, releasing her hand. "I've had worse."

"Ollie, what happened?" Imogene grasped his forearm to survey the burn. "You need to get butter on that right away."

She tried to ignore the strong corded tendons beneath her fingers. Ollie wasn't a bruiser, so she hadn't expected him to feel muscular. But he was manlier than she'd originally given her old neighbor credit for.

"I don't need butter." He stepped closer, his voice tense, his eyes burrowing into hers.

Imogene swallowed. She studied his face, the soot, the slightly

271

singed hair on the side of his head. "Tell me you didn't start the fire."

She didn't know why she said it. Didn't know why she suddenly had visions of Ollie making a homemade bomb for the post office either, but she did. She was turning into a horrible person! Suspecting everyone near and dear to her.

And Ollie *was* dear. He was an old friend. He had been since they were kids. He was just Oliver Schneider, the neighbor who'd gone off to war, who'd remained vaguely in the back of her mind while he was stationed overseas, who'd come home and walked the trails between their adjoining land in his overalls and rolled-up shirtsleeves. He was Ollie.

He was kissing her.

His hands had come up and cupped both sides of her face. His mouth moved against hers hungrily, as though she was his—had always been his. As though he'd somehow come close to losing her.

Imogene whimpered and tried to pull away.

Ollie released her, but his face was a breath away, his eyes driving into hers.

Imogene's breaths came in short puffs. She realized her hand had come up and was clutching the front of Ollie's shirt where it showed above the bib of his overalls.

"What in tarnation?" she breathed.

Ollie leaned his forehead until it rested against hers. "I'm sorry, Genie. I got a phone call. Some guy on the other end said to hurry. That you were in the town hall and it was on fire."

"What!" Genie cried.

"So I ran in. The flames, the smoke. I couldn't . . . I couldn't get to ya."

"Oh dear . . . !" Horror filled her, and along with it a strange jubilation that her soldier had come home from war only to rush without thought into a burning building.

Ollie stole another kiss. There was desperation in him. Relief and joy mixed with something else altogether.

"Ollie—" Imogene tried to speak, but he kissed her again. This time her lips moved in response, and she returned it. It was heady. Surreal.

It was Oliver Schneider.

"Ollie—"

"Don't." Ollie pulled back, lifting his burned hand and brushing his knuckles down her cheek. "Don't say nothin'. It won't happen again, but I just—" his breath came out in a great sigh—"I just couldn't stand the thought of losin' ya, when it was the thought of havin' ya that brought me back."

"What?"

Ollie's chest heaved as he took in a deep breath of air to make up for what he'd released. He stepped back from her and glanced down at his burned hand. "Yeah. Okay. It's stingin' now."

"You need butter," Imogene said, but her voice was weak as their eyes remained locked together.

Ollie nodded. "Yeah. Butter."

"My mother has butter."

"So does mine," he responded.

"Okay," Imogene nodded.

"Yeah." Ollie spun on his heel and hurried away, leaving her in the middle of an empty park, staring after his retreating form and wondering where on earth this side of Oliver Schneider had been hiding all these years.

Chapter 31

It was arson. Plain and simple, Chet said. Just like the post office had been a homemade bomb. Imogene eyed her brother across the dinner table as Mother served up a roast with potatoes and carrots. Chet half lived at the police station when he wasn't at his tiny apartment. It wasn't unusual for him to join them for a home-cooked meal. Mother said she'd invited Ivan to stay after field work and have his wife join them for dinner, but Ivan had turned them down. Typical. He avoided them, avoided socializing, and as a result, Imogene hardly knew her sister-in-law.

"Does anyone have a reason for burning down the hall?" Daddy shoveled a forkful of roast into his mouth as Mother poured him a glass of milk.

Chet snatched a dinner roll from the basket in front of him. "All sorts of possible reasons. Someone doesn't like the government? Doesn't like our community? They're public buildings, so maybe they just don't like people."

"That's very nonspecific," Imogene said, reaching for her water glass.

Chet eyed her. They hadn't spoken much in the last week. His mouth tightened. "Yeah, well, I do what I can."

Imogene gave him a look that told him she didn't believe

that. Chet narrowed his eyes at her, and then they both looked away from each other.

Mother sat down and laid a napkin over her lap. "Myrtle Simmons said she heard on the party line that someone called Oliver Schneider and told him *you* were in the building, Genie!"

Mother seemed remarkably calm about it, but then she'd probably heard of it after Imogene had already returned home from work, completely unscathed.

"Myrtle needs to stop listening in on other people's conversations." Daddy prodded the air with his fork.

"Ollie stopped by the station to let me know that." Chet lifted his eyes to Imogene. "Any reason why someone would want to send Ollie charging into a burning building you weren't even close to?"

"Of course not!" Imogene fingered her fork.

Chet frowned. "Well, twice in one week isn't putting me at ease. Someone hits you with their vehicle and you don't recognize it or the driver? Now this?"

"Is there some conspiracy goin' on around Mill Creek?" Daddy inserted.

Chet shrugged. "I dunno. If there is and anyone in my department knows of it, it's above my pay grade."

"Can we—not talk about this?" Mother's voice shook, and the three of them looked at the matron of the family. Mother's face had whitened, and she held her hands in her lap. "I just—I can barely get by each day as it is. I can't speak of losing another daughter. I hardly got through the last few years with my boys overseas. Every day I waited for that knock on the door with the telegram. You finally made it home and then . . ." She suddenly stood, her chair legs scraping on the floor. She balled up her napkin and threw it on the table. "Excuse me."

Mother hurried from the dining room.

Chet set his fork down, clanging it against his plate.

Imogene couldn't ignore the same ache that throbbed inside her.

Daddy wadded up his napkin, wiping it across his mouth. He threw it on his plate, the material sopping up gravy. "Goin' to have to sell this farm." He cursed. "Your mama's goin' to lose it pretty soon. She won't even go up to the attic."

He left the kitchen, following after his wife.

Chet and Imogene sat in silence.

Chet cleared his throat.

Imogene patted the comb in her hair in an absent, preoccupied gesture.

"Dad's right," Chet finally said.

"Sell the farm?" Imogene echoed her father.

Chet gave her a poignant look. "Well, sure. Mother's goin' crazy livin' here every day with Hazel's room upstairs. Didn't help we had people clean it up. You can still see—her blood is still on the wallpaper, Genie. Has anyone even gone upstairs since the place was cleaned up?"

Imogene nodded her head. "I have." She'd considered moving into it. To be closer to Hazel, wrapped in the faint, lingering scent of her. Unlike Mother, Imogene wanted to cling to Hazel's tangibility and see what remained of her. Mother saw only the violence. But that violence was imprinted in Imogene's mind anyway, whether she was in the room or not. Still, it hadn't been practical to relocate her entire bedroom there, so instead she'd allowed herself evenings sitting cross-legged on the floor by the window, staring at the stains and trying to remember— remember anything that would tell her who had killed her sister.

"Only you, though." Chet grabbed his fork and took a bite of roast. He seemed to be the only one in the mood to eat. "That room is goin' to haunt us all till the day we get rid of this place. Just like we sold the land to the plant. Start over. Move into town. Move away. Heck, there's not much left of our family anyway."

"Yes, there is," Imogene argued. But it was weak. Even to her own ears.

"You think so?" Chet challenged. "'Cause with Ivan taken a jump off the deep end, and Hazel gettin' killed, and me not able to do a dang thing about it . . . seems the only one holding Mother and Dad together is you, Genie." He swallowed his roast and gave her a dark stare. "And at the rate you're going, you'll be dead before the month's out. Unless I can find whoever wants to hurt you, same as I need to find out whoever is targeting the public buildings."

It was coarse. Tactless. But true.

Imogene released a shuddering sigh and tried to catch her brother's eye. He wouldn't look at her. "I'm not going to die, Chet. I'm just going to help you figure out what's going on."

"Don't, Genie."

"I promised Hazel I would."

Chet dropped his fork and leaned forward on the table, skewering her with his green eyes. "Hazel is *dead*, Genie. She's dead. Leave her there and walk away before we have to bury you too."

—⁂—

"He's right, you know. You're dead." Imogene finished dabbing the last puddles of blood-red paint on the floor of the miniature attic bedroom.

But you're not letting me go. Hazel argued back in Imogene's mind.

She sniffed, the air pungent with the tang of old straw and the lingering scent of cow manure that always tinged the air. Imogene put the paintbrush in a Mason jar of water and watched the red swirl in the clear liquid, staining it, claiming it, marring it. She picked up the doll she'd chosen to imitate Hazel.

This was where it became the most difficult. The most suffocating and bitter.

"I'll never let you go," Imogene whispered into the air as she positioned the doll in its pretty shirtdress facedown in the expanse of blood that Imogene had painted on the floor. Her breath caught, and she bit the inside of her cheek—hard—tasting her own blood while arranging Hazel's limbs into the position she'd lain when Imogene first found her.

"Hazel?" Imogene reached the top stair of the attic. Her hand braced against the doorframe as she peeked into the bedroom. Foreboding choked her. She could feel her throat constricting with premonition.

Hazel didn't answer.

The room was empty, darkening as dusk settled over the farm. Time stalled for a moment while Imogene scanned the bedroom. Dresser, bed, chair, table and radio, a desk, an easel in the corner with a canvas of the farm Hazel had painted last year. The flowered wallpaper—

And then it all came true. The agonizing scream that tore from her and left her throat sore for hours later as her gaze realized it wasn't all flowers on the wall. It was splatters of red. A foot on the floor peeked out from the end of the bed.

Imogene's knees gave out, and she crawled across the floor toward the feet. Bare feet in nylon stockings stained on the bottoms as though they'd stepped in their own blood.

She shrieked Hazel's name. Repeatedly as she sat back on her knees, rocking back and forth. Hazel's body lay facedown. The back of her hair was matted with the evidence of violence. It was smeared on the floor, and a footprint—Hazel's—had left its mark just before it was dragged across the wood floor like a paintbrush across a canvas, ending where Hazel fell.

Imogene relived the moment as she dragged a tiny brush from the blood splatter to the bottom of the doll's foot. Her hand was shaking viciously, and Imogene gripped her wrist with her right hand while her left lifted the brush to begin transposing red paint to the back of the doll's head.

Why are you doing this? Hazel's voice begged Imogene for an answer. Imogene knew only she could hear it. It was in her head—in her very soul—Hazel's voice.

"Because." Imogene let a drop of paint run down the back of the doll's neck. "I need to remember."

But why?

"Because I need to know who did this."

Why am I not wearing shoes?

Imogene's paintbrush stilled above the doll. "I-I don't know." She furrowed her brow in consideration. Hazel was right. She always wore shoes. Especially when cooking, because of the time when she was ten and dropped a can of Spam on her big toe. So where were her shoes? They were simple black oxfords with a short heel. Hazel owned only one pair of oxfords and then a pair of sling-back heels for dressier wear. Shoes had been rationed the last few years during the war.

She dropped the paintbrush into the jar of water and wiped her hands on her apron. Shoes. Why would shoes be important? And an unidentifiable sketch from the nightstand? Imogene hadn't a clue why, but the minute details of the scene seemed to shout at her. Begging for her to put the pieces together to form the story of what had happened that dreadful day.

Hurrying from the barn, Imogene skirted a farm cat that was flipping a dead mouse into the air, toying with it. She shuddered. She'd never paid attention to the little omens of death before, the ones that hung around a farm. Cats and mice, the occasional death of a cow, the deer carcass when the boys hunted for venison in the autumn and winter months. It was all part of country life. But now it was too much a part of life.

She pushed the screen door open, its hinges squeaking as it swung out, and then its frame slamming as it closed behind her. Mother was in the kitchen. Imogene could hear her as she peeled potatoes. The *swish-swish* of the peeler as it stripped the spud of its skin.

"Mother?" Imogene burst into the room, taking in the domestic scene of the family matron bent over a porcelain-coated metal pan. Skins from the potato stuck to the inside. Her hand gripped the red handle of the long peeler and moved deftly and with experience.

The Saturday midday light shone through the window with the frilly white eyelet valance bordering its top. Mother's shin-length cotton dress, practical stockings, and kitchen apron were neatly in place as always. Her own pair of oxford shoes were scuffed but well-cared for.

"Where are Hazel's shoes?" Imogene blurted out, not waiting for Mother to greet her or to lift her head and acknowledge Imogene's flustered kitchen entry.

The peeler flipped from Mother's hand and landed in the pan with a clank. Mother's hands gripped the counter, and she steadied herself as she jerked in surprise. "Hazel's shoes?" She gave Imogene a startled look. There was a distant expression in her eyes that unnerved Imogene. Like Mother had been far away in her mind, and Imogene's question was a rude jerk back into the present.

"Yes. She had two pairs."

"I know she did." Mother reached to fish the peeler from the bowl.

"Where are they?" Imogene pressed.

Mother held the peeler aloft as she twisted toward Imogene, her eyes wide and pleading. "I don't know. In her room?"

Please don't talk of Hazel.

Imogene knew immediately it was what Mother really wanted to say. Still, she had to ask. "Which—which shoes did she wear when we buried her?"

Mother reached for a potato, her hand visibly shaking. "Her sling-backs."

Guilt stung Imogene, and to make up for the agony she'd just put Mother through, she drew close and pressed a kiss against Mother's cheek. "Thank you."

Mother nodded but didn't answer. Her peeler took a decisive swipe, and a strip of peeling flipped into the bowl.

Imogene exited the kitchen and hurried up the stairs, passed the second-floor bedrooms, and without giving herself time to pause—time to reconsider—she darted up the next set of stairs to the attic bedroom. At the top of the landing, she ignored the room to the right where they stored boxes of unused items. Turning the knob, Imogene flung open Hazel's bedroom door.

The air had already turned stale from lack of use. A faint smell of cleaning chemicals reminded Imogene that people had come to remove as much of the evidence as they could of what had happened. The floor was clean. Bleach had discolored the wood. The bed had been stripped, the spread folded neatly after having been washed, now lying across the foot of the bare mattress.

All of Hazel's personal items were still where she'd left them.

Imogene hurried to the dresser, pulling out the drawers. She rummaged through them. Underclothes, stockings, ribbons, and a few slips. She knelt on the floor and looked under the bureau. Hazel had often kicked her shoes off and accidentally sent them deeper beneath the furniture than she'd intended.

Nothing.

Imogene moved to stand when a strip of white on the bottom of the dresser caught her eye. She reached for it, tugging until the small piece of torn paper would release.

Hazel's handwriting caught her attention immediately. A tiny cursive on one side of the scrap.

Propellant.

A knot formed in Imogene's stomach. It was a word often bandied about at the plant. The smokeless powder propellants. Ammunitions.

But why would Hazel care? She worked in the laundry where she cleaned the coveralls the workers wore when working with the nitric acid used to create the propellant. Imogene fingered the piece of paper. Ollie worked at the plant, except he was in the administration building. She wasn't sure what he did there, but it wasn't working on any of the lines. Sam worked on the C-Line, where they took the nitrocotton and formed it into pellets of the smokeless propellant.

She flipped the scrap over, and a different handwriting met her. It was narrow and thin, reminding her of Daddy's chicken scratchings.

Waddall Farm
Grayson Field
Pickett Farm
Jakowski Farm
And beneath these, three more locations.
Post Office—pellets
Town Hall—cotton
Courthouse—??

The shock of what she read wrapped itself around Imogene, catching her breath. The paper dropped from her limp fingers, floating back and forth until it landed on her lap.

Hazel had hidden a plan to destroy public buildings. Imogene ached to believe that Hazel had maybe stolen this and tried to hide it away to thwart the plan. But a nagging sense of truth gripped her as she reread the words *Grayson Field*. Hazel had somehow personalized it all. And it seemed, for some reason, it had become personal in return.

CHAPTER 32

Aggie

She'd slept for twelve hours. On awakening, Aggie made a frantic grab for her phone. Two missed calls. One from Mrs. Donahue, one from the police station. She made fast work of checking her voicemail. Mrs. Donahue's reassurance that nothing had changed, and that a handsome young man named Collin had come to "keep vigil" didn't necessarily bring Aggie much relief. The next voicemail was in response to the inquiry she'd made earlier regarding finding and accessing the cold case file on Hazel Grayson.

Maybe they still had it.

The evidence would need to be searched for in storage.

No, a civilian would not be able to attain access to the evidence.

The case would need to be reopened and a detective assigned to it.

Please let them know if there were new developments such as witnesses or evidence that might influence reopening a seventy-year-old case.

Aggie deleted the message and tossed her phone on the bed. Well, that was that. New witnesses? She let out a wry laugh that echoed in her otherwise empty bedroom. Outside of Mumsie, potential witnesses were more than likely deceased.

She slipped out of bed and jammed her feet into a pair of slippers. She needed a hot shower, some coffee, and then she'd head over to the hospital to relieve Collin, who had promised her he'd stay all night with Mumsie. But she was antsy now. She needed to see Mumsie. To touch her hand and push her hair back from her forehead, feeling the warmth of her skin and reassuring herself that Mumsie was still alive.

Aggie grabbed a few things and headed toward the bath. She paused outside of the room with the dollhouse. A vague recollection nagged at her. Honestly, it was something she'd seen on a TV crime drama once. She veered off course from the shower and reentered the room, beelining for the dollhouse.

The rookie detective on the case in the drama had been so focused on the forensic evidence from the crime scene itself, he'd ended up getting shown up by a fellow detective who cracked the case when he took a broader view and found evidence in a completely different room.

Aggie positioned herself in front of the dollhouse, only this time she ignored the gruesome, re-created crime scene and studied the other rooms in the dollhouse instead. If Mumsie had created this after the murder, then her intent was to add detail from the day of the crime. Had she focused only on the room where Hazel had been killed, or had she . . . ?

Her fingers snapped in exclamation, and Aggie pointed to the model kitchen as though someone stood beside her.

"There you are," she muttered. She leaned closer, studying the room. At one point, it looked to have been carefully arranged to replicate the actual Grayson farmhouse kitchen. A tiny hand-sewn eyelet valance over the kitchen window was only one of the minute details. But what wasn't customary were the objects in the room that seemed to imitate a photograph. The instant a picture had been snapped to freeze time and capture exactly what the room looked like in a precise moment.

A miniature mixing bowl sat on the counter.

On the kitchen table was a delicate teacup. Someone had been sipping tea, it appeared. Aggie's eyes roved from the kitchen into the hallway. She noticed the lineup of black-and-white photographs on the wall. Sketches really, created by the dollhouse's designer, but drawn beautifully to show the actual photographs that had hung in the farmhouse. Aggie narrowed her eyes. There were eight picture frames. Five had people posing from different eras. Older ancestors, she assumed, and impossible to make out the specifics in their minuscule features. Three of the photographs were landscapes. One of the farm, one of a valley, and the other a rather depressing sketch of field grasses around gravestones. Not a typical picture someone would wish to hang on the wall.

Aggie fumbled for the magnifying glass Mumsie kept on the table by the dollhouse. She held it up to the imitation photograph. The markers on the graves were sketched in pencil or maybe charcoal, and the artist had taken the time to etch in pinpoint letters, the names that must have been on the actual stones.

Billy

Tom

Aggie lowered the magnifying glass. Children maybe? Siblings of Mumsie? She'd heard of graves being significant enough to capture in a photograph or sketch. Specifically if they were children. She couldn't put a finger on why it felt important, but it did. Not to mention, that photograph was the only one out of the eight tilted and hanging at an extreme angle to the others.

"Why?" Aggie tapped the picture frame glued to the dollhouse wall. "Why would Mumsie deliberately hang this out of sorts to the others?"

It must have been out of sorts the day of the murder.

Aggie set the magnifying glass on the table and shook her head to clear her mind. She was grasping at straws for sure. Giving importance to things that more than likely had none.

Walking from the room, Aggie started the shower and made quick work of hopping in. She poured cherry-scented shampoo into her hand and worked it through her hair. Yet she couldn't stop picturing the stalled baking scene, the tilted picture, the gravestones.

Gravestones!

Aggie stilled as the hot water beat against her head, sending streams of soap down her neck and body. If "Billy" and "Tom" *were* Grayson gravestones, then there *was* a family graveyard. Somewhere outside of the Mill Creek Cemetery. Outside of Fifteen Puzzle Row. But for some reason, only Hazel was buried there. The rest of the Grayson family—Chet, Mumsie's other brother Ivan, even John Hayward, Mumsie's husband and Mom's father—they were all missing. She'd not even found evidence in the logs she'd half organized that any Grayson or relative thereof existed in the Mill Creek Cemetery.

She quickly rinsed her hair and shut off the water. Stepping out of the shower, Aggie wrapped a towel around her body and met her eyes in the reflection of the mirror. The librarian's mention of a cemetery at the old powder plant acreage raced through her memory. It was the only other one she'd heard of in the area.

"An old family cemetery on government land?" Aggie asked her reflection. It felt key not only as to why Hazel was buried in Fifteen Puzzle Row, but also why Hazel had died in the first place.

—⟊—

"Of course, dear!" Mrs. Donahue patted Aggie's arm. Jane stood sentinel next to her, with Mrs. Prentiss balancing three to-go cups of hot tea in a cardboard carrier. "We're thrilled you called."

Aggie glanced at Mumsie, who still rested in the hospital

bed. She'd seemed a tad more responsive today. Her fingers had moved and at one point squeezed Aggie's hand. The doctor indicated it was a good sign that Mumsie didn't have paralysis. At least on that side. She still hadn't awakened, and her awareness seemed nonexistent. Aggie was going to go stir-crazy sitting in the hospital. Now that she'd had a twenty-four-hour fix of reassuring herself Mumsie was still very much alive, she was aching to find out more about the gravestones. Added to that, Collin had sent her a text message saying exhumation of the mystery grave was starting this afternoon. Part of her wanted to be there for that as well.

"I'm so appreciative the three of you are willing to stay with Mumsie." Aggie gave the elderly ladies a smile.

"Nonsense." Mrs. Prentiss waved her off. "You can't leave her here all alone."

"Well, she could," Jane interrupted pragmatically. "It's not as though we're adding to her physical well-being by being here."

"We are to Aggie's, though. She can rest in good conscience while she goes out and brings home the bacon." Mrs. Donahue gave Aggie a reassuring smile.

"I don't think you're supposed to say that," Mrs. Prentiss frowned.

"What? Bring home the bacon?" Mrs. Donahue cocked her head and looked sideways at her friend.

"It's offensive to animal rights activists and vegetarians," Jane inserted.

Aggie bit her lip. The women were entertaining of their own right.

"Now, doesn't that beat all!" Mrs. Donahue clapped her hand over her mouth. "I'm sorry." She shot Aggie an apologetic look. "I just never know what I can say anymore these days."

"It's okay," Aggie reassured. "I'm not a vegetarian, so no offense taken. And I haven't taken a membership with my local animal rights organization."

"Your what?" Confused, Mrs. Prentiss furrowed her brow.

"That's wonderful!" Mrs. Donahue heaved a sigh of relief. Jane rolled her eyes.

Aggie began gathering her purse and phone and a few other items when the thought crossed her mind. She hesitated, then decided to go for it. "Do any of you know anything about the cemetery on the old powder plant property?"

Mrs. Donahue shook her head.

Mrs. Prentiss was busy removing the cups from the carrier and setting them on the hospital table by the bed.

Jane nodded. "A little."

"Could you share it with me?" Aggie asked.

"Of course! I was ten, I think—ohhh, maybe five or six—doesn't matter. I was a young thing when the government erected the plant." Jane tapped her chin with her finger. "I believe the government tended the cemetery, but after the plant was bull-dozed several years ago, the cemetery was made available to the remaining relatives."

"Do you know who's buried there?" Aggie inquired.

Jane shook her head. "Not specifically—Graysons, I think. I'll be in one soon enough. No need to go exploring there before my time."

"You'll be buried in Mill Creek Cemetery." Mrs. Prentiss handed Jane her tea. "Not that old one out at the plant."

"Very true." Jane nodded, taking the tea.

"I remember, when I was in my twenties, there was a big to-do made by the Grayson family," Mrs. Donahue mused aloud.

"Mumsie's family?"

"Mm-hmm. Of course, Imogene wasn't here then. She'd moved out of the area. It was later when she moved back. But her brother, Ivan, pitched a fit like none I've ever seen after their parents died. Died within days of each other, like two souls who couldn't stand to be apart."

"Oh, how romantic!" Mrs. Prentiss clapped her hand to her heart.

Aggie tossed her a glance but kept her attention riveted on Mrs. Donahue. "Ivan would have been my great-uncle. What did he pitch a fit about?"

"Well, he wasn't a nice man, and I vaguely recall it had something to do with wanting to bury his parents at the old cemetery by the ammunition plant. I don't know why. I think—he had a sister at Mill Creek Cemetery, so I'm not sure why his parents were too good to be buried there." Mrs. Donahue took a sip of tea.

Jane's small sigh of exasperation puffed out her round, powdery cheeks. "Well, of course anyone would want to be buried with family. If the Grayson family plots were on the plant property, they couldn't have buried Hazel there when she died, because the plant was in full production. The government wouldn't allow it."

"Oh. Well, to be sure then." Mrs. Donahue nodded.

"So, Uncle Ivan somehow obtained permission to bury Mumsie's parents in the old family cemetery on government property?" Aggie ventured.

Mrs. Donahue nodded. "I think so? It's amazing I even remember that much."

"They probably didn't want to be buried next to Hazel anyway," Mrs. Prentiss said. "I remember my mother saying Hazel died and was a bit of a town pariah. Everyone tried to ignore the fact she'd existed."

Aggie drew back, dropping her car keys on the table next to the tea and sinking onto the edge of the bed by Mumsie's legs. "Mumsie never said anything about that."

"Oh, she wouldn't!" Jane said quickly. "Her life has been devoted to honoring her sister."

"Then—why was Hazel a pariah?"

Mrs. Donahue coughed and drank her tea, making a pretense of looking out the hospital window. Mrs. Prentiss busied herself with breaking down the cardboard cup carrier so she could stuff it into the room's recycling bin.

Jane looked between the two, narrowed her eyes, and then patted the side of her head as though she needed to remember clearly. She met Aggie's eyes. "Rumor had it that Hazel helped with the destruction of the post office and the town hall. One was an explosion, the other a fire."

Aggie recalled the newspaper articles she'd read at the library. "But—she was already dead? How could she have helped?"

Jane clicked her tongue. "No one knows. That's why it's just a rumor. They say Hazel got mixed up in some snafu against the United States and got killed for it."

"Oh!" Mrs. Donahue protested, casting a corrective look at Jane. "No, no. She wasn't involved in *espionage*!"

"I never said she was!" Jane snapped.

"That's so exaggerated!" Mrs. Prentiss tapped her finger on her teacup. "It sounds like a spy novel. Next you'll say she fell in love with a Nazi and they planned to rally the strong German population of our town and create a new society!"

"Careful." Jane's voice lowered. "Also not politically correct."

"Oh, for heaven's sake." Mrs. Prentiss rolled her eyes at Jane and leveled a frank look at Aggie, who was about ready to shout at all of them to stop bantering in circles and speak only the facts.

"The fact is," Mrs. Prentiss began to Aggie's relief, "it was a local skirmish. They caught whoever it was. End of story. Whether Hazel was involved or not was simply part of town gossip. Nothing more."

The hospital room was quiet for a moment, and then Mrs. Donahue cleared her throat. When she spoke, her voice sounded a bit wobbly, as though weepy at some distant memory. "My mother told me that when the boys came home from the war, people thought the world would go back to the way it was before. But it didn't. The war lived on in souls for years after, and people were just never really the same again."

CHAPTER 33

I t appears female." Collin's voice through the phone brought an odd thrill to Aggie. She really needed to get past this flip-of-the-stomach thing whenever he was around.

"The body?" Aggie adjusted her grip on her phone as she made her way across the hospital parking lot.

"Skeleton, actually."

"Ah, wonderful." She tried to sound flippantly interested, but Aggie was more than happy now to *not* be at the mystery grave's exhumation.

"It's going to be a beast to determine the individual's age. For that matter, how long she's been dead. Although, on my initial assessment, she appears to have wisdom teeth, so that would put her age to be eighteen or more at time of death. And the fact it's strictly skeletal remains tells me it's more than likely been many years. Still, decomp and time deceased are wonky things to try to calculate."

Aggie opened her car door, tossing her bag onto the passenger seat. "How will you find out?"

"I'll complete my initial assessment here in a bit, but they'll take the remains to a lab for an assortment of lovely tests in order to make more accurate determinations. Will you hop down to see her before she goes?"

Aggie choked, coughed, then slipped into the driver's seat, shutting the car door. "I wasn't planning on it."

"You really should! It's quite remarkable. I assure you, she's not gruesome in the slightest."

"I almost passed out at the fake skeleton in Mumsie's yard the first day I arrived in Mill Creek. How do you expect me to stay standing when I know I'm staring at a real one?"

Collin's chuckle seemed far too relaxed considering the topic of conversation. It just went to show how familiar he was with his field of work. "Very well then. I shall do my work here on my own and *text* you my theories."

She didn't miss the inflection on the word *text*. At least he was a fast learner and knew her preferred form of communication. Aggie didn't want to be guilty of abusing too much time off from the cemetery, but today seemed like a marvelous day to avoid work.

"If Mr. Richardson is there, will you tell him that I plan to return tomorrow? I have a few errands I need to run today for—um—Mumsie." She faltered. It was a tiny white lie. Mumsie hadn't exactly *asked* her to visit the old cemetery and check out the graves there. But if Hazel was somehow the black sheep of the family, Mumsie's devotion to her memory told Aggie that Mumsie didn't believe the accusations against Hazel were real. It was as though, by having a stroke, Mumsie had dropped her mantle of dedication to finding proof, and Aggie had inadvertently picked it up and could now not set it down.

"Certainly, I can do that." Collin paused. "Are you all right, Love?"

His question was straightforward and really shouldn't have mattered much to Aggie, but somehow it did. She blinked furiously as her eyes filled. "I-I'm fine."

"You're such a horrific liar, Agnes."

"No, really, I'm fine."

"And I'm the king of England. Very well, do what you will. If you need, drop me a line, eh?"

Drop him a line? Aggie had the sudden desire to race over to the cemetery—skeletal remains or not—and hide her face in his chest, breathe in that old spicy aroma, and feel the crisp cotton of his perfectly ironed shirt.

"Okay." It was all she had to offer in response.

"And, Love?"

He really needed to stop calling her that! "Yes?"

"A wise man once said, 'When you walk a lonely road, take hold of the hand of a friend when it is offered to you.'"

That belonged on a calendar. Aggie smiled a resigned smile into the phone. "And who was the wise man?"

Collin's voice held a bit of humor laced with a large measure of intent. "Me."

Aggie wasn't sure what to say to that. Friendship was a great thing and all, but sometimes it was offered and then withdrawn when the going got tough. And something deep inside told Aggie that she had yet to experience the *tough*. If Collin was anything like the typical male of her experience, he wouldn't have enough stamina to stick with her.

"Sometimes walking alone is safer," Aggie responded at last, turning the key to fire up her car's engine.

"Self-preserving, yes. But satisfying? Hardly." Collin's words pierced her. Made her wish for a moment that she could really believe him. Truly believe that, somehow, God reached down from heaven and plopped someone next to you to be His hands and feet in your life, and that they would carry you when you couldn't walk on your own.

Aggie rested her hand on the steering wheel, even though she had yet to put the car into reverse and back out of the parking spot. "How do you know that God is truly real, and if He is real, that He cares?" The question came out of nowhere, surprising even her. "It doesn't seem evident He's all that concerned with sparing us from pain."

Collin was quiet. Aggie pulled the phone away from her

ear and glanced at the screen to check whether the connection had been cut. She heard his voice and raised the phone again so she could listen.

"People make the mistake of thinking if God were real, we'd live in some sort of Utopia. But we won't, not when we're human and have the nasty habit of making awful errors. Not to mention, God did sort of create a Utopia—the Garden of Eden—but that's another topic for another day. All I can say right now is that we sell God short when we look at the pain. Instead, we should focus on what He's provided us to help us heal."

"Magic juice?" Aggie quipped.

Collin chuckled. "No, Love. His medicine comes in various forms, although I've found the best is simply being in the company of those willing to fight for you. One person can easily be overpowered, but two? They can defend themselves. Add a third, and it's a very difficult combination to break."

"I'm not sure what you want me to do with that explanation." Aggie had to be honest. Religion, faith, *God*—none of these were new concepts to her. They just weren't practiced.

Collin answered with a softness that wrapped around her soul. "Just call me if you need to. It's really quite simple."

Aggie ended the call, setting her phone on the seat beside her. She gripped the wheel and stared through the windshield at the hospital that rose in front of her. Mumsie's room window was on the fourth floor, sixth window in. She fixated on it.

Just that simple.

One of these days, she knew she was going to break. That the dam that held back the tears since the day she'd heard the last breath slip from her mom's lips would collapse. The very idea that she could move beyond Mom's death—experience *life* without Mom—that was what kept her from healing, from taking comfort and strength from others. It was a betrayal. A betrayal to Mom and everything they'd experienced together. Their closeness, the intimacy of mother and daughter, the way

Mom could read her soul by just looking into her eyes—how could Aggie move on and close that chapter of her life? It was better to leave it a raw, gaping wound. At least then, Mom was still with her, even if Aggie's spirit was slowly dying its own death at the hand of a tenacious grief. At least then, Aggie didn't close the door and walk away, leaving Mom behind.

Mumsie's window reflected a beam from the afternoon sunlight. For a moment, it blinded Aggie, then blinked away as a cloud dimmed the reflection. Aggie chewed the inside of her bottom lip and nodded. It was the same for Mumsie—it must be the same. All these years, she'd kept Hazel alive, kept her breathing and vibrant by not closing the door.

Aggie wondered if part of why it'd been seventy-plus years since Hazel's death remained unsolved was not only because it was a murder case gone cold, but because if Mumsie did find the answers, then Hazel would really be dead. Her story would truly be over. Her grave would be final.

"We're too much alike, you and I," Aggie whispered up at Mumsie's window. She could see it now. Two peas in a pod. One old, one young. Both festering in the raw agony of grief. And it terrified Aggie. It terrified her to know that bloody rawness would still be as painful seventy years from now.

Unless she somehow found a way to say goodbye.

—⁂—

Aggie stopped for a bottle of water at a gas station and filled up her car's tank. Her drive to the old cemetery didn't take long, and as she came over the top of a steep hill bordered by woods, she was impressed by the broad expanse of fields in the valley beyond. Cornfields made up part of it, but there were also large sections of acreage of yellow grass, along with spacious patches of gravel and dirt where buildings had once stood. Her car curved down the road, entering the pass, and she noted one white, two-story rectangular building on the left side of the road. Slowing, she read the sign posted to a chain-link fence that bordered approximately three acres.

Mill Creek Ammunition Plant
Museum and Records Office

Good place as any to start. Aggie pulled in and parked. She made quick work of exiting her car and walking the few steps to the front door. A bronze plaque was mounted to the right of the door.

Power Plant Main Office, 1942–1999

Aggie pulled open the door and stepped inside. Displays were scattered about the room. Black-and-white pictures, memorabilia behind glass cases, and bookshelves with binders and books.

"Can I help you?" The voice came from a small office just off the back. A young woman wove her way through the displays. Her blue jeans were torn at the knee, and she wore a pink T-shirt emblazoned with the logo of the Ammunition Plant Museum. Aggie guessed she was maybe in her mid-twenties.

"Yes, I was looking to speak to someone about accessing the old cemetery on the ammunition plant's property." Aggie hoped she didn't have to go through some strange political red tape to gain access to the private property.

"Oh!" The woman smiled and extended her hand. Her red hair curled in a frizzy ponytail, and her blue eyes sparkled. "Hey, that's awesome! We don't get very many people interested in this place anymore. It's sorta dying a slow death."

Bad choice of words. Aggie hid her wince.

"I'm Terra, by the way. I work here part-time. We have private supporters who fund the museum."

"Cool," Aggie nodded, but she really wasn't concerned with how Terra was paid.

"So what interests you about the cemetery?" Terra leaned against a display of old bullets and grenades.

Aggie figured there was no reason to hide her purpose. "I'm

Imogene Hayward's granddaughter. She was a Grayson during the war, and I guess they owned some of the property the
plant was built on. I was going to venture a guess that it has a
cemetery on it?"

"Sure!" Terra nodded, her ponytail bobbing. "Yep. So, the
acreage the cemetery is on was purchased quite a while ago by a
private company that granted burial rights back to the Grayson
family. Super generous of them, I'd say, to let the family have
their cemetery. There was quite an uproar when the government
moved in and bought the property from the farmers."

"But they bought it," Aggie countered. "That has to count
for something."

Terra gave her a look that indicated she was understanding
but not sympathetic toward the government. "Sure. Underpriced
value, and the farmers didn't have a choice. So really it was
shut-up money."

"Oh." Aggie didn't know if Terra was a natural-born activist
or just an accurate historian. She'd no desire to start debating
the implications of government need versus personal need. War
was messy. Period.

"Anyway! Yeah. You can see the cemetery. It's not too far
from here. There's a road back in, and the owners have made
it public access. Really, no one cares to go back there anymore.
The last burial there was . . . oh, maybe twenty or so years ago?"

Aggie was anxious to visit it. To see if Mumsie's husband—
her grandfather—was there. To see the other names too. To
miraculously find something that would trigger more clues,
more information to piece together to make Hazel's death finally make sense.

"Want me to go with you?" Terra offered.

Why not? Aggie shrugged and nodded. The chatty tour guide
might be helpful.

After a short few minutes of driving down a gravel road,
the old cemetery opened in front of them. There was nothing

marvelous about it at all. An iron fence bordered it, with fifteen or twenty stones inside.

"The government agreed to care for it when they bought the land from the Graysons back in the forties," Terra explained as she hopped out of Aggie's car. She slammed the door and starting hiking for the entrance. "And to their credit, they did. Around the time of the Vietnam War, they hired a blacksmith to forge the fence you see here now, funded by the maintenance budget and some private donations."

Aggie studied the fence. It was simple in its design, the iron-work evidently hand-forged, textured from the hammer as it had tapered the ends into gentle scrolls. Her eyes skimmed the stones, reading what she could of the etchings and noticing a lot of them were weatherworn. All in all, it was a peaceful cemetery, unassuming in its elegance, understated in its years.

"Now," Terra said as she reached for the latch, flipped it, and swung open the waist-high gate, "the current owners pay homage to the dead and have someone come by every week or two as needed to mow and weed-whack the place."

Immediately, Aggie's eyes landed on a pair of headstones, the names inscribed on them grabbing her attention.

Billy Grayson

Tom Grayson

So they *had* been children, as was evident by the dates showing they'd both died as babies.

Ivan Grayson

Chet Grayson

Mumsie's brothers, if she recalled correctly. There were a few other graves too, older ones, in the same area. Then Mumsie's parents. Some cousins perhaps? Ivan's and Chet's children?

"There's no headstone for John Hayward." Aggie frowned, noting the absence of her grandfather's grave.

"Who's he?" Terra asked with a curious cock of her head.

"My grandfather. He was married to Imogene Grayson, who

is the sister to Ivan there"—Aggie pointed to his headstone—
"and Chet, and also their sister Hazel, who's buried in Mill
Creek Cemetery."

"Ohhhhh!" Terra's brows rose. "Interesting! Yeah, I don't
know anything about a John Hayward. That's weird. Was he
living in Mill Creek when he died?"

Aggie strained to remember the details of family history
Mom had shared with her over the years. Her grandfather had
died when Mom was a toddler. According to the Three Stooges
back at the hospital, Mumsie wasn't living in Mill Creek when
her parents passed. Aggie glanced at their stones again, com-
puting dates and circumstances in her mind. So that meant . . .

"No. I guess they didn't live here when my grandfather
passed."

Terra smiled. "Got it. So, most likely he's buried wherever
they lived at the time."

California. The answer supplied itself in Aggie's head. She
recalled Mom telling her that she was born in California, and
Mumsie had stayed there with her until her early teens. They'd
moved back to Mill Creek when Mumsie's brother Ivan took
sick, and never left after that.

Aggie wished there was more here. She wasn't sure what.
Her grandfather's grave would be nice, but now that she was
level-headed enough to put two and two together, it made sense
it wasn't here.

"What do you know about Hazel Grayson?" Aggie asked
the young historian. "I've been told she didn't have the great-
est reputation."

Terra pursed her lips, and her gaze swept over the small
cemetery. "I know more about the plant than I do any of that.
But I did learn about the post-office explosion and town-hall
fire back in the forties, 'cause the authorities thought someone
had probably smuggled supplies from the plant to make the
homemade bomb and start the fire."

"Did they ever prove that?"

Terra nodded. "Oh, sure. I mean, they locked someone away for it."

"Who?" Aggie asked.

Terra shrugged. "Like I said, I'm not as familiar with that story. Just how it related to the plant here. But . . ." Her words dwindled as she caught sight of something. "Well, that's weird." She took a few steps forward, craning her neck, her eyes fixed on something.

"What is it?" Aggie looked in the direction of the cemetery that Terra was walking toward, but from her angle she didn't see anything other than a row of basic gravestones.

"This." Terra squatted in front of a gravestone a few rows away, toward the far east side of the small piece of property. She lifted something from the base of the stone.

A wilted rose.

Something shifted in Aggie. She skipped around the headstones and hurried to Terra's side. She snatched the rose from her, and Terra gave her a startled look. Thumbing through the petals of the pink flower, Aggie looked for black ink. For the words *It's not over.*

"Nothing's written on it," she mumbled. A wilted rose petal broke off and fell to the yellow grass at their feet.

"Written on it?" Terra drew back. "On a flower?"

Aggie shook her head in dismissal. She didn't want to answer Terra's question. It wouldn't make sense. But the fact a pink rose had found its way to the old family cemetery could not be happenstance. Someone—*someone*—was as intent on Hazel's seventy-year-old murder as she was. As Mumsie had been.

"There is some writing," Terra offered.

Aggie's head snapped up. She leveled Terra with one of Mumsie's infamous green-eyed stares. "Where? What?"

Terra motioned to her. "On the back of this gravestone. I've seen it before. It's curious because most people put epitaphs on the front, but this one was chiseled on the back."

Aggie moved around the stone to stand beside Terra, who pushed her hands into the pockets of her jeans. Terra gave a redheaded nod toward the stone. "See? A strange epitaph too."

She didn't deserve death. He didn't deserve life.

It matched the note left at Mumsie's. The note with the fragments of pig bone. Meant to terrify them, or creep them out, or what? Stop them from trying to figure out Hazel's murder?

"Whose grave is this?" In her rush to the rose and then to see the epitaph Terra pointed out, Aggie hadn't paused to read the name of the soul laid to rest there.

Terra spoke it as Aggie rounded the stone again to read the name. "Samuel E. Pickett."

"Pickett? I'm not familiar with that family name at all." Aggie couldn't figure it. Nothing fit. What was someone with a non-family name doing buried in the Grayson cemetery? She eyed the date of death. "He died in 2014."

"Not too terribly long ago." Terra's words acknowledged Aggie's observation.

Aggie studied her. "Do you know how or why he was buried here, if he wasn't a Grayson?"

Terra shrugged and sucked in a thoughtful breath, narrowing her eyes in thought. "The only thing I can think of is a Grayson would have given permission. They were probably approached by the corporation that owns the property after someone put in a request to bury the body here."

"That's the process then—to be buried in this cemetery?" Aggie still held the rose, though several of its petals had fallen off now and rested in a pattern on the ground, not unlike the pattern a flower girl might have left for a bride.

Terra nodded. "It's not complicated. The owners don't have any interest in the cemetery, but they also have no intentions of having more plots provided than what the allotted acreage allows. So, they look for proof of relation to the Grayson family."

"But my grandmother is the only living Grayson." Besides herself, of course.

"Then she would've been the one the owners contacted," Terra replied.

"I need to talk to the owners." Aggie waited, expecting Terra to provide the name.

Terra gave her an apologetic wince. "Yeahhhh, well. Good luck. They moved their main offices to New York, and now it's a heck of a job to get ahold of anyone."

"New York?" Aggie wanted to bang her head against a wall. "Well then, how do I get their attention? I need to find out who requested to bury Samuel Pickett in the Grayson cemetery. What do I need to do?"

Terra blinked, and her response was innocently frank, but ran a chill down Aggie's spine. "They might respond faster if you needed to bury someone here." She gave a little laugh, not realizing the impact of her words. "I guess the quickest way to get their attention is to die."

CHAPTER 34

Imogene

She couldn't get to Chet fast enough. Hazel's list of names, of explosives . . . it was horrific. Somehow Hazel had gotten mixed up in something bigger than herself. It had to be that! There was no way Imogene would believe Hazel had somehow masterminded such a hateful act of revenge.

Imogene wanted to call Chet—it'd be quicker—but of course, someone would be listening in, and knowing Imogene had called the police station, the news would be all over Mill Creek before she even had a chance to get to town.

She was wary of walking. The distance didn't bother her, but the last time she'd walked alone—well, if someone was targeting her, she didn't mean to make it easy for them. Imogene had hesitated for a long moment before lifting the handset and asking the operator to dial the Schneider farm. She'd asked for Ollie. He'd answered. Now she sat beside him in his truck as they bounced down the rough road to town.

Imogene glanced at him from the corner of her eye. She hadn't talked to him since the town hall burned down two days ago. Hadn't let herself think about his kiss. His *kisses*.

Holy Joe, she didn't even know *what* to think about it, other than she wanted to kiss him again. Her heart was all aflutter, and this was the worst time to suddenly want to go out dancing with Oliver Schneider. To cast him coy looks and little *come hither* winks that would make Mother blush and then lecture Imogene until kingdom come. Fact of the matter was . . . she'd changed. Imogene realized her *not* wanting to go out dancing and flirting with Ollie seemed disrespectful to the man somehow.

She looked down at Hazel's note gripped in her hand. No. She just wanted this all to be over so she could go on a simple country stroll with him. Maybe have him steal another kiss. Think about a quiet life—on a farm? Sure. Why not? She'd even lost her stomach for style and fame and Hollywood. Hazel's death had turned her solemn, and now she'd pay just about anything to have back the normal life they all thought they could have when the boys came home from the war.

"You're awfully quiet." Imogene tried to break the silence between them.

Ollie's arm rested on the open window of his truck. Wind ruffled his hair, pushing it off his forehead, making his chiseled features more pronounced. He shot her a quick glance.

"I'm just glad you saw fit to call. No reason you should be walkin' alone right now."

"No. Of course not." Imogene bit her bottom lip. She eyed the bandage on his hand. "Is your burn awful bad?"

Ollie gave it a tiny wave. "Nah. It's nothin'."

Nothing compared to what? Imogene jerked her attention to the view of Mill Creek coming closer on the horizon. Compared to his buddies getting blown to bits? She'd heard the stories. Whispers of them from some of the boys willing to talk. Boys like Sam Pickett, whose charismatic personalities lent toward bragging—bragging up their bravery. She couldn't blame him for it. Sam had put himself on the line just like

Ollie, just like Chet and Ivan. Heck, they had all put themselves on the line, so whatever they had to do to cope with it, she was fine with that.

"Listen," Ollie began, his throat bobbing as he swallowed hard.

Imogene's hand shot out and grasped his wrist above his burned palm. She held it lightly. He looked at her, searching her eyes, then shifted his attention back to the road ahead.

"Don't, Ollie." She didn't want him to apologize. She didn't want to figure out what they were feeling, or thinking, or even needed from each other right now. "Leave it be. It's okay."

"You sure?" There was resignation in his voice, also a tiny thread of hope. Future hope. As though he hadn't potentially ruined things between them.

"I'm sure." Imogene squeezed his wrist before releasing it. "We can talk, but another time." She didn't know when that would be. *How* it would be.

They entered Mill Creek. She noted the white Baptist church steeple rising over the rooftop of the police station. Funny how faith cast a shadow over the wickedness represented by the need for law enforcement. No one in her family was outspoken about God, but they'd always been churchgoing people. Good people.

"You suppose God knows what's going on in Mill Creek today?" she ventured.

A wan smile touched Ollie's mouth. "He knows. Just don't know if He's gonna do anything about it."

Imogene nodded. There it was. He said what they were thinking. What many were thinking before, during, and after the war. The economic crash, the droughts, the struggles not to lose farms, the war, boys getting killed, and now Hazel and all this other stuff at the post office and town hall? It was one catastrophe after another. Every now and then Lola said something about the "end days being close." End days or not, Imogene hoped God had some sort of plan. 'Cause right now He'd done a sore job of making anything make sense.

———ᴍ———

"What's a looker like you doin' walking alone?" Sam Pickett jogged across the street to meet her.

Imogene couldn't hide the instant smile, even as she glanced over her shoulder for Ollie, who'd told her he'd catch up to her at the station, but first he needed to stop at the drugstore for his mama.

"I'm not alone," she tossed back coyly. "I'm with Ollie Schneider." Something in her enjoyed saying that maybe a little too much. Gone were the days when she didn't want to *belong* to anyone. Now there was some security in leading even Sam to believe she and Ollie might be an item. Not that she needed protection from Sam—regardless of what anyone said.

Sam's jaw muscle twitched, but his eyes remained smiling, or glassy, Imogene wasn't sure. He seemed a little too happy—on the tail end of tipsy maybe. He made an exaggerated display of looking around them as he kept up pace beside Imogene. "Well, that's a gas! I don't see Ollie anywhere."

Imogene laughed a little, rolling her eyes as she stepped away from him. A little distance from the handsome man was wise if he'd spent the night with a bottle. "He's meeting me at the police station."

There was a small hitch in Sam's gait, but then Imogene noticed his toe had caught a lip on the seam of the sidewalk.

"Goin' to see your brother?"

"Mm-hmm." Imogene didn't mention Hazel's note that she'd tucked safely away in her clutch.

"Any news about your sister?"

Now it was Imogene's turn to trip. Sam's grip on her elbow steadied. She pulled away. "Um, no."

Sam appeared genuinely empathetic. There was a recognition

of grief in his eyes. He was no stranger to loss himself. "I keep hopin' they'll find who did it."

Imogene went cold inside. The kind of cold that made it possible to carry on without Hazel. "What do you care anyway? You weren't even her friend. Ida was." She heard the snap in her voice. The lack of social tact and etiquette, and darn it, she didn't care.

Sam halted, and Imogene faced him. His eyes were deep with hurt, and a pang of regret speared her heart. She *should* care. It wasn't fair to transpose her agony onto Sam. Not when he carried his own, in his own way. They all needed to cope. Booze for one, a Bible for another. But what did she have?

"I'm sorry," she mumbled. Half meaning it, half not.

Sam's finger trailed briefly down the side of her cheek. Just a brush, a swift touch. "I get it. I get mad too. Losin' a loved one ain't ever easy."

"No, it's not." Imogene glanced at the station door a few yards away. Hazel's note was burning a hole in her purse. "I-I need to go see my brother."

"Sure." Sam took a step back, shoving his hands in the pockets of his trousers. "Hazel was a good gal, you know. Always hummin' and wearing pink roses on just about every dress she owned. Sorta like the paintings she loved to paint. Always a streak of pink in 'em somewhere."

Imogene stilled. "You noticed that?"

Sam blinked and squeezed the bridge of his nose as though he were relieving a headache. He gave her a quick smile. "Of course. She was as pretty as her sister."

Imogene stared at him quizzically. It was the first time Sam had said anything personal about Hazel. "I didn't think you knew Hazel all that well."

Sam shrugged, his expression dull. "She was Ida's friend."

"But"—Imogene frowned—"you knew that Hazel loved to paint?" It wasn't that it was a secret hobby, but Hazel didn't announce that she dabbled in artistry, let alone show anyone she barely knew one of her paintings.

Sam blinked and shrugged again. "She never made it a secret."

But she had. That side of Hazel was on the easel in her bedroom, hidden in the stall of the barn, framed in an unaccounted-for frame with a landscape Imogene was hard-pressed to recall.

"I see," Imogene nodded. She wasn't sure what to say. Wasn't sure how to process the fact that Sam Pickett knew one of the more intimate details of Hazel's life. She offered Sam a shaky smile. It didn't sit well. Especially with the Pickett name on the list of farmers who'd lost their property to the powder plant.

—ɯ—

"Who've you shown this to?" Chet's expression was grave. Imogene could tell he was calculating it all in his head. The list of properties, Hazel's handwritten word *propellant* . . . plus the recent attacks on local government property and Hazel's death, and it was all adding up to an obvious conclusion. Except for why Hazel had died—and who had killed her.

"No one," Imogene assured him. "Well, Ollie."

Chet didn't seem bothered by that. "Have you talked to anyone on this list since you've taken the job at the plant?"

Imogene hoisted herself onto Chet's desk next to his chair. He gave her a half scowl for perching on his desk, but he was too focused on this latest piece of evidence she'd hand-delivered to him to rebuke her about it.

"The Picketts, obviously. Ida and Sam. I know I've chatted with some of the others. Several of them have kin who work at the plant or took jobs there themselves."

Chet ran his index finger down the list of names. He clicked his tongue. "Picketts were mighty upset when they had to sell their land, and I wouldn't put something like this past one of them. But, honestly, it was Mr. Jakowski who made the biggest stink."

Imogene crossed her ankles and pointed at the Jakowski name on the paper. "I think their son works in the A.O.P. building."

Chet looked up at her from his seat in his wooden chair on rollers. "Remind me what that is again?"

"It's where they work with the ammonia. I think he helps unload the ammonia off the train when it arrives."

"You ever talk to him?" Chet asked.

Imogene maintained her casual air, but her insides were churning. If she'd inadvertently talked to someone who'd had intentions of sabotaging the town . . . The thought made her sick to her stomach. Not to mention, a fierce rage rose in her when she thought of Hazel. The kind of rage that made her wonder if she were ever face-to-face with the man who'd taken Hazel's last breath, would she be able to refrain from breaking one of the most specific commandments? *Thou shalt not murder.* Turnabout was fair play, after all.

"Genie?" Chet's question snapped her attention back to him.

"What? Oh. I don't know. I'm sure I have talked to him. I talk to all sorts of the boys—and women—who work there. I mean, they have to eat."

Chet nodded. "But nothing that stands out?"

"No." Imogene's frustration increased. She uncrossed, then recrossed her ankles and, shifting on the desktop, rustled papers beneath her hips. "Daddy's name is on that list." She ventured it, the suspicion. The nagging taunt that somehow this could be far closer to home than any of them realized. She tried to gauge Chet's reaction. Not his defense of Daddy so much as whether he showed any sign of guilt himself.

Chet reared back in his chair, green eyes widening until she saw the flecks of yellow in them. "That's more than a bum rap you're puttin' on our father, Genie!"

Imogene leaned over the desk, bracing her body on her right palm with fingers splayed across his desk mat. She leveled eyes with her brother. "Or Ivan, then."

"Genie!" Chet's explosion caused him to glance around the station. It was mostly empty this afternoon, but a secretary toward the front raised her head for a moment before returning to her typewriter. Chet leaned forward, his elbows on the desk. Imogene could smell tobacco on his breath from his last cigarette, and maybe a hint of mint from chewing gum.

"If you want to play the game that one of ours is behind all this, then you're—" He stopped.

Imogene noted the hesitation in his eyes. "See?" She sat upright. "See? It's not all plain as day, is it? It's as ugly as a bug's ear, but the fact is you can't tell me Ivan—or Daddy—doesn't have their own grudge against the U.S. government."

Chet cocked his head to the left. "But Hazel . . ." He snatched up the paper and wagged it in Imogene's face. "*She* was the Grayson messed up in all this. *She* was the one who got herself killed. There's no way on God's green earth you could convince me that Daddy or Ivan did that."

"You couldn't convince me that Hazel was involved either, but there it is in black and white! Besides, Ivan's changed, Chet." Imogene brought her voice down a bit and glanced over her shoulder at the secretary, then back at her brother. "He's not the same since he got home."

Chet's eyes darkened. "Genie, *none* of us are. Now, I've gotta talk to the captain about this note. This, along with the last two incidents to government buildings, is goin' to get this taken out of my hands faster than you can spit out a riddle. The government isn't going to play around with this. I think they've already got someone from the military goin' to investigate at the plant. This is a national issue of security, Genie, not just some small-town scrape."

Imogene hadn't considered that. She hadn't thought about

the fact that it potentially involved the powder plant where the government was making supplies for the war effort.

"Things are tense right now." Chet set Hazel's paper back down on the desk. "I don't know what Hazel got herself mixed up in, but it wasn't good."

"But the war is over . . ." Imogene knew that it didn't matter. For many, the war would never end—not really—and all for very different reasons. Some grief, some anger, some just lost and wandering.

Chet pushed back in his chair and stood. He looked down at her, and for a moment a softness touched his face. The kind of brotherly affection Imogene missed from Chet—from Ivan even. "I know none of us were behind this, Genie."

"That's conjecture," she argued back, using her brother's own law enforcement logic.

Chet ran his hand over his head and blew out a puff of air. "Doggone it, do you *want* it to be one of us?"

"No!" Imogene quailed at the very idea, but she wanted to feel safe too. She didn't want to look over her shoulder when she was working on Hazel's dollhouse for fear Ivan was going to come in and strike her from behind. She didn't want to doubt Chet's honesty when he protested too much against one of her theories. She wanted their names cleared without a doubt—and not just because she was loyal to family.

Chet nodded and reached for his cap. "There's nothing that says a Grayson is behind this. Ivan was in the fields with Daddy when the post office blew up, and he was with the veterinary working on that old sow's cut leg when the town hall caught fire."

Imogene couldn't help but release a breath of relief. Chet noticed it and gave her a grim smile, but one filled with disapproval that she'd doubt their brother.

"'Sides, it was a field, just a field that we sold."

"And Mother's cemetery." Imogene winged a brow upward.

Chet nodded. "Yeah. What? You think *Mother* did all this?"

No. Imogene shook her head. No. Mother wouldn't know how to build a bomb. Heck, Mother didn't even know how to hold a grudge, truth be told. She was just a silent, stoic warrior through her pain of losing babies, and loved ones, and now Hazel.

"Then the Picketts." Imogene redirected the attention away from her family. Chet had made his point, and she was satisfied—relieved.

Chet braced his hands at his waist and stared at her. "Like I said, I wouldn't put it past them. But which one? You know Sam and Ida, but there're cousins too, and I thought they had an aunt or something. She may have a vested interest, especially if she shared any of the ownership."

Imogene struggled to see through her cloud of suspicion. "I was with Ida on the bus when the town hall went up in smoke, and Sam was with me when the post office blew up."

Chet frowned. "He was?"

"Well, yes. Right after anyway. He and Ollie took me home, remember?"

"Huh." Chet scratched beneath his nose. "Doesn't mean they're cleared. I'll check it out, and the Jakowskis and this other family. Hazel saw some connection there somehow. It can't be coincidence all of us on that list lost land for the plant to be built."

"And you think someone wants the government to pay for it?"

Chet opened his mouth and then snapped it shut. "I think you should go home and help Mother with supper. You've done what you needed to do. You found this paper and got it to me. Hazel would be proud of you. Now stay out of the rest, Genie."

She slid from the desk and laid her hand on her brother's elbow, giving him a slight nod. He was right after all. This was getting deeper—bigger—than she'd imagined. She had helped Hazel, though she still needed to figure out why Hazel's oxfords were missing and what that missing sketch in the bedside frame had been of. They had to be clues. They *had* to be.

"I'll go home, Chet." It was the least she could do. He had assuaged her worst fear. The fear that Ivan was behind it all, or even Chet himself. But no. Their family was clean. That was the way it was supposed to be.

"Genie?" Chet reached out and gripped her wrist lightly.

She turned, question in her eyes.

Her brother hesitated, tightened his lips, then gave a small click of his tongue in resignation against whatever internal battle he was fighting. "Hazel—she'd be proud of you wantin' to figure out what happened to her."

Imogene blinked back tears that immediately sprung to her eyes.

Chet gave her a nudge and a shaky laugh. "She'd tell ya you were half a stick of butter short of a recipe too."

"I'm not losing my mind." Imogene's own laugh in return was equally as wobbly.

Chet's smile was sad. "Get home, Genie, and stay outta trouble."

She tossed him a flippant wave and a wink over her shoulder as she walked toward the door. "It's what I do best!"

CHAPTER 35

It was supposed to have been a quick exit from the station. Imogene left the building and looked up and down the street for Ollie. Maybe he'd stopped at the drugstore or got caught up chatting with someone when he parked the truck.

Whatever the reason, Ollie hadn't been there. Someone else had, and now his hand was hot over her mouth. Imogene could taste the sweat of his palm, feel the calluses against her tender lips, and worst of all, hear the roaring rush of pain in her ears. The back of her head throbbed, and she was being dragged across the floor of an empty warehouse room. The cement floor scraped against Imogene's heels as she half tripped, half walked backward, her head trapped between his hand and his chest.

"Why can't you just stay outta trouble?" His words were eerily reminiscent of Chet's last warning.

Imogene wasn't surprised, not really, when Sam Pickett appeared out of nowhere by her on the sidewalk. But his offer of a soda at the drugstore had been a distraction, and she'd hoped she'd spot Ollie on the way. Sam strolled beside her for a few blocks. Then he'd diverted into an alley. A cat, he'd said. He'd seen a cat drag itself behind the stack of old crates leaning against the wall of the building. Looked injured, he'd said.

All Imogene could think of was her brother Ivan taking a foot to their barn cat and sending it careening across the building. Her sympathies went up. Her guard went down.

It was the last thing she remembered.

She tried to talk now, but her voice only muffled against Sam's hand.

"Quiet." His word was a plea. Not harsh, but rather desperate. "Please, be quiet."

Imogene hadn't a clue where they were, until she heard familiar sounds. A train. Steam. She smelled the acrid scent of the plant. This must be one of the storage buildings. How Sam had gotten her here, she'd no clue. Would probably never know.

Sam dragged her behind large wooden boxes and released her with a light shove. She fell to the floor, her dress coming up around her hips, revealing the cuff of her stocking and the clips of her garters. Imogene palmed the cold floor as she scooted backward on her behind, away from Sam. Her back hit the solid wall of boxes.

"I'm going to scream." She didn't even know why she warned him. But she did, and then her scream followed.

Sam launched himself on the floor next to her, slamming his hand so hard against her mouth that Imogene felt her teeth bite into her inside upper lip. Her already pounding head rammed into the wood crate behind her. Dazed, Imogene stilled for a moment, her eyes searching out Sam's.

His were disturbed. Panicked. He was afraid.

"Shut up, Imogene. Please." Sam's fingers dug into the flesh just below her cheekbone. His charming grin was replaced by nervousness. "I need you to be quiet. Let me think."

Imogene nodded, her eyes wide. Anything. She'd zip her lips like a priest hearing a confession if it meant he'd lighten his grip on her mouth. She could taste blood.

Sam lowered his hand. He stared into her eyes for a second

before collapsing beside her, his own back against the crates. He tilted his head back toward the warehouse ceiling, his chest heaving in a sigh that emphasized his anxious energy.

"Why'dya have to go nosin' around like that, Imogene? First day you came to the plant, I tried to warn you to back off. I could see it in your eyes. But you ignored my note." His whisper was half plea, half anger.

"That was you who bumped into me!" Imogene reached to tug her dress down from her hips. The back of her head ached from where he'd clubbed her. She shifted her feet, catching sight of her shoes. Sensible pumps. Not unlike Hazel's missing ones. "Did you kill her?" Imogene hissed, accusation seething from her eyes.

Sam pulled back as if she'd struck him. "Heck no! Never. I would—*never*." There was enough vehemence in his voice that any other time, Imogene would have believed him.

He raked his hand through his dark hair, strands sliding between his fingers. "Gahhhhh!" His growl was fierce. He banged the back of his head against the boxes behind them.

"You need to let me go, Sam." Imogene edged an inch away from the man. Ida's brother had shifted dramatically from the charming, grief-stricken widower, who seemed to try to hide behind flirtation, to a troubled, agonized man that angered Imogene, but also—for some twisted, unexplainable reason—tugged at her empathy. It was like the man was trapped. Cornered. Fighting his way out of a battle he couldn't win.

"I-I can't let you outta here." Sam shook his head. "Not now."

"Why are you doing this?" Imogene pressed. "What did I do to deserve this?"

"Nothing. And neither did Hazel—but she's dead too." Sam leaned his head against the boxes again and this time closed his eyes. "I loved her so."

The declaration struck Imogene like a fist to the side of her face. She lurched away from him, staring in disbelief.

Sam held both palms to the sides of his head, his eyes still squinting shut. "It all got so messed up." He groaned.

Imogene shifted, positioning her feet beneath her. She was going to run. She had to. Or else her fate wouldn't be unlike Hazel's, and she had no intention of dying today. But questions raced through her. Sam loved Hazel? Then if he had, why had he killed her—unless his denial was true?

"You blew up the post office, didn't you?" Imogene distracted him from Hazel.

Sam opened his eyes and studied her face but didn't seem to notice she was perched on the flats of her feet, knees bent to spring upward.

"Didn't you?" Imogene pressed.

Sam laughed then. A sobbing, defeated type of laugh. "You learn all sorts of stuff when you fight in a war. Dumb thing is, you'd think you'd learn to love what you're fighting for. Like your own country."

"Are you—are you a—?"

"A Nazi?" Sam's eyes went wide. He curled his lip in derision of the thought. "Those beasts deserve what they got. Now and in the afterlife."

"But you blew up the post office. And the arson? You set the town hall on fire too, didn't you? You could have," she realized. "Your shift ended before Ida's and mine, before we got back to town."

Sam sniffed, rubbing his fingers in a violent sweep back and forth beneath his nose. He leaned toward her, his eyes narrowing. "I came home like all the boys. Slack happy the war was over. We'd fought for a cause, and dang it, we'd won."

"And that was swell of you," Imogene assured him. Maybe if she was nice, maybe if she used honey and sugar instead of sour . . .

"My aunt didn't write to me and let me know they took the farm." Sam rolled his lips together, then sucked in a breath between clenched teeth. "I came home to a dead wife and no farm. Nothin'!" He gave his arm an exaggerated wave, indicating the building surrounding them. "This here warehouse was built right where my barn stood. That tree outside the administration building?"

Imogene nodded. It was all she could do.

Sam gave a short laugh. "I planted that tree when I was a kid. Planted it right outside my mama's bedroom window. I was a mama's boy, see? And I thought if I put a tree there, she'd never forget me. Well, the tree's still there. House ain't, though. Guess it wasn't even good enough for an office. The *United States government* had to tear it down."

Imogene swallowed hard. She wanted to argue with him. Wanted to ask what choice had the government? On someone's property an ammunitions supply plant needed to be erected. The soldiers needed weaponry. Weaponry needed firepower. But she dared not argue with Sam. He didn't *seem* like a killer, but then that was probably why Hazel had trusted him and let him inside the house.

She sensed the color drain from her face. Good heavens above, Hazel had taken Sam to her *bedroom*.

"What were you doing in Hazel's bedroom?" She'd accused him, still balancing on her feet.

Sam looked to the ceiling and gave another brief laugh. "You'll never believe me anyway."

Imogene tilted her head to study him. "Why do you say that?"

Sam met her gaze. "'Cause you've already decided I killed her. Well, I didn't. I loved your sister. She saw something in me. In this broken shell of a man who came home to nothing."

"You came home to a son," Imogene argued.

Sam's expression darkened. "I came home to nothing. Leastways, that's what I thought. Hazel, she was all flowers and dreams. Perfume and imagination. She was shy and yet she could tell it like it was."

Yes. That was Hazel. Imogene's eyes teared.

Sam continued. "I didn't mean to love her." He sounded apologetic. "I didn't mean to involve her in this. She was someone I could talk to. She knew what it was like—having the land taken. Hazel told me about your little brothers your mama buried here, Billy and Tom. Some of your other relatives too. Heck of a thing to lose your family graves, and for a pittance. The government thinkin' they can offer money to relocate us? You can't relocate memories. They stick to the place they were born in."

Sam was right. Imogene realized it was partly why she was drawn time and again to Hazel's dollhouse. To the scene she'd re-created there. Every nuance she could remember in the vivid details of her mind. It was the most startling memory of all her memories. One she would carry with her until death, no matter what happened to their farm decades from now.

"Hazel would never have condoned your damaging public property like that. Endangering lives? She never would have gone along with it." Imogene couldn't help the protest that squeezed from her. She couldn't believe that of Hazel. Couldn't believe Hazel—*good* Hazel—would be sucked into a homemade vendetta of hate. Especially after the war. Especially after seeing what violence did to families.

Sam tipped his head back once more, closing his eyes as if to watch some scene play out in his mind. "You're right," he muttered. "She didn't go along with it. It's why she's dead."

"She was going to rat you out, wasn't she?" Imogene hissed. "You killed her for it."

Sam didn't open his eyes. Didn't shift his expression. Didn't even bother to move when Imogene stood, accidentally hitting a wooden crate with her elbow.

"You just go on believin' what you want. If you think I killed her, then fine. Doesn't matter anymore anyway."

Imogene stared down at him. Sam's entire body sagged in

resignation. Maybe even in relief? She couldn't tell. But she only had two options now. Run, or kill the man who sat on the floor beside her. Kill him with her own two hands and become no better than he was. Exacting deeds out of vengeance and demand for restitution. But no amount of bloodshed, no amount of gasping as she strangled the breath out of him would satisfy her. Hazel was dead. Sam's death wouldn't bring her back.

Nothing would bring her back.

CHAPTER 36

ello?" The front door of Mumsie's house was open. Aggie entered, glancing around. The late afternoon was cloudy, the leaves rustling in the autumn breeze. "Rebecca?" she called out. There wasn't any reason for Mumsie's caregiver to be at the house, yet she was the only other person with a key.

"Hello?" Aggie took a hesitant step toward the kitchen.

"Aggie?"

"Ahhh!" Aggie startled at the voice behind her, spinning, clutching at her throat—as if that would do something miraculous in an emergency—and leveled eyes on the caregiver. "Rebecca!" she gasped. "You scared the living daylights out of me!"

The younger woman winced. "I'm sorry. I left my book here from the other day and I wanted to retrieve it. I didn't want to call you since I figured you were at the hospital with Mrs. Hayward."

It made sense. Silly, but it made sense.

Rebecca dug in the front pocket of her hoodie sweatshirt.

"This was at the door when I arrived. I was just heading to put it on the kitchen table for you."

Aggie eyed Rebecca as she reached for the envelope, then opened it. She glanced down and came just short of launching it across the room. "Call the police," Aggie said. She heard the graveness in her voice. Felt the sensation of urgency, mixed with the necessity not to panic, flood her body.

"What is it?" Rebecca's eyes went wide.

"I said, call the police." Aggie spun away from the caregiver once she saw Rebecca fumbling for her phone. She hurried into the kitchen and placed the envelope on the table.

More bone fragments.

No note this time.

Just—

Her phone trilled. Aggie jumped, squelching a squeal, and answered it.

Collin's voice sounded harried and urgent. "You need to come straightaway."

"Where?" Aggie clutched the phone tighter, glancing at the envelope with bone fragments as if it were going to fly away.

"The cemetery, Love. I need you to come straightaway."

"I-I can't. I . . ." This was surreal. She didn't even know what to say.

"There's something here you need to see." Collin wasn't giving up.

Neither was she. "Collin, there's something here *you* should see."

"Bone fragments," they both said in unison.

"What?" Again in unison.

Aggie waved her hand to shut Collin up, even though he couldn't see her. "No, no, *I* have bone fragments here. At Mumsie's. In an envelope."

"Same, Love. Left on the desk in the office. Left there *while* we were at the grave we exhumed."

"I've called the police," Aggie announced.

"I have them here." Collin had bested her. "I'm guessing by the looks of it, it's probably pig—just as before. But I've no clue what you're holding there. Oh. The detective says not to touch it."

Aggie nodded. It was why she'd set it on the table. It'd been tampered with enough as it was.

"They've dispatched a unit," Rebecca said from the doorway, looking about as worried as Aggie had to assume her own face showed.

"Collin, the police are on their way."

"Fine. Finish there, but then you still need to come. There's—more."

"More?" Aggie frowned. "What do you mean 'more'?"

Hesitation. Then, "Just come as soon as you can."

———

"I came as soon as I could." Aggie arrived breathless, which made little sense since she'd driven. Still, it felt like she'd run a marathon.

Collin looked up from the desk in the cemetery office. Dusk was settling. The police had left Mumsie's home with the bone fragments after interviewing herself and Rebecca. It appeared they'd left the cemetery as well.

"You'll want to sit down for this." Collin's ever-present twinkle was gone from his eyes. The depressions in his cheeks were shallow, not deep from the impact of his smile.

Aggie plopped onto a nearby chair, ignoring the hardness of its plain wooden frame. "What is it?"

Collin turned back to the desk and slipped on cotton gloves. He reached for something, turned back to her, and extended his hand.

A ring lay in the middle of his palm. A gold band. No jewels. No diamonds. Aggie knew instantly that it was meant to be a man's ring. It was dirty, almost tarnished, as if it'd been dug up from some hole in the . . .

Aggie blanched. "Please tell me you did *not* take that off the skeleton."

Collin shook his head. "On the contrary. I uncovered it in the grave. Underneath where the body had been disposed of."

She raised a brow, eyeing the ring with suspicion. "And why do I need to see it?"

Collin paused, then lifted the ring between his index finger and thumb, holding it out for Aggie to see. "The inscription, Love."

Aggie leaned forward, squinting to read the finely etched lines on the inside of the ring.

Forever Yours

Aggie locked eyes with Collin.

He tipped his head. "One more word."

One more word? Aggie looked back at the ring.

Hazel

The quietness that stretched between them felt thick.

Finally, Collin cleared his throat and dropped the ring back onto his gloved palm. "There were few remnants left in the grave. The decomposition indicates it's been several decades, if not longer, that the body was left there."

"I-I don't understand. Did you dig up—did you dig up *Hazel?*" Aggie couldn't help that her sentence ended in a slight screech.

"No. No, I don't believe we did. There is very little chance that someone would place a marker over the wrong grave. Not to mention, we can confidently assume Hazel was properly buried in a coffin. This woman was not."

Aggie drew in a shuddering breath. She had no words as Collin twisted in his chair and set the dirty ring on a piece of clean cotton. He reached for something else and turned back.

"I found this too. It appears to be part of a shoe heel, perhaps one the woman was wearing when buried."

"A shoe heel?" Aggie pushed out from her tight throat.

"Yes. From what I can tell . . ." He let his sentence hang as he swiveled back to the desk and deposited the piece of shoe heel there. He hit a key on his laptop's keyboard, bringing up a software program with pictures of shoe heels. "It appears to be from what women called an oxford."

"Like a short-heeled loafer?"

"Exactly." Collin clicked on a photograph. "If so, the style dates the shoe to the forties, maybe fifties."

"Around when Hazel died?"

"Likely, yes." Collin scratched the back of his neck, arching it to examine the heel on its cloth. "There's no manufacturer imprint. It's possible they were handmade. Still, the style—"

"The style looks like some shoes I have in my own closet!" Aggie interrupted. For some reason, Collin's line of thinking irritated her. "You can't say that body was from the forties because a bit of a shoe heel has somehow evaded the merits of time and earth to imply a date."

"Actually, Love"—Collin spun on his chair to face her—"I can. Of course, I'll have the remnants tested in a laboratory, but this is where common sense may be used to build a case. A ring from Hazel—"

"Assuming it's our Hazel," Aggie cut in.

Collin gave a short nod. "Very well. A potential ring that Hazel gave to someone, a body, a partial shoe consistent with the style and making of a 1940s cobbler, and the pieces fit. Somehow this body was dumped just plots away from Hazel Grayson, with *her* ring."

"It's a man's ring, though," Aggie protested.

"Did your grandmother's sister have a lover?"

Collin's question was simple and, in this day and age, shouldn't have been shocking. Even so, Aggie felt a blush creep up her neck. She looked away. "I highly doubt it."

"Why? It isn't farfetched. We should find out."

"But you said the skeletal remains were that of a woman?" Aggie frowned. "Why was a man's ring buried with an unknown woman's body?"

Collin nodded. "I didn't say this wasn't still a monster of a mystery."

Aggie rolled her eyes as her phone trilled. Stifling a growl, she dug in her jeans pocket for it. "Hello?"

"I'm just calling to check in!" Mrs. Donahue's airy voice was the last straw to Aggie's worn patience.

"If she's not dead, then don't call me!" Aggie snapped.

Collin's hand shot out to her knee to calm her down.

Mrs. Donahue cleared her throat nervously. "Oh . . . well, I—and if she's awake?"

"What?" Aggie batted Collin's hand away.

"Yes," Mrs. Donahue affirmed, "your sweet Mumsie is awake now. She's asking for you."

Aggie bolted from her chair, hanging up on the elderly woman. "It's Mumsie! She's awake." She left Collin behind, but as she slipped into the driver's seat of her car, he surprised her as he hopped in the passenger side.

"What?" He met her surprised stare. "I happen to like your grandmother. The dead woman can wait."

"Where's the ring? The shoe?" Aggie asked as she started the engine.

Collin patted the leather messenger bag he carried with him. "In here. As wonky as this day has become, I'm not leaving it behind to mysteriously disappear."

"Or to be sprinkled with the dust of bone fragments?" Aggie joked, but didn't feel any humor as she said it.

Collin's jaw was covered in reddish whiskers. His crease deepened as he tossed her a smile. "Ahh, Love, you're such a pessimist."

"I'm a realist." Aggie shifted into drive and pressed the gas pedal, pulling out of the cemetery drive. "And the realist in me says someone didn't want us to exhume that body—or find that ring and shoe."

Collin twisted his face in a grimace of agreement. "A seventy-year-old ghost perhaps?"

"I'm going to find out." Aggie's tires squealed a bit as she turned onto the main highway in a beeline for the hospital. For Mumsie. For the truth.

—⁓—

"You mustn't stress her, the doctor said so." Mrs. Prentiss was hot on Aggie's heels as she marched past the waiting area down the hospital corridor toward Mumsie's room. She didn't know when she'd grabbed Collin's hand, but she had. She was holding it, and she liked that she was holding it.

"Imogene is a bit disoriented," Jane hollered from behind Mrs. Prentiss.

"Ohhh, and she hasn't had her supper!" Mrs. Donahue added.

Aggie spun, hauling Collin around with her. She glanced at him. He looked about ready to chuckle at her intensity. She tempered herself.

"Ladies. Thank you—for your—*devoted* vigil over Mumsie. But, if it's okay with you, I'd like to see Mumsie alone."

"Oh yes!" Mrs. Donahue nodded vehemently.

"Certainly!" Jane affirmed.

"Come with me." Mrs. Prentiss slipped her aged arm through the crook of Collin's elbow, much like an old woman intent on snagging a younger man.

"Ohhhh, no." Aggie tugged on Collin's hand and gave Mrs. Prentiss a gentle but not-so-subtle *back off* raise of the brows. "He's coming with me."

"Ahh." Mrs. Donahue smiled, nodded softly. "Sweet love. Yes. Leave them be, Prentiss."

"Go, go." Jane patted Collin's arm.

Mrs. Prentiss released him with a little snort of disappointment.

Aggie rolled her eyes to herself and muttered "Sorry" to Collin from the corner of her mouth.

"Whatever for?" He grinned as they made their way at a slower pace to Mumsie's room, the three old ladies staring at them as they departed.

"Sweet love?" Aggie shook her head.

Collin tugged her hand and leaned to whisper in her ear, "You need to be more romantic. Not everything is dark crypts and murderous schemes, you know."

"Honestly!" Aggie sniffed. Then, hearing herself, she realized how remarkably like Mumsie she sounded, the bitter and the jaded included.

They entered the room, and Aggie jolted to a stop.

An older man bent over Mumsie's bed. His shoulders were stooped and thin, covered with a sweater. His hair consisted of a narrow ring around his otherwise bald head, gray mixed with white. He balanced on a cane that resembled a shepherd's staff, hook included.

The two of them were speaking in murmurs. Mumsie's voice was strained.

"Mumsie?" Aggie stepped toward the hospital bed, dropping Collin's hand.

Collin moved just a tad in front of her. "Who are you, sir?" he demanded.

The elderly man turned. His face was wrinkled, with sky-blue eyes that appeared kind but with a tinge of anxiousness to them. He looked back at Mumsie.

"I'm so sorry. I never meant . . ." the man started to say.

"It's over," Mumsie said. "Leave me at peace now." She waved toward the door. Her hand shook. A tear rolled down her face.

"But—" he protested.

Mumsie speared him with a vibrant green glare that never

faded as she aged, her eyes never losing their fervor or zeal. "You've done *more* than enough."

The elderly man staggered past Aggie, his shoulder brushing hers, leaving a whiff of tobacco and cinnamon in his wake.

Mumsie watched him leave, then shifted her attention to Aggie. She was pale. Her wrinkled skin still powder soft, but the rosy blush on her cheeks gone. Still, a determination entered her expression as she leveled her gaze on Aggie. "Come to see me rise from the dead?"

Her hint of a smile warmed Aggie's soul, even as she cast a questioning look over her shoulder to where the strange old man had fled through the door. Mumsie was back. That was what mattered right now.

CHAPTER 37

Mumsie refused to explain who the elderly man was. Aggie pressed. Collin changed the subject. Aggie glared at him. Collin winked. Mumsie dozed on and off until finally a doctor came in and recommended they let her rest. Her vitals looked good. He was pleased to see there didn't appear to be lingering damage to her brain from the stroke. The doctor insisted they go home.

Mumsie was deep asleep by the time he was finished.

Now Aggie half fell onto a kitchen chair. She grabbed her tablet from her purse and powered it up.

"Coffee?" Collin asked, but he was already making it.

Aggie did some web searches. *Samuel Pickett, Mill Creek, 1946.* It didn't take long to find information on him.

"So, *he* was the one who blew up the post office and burned down the town hall?" Aggie stared at a black-and-white image of the man. He was once a "looker," Mumsie would have said, and Aggie agreed. But it made no sense why a local terrorist had been buried in the old family cemetery, while their murdered sister was laid to rest in a cheap grave in Fifteen Puzzle Row.

Collin straddled a chair beside her. He was wearing jeans. Dark-washed, ironed jeans, but jeans nonetheless. His spicy aftershave made Aggie a bit heady in her weariness from the shocks of the day. Yet she ignored him for the moment, flicking her finger on the screen to scroll up.

"Apparently, he fought in the war, came home to find his family farm had been sold to the government for the ammunition plant to be built there, and developed a case of vigilante justice." Aggie skim-read for them both.

"And why are we suddenly interested in Samuel Pickett? Is he the gentleman from your grandmother's room tonight?"

Aggie gave him a sideways glance. "Um. No. Samuel Pickett is dead. He's buried in the Grayson family cemetery—also on old ammunition plant property."

"That's rich." Collin pointed to a link off the newspaper article. "Notice that headline?"

Aggie leaned forward, then exchanged looks with Collin. "*Man Suspect in Local Girl's Murder.*" She clicked the link. In silence they both read the article. How Samuel Pickett was also being investigated for the murder of Hazel Grayson. Aggie did a few more cursory searches but found nothing of import to conclude Samuel Pickett had ever committed the act.

"I'm a tad confused as to why the Grayson family would allow Samuel Pickett to be buried in their cemetery." Collin's face quirked as he tried to make sense of this.

Aggie blew out a breath, lifting a few strands of hair that then fell against her eye. She pushed them out of the way. "Decades later." She twisted in her chair to face Collin. "I don't understand. The girl at the Ammunition Plant Museum told me that to be buried in the Grayson cemetery you needed permission from the landowners, and the landowners verified familial connections with a living Grayson. The only one alive would be Mumsie. So why on earth would she authorize Samuel Pickett to be buried in the cemetery when he's not family and he's potentially Hazel's *killer*?"

"We're missing something." Collin unwrapped himself from

the chair and adjusted his wire-framed glasses. His hair sparkled a cinnamon-red in the dim kitchen lighting, but his eyes were intense with a determined glow. "Come." He held out his hand.

Aggie took it—because not taking it seemed like a lost opportunity—and trailed behind him as he led her up the stairs. Collin pushed open the door to Mumsie's study, but instead of entering, he stood in the doorway. Observant.

"The bed and the bedside table are positioned exactly like in the dollhouse," he said, repeating what they already knew. "The spread appears to be the same one, as indicated by the stains."

Aggie hadn't let go of his hand, and he hadn't released hers. She waited, allowing the archaeologist's mind to turn. He stepped into the room, narrowing his eyes in thought.

"In 1946, they knew far less about forensic science than we do today. So how they looked at the crime scene—how your grandmother looked at the scene—may have been shortchanged by their lack of knowledge."

Collin drew her over to the dollhouse. "What do you see?"

Aggie remembered the tilted frame of the gravestones in the Grayson cemetery. She pointed to it. "The frame—it's tilted."

Collin nodded. He stood silent, observing, his eyes sharp. He pointed. "Notice the blood in the bedroom?"

Aggie nodded.

He looked at her, waiting, as if something was supposed to click into place. But it didn't.

"What?" she asked, impatient.

"The blood is pooled around Hazel's head. She was struck on the back of the head."

"So?"

"So, why is there blood spatter on the bedspread?"

Aggie frowned, leaning in to the diorama.

Again, Collin pointed. "If a person were standing and came up behind Hazel from the bedroom door, with Hazel facing the wall, and they struck her, the blood would have projected back on them, and onto the floor by the door, probably missing the bedspread altogether."

Aggie nodded. "But it's on the wall, so the killer had to be standing between Hazel and the wall with Hazel facing the door."

"Correct." Collin drew his fingertip down to an empty space on the wallpaper. "There's a void here. The spatter is around it. Someone caught the brunt of the spatter, probably on their face and chest, blocking that portion of the wallpaper."

"But . . ." Aggie curled her lip as she thought. "How did Hazel end up lying facedown with her head *toward* the wall?"

"She was moved," Collin stated. He drew a path in the air with his finger inside the attic bedroom. "If Hazel was facing the door and her killer was behind her with the wall to the killer's back when they struck, Hazel would have fallen facedown with her head pointing toward the door. But, notice . . ." He indicated the spatter stains on the bedspread near the foot of the bed.

"Was she hit again?" Aggie didn't like the way her stomach clenched. She could almost see it happening in her imagination. A killer striking Hazel. Hazel falling, then trying to get up, another strike, this time spreading blood on the bed. Maybe Hazel turned then, or maybe the killer moved her, but she died facing her killer.

"Hazel probably tried to get up." Collin grimaced. "After the second strike, she turned herself before collapsing at the feet of her killer."

"How can you know that?" Aggie whispered. She glanced at the window and the darkness outside. Night had fallen. Talking murder—a very real murder—in the yellow light of the room's lamp was downright chilling.

"Assuming your grandmother re-created the crime scene accurately—which, given the amount of detail in this house, I have to conclude she did—there is a smear mark on the floor, but it's rather light. If Hazel had been killed facing the doorway and then dragged to face the wall—"

"Oh." Aggie realized where Collin was going with his reasoning. A large swath of blood would have traced the floor from her head wound.

"A pool of blood beneath her head suggests she collapsed, facing her killer, and bled out," Collin concluded. "And note how there's blood on the bottom of her foot. She stepped in her own blood."

Aggie covered her mouth with her hand. "Did Samuel Pickett really do that? I can't imagine . . . How could Mumsie allow him to be buried in the family cemetery?"

Collin leaned into the dollhouse. He clicked his tongue. "She's not wearing shoes."

Aggie shot him a questioning glance. "So?"

"We found the heel of a woman's shoe in the grave today."

"The woman buried there could have worn them," Aggie countered.

"True." Collin nodded. "Yet, follow my theory. Say someone killed Hazel, took her shoes, took a *ring* from Hazel, and there—see?" Collin turned to look at the life-sized table behind them. The empty picture frame.

"That frame represents this frame in the dollhouse. Except the real-to-life version here on the table is empty. The sketch that's in the dollhouse version has apparently disappeared in real life. Very curious, don't you think?"

Aggie nodded. It was starting to play in her mind like a TV crime show. "So the killer knows Hazel is dead. They take the ring, her *shoes*—according to your theory—a sketch from the bedside table. They run from the room. On their way down the stairs, they stop to tilt the cemetery picture sideways?"

Collin shrugged. "That, or they stopped to touch it. Look at it. Or perhaps tripped and bumped into it."

It was outlandish. All of it. She eyed Collin, crossing her

arms. "So, what then? The killer ran to the Mill Creek Cemetery, dug a grave, threw in Hazel's shoes and a *man's* ring—which still makes no sense—then jumped in after and buried themselves?"

The sarcasm in her voice brought Collin to a stillness that unnerved Aggie. He straightened from his anticipatory examination of the dollhouse and looked into her eyes.

"I don't know, Aggie. But it isn't a coincidence that bone fragments were delivered here *and* at the cemetery the day we exhumed the body. It isn't coincidence that I still have stitches in my head from someone quite talented with a shovel. It isn't coincidence that your grandmother gets a cryptic note stating, 'She didn't deserve death and he didn't deserve life.' None of this is *coincidence*. And while speaking the theories out loud implies a sort of insanity, isn't that what crimes are? They don't often make logical sense, unless predesigned by a psychopath. There's nothing in this scene or in any of the story to indicate calculated killing. It's all very passionate. Very intimate. Very *personal*."

Collin drew closer to her as if to convince Aggie to allow her imagination to consider things outside of the box. She was only an inch shorter than Collin, so his eyes were almost level to hers, boring into her with an intense seriousness she'd not seen in Collin. She swallowed. Nervous. Nervous by the idea of murder. Uneasy by the darkness and the mock-up murder scene. Agitated by the way her senses came alive with Collin's nearness. The determination in his voice. The magnetism of his attempts at piecing together *her* family mystery, to put to rest Mumsie's lifelong disturbance.

She stumbled back a step. "Collin," she whispered before whirling and racing from the room.

"Agnes!" he shouted after her.

She tripped down the stairs, hurrying away from him. She wasn't afraid of Collin, but she had to get away from him. He was too close. *She* was too close. And his concern over solving the puzzle of Hazel's murder and uncovering the identity of the unknown body in the cemetery was very passionate, very intimate, very personal. But it wasn't *his* story. It was *hers*. Yet he'd inserted himself into it. He'd become a part of her and Mumsie's story. He knew grief and yet had somehow moved past it. He watched her and Mumsie wallow in it, live in it, drown in it. That was why he wouldn't let up. It wasn't just his archaeological instincts for a good historical mystery. It was that he saw both her and Mumsie being slowly strangled by a grief he'd successfully fought off. He wanted to rescue them.

"Leave me alone!" Aggie shook off his hand as Collin landed at the bottom of the steps next to her. Tears burned—oh, how they burned—and she refused to release them.

Collin held his hands up, palms out. "I won't touch you, Love. Just pause for a minute."

They were in the foyer of Mumsie's house. The kitchen to her right, Mumsie's sitting room to her left, and the door—a way of escape—to her back.

"Death is *personal*." Aggie spat the words she'd heard in her head the moment Collin had finalized his theory. "Death is personal!" She slapped at his chest. She didn't know why, but she did. The anger, the loss, the agony of watching Mom slip into eternity. What did the Scriptures say? "O death, where is thy sting?" It was here! It was stabbing her in the heart, in her soul. It more than *stung*. It was agonizing.

Collin lowered his arms to his sides.

Aggie's chest heaved as she sucked in a sob. A sob that never should have surfaced. She wagged her finger in his face. "You don't understand. You don't! Just because you lost your sister— it's different. This was *murder*. Mumsie lost her sister by the hand of someone else. It's not—it's not the same as a car accident."

"What's your explanation?" Collin's question pierced her.

Aggie squinted, shoving back furious tears. "My *explanation*?"

336

"Your mum wasn't murdered. She died of cancer. One might say it was more natural than my sister's drunken accident."

"You dare to compare deaths to my mom?" Aggie glared. He was wickedly bold! Antagonistic. She detested him.

"You dared to compare Hazel's murder to my sister." His was a quiet observation.

She loathed him.

"My mom was *stolen* from me. Death stole her," Aggie hissed.

"It stole my sister too."

She despised him.

Aggie took a step toward Collin. Her eyes collided with his. A lone tear escaped and trickled down her cheek. She angrily swiped at it. "You don't have a right to be happy."

Silence.

"*I* don't have a right to be happy!" Aggie pushed Collin's chest, the cotton of his shirt soft beneath her palms.

No answer.

"I hate it." She choked, suffocated by two years' worth of tears collecting in her throat. "I hate it. I hate—I hate that Mom died." Aggie sucked in air loudly. A gasp. She stumbled back, lifting her arms as if to shield herself from someone striking at her.

Collin grasped her forearms gently. "Come here."

"I want my mom." Now she sounded like a lost little girl.

"Come." Collin tugged her toward him.

Aggie resisted. "Mumsie needs her sister. She *needed* Hazel. Why would God—why would He—?"

"Allow it?" Collin supplied, still holding her forearms.

Aggie locked eyes with him as though now, if she looked away, she would surely drown in the hidden horrors of Death's wake.

"There's no good answer for that. We can't understand the mind of God, and nothing I can say will make what happened feel any better. I can just be there for you, as I believe He is, and pray that one day you will find peace in spite of it all."

Aggie crumpled then. Her strength was sapped.

Collin hauled her to his chest, and Aggie curled her fingers into his shirtfront. She would cry tonight. She would weep for Mom, for Hazel. She would weep for Collin's sister. But most of all, she would weep for the lost memories that never took place, for the gaping holes loved ones left behind when they died, and weep for the fact that somehow—someway—God shared her pain.

CHAPTER 38

She'd run. Sam had let her. He'd lost all desire to fight, and all Imogene could hear reverberating in her mind was "I loved her." Sam had loved Hazel! Had it been reciprocated? If it had, then why had he killed her?

Imogene's feet pounded the pavement. People came into view as she raced from the all-but-abandoned warehouse toward the populated area of the ammunition plant. Sam had driven her here. She'd seen his pickup truck as she'd raced from the building.

Within minutes, people were responding to her cries for help. Hands were ushering her into a chair, then onto a stretcher to take her to the state-of-the-art medical facility the government had built for the plant workers and their families.

She heard the faint sound of sirens.

"Chet . . ." she mumbled, but the word came out hazy.

Imogene squinted at the form bent over her. A woman, her dark hair pulled back in a ribbon. Her dress was dotted with pink flowers.

"Hazel?" Imogene lifted her hand to touch her sister. For some reason, she couldn't reach her. "Hazel!"

Shhhh. Genie. It's swell, all right? I'm swell. You shush now. Let Chet take care of you.

"Hazel!" Imogene cried, trying to sit up in the stretcher. Someone pushed her down firmly.

Hazel still leaned over her, blurry and almost luminescent.

Imogene tried to reach for her again. "Hazel, he killed you!"

Shhhh. Hazel smiled sadly. *No. He didn't. I loved him, Genie. But he was wrong—we were wrong. I had to stop it before people got hurt.*

Imogene whimpered. Her head pounded. Voices echoed in the distance. Or maybe they were close. She couldn't tell. All she could see was Hazel. Hazel. Hazel.

Rest now, Genie. I am resting. You should too.

"Hazel!" Imogene screamed as the vision of her sister faded and blackness enveloped her.

Imogene stared at the dollhouse. She loathed it and needed it at the same time. She sat in a chair, hugging her sweater around her torso, just staring into the abyss of the miniature attic bedroom. At the doll's body. At the tilted picture frame she'd just remembered hadn't been straight the day of the murder. Someone had lifted it off the nail, then rehung it. She could tell because there was a smudge on the frame's glass. A red smudge. Someone with blood on their hands had held the framed cemetery photograph and stared at it, then replaced it on the wall. Imogene hadn't the courage to replicate the smear of blood. She was finished painting Hazel's blood. Instead, she would fine-tune the house, as Hazel would have. Adding the minute details of the day. It was easier to re-create a fake cup of tea than to paint more blood.

"What are you doing in here?" Chet's low voice broke the eerie silence.

He stepped in and caught sight of the dollhouse. Imogene

could tell the moment he did. There was a sharp intake of breath, followed by his hand coming down to rest on her shoulder.

"What have you done?" His whisper wasn't accusing. It had a hint of admiration but was mostly sad. Resigned.

"I promised Hazel." Imogene's voice was flat. She didn't feel anything now. She couldn't *feel*.

Chet didn't respond for a long moment. Finally, when he spoke, Imogene knew he'd never realize—never understand—how unsatisfactory his words were.

"It's over, Genie."

No, it isn't.

Imogene heard Hazel's soft whisper in her mind, yet she didn't respond. Instead, she shifted a sorrow-filled smile to her brother. A small nod.

"Sam confessed. To the post office and the town hall."

Imogene nodded again.

Chet's hand remained on her shoulder. Squeezing. Affirming. "He'll confess to Hazel's death. It's only a matter of time."

Imogene reached up and patted her brother's hand. She offered him another small smile. "And if he doesn't?" Sam had insisted he hadn't killed Hazel. Insisted instead that he'd *loved* her.

Imogene's gaze drifted back to the dollhouse.

Chet cleared his throat. "He didn't punch the time clock on the day of Hazel's death, Genie. Sam was supposed to be at work, and he wasn't there. He admitted that Hazel knew of his plans. He admitted she tried to stop him—tried to talk him into restraining himself. She threatened to turn him in, Genie. Our Hazel. She did what was right."

Imogene turned to face her brother, the dollhouse to her back. "And you think Sam killed her before she could ruin his plans?"

Chet tipped his head, studying her. "And you don't?"

Imogene blinked, seeing the silhouette of her eyelashes as

341

they brushed her lower lids. She didn't know. All she could hear was Hazel's voice whispering in her mind.

It's not over. It's not over.

But maybe it would never be over. Maybe, when all the evidence came in, when the clues aligned, when Sam confessed, Hazel's death would still pound with the reality of its very existence. She was dead. She was gone. That soul-splitting grief could never be over.

Aggie

Aggie hadn't slept until Collin had half lifted her onto her bed. She was physically and mentally exhausted. Her eyes hurt from weeping, and even as Collin shook out a blanket and laid it over her, she'd continued to have tears seep from her eyes and wet the pillowcase.

Collin had leaned over. Pressed a light, comforting kiss against her temple. "Sleep, Love."

His whisper created a deeper need for him. Not a physical one, not one that had any hints of sensuality. Just a need to be cared for. To not be alone. To soak in the essence that was Collin's peace in the middle of a raging storm.

He'd moved to leave when Aggie reached out and grabbed his hand. Their eyes connected, and Collin's thumb rubbed hers.

"Stay," she pleaded.

His eyes narrowed with emotion and maybe something else. "I can't, Love. I'll just be downstairs."

"Please." She'd squeezed his hand tighter. "Just sit with me?"

So he had. He'd lowered himself, and the bed sank beneath his weight. Reaching out, Collin brushed back her silky hair from her face. His touch was reassuring. Safe. Aggie's eyes had closed then, and she'd slept.

She didn't know when Collin left her room. She'd found him in the kitchen that morning, looking the most rumpled she'd ever seen him. Ginger hair askew, his cotton oxford shirt untucked over his jeans, which were now less pressed and more wrinkled.

He'd given her coffee with cinnamon sprinkled on top of whipped foam. A poached egg cupped in the middle of a piece of hollowed-out toast. A slice of cheese. Bacon.

Aggie couldn't really say anything. Her throat still felt tight. Her eyes ready to release more tears at any given moment.

When she announced she needed to see Mumsie, Collin had offered to stay and clean up the kitchen. Before she'd exited, he covered the floor in three steps and combed his fingers through the sides of her loose, straight hair. His thumb stroked her cheek, brushing her freckles.

"The answers will come."

Aggie nodded, raising questioning eyes. "And the woman in the grave? With Hazel's ring and shoes?"

Collin's face reflected her own doubts. "We may never know. But we'll do our best to find out."

She'd taken assurance in his confidence, and confidence in his assurance.

Now Aggie opened the door of her car and climbed out, looking across the parking lot at the hospital. Noting Mumsie's window. The light was on. She must be awake. Aggie had so many questions, and she wanted to pepper Mumsie with them.

If Samuel Pickett had killed Hazel, why did Mumsie still treat Hazel's death as unsolved?

If Samuel Pickett had killed Hazel, why on earth had Mumsie given permission for him to be buried in the family cemetery? More pressing, if Samuel Pickett had killed Hazel, then why was there another dead woman only a few graves over, buried with Hazel's belongings, and why was someone threatening them with bone fragments and notes and roses that insisted it was *not over*?

Aggie shut the car door.

"Miss Dunkirk?"

Aggie yelped at the deep, gravelly baritone behind her. She spun, her eyes taking in the old man from Mumsie's room. His green wool sweater. His shepherd's-crook cane. His blue eyes and gray hair. It was a nondescript face, and he wore brown glasses. He was clean-shaven. His shoes were black orthopedics. There was nothing threatening about him at all and yet, deep inside, something made Aggie take a step back, her legs pressing against her car.

"Who are you?" Her question came out hesitant. She swallowed and tried again, infusing more confidence. Summoning the inherited spit and vinegar that Mumsie had perfected. "Tell me who you are."

The man couldn't be as old as Mumsie. If Aggie had to guess, he was in his early seventies.

"I'm sorry." His voice shook. He stepped closer to her. Aggie could smell tobacco. He ran the hand that didn't grip the cane over his head. "I never meant for this to happen."

Aggie frowned. She edged away from him, telling herself he was old. She had a physical advantage, and he'd done nothing threatening. Still. Something didn't feel right. It was off. Especially since he wasn't telling her his name.

"You were in my grandmother's room last night, and she was obviously not fond of you. Was it you who called her the other night? Did you cause her stroke?" Aggie demanded.

"I just wanted . . ." His eyes shifted to his cane. His knuckles were white, and he teetered a bit, then repositioned the cane's tip with its rubber stopper on the asphalt. When he brought his eyes up to meet hers, there was a dimness in them. A hollow gloom. "You don't understand. You can't understand."

Aggie wasn't going to stick around and humor an old man talking riddles. She started toward the hospital, but the man lifted the tip of his cane and pressed it against the side of her car. He tilted a little and then gained his footing. The cane was a flimsy but effective barrier as it pushed against the front of her thighs. There was something that went against Aggie's instinct to kick the cane out of the way. It'd make the elderly man more unsteady on his feet. Even if he deserved it, striking back at someone in his condition seemed wrong.

She leveled an offended glare on him. "Pardon me, but you *will* let me go."

He gave his head a vehement shake. His eyes were a bit magnified behind his glasses. Aggie could see the lines of his trifocals and the thick glass lenses that jutted out from their frames. He was not going to fall into the category of a *cute old man*. He wasn't even grumpy. He looked distressed. She couldn't tell if it was mental or emotional distress—perhaps it was both.

"It's not over." He pulled his cane back and rammed the tip against the car again to make his point.

"What's not over? Hazel Grayson? Hazel's death?" Aggie went straight to the point. He had to have been the one to leave the flowers with the handwriting on the petals. Had to be the one behind the cryptic note and bone fragments.

"You figured it out then?" he asked.

"It's not hard to. You're a stalker. A mean old stalker. Did you attack Collin too? With the shovel?"

The man's lips thinned into a wry smile. "Sort of makes an old guy like me feel pretty good to take out a younger man."

Aggie accused. "Why would you do that?"

"No." The old man's eyes widened. "No! It's all just gotten so—so out of control. The story of what happened . . . you weren't supposed to find it *all*."

"Find it all?" She didn't understand the emphasis on the word *all*.

"Never mind," he spat.

"You're talking about Hazel. But you're not even old enough to remember her," Aggie baited him.

His face darkened. Again he prodded her car with his cane. "*Never* say I'm not old enough to remember Hazel. Never."

The fierceness in his voice stunned Aggie into silence. Before she could react, his cane cracked against her knees. Aggie cried out. The shocking pain against her kneecaps made her legs collapse. She fell to the parking lot. The old man stood over her, lifted his cane, and shoved the tip into the side of her knee.

Aggie bit her lip against the pain. She didn't want to cry out and give the old man the satisfaction. Whoever he was, she didn't want him feeding off her hurt.

He clicked his tongue and shuffled his feet to maintain his balance. "If you'd just left the grave alone . . ."

"Hazel's?" Aggie bit out.

He gave a short laugh. "No. I *wanted* you to see Hazel's grave. *He* didn't deserve to die with her blood on his hands."

He had to mean the mystery grave. Aggie moved her leg, but the man's cane pressed harder into the soft flesh on the inside of her knee. She winced.

"Whose grave is it?" Aggie clenched her teeth. It wasn't possible he'd broken her kneecap with his strike, but she could tell it was wickedly bruised.

"Whose grave?" He tucked his chin in surprise. "You haven't figured that out?"

"No." Aggie shook her head.

"Ida's," he choked out with a cynical laugh. "Ida's grave."

"Who's Ida?" Aggie couldn't hide her bewilderment.

"My aunt. My very, *very* dead aunt."

CHAPTER 39

With a quick twist, she could grab the old man's ankles and yank. He'd come down fast and hard, and she could run. He'd probably break a hip. Aggie wasn't sure if she cared—or if she *should* care.

"Get up." The old man nudged her leg with his cane.

Aggie complied, holding the car as she limped to her feet. Though her knees throbbed, she found she could stand.

"Let's go."

"Where?" Aggie adjusted her grip on the door handle.

"Your grandmother's room."

Aggie had no desire to take this crazy old man to Mumsie's room. The last thing Mumsie needed was another stroke. She'd tolerated far more than enough.

"No. No, we're not going to see Mumsie. You're telling me right here and right now who the heck you are—and who this *Ida* is—or I'm calling the cops."

The man gave her a thin smile. "I'll use my cane again."

Aggie glowered at him. "And I'll fight you for it and return the favor. If you want to go up against a younger woman, feel free, but I'm afraid my bones are tougher than yours."

He blanched, lowering his cane and leaning on it. The fight appeared to be seeping from him. He rubbed his eyes with his free hand and shook his head. "I didn't want you to find Ida's grave. I just wanted my daddy's name cleared from Hazel's death."

"Who's your father?" Aggie demanded.

"Sam Pickett." He heaved a sigh. "I'm Sam's son. Glen."

Aggie leaned against her car, crossing her arms, tendering the knee that had taken the brunt of the old man's strike. "Glen Pickett?"

"Yes." Glen nodded. "My aunt Ida is the dead woman your archaeologist friend is trying to get identified."

"How do you know this?" Aggie narrowed her eyes at him.

Glen shifted his weight again.

She raised an eyebrow. *Don't make me hit you, old man.*

He seemed to get the unspoken message. "Can we sit down?" he asked.

As if they were going to exchange pleasantries and forget the caning incident? Aggie shook her head. "You sit." She motioned to the cast-iron bench on a small strip of grass by the sidewalk. "I'll stand."

He hobbled to the bench and eased onto it. Aggie stood over him. Her knees continued to throb in pain. Stupid old man. He was lucky she hadn't called the cops—yet.

"Start from the beginning. No riddles. I still hold you responsible for Mumsie's condition."

Glen nodded. Aggie noticed a smattering of age spots on his sagging cheeks. Standing over him, he was far less threatening and more pathetic. A pathetic, sad old man with a spiteful streak.

"My father, Sam, was in love with Hazel Grayson. They were gonna get married. I still remember Hazel. Sweetest thing ever. She used to bring me lollipops. Never told anyone they were courting. My daddy didn't have a nice reputation around town."

"Shocking," Aggie muttered.

Glen shot her a look. "They had a mutual interest, my daddy and Hazel."

348

"Their properties the ammunition plant bought out?"

"Figured that much out, did ya?" Glen raised his brows.

"But I can't figure out why Sam's buried in *my* family cemetery."

"Your grandmother," Glen supplied frankly. "She knew my daddy and Hazel loved each other. I don't know *how* she knew, but she did. Years ago, when Daddy died, I realized for the first time that maybe he wasn't guilty of everything they accused him of. Maybe he didn't kill Hazel Grayson. 'Cause, see, that never made any sense to me. Even as a five-year-old lad, I knew they loved each other. Hazel had given him a ring even. I heard her tell Daddy that it was backward—her givin' him a ring—but she didn't dare wear an engagement ring. Not yet. Not until her family understood."

Aggie adjusted her weight onto her other foot, crossing her arms and glaring down at Glen. "So he killed her? And what does your aunt Ida have to do with all this?"

Glen reached for the deep pocket of his coat.

Aggie took a step back, holding out her palm. "Hold on."

The man lifted aged eyes, a hefty amount of exasperation in them. "I don't have a gun."

Aggie glowered at him. "You cracked me on the knees."

Glen nodded as he pulled a phone from his pocket. "That I did."

"And you left roses on Hazel's grave."

Glen's eyes had a nostalgic film over them. "I did that too. It's not over. My daddy's name needed cleared."

"But he blew up the post office and burned down the town hall," Aggie argued.

Glen shrugged his bony shoulders and readjusted his grip on his cane propped between his knees. "But he didn't kill Hazel. She didn't deserve to die. My daddy didn't deserve to do life in prison."

Aggie leaned forward and stared directly into the old man's

eyes. "He blew up the post office." What couldn't the man understand? Even if Sam hadn't killed Hazel, he certainly didn't deserve to walk away free after that. "Well, what about the pig bones? Why send my grandmother those bone fragments?"

Glen gave her a narrow-eyed look from behind his thick lenses. Studying her. Thinking. "Your grandmother's getting old. She's gonna die one of these days, and she's the only person left who believes my daddy didn't do it. I needed to shake her up. Get her to talk. And she wasn't doing a thing. Just sitting in that old house waiting to die."

"So you tried to scare the life out of her? Whatever happened to an old-fashioned house call and a conversation?" Aggie wasn't sure she'd ever sensed such a fierce protectiveness course through her.

"I tried. A couple of times about two years ago. She knew me well enough to understand who I was. She didn't want to talk to me. She'd hang up on me when I called." Glen shook his head. "I never meant to hurt her, but I had to get her attention. I figured she'd see I was serious. The roses—Hazel's favorite pink ones. The note. The bones—sort of like an unsolved crime, you know? She should've got the message. But she chose to turn a blind eye. Maybe it was all too painful, I don't know! But she finally answered her phone the other night when I tried the 'old-fashioned way,' as you put it. She kept telling me it was over. But it's not! My daddy doesn't deserve to be tagged with that girl's death!"

"And you're not sorry," Aggie surmised. "About any of it? You're unhinged."

Glen looked up at her and shrugged. "Sometimes it's too late for 'I'm sorry.'"

"What's that supposed to mean?" she snapped back.

He swiped at his phone screen, tapped it, tapped it again, then held it out to Aggie. "Watch."

She reached for the phone, shooting a cautious look at him.

It was a paused video of a TV screen. The image on the set was blurry, but she could make out an elderly man's profile, blued by the coloring of the video.

"Who is it?"

"Press *play*." Glen was picking at his thumbnail.

Aggie braved the bench and eased down at the far end of it, away from Glen. She tapped the phone screen. The video was a bit shaky. Someone had held up the phone and recorded another video playing on the TV.

The man on the screen was speaking. It was garbled. Difficult to hear. Aggie drew the phone closer to her face.

"My name is Sam Pickett . . ."

Aggie gave Glen a startled look.

He was gone.

She surged to her feet, his phone still in her hand, Sam's voice playing in the background. "Glen!" Aggie shouted. She spun in a circle, scanning the sidewalk. There he was. Moving fast for an old man with a cane. "Glen!" she shouted again. But he ignored her. Payback for being ignored the last many months? Perhaps. Aggie had no intention of launching bones at him to regain his attention, though.

Besides, Glen had left behind answers. Maybe all the answers even. In the voice of a man who seemed to connect them all.

Imogene had rung Lola. Their chat was brief. Lola said that the entire town was subdued since Sam Pickett's arrest. She told Imogene she'd gone to visit Sam's aunt and Ida—to take them a loaf of bread and some muffins—but Sam's aunt said Ida hadn't been home since before Sam had been arrested. She'd found a note from Ida saying she was hopping a train and going to New York City.

"What about Sam's son?" Imogene asked her friend.

"He's with their aunt," Lola responded.

"I hate everything about this," Imogene mumbled into the phone.

"You and me both," Lola said.

Imogene hung up the phone. She found Mother sitting at the table. She looked up at Imogene and pushed a teapot toward her.

"Have some," said Mother.

Imogene nodded and sat down. Pouring the lemon tea—Hazel's favorite—Imogene watched the honey-brown liquid slosh into the blue cup.

"I did it." Mother's declaration was soft but firm.

Imogene glanced up, setting the teapot down with a *thud*. "You did what?"

Mother met her eyes. "I poured Hazel's tea. That night Daddy shot the raccoon? I'd been up just minutes before. Made tea. Poured it. I was drinking it on the front porch. Then I heard the raccoon and figured Daddy would hear it rustling around out there. One of the dogs was sure to bark. So I came back in. 'Course, I didn't latch the door, so the wind blew it and scared you silly, but I hightailed it back to bed. I'm so sorry I never said anything."

"Why?" Imogene remembered the steaming cup of tea. That feeling that Hazel had been there—but wasn't. "You didn't do anything wrong. Why not just tell me? Or tell Chet? So we didn't wonder?"

"Because . . ." Mother's voice dropped to a whisper. "I missed her. I just—missed her. I wanted to remember."

Imogene reached across the table and took her mother's hand in hers. Their eyes locked in mutual understanding. "I'll never stop missing her," Imogene murmured. Because it was true.

"Red in the mornin' . . ."

The words knifed her heart as Imogene stared across the valley, the brilliance of the sunrise stretching over Wisconsin farmland like a wash of blood reminding the world what had been shed in recent times. Reminding Imogene what she had lost.

She gave Ollie a sad smile as he strode up beside her on the hillside, hands buried in his overall pockets. His hair was damp, like he'd just showered.

"They all want me to say goodbye to her." Imogene's admission was quiet and drifted into the morning air. She watched as Daddy strode across the yard toward the barn, his frame small from their vantage point on the hill. The dog bounded beside him and then paused, catching sight of a cat. He barked and took off after the feline. The tabby scurried under the fence and toward the cows, dodging the Holsteins' hooves and escaping the playful dog.

Ollie cleared his throat. "I never found sayin' goodbye to be worth the while."

Imogene tugged her hand-knitted sweater around her dress as the breeze brushed a ghostly reminder over them, as if Hazel had swept by hoping they'd take notice.

It'd been days since Imogene had heard Hazel's voice. She knew it was her own heart that kept Hazel alive. She knew Hazel didn't really talk to her, that Hazel was dead. Still, everything in Imogene wanted to converse with her sister. Somehow *see* Hazel just as she had the day she'd escaped from Sam. Beautiful, gentle, soft, sweet Hazel.

"I don't think he did it, Ollie," Imogene whispered.

She noticed Ollie's face shadow at her words. He looked at her, his shoulder brushing hers as he stood beside her. "Still think Sam's a good guy, huh?"

Imogene shot him a quick glance. "No," she answered quickly. Maybe too quickly. Ollie didn't look as though he believed her. She took a step away from Ollie. A little distance. A little distance might be helpful. The headiness of having him standing beside her caused a battle of emotions to swirl inside. She wanted to launch herself in his arms, have him hold her, kiss her, pretend that life was fairy tales and handsome soldiers returned heroic from war. But she also knew that life wasn't like that. It was dark, empty, and all too often void of satisfactory answers.

"I just don't think he killed Hazel," she said belatedly.

Ollie grunted.

"Do you?" Imogene wanted to know. *Needed* to know what Ollie thought.

His shoulders rose in a shrug. "Reckon I don't know. Makes sense he did, though. 'Specially if she was gonna blow the whistle on him. He tried to hurt you. Even admitted to hittin' you with his truck. Tryin' to get you out of his way. Get you to stop nosin' around his business. He confessed to callin' me to rush into the town hall to save you when you weren't even there. Thought somehow even I was catchin' on to him. So he tried to kill me too. Heck, he destroyed buildings out of revenge, Genie! I don't see why anyone could think he ain't capable of murder."

"But why would he—?" She stopped, hesitated, then plunged forward, voicing her doubts to the one person she ached would understand her. "Why would Sam confess to all that and not to Hazel's death? He's already going away for the rest of his life. What does it matter if he admits to murder too?"

Ollie was quiet. He either didn't have a response or simply knew Imogene wouldn't agree with his response. No one would understand her reticence to blame Sam. Not really. Logic said all the evidence pointed to him. But other pieces—the dollhouse pieces—didn't. The cockeyed photograph of the family cemetery. It should mean nothing to Sam, so why stop to look at it, touch it? Hazel's missing shoes . . .

"We're never going to agree," Imogene admitted quietly. It was like an unscalable fence had suddenly risen between them.

Ollie glanced at her before refocusing on the horizon. "There ain't always answers for everything. Sometimes you just gotta move on, even when you're screamin' *Why?* on the inside."

His words were spoken from some deep place inside him. The wounds that festered and that he never spoke of. The agony that Ollie had packed within himself when he came home, like he'd packed his Army trunk when he first went to war.

"How do you move on?" Imogene took a step closer to him. The distance between them was painful, especially now as a tingling of worry rose that they wouldn't be able to heal from their grief to start anew.

Ollie glanced at her.

Imogene filled in the blanks of his unspoken question. "War. Losing buddies. Watching people die."

The only response was the breeze. Then the crooning warble of a mourning dove. The lonesome, guttural moo of a cow.

"I haven't" was Ollie's reply. "I just keep tryin'."

She had no response. Keep trying. It wasn't what Imogene wanted to hear. The closure she was aching for seemed so far away. Hazel's death hung like a black flag draped over life, reminding her every day that someone had been stolen from her.

"But you brought me home." Ollie's quiet admission caused Imogene's breath to stick. She looked up at him. He met her eyes and turned. "I remembered you. Every day. I needed a reason to make it home."

What was her reason? Imogene couldn't ask the question. It was remarkably selfish in light of the care and honesty that emanated from Ollie's eyes.

"Ollie . . ." She didn't know what to say. Two months ago, before Hazel had died, she might have laughed. Might have toyed with Ollie, flirted, maybe even melted a little under his brooding look. The loyalty there, the sincerity—a girl should love it. But it only caused more pain. A dull, aching sensation deep in her heart that told her she couldn't climb the insurmountable agony of loss to get to the place of hope she wanted to be in.

A knowing look washed over Ollie's face, replaced then with defeat. "I get it." He nodded. "I know."

Imogene reached out, laying her hand on his arm. "Ollie, I don't . . ." She didn't what? Didn't love him? Didn't at least have feelings for him? She did! Oh, she did, sure as shootin', but . . . "I don't have anything to give you right now."

They were the whispered words of a broken heart. Flayed open in all their truth, painful and raw. A truth that ruined good things as the bad crept across the final remnants of optimism, suffocating her future along with her joy.

"Nothin'?" Ollie's question pierced her.

Imogene's eyes brimmed with tears. She let them spill over onto her cheeks. "Do you? Do you have anything to give?"

The way he blinked. The way his face winced. The way he looked over her shoulder and away from her eyes told Imogene all she needed to know.

Ollie was right. Saying goodbye wasn't worthwhile. So, she wouldn't. Not today. She wrapped her arm around his and leaned her head against his shoulder. But someday. Someday soon she would, and Ollie would live his life and she would live hers. Forever in the shadow of grief and a longing for what should have been.

Maybe one day a sunset would come, sweep the valley in its red delights, and promise a new beginning.

Today was not that day.

CHAPTER 40

Aggie

Mumsie sat up in the hospital bed. The blush had returned to her cheeks. Her eyes were aware, and she lifted her own cup of coffee to her lips. "Honestly—" she paused to swallow the brew—"one would think I almost died. All this attention and fuss."

"You *did* almost die." Aggie ignored Mumsie's veiled complaint and adjusted the ties of her grandmother's hospital gown.

"For pity's sake." Mumsie batted Aggie's hand away, but there was a sheen over her eyes. The unspoken affection and gratefulness that Aggie knew Mumsie simply didn't know how to voice.

"Well, Cricket," Collin said from the other side of the bed, his eyes connecting with Aggie's before meeting Mumsie's soft smile at the newest moniker to be bestowed on her by Collin, "you have enough sass to live for another twenty years."

Mumsie gave a curt nod, and her smile at Aggie insinuated that at least Collin understood she was all right. "I will. I plan to make it to one hundred and ten, and then if I keel over, so be it."

"Why one hundred and ten?" Aggie couldn't help but ask.

"Well, by then the game-show host of my word puzzles show will have retired—or died—and then it won't be worth watching anymore."

Of course.

Aggie exchanged amused glances with Collin, but then the seriousness of what had occurred earlier that morning returned. She'd called Collin from her phone the minute Glen Pickett had walked away. After telling Collin of Glen's claim that the dead woman in the mystery grave was his aunt Ida, Collin had made some fast calls to follow up on that story. She wasn't sure who he'd called—didn't even know what, if anything, he'd uncovered. She certainly didn't understand what Glen's aunt Ida had to do with any of it, or why Glen had been so quick to leave his phone with Aggie after going to all the trouble of dropping a trail of threats to gain attention.

Aggie had yet to watch Sam Pickett's video. Mumsie needed to be with her when she did so. If it was a confession of Hazel's murder, Mumsie should hear it. Aggie was glad they were in the hospital. The idea of inducing another stroke was a real concern of hers.

"What is it?" Mumsie looked between them. "Someone die while I was asleep?"

"No." Aggie shook her head. "Your friends were here, though, to be sure you didn't."

"The Three Stooges?" Mumsie squeaked, lifting her brows.

Aggie laughed. More evidence she and Mumsie were so similar. They'd even attributed the same title to Mumsie's friends.

"Oh, they're good sorts." Mumsie's smile was a satisfied one. She handed her coffee to Collin and adjusted her blanket. "A person needs family—even church family."

Aggie fingered the phone in her pocket that Glen had left behind. She should call the police. But her knees felt better now, though bruised, and somehow calling the cops on old Glen Pickett seemed . . . cruel. She didn't like the man, but at

358

the same time, something about him just seemed so defeated. If anyone called the police on him, it would be Collin's right. Glen's admission to striking Collin at the cemetery still made no sense as far as motive, but it was enough to have him arrested.

"Mumsie?" Aggie started, pulling the phone from her pocket. "Glen Pickett visited me this morning."

"That boy?" Mumsie scowled. "Trouble in a handbasket."

"Like his father?" Aggie led.

Mumsie gave her a quick look. "Sam Pickett was troubled. He did some bad things, but—"

"But he loved Hazel," Aggie finished for Mumsie.

Mumsie's expression confirmed Glen's story. "Sometimes a person can't help who they love." There was a wistfulness in her voice, and a faraway look entered her eyes. Then she blinked and it disappeared as fast as it came.

Aggie glanced at Collin, who was eyeing her from across the bed. She dropped her gaze.

"Glen gave me this." Aggie showed the phone screen to Mumsie.

Mumsie's eyes widened. Her mouth opened in a small *o*. "Sam," she breathed. Her eyes locked with Aggie's. "People said he killed my sister. But he didn't. I've always believed him."

"Is that why you allowed him to be buried in the Grayson cemetery?" Aggie reached for a chair and scooted it next to the bed. She lowered onto it. Collin followed her lead and leaned onto the sill of the window that overlooked the parking lot.

Mumsie's lips tightened. "Yes. No one seemed to care about Sam Pickett after he was sent away. Everyone thought it was all over, though he never once confessed to killing Hazel. That dollhouse? I've spent seventy years looking at it. Pondering it. No matter how I studied it, how I try to remember, I can't fit the pieces together. I know he loved Hazel, and . . . and I believe she loved him too."

Collin adjusted his weight on the broad windowsill, his hands bracing on either side of him. "Did you notice anything missing from Hazel's room after she died?"

Mumsie shifted her gaze to him. "I did." A swift nod followed. "Her shoes. A pair of short-heeled oxfords. And a picture—one of her art pieces. She had one by her bedside. Although, for all the details I recall, I've never been able to remember what it was of. I even asked my mother and daddy, and my best friend, Lola. None of us had ever paid it much mind."

Collin cleared his throat, and the sound drew Aggie's attention. He stood and returned to Mumsie's side, taking her hand and easing down onto the bed. "Cricket, we found Hazel's shoes. Well, the heel of one."

Mumsie's eyes widened. "You did? Where?"

"In a grave. Buried in Fifteen Puzzle Row," Aggie supplied.

Collin nodded. "At least I *think* it's hers. There was also this." He pulled the man's ring from his pocket and handed it to Mumsie.

Mumsie held up the ring, reading the inscription. She laid it in her palm, cupping it with her other hand, breathing in a deep sigh and closing her eyes. "Ohhh, my sweet Hazel. What did you do?"

Collin shot a glance at Aggie. "I've been doing some records searching. Hazel and Sam—they were married. About two months before Hazel died."

Aggie clamped her hand over her mouth, biting back her cry of surprise.

Mumsie didn't open her eyes. A sorrowful smile touched her lips, with hints of hurt at the corners. "Oh, Hazel," she breathed, "you could've told me." She slid the ring on her thumb and opened her brilliant green eyes framed in gray-black lashes. "I'm not surprised. I knew there was more to the story."

"I think we should hear the rest from Sam." Collin gave Aggie a meaningful look.

She didn't want to upset Mumsie. She would throw the phone into the garbage and live her life with no answers if she had to.

Mumsie's hand—the one with Hazel's ring on her arthritic, curved thumb—reached out and felt for Aggie's. She searched Aggie's face and offered her a small smile. "I need to know, Agnes. I've waited . . . seventy years."

Drawing in a deep breath, Aggie lifted the phone, swiped at the black screen, and hit play.

"*My name is Sam Pickett. I spent most my life in prison, and now I s'pose I wasted most of it. Problem was, I was angry. A man gives his all for his country and comes home to find his country took it all . . . well, that's not why I'm recording this. I want you, Glen, to know once and for all, and from my mouth for the thousandth time: I did not kill Hazel Grayson. When I came home from the war, my first wife, your mama, had died. I was alone and had no land. My sister Ida and I had to beg off my aunt for a place to live. But I loved Hazel. I did. We met at the plant. She was Ida's friend. Young, pretty thing, with a smile that could light up heaven.*"

Aggie glanced up from the phone to Mumsie. Mumsie nodded, agreeing with Sam. A lone tear trickled down her cheek.

"*I told Hazel what I wanted to do. Make the government pay for movin' in on our farm. On her family land and cemetery. Then, when Ida reminded me that the Graysons had been so kind as to let them bury your mama there—my Bonnie—I was doubly mad. But Hazel, she got a bit of conscience, said God wouldn't approve, that we were raised better'n that. That God would bring somethin' good out of it all.*"

The image of Sam Pickett blurred, then came back into focus. Sam cleared his throat and rubbed his hands over his eyes. His wrinkled skin sagged, jowls on the sides of his chin. He looked directly into the camera.

"*I still don't see what good God brought of it. Hazel was killed. My new wife. Killed 'cause Hazel threatened to tell on*" me. Well, Hazel should have! She was right. What I did wasn't worth wastin' my life over! Wasn't worth the hurt I caused you, Glen. But she was angry and scared . . . she killed Hazel."

"Who?" Mumsie leaned forward, her voice shaking. "Who was angry at Hazel?"

Sam seemed to look past the camera. His voice became garbled.

"I'd do it all over again. She had no right. No right to take Hazel from me. A few weeks after Hazel died and Ida was suddenly wearing new shoes. We didn't have much money between the two of us, and plain as they were, I recognized Hazel's shoes. I knew. I knew right away what Ida had done and what she'd kept quiet all this time."

Mumsie's gasp was loud. She sagged against the pillows. Aggie reached to pause the video, but Collin's hand stilled her. He gave his head a small shake.

"Ida told me she went to talk to Hazel. To tell Hazel she needed to let me do what I needed to do. Ida was so shy, I didn't think she had it in her. She said Hazel took her up to her bedroom to talk. Ida said she got so mad that she hit her. Hit Hazel when she turned to go back downstairs and start supper for her family. When Ida told me Hazel begged her—begged her to stop—Ida didn't. Then she had the guts to come runnin' to me in Hazel's shoes. Thinkin' I'd somehow be thankful. Thinkin' I'd understand. Well, I didn't understand. I'll never understand. I for sure had no intention of understandin'!"

Aggie's hand was shaking. Collin relieved her of the phone as Aggie crawled onto the bed next to Mumsie. Mumsie leaned into her, and Aggie held her. Held the woman who had raised Mom, who had lived alone all these years, who'd been accused of being persnickety and eccentric. The woman whose heart had been broken all those years before and never healed.

"I don't remember much. Just remember going to Hazel's grave after Ida and I had it out, and cryin' in the rain. Then I *dug a hole way down and threw in my ring. Then Ida. Burying my sister not far from Hazel, I just became numb. Been numb ever since. Left a note for my aunt from Ida sayin' she went to New York. I got arrested after gettin' in a tussle with Imogene Grayson. As for Ida's grave, no one visited that section of the cemetery. It was old. Untended. I figured no one would spot the grave an'—well, if they did, so be it. It wasn't where Hazel shoulda been buried. I shouldn't have buried Ida there neither. God save me if I didn't love them both, Hazel and my sister. And yet after all of it, they were both dead. Just dead. I couldn't go back and change nothin'."*

The video bugged out for a brief moment, then came back.

One last glimpse of Sam's face. One last thought. *"It'll never be over. Not till we choose to move on, and . . . and it's too late for me."*

—⟊⟊⟊—

Collin had turned off the phone a few minutes before, but no one spoke. Mumsie reached for a tissue, her hand trembling. Aggie brushed a curl off Mumsie's face.

"You okay?" A silly, inept question.

Mumsie drew in a shaky breath. "So much loss."

Collin eased off the bed, setting the phone on the hospital table. He caught Aggie's eyes. "I'll leave you two to chat, all right?"

Aggie wanted to reach out for him, to ask him to stay, to hold his hand and insist he was one of them. Part of them. Somehow. But she couldn't—she didn't. She watched him lean over and give Mumsie a kiss on her cheek.

Mumsie patted his cheek in return. "Well. Chivalry isn't dead then," she quipped.

The creases in his cheeks deepened. "Not dead. Very much alive."

"Thank the Lord." Mumsie patted his cheek one more time.

"You remind me of someone I once knew—he was a good man too."

Collin smiled. "I'll take that as a compliment."

"You should," Mumsie stated.

Collin gave Aggie a lingering look, then exited the room, leaving behind a waft of spicy cologne and the memory of his soft eyes and caring warmth.

Aggie shook off the undefinable feelings and adjusted herself next to Mumsie. "It's just you and me now, Mumsie. I won't leave you. I promise. I should have come home after Mom died, but I—"

Mumsie squeezed Aggie's hand. "Death deals a wicked hand. We all respond differently, and not always the way we should."

Aggie pulled away so she could look down at Mumsie, who rested beside her. "What do you mean?"

Mumsie's voice shook a little. Whether from age or emotion, Aggie wasn't sure. "After Hazel died, I . . . I had a chance for happiness. I probably had the opportunity to heal, but I couldn't. Hazel lived with me, both in my mind and my heart. It wasn't resolved." Her eyes drifted to Glen's phone on the table. "I guess it wasn't resolved for most of us."

Aggie nodded. "Why do you suppose Glen did that? Left the flowers, the notes? Attacked Collin at the cemetery?"

"I should've listened to the boy. Let him in the house, taken his phone calls. He always was just a step away from crazy—the Picketts always were. I suppose poor Glen finally just gave up trying to talk to me, to get my attention, and just threw in the towel."

Aggie shrugged. "It would've saved everyone a lot of hassle if he'd just brought you the phone in the first place and asked you to defend Sam's name."

Mumsie pursed her lips and sighed. "If only humankind would do things the simple, honest way. But we don't. For whatever reason, we have to take the hard way."

"What good is it for Glen to clear his father's name anyway? The rest of the world wouldn't care." Aggie hated to be harsh, but the truth was the truth.

"Justice." Mumsie's response was quick. "Justice."

"How is that justice?" Aggie felt restless. She sat up from beside Mumsie and eased herself onto the floor. She moved to the hospital window. "Is it justice to send an old woman into a stroke?"

"He wanted his daddy's name cleared of Hazel's murder," Mumsie answered. "She wasn't supposed to die. If you look at it from Glen's point of view, Hazel was going to be his new mama."

"A happily-ever-after," Aggie said.

Mumsie nodded. "And then you and Collin started to dig around the cemetery. Well, *that* part didn't need unburied. That'd only prove what Glen wanted to disprove—that his daddy was a killer. Just not who everyone thought he killed."

The puzzle pieces came together in Aggie's mind. She spun from the window. "Glen wanted to instigate us into researching Hazel's death. He wanted us to figure out that Sam didn't do it, but he didn't want us to uncover more of Sam's grievances. And the fact he'd killed his own sister, Ida."

"That's what I'd guess." Mumsie tapped the table with Glen's phone on it. "And he'd have saved a lot of trouble if he'd taken the simple way. But then I can't say a word, seeing as how I've never taken the simple way myself."

"Didn't you suspect Glen? With all the weird things happening lately?" Looking back, the pieces were falling so well into place that it all seemed obvious now, almost too obvious.

"Agnes, I've suspected so many people my entire life, I've learned to dismiss myself as much as I've believed myself."

There was an eerie ring of truth to Mumsie's words. Her sister's murder had rested on her shoulders for decades, with every clue, every lead, every suspicion ending in nothing. It was no wonder she'd dismissed Glen's advances. Foolish perhaps, but no wonder.

"We'll have to get the police involved," Aggie said.

"Of course," Mumsie replied. "Sending an old woman pig bones and dropping a dummy skeleton into her backyard is a bit of an overstep."

"You think he left the skeleton there too?" Aggie supposed it made sense.

Mumsie rubbed her eyes. "I think it's likely. But then, like I said, the whole Pickett family has always been a little off."

Aggie absently reached for her knees, rubbing them.

Mumsie picked up Glen's phone and handed it to Aggie. "Go. File your police report."

Aggie took the phone and rounded the bed. As she reached for her purse, a nagging thought pressed into her. She turned, studying Mumsie for a moment.

"Spit it out, Agnes," Mumsie directed.

"John Hayward, my grandfather . . . did you bury him somewhere else?" While Aggie knew the answer was probably yes, the unresolved element of her grandfather's missing grave irked her.

Mumsie's smile dimmed, and she nodded. "I did. After Hazel died, I moved to California for many years. He died there, and after that I moved back home to Mill Creek." She gave a sad laugh. "I thought if I kept moving . . . maybe I'd forget. Somehow."

"But you didn't?" Aggie sank into the chair she'd abandoned earlier.

Mumsie took a deep breath. "Never. I met and married John— your grandfather—not long after I moved to California."

Aggie narrowed her eyes. There was something in the way Mumsie said it . . . "Did you—weren't you happy?"

Mumsie looked down at her hands. "I was happy. As happy as I could be."

Aggie sensed a big hesitation. "What is it?" She leaned forward in the chair.

Mumsie lifted her eyes. "Agnes, don't let grief tie your years up into a lifetime of regrets. Let the good Lord take care of your aches and heal you. So that you don't miss out on the good—on the blessings He hides in the middle of all that hurting."

The lump in Aggie's throat grew. "I don't know what you mean."

Mumsie reached out, and Aggie took her hand. Mumsie's familiar green eyes crinkled at the corners as her lips shook with emotion. "Grief can become its own prison, Agnes. Once there, getting out is—nigh impossible."

The image of Mom flooded Aggie's memory. She swiped at her eyes as tears filled them. "I miss her. I hate cancer, Mumsie. I can't—I don't know how to move forward."

Mumsie squeezed Aggie's hand. A warmth Aggie had never seen in Mumsie spread over her face, consumed her eyes, and crossed the space between them, drawing her in.

"You stop moving," she whispered. "You go ahead and let the grief consume you, because then it will heal you, free you, and the good Lord can move into its place and show you promise. Promise that there is so much more life to live. So many more people to love. And the footprints of those who've gone before you? They'll still be there. Memories to warm you when you're old."

"Did you? Stop moving?" Aggie lifted Mumsie's hand to her cheek.

Mumsie nodded. "Finally. After your mama passed. Saying goodbye to my daughter . . ." Mumsie choked up, pinching her lips together. "No mother wishes to have their baby go before them. But I was tired of living in that dark place all these years. And"—Mumsie met Aggie's eyes—"I was done wasting my opportunities with the people I cherished. That's when I wrote you and told you that little white lie."

Aggie laughed. "That you broke your hip?"

"Heaven knows I had to bring you home *somehow*." Mumsie's

eyes were shadowed, yet there was contentment in them. "I lost many chances, Aggie, but I still have you."

"For always." Aggie leaned into Mumsie's hand.

"So long as you stop throwing away the plastic baggies and learn to wash them!" Mumsie scolded.

"I promise," Aggie laughed.

"Now, go find your archaeologist and let him know."

"Let him know what?"

Mumsie tilted her head and gave Aggie a knowing look. "If you don't beat all, girl. Let the boy know you're gonna stop moving."

CHAPTER 41

She'd looked for Collin in the hospital cafeteria. Called him. No answer. Looked for him at the police station. Filed her report and gotten a rather confused but confident response that they'd investigate Glen Pickett—and the cold case of Hazel Grayson, along with the case of Ida Pickett, whose life had been dramatically cut short.

She found Collin at Mumsie's. In her study no less. Standing in front of the dollhouse, hands in wool trouser pockets, a studious look on his face.

"Collin?" Aggie hesitated as she entered the room.

He looked up. His blue eyes gentle behind his glasses. "There you are, Love."

"How'd you get in here?" She took a step toward him.

Collin turned. "Your Mumsie told me where the spare key is. I do believe I figured this beast out."

Aggie frowned. "Figured what out?"

Collin waved his hand at the dollhouse. "The missing picture in the empty frame. The one your grandmother thought disappeared the day Hazel died."

Aggie took another step into the room. "What do you mean, 'thought'?"

"It didn't disappear." Collin motioned with his hand. "Come here."

Aggie approached him, allowing Collin to pull her close to his side. "Look. The frame where the sketch was supposed to be?"

"Yes?" Aggie gave him a questioning look, as if she were supposed to see in minutes what Mumsie hadn't in seventy years.

Collin ran his finger over the bedside table. "There never was a picture in the frame. You see? Your grandmother did remember—she just didn't realize it." He pointed to the empty frame on the table by the real bed. "It was where Hazel wanted to put her sketch, so she did a vague impression of it in the dollhouse but never mounted it in the frame in real life."

"How do you know this?" Aggie struggled to comprehend Collin's train of thought.

He pointed to the tilted frame of the gravestones on the stairs. "The gravestones were a reminder of what your family had lost. If you take this miniature frame"—Collin did so, holding up the tiny picture—"and hold a magnifying glass over it"—he pulled a magnifying glass from his pocket—"you can see it's a landscape marked distinctly with a farmhouse and a large tree in front. I went online and checked old photographs of the farms before the government moved in. This miniature sketch is of the Pickett homestead. Before the ammunition plant was built. It would have meant something to Hazel, but there's no way she could have framed it like she obviously wanted to. There'd be too many questions."

"But how—?" Aggie couldn't fathom how Collin had surmised all of this just by standing here and studying the dioramic crime scene.

"Come." Collin returned the tiny framed sketch to its place in the dollhouse and straightened the original, life-sized empty frame by the bed, then led Aggie from the room. She trailed after him, curious, until he moved into Mumsie's room. Opening the door, he then closed it once they'd entered. Behind the door hung the original sketch of the family gravestones.

"How did you find this?" Aggie stared at it in disbelief, wondering how she'd ever missed it. But then she hadn't exactly been looking either.

Collin wagged his brows. "I snooped. As any good archaeologist would do. And on a hunch . . ." He lifted the framed picture from its nail and slid off the back of the frame. "Ta-da."

A small sketch was revealed. Saved against the land the Graysons had lost was Hazel's sketch of the Pickett farm.

"My guess is," Collin explained as Aggie reverently took the picture from his hands, "when Ida was running down the stairs, she saw the picture of the gravestones. Maybe she even was tempted to take it—how was she to know what Hazel had hidden inside? A sketch of their own home."

Aggie stepped back and slouched on the edge of Mumsie's bed, Hazel's sketch in her hands. She hovered a palm over it before lifting her eyes to Collin. "Hazel really did love Sam, didn't she?"

He nodded, staring down at the picture. "I believe she did. She left quite the impression on Glen Pickett. All these years, he's seen her as more of a mother than even his great-aunt who raised him."

"How do you know that?" Aggie handed the picture back to Collin, who busied himself returning it to its place behind the door.

"Well, it helps that I stopped by Glen Pickett's place and gave him what for."

"Gave him what for?" Aggie's brows went skyward. "Did you confront Glen?"

Collin nodded. "Probably wasn't proper of me. The police should be the ones to confront him. But Glen did, after all, give me stitches. He owed me an explanation."

"And what did he say?" Aggie stood, stepping toward Collin as he finished rehanging the gravestone sketch on the wall.

"He was quite apologetic for the bump on my head. Apparently, he thought that breaking into the office and stealing the computer would somehow thwart our efforts to remap the cemetery. Poor man knew I'd find his aunt's grave, which wasn't going to help clear his father's name at all."

Aggie released a heavy breath. She was tired. Bewildered and tired. She moved to go downstairs. Coffee would be good.

Collin followed her, his steps sure behind her on the stairs.

As Aggie entered the kitchen and began making coffee, she debated with herself about whether to ask Collin anything further. Her conversation with Mumsie replayed in her mind. But there was something vulnerable in her asking Collin, something frightening. That she would open herself to him more than she already had. Yet she desperately wanted to know his thoughts.

"Collin, do you believe grief can ruin lives?"

Collin met her questioning eyes. "Of course. Grief isn't wrong, but it can paralyze. It can thwart a life. A person can choose to let time stand still, and while they hold the pieces of the past, the hope of their future passes them by." He reached out and took the coffee scoop from her hand, laying it down on the counter. His fingers lightly nudged her arms and turned her toward him. Collin's voice was soft, gentle, but most of all, understanding. "A person shouldn't miss the promise."

His hand rose, and his thumb brushed over her freckles.

Aggie leaned into his hand. "The promise of what?"

Collin smiled. It reached the corners of his eyes, crinkled them, and made his cinnamon brows rise. "The promise of whatever is in store. Grief is like the moment you close a chapter in a really good book. It leaves you suspended, unfinished, even remarkably unsatisfied. But it doesn't mean the story is over. You just have to—"

"Keep reading?" Aggie took a step closer to him.

Collin's eyes widened in pleasant surprise.

She reached up and, in typical Grayson Girl fashion, let her boldness overtake her caution. Aggie pressed her lips against his, and it was only a moment before Collin's arm wrapped around her.

"What was that for, Love?" he murmured against her mouth.

Aggie drew back and winked. "I think I should keep reading." She brushed at the remnants of her lipstick on his mouth, mimicking his accent. "I daresay, red looks good on you."

Collin's eyes darkened with feeling, and he pulled her hand away. "It looks much better on you, Love."

She knew it was no accident he called her Love. And it was more than okay that he kissed her again.

———

The trees were blazing in their autumn glory as Aggie led Mumsie into Fifteen Puzzle Row. Her walker added extra support to the elderly woman, but Aggie held on to Mumsie's arm just to be sure. The silence between them was mutually understood and respected.

They paused in front of Hazel's grave. This time there was no pink rose.

"It truly is over," Mumsie whispered. Her eyes caressed Hazel's marker. Then they shifted to Ida's unmarked grave just plots away. It had been filled in. Her remains were to be reburied. Mumsie hadn't the heart to grant permission for Ida to be buried in the Grayson cemetery next to Sam, so a small plot had been acquired and she would be interred at the Mill Creek Cemetery. Hazel, however, was to be moved. In a few weeks, Collin would oversee the exhumation of her coffin and the relocation to the family cemetery. Next to her brothers, her parents, and next to the man she had loved.

Walking back to Hazel's grave, they stood and bowed their heads. Aggie looped her arm through Mumsie's elbow and held her close. There was such finality in the air. But it was a calming end. Resolution. Answers. The moment they could finally close Hazel's life with knowledge, tears, and the resolve to continue on.

"Do you . . . ?" Aggie hesitated, then leaned her head against Mumsie's gray curls. "Do you ever talk to her? To Hazel?"

It was a strange thing to ask, she knew, yet there were times, even now, when she thought she could hear her mom's voice. That she knew what Mom would say. And she would respond too, when no one was listening. For some reason, it made Mom seem closer to her and not so far away.

Mumsie's soft chuckle drifted over her sister's grave. "Every day." She turned to look Aggie in the eyes. "Every day."

"I suppose I should pray instead of talking to Mom, huh?" Aggie admitted. The thought stung a little. Not that sharing her heart with God wasn't adequate, but that not speaking to Mom would be so final. So . . . ending.

Mumsie patted Aggie's hand that still curled around her arm. "Ohhh, Agnes. Regardless of where faith may take us and what the good Lord has in store, we'll never stop hearing their voices. The voices of the ones we've loved before."

The faraway look filled Mumsie's eyes again. Aggie followed her gaze but saw nothing but gravestones across the near and the distant grass. She skimmed them. The names.

Edward Jenkins
Penelope Hinden
Oliver Schneider

. . . names of people Aggie would never know, whose names meant nothing to her but who had all lived lives and had all left loved ones behind.

Aggie looked at her frail grandmother. Mumsie seemed fixated on one of the stones, although Aggie couldn't tell which one. Finally, her grandmother drew in a quick breath, a quiet determination settling over her face.

Mumsie smiled at Aggie, then squeezed her hand. "Yes. Their voices will always echo, here, among the stones, and in our hearts. It is how it was meant to be."

QUESTIONS
FOR DISCUSSION

1. Aggie's and Mumsie's internal and spiritual struggles parallel each other's journeys. In what ways were they similar, and in what ways did they resolve them differently?

2. Imogene had a few steadying forces in her life. How do you think Lola and Chet specifically affected the way Imogene viewed the tragedy around her and the future without Hazel?

3. Battling with grief and its long-term effects is a major theme that runs through Imogene's life. In what ways do you believe Imogene could have handled her sister's death differently that might have influenced Imogene's life story in a more positive way?

4. How did the church ladies contribute to Mumsie's story of healing and regeneration? How have others helped you during difficult times?

5. Aggie uncovered some unique habits that Mumsie had carried over from her childhood during the Great Depression and through the war rationing program. What habits did your family pass down that you think may have originated during those years of struggle and hardship? In what creative ways have you adjusted your lifestyle when finances became tight?

6. Why do you think Ollie and Imogene weren't ready to pursue their fledgling romance? Do you think, had circumstances been different, they could have built a happy life together?

ACKNOWLEDGMENTS

Book four has winged its way to my amazing editors, Raela and Luke, the remarkable team at Bethany House, and my stellar cover designer, Jenny. This was speed-writing at its best, and I loved the race as this story came to life through trips, plane malfunctions, hotel stays, coffee runs, and the sheer joy of knowing you all!

My agent-momma, Janet Kobobel Grant, who has my back like the fierce little mother she is. You are strength and savvy personified. I hope I can be even a little like you when I grow up.

Amy Green, you emailed me a podcast that launched this book and its dollhouse-forensics theme into happening. Thank you for thinking of me when you hear of murder and mayhem. Arsenic cheers to you and a friendly tap of the sword tip!

Natalie Walters, you put up with an awful lot of texts during this novel's writing. You also saved Mumsie and Aggie from the proverbial garbage can and convinced me that Collin was, after all, salvageable as a hero (though not at *all* my type). Thank you for your grace, your love, but most of all your daily support. I love doing life with you.

Linsey Adair, my own personal cemetery secretary. Well,

not *literally* my cemetery secretary, because I'm not dead yet and you live in a different state, but the cemetery secretary who truly brought this story to life with ideas, insights, expertise, and dedication. Thank you. Let's do coffee. Soon.

I must add in some extra thanks to my gramma Lola, who taught me to wash baggies at a young age and would catch me throwing them away in the garbage long after I was married. I love the way you taught me to conserve what God has given us, and not to take for granted the life we have, be entitled and expect we deserve more, and how to hoard bread-bag ties like there's no tomorrow.

Halee Matthews, you always, ALWAYS have my back. This time in the what-the-heck-do-I-title-this-book department. As usual, your insight and poetic nature provided the perfect one, and we all agreed it was meant to be.

There's a long list of folks I always want to thank. Most of them are family, like my parents, my in-laws, my brother, my sisters . . . you all are the frosting and sprinkles on the cake of my life and I love you!

My Cap'n Hook, you're a pirate of the worst sort. I'm still held captive after almost twenty years. Or maybe that's the best sort of pirate . . . I need to think about this. LOL, I love you.

To CoCo and Peter Pan. You know every book is for you. Someday you'll be old enough to read murder and mayhem and learn a whole new side to Mommy that you never knew existed. Sorry if I scare you a little. We can always just drink coffee and pretend I'm normal.

Jaime Jo Wright is winner of the Christy, Daphne du Maurier, and INSPY Awards and is a Carol Award finalist. She's also the *Publishers Weekly* and ECPA bestselling author of three novellas. Jaime works as a human resources director in Wisconsin, where she lives with her husband and two children. Visit her at jaimewrightbooks.com.

Sign Up for Jaime's Newsletter!

Keep up to date with Jaime's news on book releases and events by signing up for her email list at jaimewrightbooks.com.

More from Jaime Jo Wright

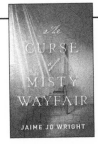

A century apart, two women seek their mothers in Pleasant Valley, Wisconsin. In 1908, Thea's search leads her to an insane asylum with dark secrets. In modern-day Wisconsin, Heidi Lane answers the call of a mother battling dementia. Both confront the legendary curse of Misty Wayfair—and are entangled in a web of danger that entwines them across time.

The Curse of Misty Wayfair

You May Also Like . . .

Annalise knows painful memories hover beneath the pleasant façade of Gossamer Grove. But she is shocked when she inherits documents that reveal mysterious murders from a century ago. In this dual-time romantic suspense novel, two women, separated by a hundred years, must uncover the secrets within the borders of their town before it's too late.

The Reckoning at Gossamer Pond by Jaime Jo Wright
jaimewrightbooks.com

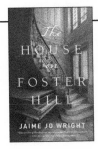

Fleeing a stalker, Kaine Prescott purchases an old house with a dark history: a century earlier, an unidentified woman was found dead on the grounds. As Kaine tries to settle down, she learns the story of her ancestor Ivy Thorpe, who, with the help of a man from her past, tried to uncover the truth about the death.

The House on Foster Hill by Jaime Jo Wright
jaimewrightbooks.com

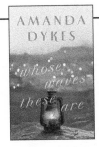

In the wake of WWII, a grieving fisherman submits a poem to a local newspaper asking readers to send rocks in honor of loved ones to create something life-giving—but the building halts when tragedy strikes. Decades later, Annie returns to the coastal Maine town where stone ruins spark her curiosity, and her search for answers faces a battle against time.

Whose Waves These Are by Amanda Dykes
amandadykes.com

◆BETHANYHOUSE

More Absorbing Fiction from Bethany House Publishers

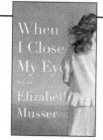

Famous author Josephine Bourdillon is in a coma, her memories surfacing as her body fights to survive. But those around her are facing their own battles: Henry Hughes, who agreed to kill her for hire out of desperation, is uncertain how to finish the job now, and her teenage daughter, Paige, is overwhelmed by fear. Can grace bring them all into the light?

When I Close My Eyes by Elizabeth Musser
elizabethmusser.com

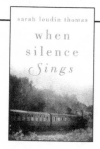

After the rival McLean clan guns down his cousin, Colman Harpe chooses peace over seeking revenge with his family. But when he hears God tell him to preach to the McLeans, he attempts to run away—and fails—leaving him sick and suffering in their territory. He soon learns that appearances can be deceiving, and the face of evil doesn't look like he expected.

When Silence Sings by Sarah Loudin Thomas
sarahloudinthomas.com

Gray Delacroix has dedicated his life to building a successful global spice empire, but it has come at a cost. Tasked with gaining access to the private Delacroix plant collection, Smithsonian botanist Annabelle Larkin unwittingly steps into a web of dangerous political intrigue and will be forced to choose between her heart and her loyalty to her country.

The Spice King by Elizabeth Camden, HOPE AND GLORY #1
elizabethcamden.com

BETHANYHOUSE

CPSIA information can be obtained
at www.ICGtesting.com
Printed in the USA
LVHW092306061219
639748LV00004B/186/P